HEART of a WOMAN

VIRGINIA C. MCKINLEY

Heart of a Woman
Copyright © 2023 by Virginia C. Mckinley

ISBN
978-1-960197-21-4 (Paperback)
978-1-960197-22-1 (eBook)
978-1-960197-20-7 (Hardcover)

HEART OF A WOMAN

VIRGINIA C. MCKINLEY

Acknowledgements

I am truly grateful to all those who have stood by me throughout my dedication of being an author with something to say. I will not forget those who listened, critiqued, and helped me along the way. To all my family, who had to listen to my dreams, that they were not sure would come true, but stood behind me anyway, with great support and trust in me. I had a vision that has never been seen throughout our family history, but my family help make it come true for me. Without the constant help and encouragement from my children, my mother, who stood strong behind me, my grandmother, who said it would happen even if she didn't live to see it and God who inspired me, this might never have happened.

Chapter 1

Love is something that comes along once, maybe twice in a lifetime and I have already used up one of my chances for true love. The consequences can be devastating, that's why I'm leaving my hometown to find fame and fortune in New York City, what some call the Big Apple, where the Statue of Liberty resides and the Empire State Building. These are places I've always wanted to see. Mama always said I had more pre-conceived notions about more stuff than anyone she ever knew but being a country girl, I never got much chance to see anything big and exciting as I'm about to see, when I get to New York. That's why I always had such big dreams.

Sitting here on this Greyhound Bus, I remind myself, that I have an intolerance for sitting for long periods of time, which gives one plenty of time to think and I'm not one for doing a whole lot of thinking. I've been known to be a very impulsive type of person and there have been times, that I've paid a heavy price for having that kind of imperfection in my character. If I fail at this attempt at life, I know I'll feel the consequences of the back draft from all the people talking their heads off, if I have to go back home. I can't help going over my life and

I certainly can't help thinking about the real reason I'm leaving Lexington Kentucky. As I look out the window of the Greyhound Bus, I think about Scooter Davis, my high school sweetheart, the man I was engaged to marry, well Scooter came home from the armed forces already married. The animosity I felt for the man was quite evident, because of his breach of promise. The man I was supposed to marry, had a wife when he returned home. My heart is still broken in a million pieces and I'm going away to find some happiness and peace of mind in New York City. My dream is to become a fashion model and make Scooter and everyone who whispered behind my back jealous and ashamed they ever said things about me. I'll show them all and make Scooter sorry he didn't marry me. I know I'm the better woman, not some mediocre half-witted woman, that can't make a man happy, but I was the right woman for Scooter and yet he chose another and left me to wallow in self pity at the very thought of what he's done to me.

If it wasn't for my upbringing, I might of thought of committing suicide, but that's totally out of the question, since I've been reared in a way that frowns on such thoughts, let alone an actual suicide act. That would have ruined my whole image, and that is, the image of an intelligent young woman trying to make the best out of her life. That is what's expected of me by everyone who has predicted that me, Callie Mason will be the first in her family to make something great out of herself. I'm just not sure I can live up to their expectations. I didn't tell mama and daddy that I would be leaving. I didn't want to get caught in the middle of the crossfire of outrage, that would proceed to take place, if I revealed my secret.

As my ride is about to end, I can plainly determine that we're nearing New York City. It won't be long now until we leave Newark and enter the infamous Lincoln Tunnel. We should be getting off the bus around nine a.m., and I'm finally going to be in Americas Melting Pot, the place where I belong where all people have a chance to make something out of themselves. It was a long and tedious ride from Lexington, Kentucky my home from birth and a home that was not bad to us colored people. It's also known as The Blue Grass State. It's my first time out of Kentucky, it seems as if I'm in a different world. They say it's pretty easy to get work in the big Apple, even if I have to start out as a waitress or something like that. I don't have so much pride that I can't do that kind of work, after all the most famous people in the world started out doing something small and meager.

I hope I can find a place to stay that doesn't cost too much money. Mama says New York is for well to do folk, and that I have no business here, but I'm going to prove her wrong if it's the last thing I do. I want to be somebody and if coming here is what it takes, then that's why I'm here to make it, just like all the other greats that got their start in this wonderful city.

When I check my watch, I find that it's 9:15a.m. and I'm standing on the street in front of the bus station in Manhattan trying to get a taxi to take me to a hotel. I'll stay in the hotel just long enough to find something I can afford. I've saved up three thousand dollars under my mattress at home, where I kept this money to come here. I have been saving for the last seven years. Ever since I graduated from high school, but from time to time, when

I was out of work, I had to pinch off of my savings and that's why I only have this amount of money to work with, cause daddy always did say, that I couldn't keep money for long, cause it burnt a hole in my pockets.

"Hey, you want a ride?" It was a taxi cab driver speaking to me as I come back to reality.

"Oh, yes please. I'm going to the hotel on 8th Avenue."

The cab driver gets out of the cab to get my bags. He looks like a football player or something. He has large biceps. He picked up all three of my bags and starts for the trunk of the taxi. While he is putting the bags in the trunk, I get into the cab, trying to act as if I had been here a dozen times. I didn't want to look like a tourist or someone who knew nothing about this fabulous place. I want to look as if I belong here.

"Where did you say you were headed?" He asked.

"It's a hotel not far from here, down the street somewhere."

"I think I know the one," the cabby said.

As I ride down the busy streets, I can see the tallest buildings I have ever seen in my life. There are literally fifteen or twenty cabs in sight. I'm trying to relax my long legs, but they seem to extend longer in the back of the taxi than there is room for them. No one knew that I had secretly wanted to be a model, because I never told anyone, not even my parents. They would have had a fit, if they knew I was thinking of something such as being a model. They want me to go to college and be a nurse, but me, Callie Mason, well I have other ideas. The large grain mill my father owns in Lexington, he named after the family name, "Mason Mills", would go on forever, but I have no intentions of my last name being Mason for very long. My biggest dream is to find my soul mate, fall in love and get married, but not to one of those domineering dogs that don't let their woman do anything, without them being there to sniff them out either, but that won't be until after I become a successful model.

"We're here," the driver says to me, after stopping in front of a very tall building.

"How much is the fare?" I ask.

"How much does it say on the meter?" The man questioned me.

"Oh I'm sorry," I told the man apologetically. The meter said five dollars flat. I gave him a dollar tip. When I get out I feel a little embarrassed, so I get out of the cab in a hurry. The man came around with my bags and took them inside the hotel for me. I'm finally here I thought, as I walked over to the man standing behind the service counter.

"How much are your single rooms?"

"Depends on the room. Do you want two beds or one?" The clerk asked?

"Just one," I replied rather irritated.

"Do you have any pets with you?"

"Do you see any pets?" I lashed back at the man.

"These rooms are too expensive for me," I'm now saying under my breath, as I get on the elevator. I just hope I find an apartment before I run out of money. I'm hoping I haven't made a mistake coming here, but I know in my heart that I'm doing the right thing. Daddy always tells me to do what I have to do, but that's only if It's agrees with his philosophy, but now I'm doing just that.

I heard the elevator making a pinging sound as it stopped on the 7th floor of the hotel. Just as I'm getting off, there is this very attractive man dressed in a suit and necktie getting on the elevator at the floor I'm to get off on. I should just stay on and ride down with him, I'm thinking to myself, but I get off the elevator and start to look for my room. The corridors are so long and I don't know exactly which way to go, but I look with great patience for my room. When I find it, I open the door to see a room that is pretty nice, but not nice enough for the pretty price I paid. People from my hometown are not used to paying this kind of money for a hotel room. This is no place for cheapskates who want to get more for their money than they are willing to pay. When my family and I went on vacations, the hotel room was more like forty-five and fifty dollars a night, but this is New York. I am glad to even get a room. All the other hotels are filled except the ones that are four hundred dollars and above, and God knows I surely can't afford anything, that's in that price range, I'm barely able to get the room I have, and if I don't get a job soon, I might just be camping out in the woods somewhere.

Once inside the room, I place my luggage on the floor of the hotel room near the closet, and decide to go and get something to eat in the hotel restaurant. Before I go, I brush my lustrous long black hair that everyone tells me is so beautiful. I smooth out my suit, while I admire my long slim body. "Yes, I am model material," I say, right out loud as if I am talking to someone other than myself. I have a habit of doing that sometimes, when I alone.

When I close the door behind me, I suddenly feel odd in this large hotel. It's kind of creepy as I walk to the elevators. Being that I have never been anywhere alone before in my whole life, I kind of have the jitters. As I stand here waiting for the elevator doors to open, I wish I had at least worn a jacket. It's cold in the corridor and when the doors do open, I see that tall handsome man in the suit again. He is standing right in front of me. I sort of clear my throat, as I step inside the elevator, without getting too close to him. My better judgment tells me not to get too friendly with anyone, until I get to know him or her.

"What floor would you like Miss?" He asks.

"The lobby please," I say, looking straight ahead and being careful not to look at him.

"Where are you from?"

"I beg your pardon," I say.

"Are you from around here? If you were, I thought maybe you could show me around."

"No I'm not from around here and if I were, I wouldn't be showing you around," I say to him, as the elevator doors open and I'm looking at him from the corner of my eye to make sure he's not going to get too close to me, and then I step out into the lobby. He enters the lobby as well. He is still behind me, as I go into the dining area, where I find a table. If I weren't so timid, I would have entered into a conversation with him, but my fear of strangers goes back a long way, when I was a child and a man tried to lure me into his car, but I ran screaming instead, and the next day I found out that he had been successful at luring one of my classmates and somehow she wound up dead. He definitely is all that, but I can't just let the first man I see in New York pick me up now can I. My parents taught me better than that and the thought of my classmate, who was killed, has never left my subconscious mind. At twenty-five, I'm still a virgin and I'm going to stay that way until the day I get married. My plan has always been to save myself for Mr. Right. After being in the church choir practically all my life, I am not about to compromise my morals now. I've made it this far and I'm going all the way to the alter and then to the honeymoon bed. Yes, mama has taught me well. She's drummed virginity until marriage into my head, ever since I was five years old. It was like a record that played over and over in my head, until I was completely brainwashed and when I became a teenager, if I even thought about sex, I felt as if I had done something so awful, that I had to say the Lord's prayer five times before I went to sleep that night.

The waiter was now standing at the table waiting to take the order. Once I had looked over the menu, I decided to have opened faced roast beef sandwich with mashed potatoes and gravy. I will splurge just this once. It is inconceivable to me that the man that was in the elevator with me, is now staring at me from across the room. Pretending not to see him, I pick up a newspaper that is lying on the table, left by someone who was here before me. As I start to read it, I peak out of the corner of my eye again, and the man is now sipping a drink and still looking at me. Quickly, I put my eyes back on the newspaper again, trying to act as if I am not noticing his stare.

When the waiter brings my food, being that I am so nervous and all, I can barley eat. I start to play with my food, then I take a few bites and quickly get up from the table and start for the cashier to pay for my order. I am just too nervous to do my usual ritual of gulping down my breakfast, because I am always in such a hurry. Now I blame him for making me waste my food, as if I can afford to waste anything. After paying for the food, I head back to the seventh floor.

Once inside my hotel room, I close the door, lock it and I'm standing here with my back against the door and then, I let out a big sigh of relief. I feel a little safer now, but to my surprise the phone starts to ring. I'm so surprised because, I told the man at the front desk that I could not afford to pay seventy-five dollars to have them turn the phone on. He must have felt sorry for me and turned it on anyway. I slowly move toward the phone and then pick up the receiver.

"Hello."

"Hello dear. It's your mother. I just want to know that you've made it safely honey. Are you all right?" Mama says, in that high-pitched voice of hers.

Yes mother, I'm fine," I lied. She had always taught me not to lie.

Why didn't I just tell her the truth, that I'm scared out of my wits? Why didn't I listen to my mother and go to college to be a nurse like she wanted me to do. Now it's too late. I have to prove to everyone that I'm right about the decision I've made to come here. I have to prove that I can make it on my own. I've always been told that I've been stubborn from the day I was born. Daddy always says that I was more stubborn then the pet mule he had when he was a boy.

"Have you eaten yet dear?"

"Yes, mother I just finished eating something in the hotel restaurant."

"Make sure you wear something warm to bed tonight. You know how cold it can get up there," she tells me, with that tone of voice that says I'm your mother and I know what's best for you.

"Yes mother, I'll wear my flannel pajamas you bought me for Christmas."

"All right dear. You call me tomorrow."

"All right mother, I'll call you then."

When I'm finished talking to my mother I fall backward onto the bed. I'm feeling quite drained and I just want to get some sleep. Sleep is what I need. I'll feel better when...

It's the afternoon, when I finally awaken, I realize that I've slept fully dressed in my clothes. That bus ride from Lexington must have worn my frail body completely out. As I sleepily get up from the bed, I go to the bath room to take a shower. I turn on the hot water and the hotter the water gets the better I like it. I need to be refreshed before I go out to look for a news paper in order to find a job. I will just find a temporary job until I get that big modeling break and a short while later, I find myself walking the streets of New York City looking in shop windows and wishing I could buy some of the most wonderful clothes I had ever seen. There are many people walking and all of them going somewhere. I don't know where they could all possibly be going in such great magnitudes, but I walk until my feet hurt and then walk some more, after resting for awhile in a restaurant and looking out of the window at all the people passing by, as they walk towards their destinations.

The rest of the evening is a relaxing one. I'm sitting in my room watching TV and reading magazines. I'm too tired to do much of anything my first day in the city, because I'm very tired from the long bus ride.

The very next morning, I shower and get dressed in my short leather skirt and my cardigan sweater, I go down to get a newspaper to look at the want ads. I also stop to get a cup of coffee before going back to my room, so when I go into the dining area where it's crowded with guests staying at the hotel, I see him. He's dressed in black dress pants and a black turtle neck sweater. Since it is January, it's appropriate for this time of year. Snow flakes have already started to fall, as I look out of the big glass window of the dining area.

I have found a table got a cup of coffee and I'm ready to hurry out of here. When I did leave the restaurant, I practically run through the hotel lobby to the elevator and it isn't long, before I'm back in my room. As soon as I collect my thoughts, I grab my leather coat and purse, hurry outside and wave to the first taxi I see. I tell the man I want to go to Macy's Department Store, because that's where I will first look for a job. Clerks in New York make more than just the average clerk in Lexington. At least I would be able to make enough to get an apartment until my big break came.

When I get inside Macy's I can hardly hold my mouth shut. It must have dropped open, because as I look around, people are looking at me funny as I move slowly through the aisles. What I see is like nothing I have ever seen before. It is so large and it's like everything is so shiny and new. As I walk through the jewelry section, I noticed that my mouth is open and I immediately closed it. A lady is standing and looking all pretty behind the counter, as I walk up to her to ask for directions.

"Do you have a personnel department?" I ask the woman, who is dressed so very elegantly and willing to help me out, so she can get her commission.

"Why yes, we do," she says, as she looks me up and down, while giving me the directions.

"Thank you." She didn't seem to be very impressed with me, I'm thinking, as I stop to check myself out in one of the huge mirrors along the walls. In my opinion, I think I look just fine. I never did have an inferior complex of any kind, not even when I was growing up as a kid. What is wrong with that woman anyway? She just doesn't know class when she sees it. She will be surprised if I come out of here with a job.

That's just what happened, by the time I leave Macy's I have a job all right. I am to start tomorrow morning. When I get outside the store, I do a little dance; you know the kind we do in church when we feel happy. I then gained my composure and waved for a taxi that stopped immediately. I feel pretty good about myself. I'm in New York City and I have landed a job at one of the finest department stores ever, if not the finest. Let's see what that woman does now when I see her tomorrow and I tell her that I'm working there too. I'll go up to her and thank her for telling me how to get to the personnel department. She will certainly be surprised when she sees it's me.

Once back at the hotel, I stop at the front desk to pay for another night, which is the low point in my day. This is just too much money. My three thousand dollars is beginning to dwindle slowly. I am going to have to watch every penny I spend from this point on. I still have to get an apartment or at least a bed and a cheap television, so I won't get too lonely. Living alone I imagine can get to be pretty monotonous and I want to be prepared for those lonely nights when I'm not working. I have to stay focused on what it is I have waited for my entire life, to be a model, that is my dream. I refuse to let a man ruin my life the way I have seen so many other girls' lives ruined. Scooter Jones had broken my heart, but my life is still in tact.

The very next morning, I'm up by six a.m. I don't have to be at work until nine a.m., but I want to be ready in time for my first day on the job and I certainly don't want to be late. When I asked about the salary, the woman told me I would be making twelve to fifteen dollars an hour. I wasn't used to that kind of pay, but it's also a higher cost of living in big cities. I'll have to look for an apartment after work. I just have to find one soon or I might be on my way back to Lexington. Money is something I don't want to run out of, being this far away from home and all.

While I'm fixing the thin silk nightgown on one of the manikins in lingerie, I happen to notice a man looking at some very expensive sleepwear. He is well dressed in a cashmere topcoat and silk scarf around his neck. He also is wearing black leather gloves.

"Can I help you sir?" I ask.

"Why yes, maybe you can at that."

"Exactly what is it you're looking for?"

"What ever it is, I think I've found it," the man said, smiling at me.

I hope he isn't trying to come on to me. I've had enough for just being here for two nights. All I need is some man trying to pick me up on the job. He's smiling too much at me and I don't like it, but I'm here to make sales and I must remain as polite as I can, without enticing him.

"Well maybe you don't need my help after all."

"Oh yes, I need your help alright."

"And what exactly do you mean by that?" I ask him.

"Have you ever done any modeling?"

"Some," is my answer.

"I own a modeling agency in Paris and I'm looking for new faces and bodies of course."

"Don't play games Mr." I just don't have the time," I told him rather nastily.

He is now studying me and I'm just standing here in amazement. The look of disgust on my face should scare him away, but he just keeps sizing me up. I try to move in between clothes so he can no longer see me, but he insistently follows me while unbuttoning his coat. It is rather warm in the store, but I don't want him to get too comfortable, after all he's embarrassing me.

"Yes, you're perfect," he says to me.

"Perfect for what? I'm going to call security if you don't stop eye balling me Mr."

"Would you like to go to Paris? If you do want to go, you're hired."

"Hired for what?"

"I can make you one of the biggest models in the world," he said, as he is taking out his card and handing it to me. I just stand here reading his business card trying to make some sense of this. It just could not be happening.

I've only been here two days and without even looking, I land a modeling job in Paris. This is all to good to be true. The card does say Pierre's Modeling Agency as he holds it up for me to read. Could it be that he's legitimate? Could this be the break I've been hoping for all my life?

"How do I know you're for real?"

"Here, take my card and call the number at the bottom."

I slowly take the card from him. I read it again. It looks as if he might be telling me the truth. I put the card in my skirt pocket. He is still looking at me with excitement in his eyes. Was he really looking for models? I would soon know, when and if I called the number on the card. It must be an international number. It is not familiar to me at all.

"If you're interested, you can call me at that number on Friday. I should be in my office by then. I'm flying back to Paris on Thursday."

"If I'm interested, I'll give you a call," I told the man and he looked at me as if I were nuts. I do believe insanity does run in my family, about two generations back.

"Don't wait too long, I just happen to have a spot open."

The man left me standing here, still not able to make out what had just happened. I was nervous, irritated, and hopeful all at the same time. I can't wait to call that number on the card. I have to find out if this was for real. Knowing my luck it couldn't be real. I will probably wind up being disappointed, when I find out this guy is putting me on. Yet, I have to know for sure. I would have to wait for my lunch hour to make that call. There is no way I can wait until I'm back in my hotel room. I am just too anxious to wait that long.

I sell a few pieces of lingerie during the morning and by the time I decide to go to lunch, my heart is still racing. I look for the first phone booth I can find. When I find one, I whip out my phone card I bought before I left home. I figured I would need something prepaid, because I don't know how long my money will hold out. Now I'm glad I bought the card. It certainly is a handy thing to have right now. I find myself trying to dial all the numbers, making mistakes and trying to dial again and again. I'm too nervous to dial the darn phone number. I need to be calmer in order to get the numbers right this time.

Finally I get through to the number on the card. The phone rings several times, before I hear a voice on the other end.

"Pierre's Modeling Agency. May I help you?"

"Yes, I'm trying to find out about your agency. I have been looking for a job."

"Well, Pierre Debore is not in at the moment, and I don't know when he'll return."

"Can you tell me something about your agency?" I asked the woman, who had a very thick French accent.

"Pierre Debore has had this agency for the past ten years now, and we employ some of the biggest name models in the world."

"Like who?"

"Like Sean Taylor, Danielle Bardeau and Paul Giddeon."

Those are big names. Maybe that guy was telling me the truth.

"Thank you very much. Goodbye." I hang up the phone and my heart starts to pound.

I was in a daze all the way back to the hotel. I hardly made it through my first day on the new job at Macy's Department Store. I was already in my head, in Paris and couldn't wait to get there. The problem now is, how will I get there and will Pierre still want me at the end of the week. I hope he doesn't find someone else in the mean time. Friday is a long way off. Three days to be exact and they will be the longest three days of my life. I will definitely call Pierre on Friday, but now I'd better get my coat and punch out, because it's quitting time for me.

Before getting out of the cab I notice a man who looks as if he is homeless, begging in front of the hotel. I decide that, I will hurry past him. I don't have any money to give away. My purse is on my shoulder and I'm clutching it tightly with my hand in order to secure it, while going into the hotel.

"Hey lady, can you spare some change?" The man asks me.

"I don't have any," I tell him, as I'm trying to rush past him to get inside the hotel.

Just as I start to go past him, he grabs my arm rigorously.

"I said, do you got any money?"

"No, and let go of me right now."

"Don't get smart with me Miss. I don't like smart ladies like you."

Now the man continues to pull even harder on my arm. I'm as frantic as a scared rabbit with a hound chasing him and simply don't know what to do. He pulls on my arm and starts cursing, when a man comes out of the hotel and collars the man. To my surprise, it's the man in the hotel that had been staring at me, whenever he saw me.

"Get away from here, buddy," the man told the beggar.

The vagrant suddenly took off down the street running, with his coattail flying behind him in the wind.

"Are you O.K.?" He asks.

"Yes, I'm fine, thanks to you," I answer.

"Why don't we go into the restaurant and have a cup of coffee. It might warm you up some. You look as if you're chilled to the bone. Better yet, why don't we go to a really nice restaurant around the corner. They have excellent food there."

"Thanks, I'd like that." I can't believe I'm saying yes to this man, who had made me so frightened, when I first got here, by staring me down every chance he got. Now I'm consenting to having dinner with him. He is very good-looking and I certainly am not ashamed to be seen with him. He has on dress pants, white shirt and a black leather jacket. He is looking real good to me by this time. Being alone has gotten to me already. It will be fun to have dinner with a gentleman. After all, he did rescue me from that homeless man in front of the hotel.

We find a table near a window and sit down there. The restaurant has round tables with white tablecloths on them. I am surprised that I'm not that nervous being with him. He is like a night in shining armor compared to the day I arrived. I'm really quite glad to be in his company and I think he was surprised I had taken him up on his offer to have dinner with him.

"Thank you for coming to my rescue."

"My pleasure."

"Are you from New York?" I ask him.

"No, I'm from L.A."

"Where you from?"

"I'm from Kentucky."

"What's a nice girl like you doing here alone?"

"How do you know that I'm alone?"

"I have my ways of finding out things," he says, as he picks up the menu to read.

I look at my menu also. I don't say anything more. I just want to eat. I haven't eaten since yesterday, and I'm starved. Everything looks so good. It's hard for me to decide what to order. The menu is so exotic, I'm not sure what all of it means. I do know what fried chicken is, so I figured I'll be safe and won't look like a dummy, if I get the fried chicken and the vegetables. I just hope it's Southern fried chicken.

"Have you decided what you want?" He asks.

"Yes, I'll have the fried chicken with a side order of vegetables."

"Anything to drink?"

"I'll have a coke," I tell him.

The waiter is just about to come to our table, when I realize I don't know the man's name and he didn't know mine either. This is odd. He hasn't even asked me my name. Now I'm beginning to wonder what is his name. He probably has a name like Joe or John or something like that. He is still looking over the menu, when the waiter gets to our table.

"I'll have filet minion and a screw driver," he said.

"She'll have the same," he tells the waiter.

The waiter takes the menus and I'm in a bit of shock. He has completely ignored what I have told him about how I wanted fried chicken and a coke, and what's a screwdriver, anyway. Why do we need a screwdriver with our meal? I'm beginning to think this guy is weird. I'm too stunned to say anything about what had just happened.

"What's your name?" He asks, as he takes out a cigarette and lights it.

"My name is Callie Mason, and yours?" I ask rather stiffly.

"Johnny Parker," he said, taking a drag off his cigarette and blowing the smoke to his right side. I thought he looked like a John or Johnny. How do I know these things? I must have some psychic abilities. Mama said psychic abilities run in our family, but I'm not about to think about that now. I am too taken with this handsome man who likes to take charge. He doesn't even know me and he is taking charge of what I will have for dinner. I like a take-charge kind of guy.

When the food is served, I'm surprised that I'm not too shy to eat in the presence of this man, but I guess I'm just too hungry to care. The waiter had also brought us drinks and the drinks were not the color of coke. I take a sip of the liquid in the glass to wash down the food.

"What's this?" I ask, almost choking.

"What's the matter? Haven't you ever had alcohol before?"

"Yes, I just thought it was a soft drink. It took me by surprise." I have just lied again. I have never had alcohol before in my entire life. My parents are too dedicated to their religion and it doesn't call for alcohol. Besides, I swore I would never drink alcohol after what happened to my cousin Terry. He drank so much alcohol he threw up until he died right there on the spot. I swore from that day on, I would never put alcohol to my lips to drink it.

We pretty much eat in silence after that. Johnny did tell me that he was an actor in Hollywood and had been there for several years now. I couldn't believe my ears. Here I am in New York City and I have met an owner of a modeling agency from Paris and now the guy who couldn't keep his eyes off me is an actor. This is too much like some fairy tale, if you ask me, but a fairy tale that I am happily enjoying.

When we finish eating, Johnny just sits back in his chair and looks at me. It's as if he's trying to figure out what makes me tick. He picks up a matchbook opens it up and then takes out a pen.

"Put your number here," he says, as if it's the usual daily conversation.

"Why should I give you my number?"

"Because I want it and you want me to have it."

"You think you know it all don't you?"

"I just want to keep an eye on you while I'm here. Make sure you're all right and everything," he says, with that beautiful smile and showing his pearly white teeth, that look as if they have never missed a day being brushed thoroughly.

If ever I needed a friend, it's now. I'd be most happy to have this man looking out for me. I found out that he is only going to be in town for two weeks. He is doing a shoot for a commercial. I'm very taken by his good looks and his glamorous lifestyle. The kind I want for myself.

Yes, I want to be a star and have people know me by my first name, that will become a household word. That was and is my dream, and I will make it happen, that I promise myself. If mom and dad only knew what I had planned for my life, I would be in hot water with them forever. They have always wanted me to have some noble profession like becoming a nurse or even a doctor. I want to be a star.

"Why are you taking such an interest in me?" I ask.

"Maybe because I'm interested in you. I could be your night in shining amour."

"Maybe," I say, flirting just a tad bit.

"How old are you?" He asks point blank.

"I'm twenty-five," I tell him.

"And, how old are you?" I ask him.

"I'm Thirty," he replies.

I couldn't believe he was that old. He doesn't look a day over twenty-five.

On the way back to the hotel we're both somewhat quiet. We've taken a taxi, that was outside the restaurant and now, we're almost back to the hotel. I feel warm and cozy sitting next to this man, who came out of nowhere. A stranger who has in very little time, pretty much captured my heart. I feel protected and he has made me feel comfortable in his company. The one thing I didn't want to do, was to fall in love, and I might just have to stick to that idea. I have a lot to do in this world and it's going to take some time to do it. I don't want any relationships to get in the way. Now that I've been offered the opportunity to go to Paris, I had better go. Finding Johnny was bad timing, there can be no real love affair. I just don't have the time right now. Besides, this man is so handsome; I'll bet he has hundreds of women after him. I wouldn't stand a chance anyway.

Once inside the hotel, Johnny escorts me to my room. He leaves me at the door after he looks into my eyes and kisses my hand. He is certainly a charming devil. I watch his perfect physique from behind as he goes toward the elevators. Am I really falling for him? No, I couldn't be. I'm still on the rebound from Scooter. This just isn't the right time. I keep trying to convince myself, but who am I fooling me or the man in the moon. Stop trying to fool yourself, Callie, yes; you are falling for him in the worst way. I'll fix it by just engrossing myself in my work and put Johnny right out of my mind.

It's my third day in town and I'm sitting in the cafeteria for lunch. I play with my food as I begin to think about the night before, finding myself thinking about Johnny most of the night. He is quite remarkable all right. I'm also thinking about the phone call I'm going to make on Friday. I hope I won't be disappointed. I hope he doesn't forget who I am. Pierre Debore might just forget about the woman he saw in Macy's Department Store. That woman being me, of course.

As I ponder on what I'm going do for the next two days before Friday, a woman walks up to where I am sitting. She seems nice enough and is very well dressed. But why is she standing at my table? Could it be that she thinks I'm someone other than who I am?

"May I sit with you?" She asks.

"Sure, have a seat," I said to the woman, who is dressed very elegantly, like she's some kind of businesswoman or something. I hear that New York has very successful women who are in business or own their businesses. The cafeteria is full by now and after looking around, I can see that there really are no more seats left. The place must have filled while I was daydreaming about the future and about Johnny Parker. There are a few other black people other than myself, but most are white. I am happy to see someone of my own color and race. It gives me a sense of security, while I'm so far from home.

"How long have you been working here?" The woman asks.

"Just a couple of days. I just got here a few days ago. I'm trying to find an apartment."

"Are you looking for an apartment?"

"Yes, I am," I tell her.

"I'm looking for a room mate. You could share the rent with me, that way it won't be that much for either of us." she says to me, as if she has known me forever and then takes a bite of her chili dog, that has been put together quite sloppily, because meat is falling from her bun.

"Are you for real?" I ask, with wide eyes open. This would be perfect for me. I could stay with a room mate and it wouldn't cost me that much. This would be the right thing and I won't have to stay alone in a big city, but can I trust her? I don't know her from Adam.

"Where do you live?"

"I live in upper Manhattan."

"Isn't Manhattan kind of expensive?" I ask the woman. She looks to be about twenty- nine or thirty.

"Not really. Some friends of my dad's own the building and my rent is pretty reasonable. It's only around eight hundred a month. You can pay three hundred if you like and I'll pay the other five hundred. It would take a load off me, even if you just paid the three hundred," she says, now playing with her food with her fork.

"Sounds good to me," I said. She then gave me her phone number and address. I am to call her when I'm sure about the deal. I'm pretty much sure already. But I tell her I will meet her for lunch tomorrow and give her my answer. We get to know each other pretty well in these thirty minutes and I find out her name is Cynthia Barringer and I could tell she is the kind of person I wouldn't mind living with. Everything is falling into place. Well almost everything, but Johnny that is. I cannot let myself fall deeply in love. Not now, when everything seems to be working out the way I had hoped it would. I'm going to be staying in an apartment before the end of my first week. I still have hopes of being in Paris as one of Pierre's models, but what is the chance of that happening anyway. I have to look out for right now, and right now I need a place to stay.

When evening comes, I find myself lying on the bed, trying to put all the pieces together of what is really happening in my life, the phone rings. I hope it isn't mama. She always frets about what I'm eating and how warmly I'm dressing when I'm away from home. This is not the time to have to listen to her telling me what I should or should not be doing. It's about the fifth ring and I pick up the receiver. I'm not sure I want to answer it.

"Hello Callie."

It's him, Johnny. I hesitate before saying anything. I want to brush him off. He can only just get in my way. I really do have more important things to do.

"Hello Johnny. To what do I owe this unexpected call?"

"Just checking on you."

"I'm fine," I say. The sound of his voice is very sexy and intriguing. Just because he came to my rescue the other day, I hope he doesn't think he owns me I'm thinking to myself, as I wait for him to speak.

"How about dinner tonight. I only have a week left in New York. My shooting will end in a few days and I'll be heading back to L.A. Would you like to have dinner with me? I promise I won't make you drink alcohol, alright."

"I'm kind of tired tonight. It's my second day on the job and I need to stay in and get some rest."

"I won't keep you that long. I promise."

"I said no. Don't you understand what no means?"

"I know what no means, I'm just trying to change your mind, Callie."

"Wait, I have a better Idea. Why don't I come to your room and we order in. That way you can eat and still get some rest at the same time."

"I don't know Johnny. I don't think that's a very good idea."

"Why not. You afraid of me or something?"

"No, I'm not afraid of you. I just don't think so, that's all."

"I'll see you in ten minutes," he says, while I'm left holding the phone to my ear and now I can hear the dial tone buzzing ever so loudly. I wasn't prepared for his last words. He is on his way to my room. Now what am I going to do, I think as I'm pacing the floor, I try hard to think of what to do. Should I or should I not let him in. I don't want to seem rude after he so graciously helped me outside the hotel the other day. Now I'm trapped. He's got me cornered and I am not ready for this approach, I'm thinking and almost slip as I make a dash for the bathroom. I have to brush my hair and put on some makeup. I can't let him see me without my makeup. I fumble in the drawers for the makeup case spilling things from the drawer being too full. My hands are shaking as I try to put on eye liner, then lipstick, and then a little blush. I make a circle with my lips trying to line them with liner too. This is sick. I think to myself as I continue to hurry to put on the makeup. What do I think I'm doing? Then I answer my own question. I'm getting ready to let a man into my room.

A few minutes later after I have gotten fully dressed in slacks and sweater, there's a knock at the door. I take a deep breath and swallow hard, before going to take a look out of the peephole. It's him all right. He even looks fine through the peephole. It looks as if he is holding something. It looks as if it could be flowers. I can't tell what it is he has with him. It must be something for me, no doubt.

"Are you going to open the door?" He asks.

"Yeah, sure," I say, and at that moment I begin to unlock the door to let him in. When I see him, I just stand there not knowing what to say.

"Can I come in?" He asks, as he stands there with a bottle in one hand and flowers in the other. He hands the flowers to me, as he walks past me and sets the bottle on the table. I just stand there, as he pulls out a chair to sit in.

"I brought a bottle of wine. You must be tense from work today."

"I'm fine," I say.

"Tell you what, I'll order up some food for us, as soon as you tell me what you want." "I'm really not very hungry," I tell him.

"Sure you are. A working girl needs nourishment."

"Well, I might have some shrimp with sauce."

"Okay, I'm right on it," he says, picking up the receiver to call the hotel restaurant.

I sit timidly on the bed, while he makes the call. I am looking him over from head to toe, as me makes the order. He has on a black silk shirt, and gray dress pants. The two top buttons of his shirt are open. I can see a little of his bronze hairless chest. He's wearing a post earring in his right ear. I can tell that his gold watch is very expensive. I'm so nervous I'm almost shaking. I'm trying to keep my composure. I don't want to seem childish. As soon as he hangs up, the phone rings and startles both of us.

"You want me to answer it?"

"I'll get it," I say. It just can't be mama calling, but somehow, I know it's her. She will have a heart attack if a man answers my phone. How many times have I heard those lectures she used to give and still does, about staying pure until your wedding day? She would never believe me if I told her it's just a friend, who has helped me out in a tight spot. I just want to let the phone ring, but then mama will be worried that I'm out late and she will keep calling until she gets me, so I pick up the receiver.

"Hello?" I say, as if I'm asking a question.

"Hello honey. Did I wake you?"

"No, I was just getting ready for bed, mama." I've been here three days and this was the third time that I've lied.

"I was just making sure you were in your room safe for the night."

"I'm fine mama, really I am."

"Okay dear. Your dad sends his love."

"Tell dad I love him too mama." I hang up the phone felling a little embarrassed. Johnny was already pouring himself a glass of wine. At this point I feel I need a glass of wine just to calm my jumpy nerves. I have never been in such close quarters alone with a man before, and certainly not one as handsome and charming as Johnny Parker.

"Well, Mademoiselle Callie, would you like me to pour you a glass of Vino?"

"Sure, I think I could use one," I say. After taking a few sips, I begin to feel better. My nerves stop jumping and I am a little more relaxed. My mind is racing to know what it is that I'm to do next. He sits looking at me and I begin to twist my hair, needing to do something with my hands, I choose to twist my hair. Now I let out a deep breath, as I try to make some sense of all this in my own mind. He is still looking at me now, and I smile back at him. I'm too shy to keep eye contact, so I lower my eyes to the floor, and then I feel his hand on mine. It's warm and comforting and I like the way it feels. This time I take a big gulp of wine, as he continues to massage my hand with his hand. I should say something now to break the long silence, but maybe I should let him break it first. Oh, I don't know what to do. I haven't done that much dating in my life, and now I realize that I don't really know what a date actually consists of, or what is expected of me.

My mind seems to be racing out of control. I have never felt like this before. There is a knock at the door. Thank

God, it must be the food he ordered, I think to myself, and jumping up from the table and gliding towards the door. At this point I'm glad we've been interrupted. Who knows what might have happened if we hadn't been interrupted by the knock on the door. I open the door to find a young man in a hotel uniform holding a large covered silver platter.

"Come in. You can set the food on the table," I tell the young man.

"Is this everything you ordered?" He asks.

"Yes, this looks like everything," I say.

When the man left, Johnny and I began to eat our food. From time to time he feeds me food from his plate and asks me if I like it. Of course, I say yes. He is smiling now as he starts to feed me a large shrimp. I bite off most of it and then he eats what is left. At this point my toes are beginning to curl up. He has me completely under his spell. The city lights from outside the window are so beautiful and the atmosphere is overwhelmingly romantic. Johnny has conveniently lowered the lights, while I'm finishing up the last bit of food on my plate.

"Have you ever been to L.A.?" He asks.

"No, I've never gone there before."

"You would love L.A. There are modeling agencies out there, you know."

"Yes, I know."

Was he hinting for me to follow him back to L.A.? I have to admit it sounds very tempting? I just don't really know him yet. Maybe he's some pimp or something. I would just die if I found out he's a pimp.

I still have to call Pierre tomorrow and everyone knows, that Paris is the place to be if you want to make it big. I promised myself I wouldn't let anything get in the way of my dreams. The dreams I've had since I was a little girl.

"Are you a pimp?" I blurt out.

"No, I'm not a pimp," he says, with a frown on his face. "What makes you think I'm a pimp? Do I look like a pimp?" He asks, as if he's offended and I really can't blame him, but I just want to know for sure, I'm not dining with some Mack Daddy or something.

"I don't know. You just look so good, I guess." He just looks to good to be true.

"I assure you, I'm not," he says.

The rest of the evening went rather well. We actually had a pillow fight. I think he let me win. We tumbled on the bed as we tried to hit each other. Then we both just laid there exhausted from the fight. I turn to look at him after catching my breath, he is already looking at me as we lye here on our backs. He takes my hand and kisses it. I just continue to look at him. I am quite smitten with his charm. There is no doubt about that.

It was well after 11:00p.m., when he finally left. I have to go to work tomorrow morning and he has to do another shoot. I went right off to sleep when he left, but before he did go, he gave me a quick kiss on the mouth. I was in seventh heaven. Mama always told me, never kiss on the first date, but it wasn't that much of a kiss. It seems as if I'm breaking all of mama's rules, except the big one. I would never break that one. I know mama would know if I did break the big one, because I have never been able to hide anything from mama. She would get it out of me so fast. She just had a way of making you tell the truth.

Chapter 2

It was hard to concentrate at work the next day, and I had to call Pierre as soon as I got a chance. I hoped he was still interested, but was I still interested in going to Paris after last night. I have to get moved over the weekend. Cynthia would want to know what my decision was at lunch today and I had make up my mind to move in with her. It would help me out a lot to share the rent, instead of trying to pay rent alone. Now that Johnny had hinted for me to go back to L.A. with him, I am beginning to get confused, and I'm not as sure about becoming a model anymore. It's just that I have to do what I have dreamed I would, and that's become a star model.

I called Pierre this morning on by break, and he was very clear that he still wanted me to come to Paris. He said to let him know when I'm ready and he would send the plane ticket. I told him that it would be at least another three weeks before I could even think about coming. I figured by then I would have some more money saved up and I would not have to go to Paris broke. I also found Cynthia at lunch and told her I would move in, but that I didn't think I would be staying that long, and filled her in on what Pierre had said to me. Yes, I would be going to Paris and since talking with Pierre, I couldn't get Paris and the glamour of being a model off my mind. It's later in the day and it's almost time to punch out for the day.

I'm back to my hotel this evening after doing a little shopping. I didn't know how I was going to break the news to Johnny, but I have decided for sure that I would be taking Pierre up on his offer. Just as I was about to get into the shower, the phone rang. I wrapped a towel around me and went to pick up the receiver.

"Hello," I say.

"Hello Callie. It's Johnny."

"Oh, Hi Johnny." I tried to sound as if I were happy to hear from him and deep down inside I'm ecstatically happy. I know this was going to be a hard thing to tell Johnny what I have decided to do, so I thought I would try to explain it over a cup of coffee.

"Can you meet me in the hotel dinning room?" I ask him.

"Sure. What time should I meet you there?"

"Give me about twenty minutes," I tell him and then hang up the phone.

After my shower, I hurried and got dressed. I picked out something sheik. It was a black tight fitting dress that came up just above my kneecap. It has a V-neck with short sleeves. I put on my best perfume, when I suddenly think to myself. What am I doing anyway? Here I am going off to Paris, but I'm doing everything to be seductive to Johnny. My mind was messed up for sure. At this point I didn't know what I wanted. I just hoped whatever happened it would be what made me happy.

When I got to the cafeteria, I saw him sitting there. When he spotted me, he gave me that big beautiful smile of his. I walked slowly over to him and sat down across from him in the booth.

"Wow, he says. You look good."

"Thank you," I say, as I'm trying to act as if everything is alright.

"Hey, Let's get out of here," he says wiping his mouth with the napkin and getting up all at the same time.

"Where we going?"

"This is Friday night. Let's go clubbing," he says and holding out his hand to me. I took it and he led me back to the elevators.

"You better get your coat. I'll wait here for you."

"Okay," I say, as I pushed the elevator button and the door opened.

When I got into my room, I ran and looked into the mirror in the bathroom, and tried to fix my makeup, gave my hair several swishes and I was off.

Once outside the hotel, I looked around the streets and they were busy with lots of traffic and there were so many people on the street, all of whom were going somewhere. This was such an exciting place. It was almost dark out now and the lights that lit up the streets were magnificent and they glimmered in the blackness of night.

As soon as Johnny got a taxi we were headed for one of the nightspots. It was a club that Johnny said he found out about through some of the other actors he worked with. As we sat in the back seat of the taxi, Johnny held my hand. It felt so good. He looked gorgeous as usual, in his gray suit and tie, that he had on under his very expensive long length coat.

When we got to the night club, Johnny paid fifty dollars for the two of us to get in. To me, that seemed kind of expensive just to go to a club, but what did a girl from Lexington Kentucky know about big city life? I know the answer to that question, absolutely nothing, now that we were inside, we found a booth in a secluded corner of the place. Johnny ordered drinks as the live band played the blues. It was some local band I found out, but they could really sing. Some of my old favorites seemed to come from the band.

"How about a dance, my queen?"

"Why certainly," I say, as he takes me by the hand and we move toward the dance floor. It was a slow soft tune, and Johnny held me close. Mama didn't even know I knew how to dance. I used to practice in my room in the mirror and when I heard her coming, I would turn off the music and pretend I was studying. Daddy, would have gone to his grave, him being so religious and all, if he had known that I knew how to dance.

"I could hold you like this forever," Johnny whispers in my ear, and you know what, I could have let him hold me like that forever. That was just the way I was feeling at that precise moment. Somehow, it didn't really matter what mama and daddy thought anymore. This was the most romantic time of my life.

"I'll bet you have all kinds of girlfriends back in L.A."

"No, as a matter of fact, I don't have any girlfriends at all back in L.A. I want you to be my girlfriend," he says, while looking down at me as we danced.

"Okay," I say, smiling up at him.

The crowd was getting bigger now, and the band was getting louder. Smoke began to fill the air, and I was beginning to strangle on the smoke. I started to cough, and cough and cough. Johnny led me back to the booth.

"Are you all right?"

Yes. I just kind of choked on all the smoke and stuff," I say, a little embarrassed.

"Here, take a sip of this." He holds out the glass for me to take.

"You think this will help?" I ask, with my hand on my chest, and my eyes beginning to water. I take the drink and take a sip. I kind of pat my chest to try to clear my windpipe so I can breathe again. It worked. I was starting to feel better now that I'm breathing evenly again.

"I'm sorry, I should have gotten better seating. There is an awful lot of smoke in this area." He takes a napkin and start to fan away some of the smoke.

"No, that's alright. It could have been worse. I could have choked to death," I say, and we both begin to laugh.

When the waitress brought us another drink, it looked as if she was trying to come on to Johnny. I knew I didn't like the way she kept looking at him and talking to him and never once did she acknowledge that I was even there, but Johnny didn't give her anything to go on. He was a perfect gentleman during the whole scene.

The dance floor was really crowded by now, and everyone was rocking with the music. They played all the old time blues songs, by some of the old blues legends. There were others too that I didn't know, but it was all good. Everyone seemed so refined. This must be one of those blues clubs. Everyone kept their cool and everyone was having a good time. I could see couples dancing cozily together. The lights are dim and everyone is in their own little world. I feel as if I'm in a dream world too. When we went back to the booth to sit down Johnny held my hand until I was securely sitting, and then he continued to hold it as he moved around to sit beside me in the booth. He is looking at me now, and I'm looking at him.

"Callie," have you thought about coming back to L.A. with me?"

"Johnny, I really don't think I can do that just now. I have an offer to model in Paris and I might be going there soon."

"You can do that in L. A. Callie," he says, looking me squarely in the face.

"Johnny, I really don't want to talk about it now."

"Why, Callie? I don't want to lose you."

"You won't lose me Johnny, but this is something I have to do now. Please understand. We can still talk. The telephone has been invented you know."

"Look, I'll make you a deal." Johnny takes out a deck of cards and starts to shuffle them, I am just a bit confused at what he would do next. But I would soon find out.

"Here, I'll make you a proposition, you pull a card and I'll pull a card. Who ever pulls the highest card wins. If I win, you come back to L. A. If you win you go to Paris."

"I Don't know Johnny, it doesn't seem fair."

"You love me don't you Callie?" I had never wanted to say the word love. I wasn't ready for that word yet. Could I tell him I loved him this soon? I do love him, but I don't want to say it. I didn't want to think about that now. If I let him go back to Los Angeles alone, I might never see him again. I just don't know what to do. I wanted him and I wanted what Paris could offer me and I am just mixed up, because I don't know what I want. I guess I just want the best of both worlds. I know that I can't have both worlds, but I might just give it a try anyway.

"Answer me Callie."

"Yes, Yes, I do love you Johnny, but I can't make a deal like that."

"Of course you can. It's not that hard you know, not when you love someone," he says, now placing the deck on the table for me to pick a card. I don't want to pick a card. It's too final.

"You want to go first?" He asks.

"Yes, I'll go first," I say. I cut the deck. The top card is a ten of spades. If he beats me, will I really keep the bargain I now think to myself. He was about to cut the cards now after shuffling them again. Johnny pulled the Queen of Hearts. He had won. Now I would have to go back to L. A. With him, or I would definitely lose him. I don't want to lose him, but I also don't want to give up Paris and my modeling career.

"I guess that settles it. You're coming back with me Callie." I was happy and sad all at the same time. I didn't know if I would really do it. I made him a promise and now I was almost ready to break it, but I couldn't. I couldn't hurt Johnny like that. He was too nice for me to hurt him. The music played softly in the background. I could hardly hear it now. My mind was racing back and forth. Should I go with him, or shouldn't I go with him. Somehow I felt I had been tricked into saying something I didn't want to say. But, I did want to say it. I wanted to go with him.

Now, I don't know what I want. He pulled the Queen of Hearts, and it beats a Ten of Spades all day long.

"You'll love California, Callie. Just wait and see."

"I believe you Johnny," I say as he holds my hand.

"First I want to work awhile and save up some money, before I come. I don't want to go there without any money. I'll work here at Macy's for a few more weeks, then I'll join you there in L.A."

He didn't like the idea, but he went along with it. He promised to help me move my bags into Cynthia's apartment the next day. He would be leaving Monday morning. Everything was going so fast. My head was spinning and everything was getting all jumbled up. My plans were not going as I had wanted them to. Here I was in New York and already, I'm leaving for Paris and going to L. A. with Johnny. Make up your mind girl, I think to myself. Johnny asked me to dance again to one of his favorite songs. It was a nice slow song. He held me tight and the night was even more beautiful as one could see through the skylight in the club.

Johnny did as he promised. He came to my room to help me with my bags the next morning. He would ride over to Cynthia Barringer's apartment with me and help me get the bags up to the apartment where I would be staying with her. He never let me forget that I would be coming to him in a few weeks. He wanted me to go with him the next morning, but I could tell he wanted to give me some space. He was afraid I would change my mind, but he was willing to take the chance, or he might lose me altogether.

I introduced him to Cynthia when we got there, and I was impressed with her apartment. It was my first time seeing it. Johnny took my bags into the bedroom that I was to sleep in.

"Where did you get that?" Cynthia asked. She was saying in so many words that Johnny was fine. Any woman would be glad to have him care for them. I was lucky alright. He loved me and that was for sure. Just then Johnny came back into the kitchen where Cynthia and I were talking.

"What time do you want me to pick you up later?" He asks me.

"Why don't you pick me up around two o'clock." I say. I thought we might take a walk in Central park. I had always wanted to walk in Central Park. I must have seen it a hundred times on television, and now I would actually be there. I would be taking a walk in one of the most famous parks in the world if not the most famous.

"See you then," he says, as he closes the door behind him.

"Honey, you had just better go on to Paris. A man like that is too hard to hold, with all the women after him, I'm sure." Cynthia was saying. I was a little insecure about that, myself. How could I hold a man as well built and as handsome as Johnny?

"He's playing you girl. All them Hollywood hunks do that."

"Cynthia, you don't even know him. How could you say that?" I say defending Johnny, although I had my own doubts. What if I got out there and he dumped me. I would surely feel like a fool and look like one too. What did he want with me anyway, when he could have any woman he wanted. I was pretty alright, but them Hollywood chicks knew the ropes. What did he want with my country behind. I was just in New York from

Kentucky. What did I know compared to all those slick chicks out West.

"You better take it from me girl, you will get messed up, trying to hang with Johnny."

"Cynthia, please shut up. I'm grown enough to make my own choices."

"Yeah, and he's pushing thirty-one and he's no virgin. You know what's going to happen when you get to L. A.? You're probably going to get turned out Callie. I know your mama didn't raise no fool."

I went into my room and laid on the bed. Was Cynthia right? Had I let him move too quickly? So much was going through my mind now. Maybe this was a wake up call. Maybe God was trying to tell me something and I just didn't know it, or I didn't want to know it. I mean, I hardly know him. I just met him last week, and now I'm practically engaged. Maybe Cynthia is right. Maybe I'm in the fast lane and need to change to a slower lane. Doubt was creeping up on me. Fear started to take over. He'll be here in a little while to pick me up. I love Johnny. I really, really do love him. No one falls in love this fast, but I have fallen for Johnny. I could see that Cynthia was coming toward the bedroom. She stood in the doorway and folding her arms, she starts to open her big mouth.

"Come on Callie. I didn't mean to make you feel bad. Let me show you around the apartment. "Just come look at this lovely patio." She says, as she started back toward the patio. I got up and followed her. We both went out there in the freezing January weather. It was a lovely view of the city from Cynthia's patio.

"Isn't this a lovely view of the city?"

"You can almost see the whole city from here," I say feeling as if I am on top of the world.

"Well, not the whole city," Cynthia says, smiling at me.

It was getting cold out on the patio, so we went in and Cynthia fixed us some hot chocolate. I'm still worried about the future and that I just can't help. I don't remember having to make so many decisions when I was at home in Lexington. Everything was so simple and laid out for you. I never had to ponder and wonder and worry over what to do, what to wear and where to and when to go. Now it seems that this is all I'm doing now wondering and worrying about everything. I hear Cynthia say a curse word, because she can't find a radio station she wants to hear. I can hear her now mumbling something to herself. This is wild, I'm thinking, is this what being grown up is all about? Never knowing what to do and making hard decisions all the time. I'm starting to realize that as long as I was at home, I had never even grown up.

I'm starting to get ready. Two o'clock is almost here, and I haven't showered or changed yet. I must pick out something to knock Johnny off his feet. I pick out another leather skirt. It's dark blue and I also pick out a black silk blouse. I don't want my hair down today. I think I'll put it up in some kind of French roll or something like that. I think it makes me look more mature and sophisticated. I want to look like a woman today. Although I look good, I want to look older. Johnny is almost seven years older than I. I found out that he is almost thirty-two years old and I want to look like his woman. I'll wear my tam with the bill and a short leather jacket. I also pick out some black panty hose. As I'm getting ready, I hear the doorbell. It must be him. When I open the door, he is standing there with a bouquet of roses. I was surprised as he handed them to me.

"These are for you."

"Oh Johnny, they're beautiful. I'm going to put them in water right now. Have a seat, I'll be right back," I say, as I'm heading for the kitchen to find a vase. While I'm looking for a vase and opening all the cabinet doors to find one, I hear Johnny and Cynthia talking in the front of the apartment. It seems as if Cynthia is trying to make him feel comfortable until I return. After I put the flowers in the vase, I go back to the living room where Cynthia and Johnny are sitting.

"Those are lovely," Cynthia says to me.

"Yes, they are very lovely." I say as I keep walking to put them on my dresser in my bedroom. I'm thinking that Cynthia doesn't have to be so obliging to Johnny. Especially after what she said to me earlier about Johnny playing me. Now she's acting as if she likes him to his face. Is that two faced or what? Now I'm thinking, I'm not so sure I can trust Cynthia where Johnny is concerned. I'm going to have to listen to my heart, and not to Cynthia. What does she know anyway? She's man hunting herself.

"Ready, Johnny?" I ask, as I'm putting on my short leather Jacket and tam. My black thick pantyhose are sticking tightly to my legs, as I start to try and smooth them out.

"Yeah, lets go," he says to me.

As we're standing on the street waiting for a cab to come by, I tell him I want to see Central Park. He tells me O.K. He's always wanted to see it too. Just then we get a taxi and get into the back seat. I'm sitting close to Johnny now. I'm not as timid as I was when I first met him. We're like a couple now, and I'm scared silly. I'm scared something is going to go wrong. I've never been this close to anyone before, other than my parents that is, and I've never been in a real relationship before. I don't count what I had with Scooter anymore. It was so juvenile compared to what Johnny and I have together. It feels good to know someone other than your parents, care about you. It is my first real experience as being the center of someone's attention.

When we get to Central Park, Johnny pays the cab driver and gives him a good tip. He takes my hand and we start to walk. There is still some snow on the ground, but not a lot. It is still quite cold, so I link my arm with Johnny's arm and put my hand in his pocket and my other hand in my own pocket. We walked arm in arm for a while. I notice that Johnny is being very quiet, which is usually not like him.

"Is something wrong?" I ask.

"No, but there is something I want to say to you, Callie."

"What is it?"

"As you know, I'm leaving tomorrow, and before I go, I want to make sure that we're going to be together, so I'm asking you to marry me," he says as he's taking something out of his pants pocket. I look to see what it is and it's a small velvet case. This can't be what I think it is, I'm thinking to myself, but in reality, I know what it is.

"Johnny, are you sure, you know what you're doing? I mean, what are we doing Johnny? I don't know that much about you and you really don't know me and...

"I know enough," he interrupts me.

He opens the case and sure enough it is what I thought it would be. I'm flabbergasted and he's looking me straight in the eyes, and my knees are starting to get weak and I'm starting to shake all over because I don't know what to say, and he's waiting for me to say something, so I guess I'll have to say yes or no and I don't want to say no, but we haven't talked about this. I'm not sure what it is he wants in our future.

"Yes, I'll marry you Johnny," I say, as he takes my hand and places the most gorgeous engagement ring on my left ring finger, and I just stand there gazing at it, and then looking at him and then looking back at the ring and then looking at Johnny. He now grabs me and gives me the biggest bear hug I ever had since daddy used to give me those big bear hugs.

"Yes," he yells and thrusts both hands in the air, with clenched fists. He's smiling from ear to ear, and gives me another hug. This time it was a much more tender kind of hug. I tell myself how much I love Johnny while he's giving me this wonderful hug. He slowly pulls me closer to him. It's as if I'm melting into him. How could I say no to a man like this? I needed Johnny. He would take care of me. He's mine and I belong to him. We belong together. While I'm thinking all of this, I hope I'm not just trying to convince myself that I have done the right thing, by saying yes, just to get his proposal, but I know deep down, I want to be with Him for the rest of my life. A woman would be crazy not to except such a proposal from Johnny Parker. He was the nicest and best looking man I've ever seen, and he wanted me.

Later that evening we discussed our plans for the future. I would stay in New York for a few more weeks and then I would join him in Los Angeles in exactly three weeks to the day. Johnny was going to find a bigger apartment, because his was more like efficiency, than an apartment, and he said his woman deserved the best. I'm not sure that he's telling me everything. There is much more to Johnny Parker than what meets the eye.

I looked at my beautiful ring as we sat on the couch, where I'm staying with Cynthia. She had gone out with some friends and me and Johnny were all- alone. I'd been swept off my feet. I told Johnny that I wanted to go home to Kentucky before coming to L.A. I wanted to break the news to my parents in person. He agreed, but I would have to do this within the three weeks of the time allowed. I am so happy. He is happy too.

"Let me make you my wife before I go Callie. We're practically married anyway. It's just a matter of formality," he says, and then taking my hand and kissing it.

"We have to wait Johnny. I've always promised myself I would be a virgin when I got married. It's what I've been taught all of my life, with my parents bringing me up in church and all, it's just a part of me."

"I know baby, but in my mind, we're already married," he says, giving me that big smile of his.

"Johnny, you're pressuring me, sweetheart."

"I know, that's because I love you so much."

"I love you too," I say, straightening his necktie. I really wanted to be with him, but I couldn't do it. Mama had trained me too well and now that the temptation is right on top of me, I tell him no and that's final. I have to imagine that to be with a man like Johnny has to be to most wonderful thing that could ever be in a woman's life. I wish every woman in the world could have a man as wonderful, caring, and loving as Johnny, but that is just not the real world. Every woman deserves to have a Johnny in her life. I must have done something right to have such a man as he come along and choose little old me. I couldn't be more happier if someone gave me ten million dollars.

Chapter 3

I rode to the International Airport with Johnny this morning. His baggage was checked and I was standing there when he walked towards the plane. He had given me a long look, before he boarded. He didn't want me to forget about him, as he feared I might. I wanted to shout to the top of my voice, that I would not betray his trust, but kept quiet.

"Remember, three weeks," he had said to me.

"Three weeks." I mimicked. I held up three fingers as I said it. I watched him until I couldn't see him any longer. I watched the plane take off. It went higher and higher until it was out of sight. I stood there with my hands in my coat pockets. Suddenly I felt something in my left pocket. I pulled it out and to my surprise it was a card. It was the Queen of Hearts. I stood there almost devastated. Seeing the card almost blew my mind. It was a reminder of my promise to him. When we had cut the cards and he had won the proposal. I had pulled the ten of Spades, which didn't beat his Queen of Hearts. Now he was reminding me, by sticking his winning card in my pocket that I'm not to break my promise to him to come to L.A. I put the card back in my pocket and rushed from the airport.

Standing outside, I was able to get a taxi right away. I told the driver I wanted to go to Manhattan up on fifty-second Avenue. I gave him the exact address as I sat in the back seat with tears rolling down my cheeks. I felt so alone now that Johnny was gone. I had to get back to Lexington to my parents. I had to talk to them, because I wanted their blessings. I couldn't get married without mama and daddy. It wouldn't be right. I just hoped they would be happy for me. I'm still wiping tears away with a hanky, when suddenly I stop crying, finish drying my eyes, take out my makeup case and start to fix my face. What was I crying for? I'm the happiest woman in the world right now. This was a time for celebrating, not for tears.

By the time I get back to the apartment, Cynthia is up in her robe and fixing herself a cup of coffee. I want to tell her I'm engaged to Johnny, but for some reason I hesitate.

"Want a cup?" Cynthia asks.

"Yeah, I can use one," I say, as I sit down to the table and let out a deep sigh.

"Is something wrong?" She asks.

"No," I say.

"Come on, spit it out, Callie," she says, while pouring me a cup of coffee.

"Well, Johnny left you know and I guess I'm feeling a little lost." I tell her. I want to say and we got engaged and I'm supposed to meet him in L.A. in three weeks. I also want to say that I need a friend right now, and I want someone to be happy for me and that I'm feeling confused, because I have to tell my parents, and I'm not so sure that they will be happy for me. My parents want me to be a nurse, and I'm about to be married to an actor, but I don't tell her. I just sit there the entire time, trying to drink a cup of coffee and I really want to appease Cynthia, because she's all the friend I have right now.

"I'm leaving in three weeks Cynthia, but I'm going to see my parents this weekend."

"Callie, now where are you going so soon? You just moved in."

"I know, and I'm sorry Cynthia, but my plans have erratically changed from the day I got into town." I'm stirring my coffee with a spoon and not really wanting to drink it at all. I also don't want to debate the issue with Cynthia, because as it turns out, we don't see anything eye to eye, and besides I'm just not in the mood.

"Girl, what's gotten into you? When I first met you, it was as if you were so confident and knew where you were going in life, and now, Callie, I just don't know what to say. Are you really going to drop all of your dreams for this man you just met? Lord only knows who he really is," she says, as she takes a sip of her coffee.

"Save it Cynthia, I'm way ahead of you. Don't think I don't have my doubts, but the more you talk against Johnny, the more I want him."

"That's typical, Callie. You are so predictable," she says sitting her cup of coffee down.

It's the next day at work and I'm fixing the Lingerie, when one of the workers tells me I have a phone call. They take my place, while I answer the phone. I never would have guessed who it was if I hadn't heard him with my own ears. It was Pierre, calling all the way from Paris.

"Hello," I say.

"Hello Callie. It's Pierre."

"Well hello Pierre. I've been planning to get back to you." I lied again. What was it about being away from home that has caused me to tell so many lies.

"Callie, I just called to say that If you don't come to Paris by Sunday in time for Monday's training session, I'm going to have to get someone else to take your place."

"Can't you just give me a little more time?" I ask. I really can't believe what I'm saying to him, because I'm supposed to be in L.A. in exactly three weeks.

"All right, two weeks Callie, that's it. Call me two weeks from this coming Friday so I can arrange your airfare."

Okay," I tell him.

Callie, this is your last chance to come to Paris. Don't let me or yourself down," Pierre says, and then he hangs up the telephone, I'm standing here with the phone to my ear wondering what it was I just said, and why I was saying it. Well, I'm certainly not going to worry about it now. But the thought that I was dangling Johnny and Pierre on a string came to mind. Maybe I'm being selfish, but this is the way it has to be until I come to some kind of understanding in my own mind. The thought of being a model in Paris will not leave me alone, even though I love Johnny very much. The glamour of being on a runway in Paris has taken precedence over the love I have for my man. I look down at my engagement ring, which I hid from Cynthia and stood there twisting it around on my finger in deep thought. Going to Paris was a once in a lifetime opportunity.

That same afternoon, I'm helping a customer find the perfect lingerie for his fiancé. He is going to be married and decided he would pick out what his new bride would wear for him on their honeymoon. We went through tons of lingerie before he found the perfect piece he was looking for. His bride might be shocked when she sees what he has picked out for her. Some women just aren't into all that skimpy stuff. I'm one for flannel pajamas, robe and big fluffy house shoes myself. If Johnny bought me something like that I don't know if I would wear it.

When it was time to go home, I knew I would get a call from Johnny that evening and when I got home, the phone was ringing as I came in the door. I picked up the receiver and after speaking with him for a second, I felt that he sounded as if he were worried about something. I didn't pick up on it right away, but I could hear that he was concerned about something by the sound of his voice. He was matter of fact and gave me the impression; he was not in the mood for foolishness or games.

"How are you?"

"I'm fine, and yourself?"

"I'm just wondering, if my bride to be still loves me?"

"Of course I still love you," I say, as I start to twist my hair. I am always nervous when I talk to him. Johnny wasn't the kind of guy that joked around. He was always serious about everything. I try to choose my words carefully when I talk to him.

"So, what have you been doing since yesterday?" I ask.

"Not a lot. Thinking about you mostly," he says.

"Yeah, me too."

"Are you bundling up? I don't want you to get sick out there."

"Yep," I say. He's starting to irritate me now. He's treating me like a child. Why do men always have to treat you like a child? Either they treat you like a child or they treat you like a dog, and how do I know this, well I've watched other people's relationships for a long time. I guess it's better to be treated like a child than treated like a dog.

"I bought your plane ticket already. I'm sending it to you in the mail."

"Okay," I say.

"Callie, is something wrong? If it is, I want to know what it is right now."

"No, of course not, it's just that I just got home from work and I'm a little tired, that's all," I say. I'm really irritated, but I don't let on. I'm starting to feel as if I'm being smothered or something. I feel like I can't get enough oxygen. I'm suffocating.

"Of course not. I'll call you in a couple of days, and don't worry, everything is fine," I tell him with assurance in my tone of voice.

"Until then," he says, and he hangs up the phone. I slowly put the receiver back on the hook. I had to sort some things out. I had to figure out how I was going to tell my parents this weekend about Johnny. I didn't know what their reaction was going to be, but I would soon find out. The whole plan was tumbling to the ground. Something or somebody was rocking my world. Everything I had planned had been shot down, or I was lowering my standards. It was hard to tell what was really happening. All I know is, that I needed to do some serious thinking.

I left the airport at seven-fifteen a.m., on Saturday morning for Lexington. I wanted to see my parents. Life was so simple when I was at home with them. I never had to worry about anything. I was the only child and living at home for the past twenty-five years, had been a breeze. I have had my own room forever, and I never had to share my television, or any of my toys. I never had to wear hand-me-downs and I was always very well dressed. My parents always saw to it that I always got what I wanted. I even got my own car on my sixteenth birthday. Let's face it, I was a brat. After being on my own for a few weeks, I couldn't even make the simplest decisions. I pondered over a lot on that ride home to Kentucky. The plane landed too soon. I hadn't thought everything through yet, and now it was time to get off.

Mama and Daddy met me at my arrival gate. I'm so happy to see them both, I throw my arms around dad, as he gives he that big bear hug and then mama kisses me on the cheek. I see that dad has grown a mustache, that is trimmed very nicely, and Mama is as pretty as ever.

"Why, you look like you could use some food child. Have you been eating much, since you left home? You need to put some meat on them bones girl," mama says to me, as I hug her.

"Don't pay your mama no attention. You look just fine Callie. Clara is always trying to make somebody put on weight. She could stand to lose a little of them hips she got," daddy says smiling that big smile that I missed so much.

"You ain't never complained before Bartholomew Mason, so don't start now," mama says, as she slaps her hip with one hand. Mama has always had daddy in her back pocket, and she knew it. It was no doubt in her mind that daddy loved her dearly and that he worshipped her.

There was never an argument that mama didn't win. I think daddy loves her so much, he just let her win every time they had a disagreement. Daddy was quite special to be able to put up with mama all these years. Mama had always been feisty. That's what Daddy loved most about her.

We go to the baggage area and I pick my bag off the carrousel. We go to the parking area where my parents are parked and we get into the car. Mama is still talking, but I don't hear what she is saying. My mind is a thousand miles away exactly. My mind is on Johnny. I'm wondering what he is doing and what is it I'm going to do. I want to tell him to wait for me until I get back from Paris, but now it seems as if I'm trapped. I'm engaged to a man I love, but hardly know.

When we get home, yes, home sweet home, mama has cooked a real good soul food dinner. I can't remember the last time I ate a home cooked meal. Oh yes, I remember now, it was the last day before I left home. I'll admit, I haven't been eating right. I might have had a sandwich here or there. To tell the truth, I haven't been right since I left. Maybe being home awhile will help clear my mind. Maybe I can find some answers to the many questions that engulf my mind.

Dad takes my bag inside and mama walks with me with her arm around my waist. She's talking about something, I hardly know what, and I'm saying uh huh, like I'm listening to her, but I'm not really listening. She's saying something about Sarah, one of my best friends I used to go to high school with, and now I start to listen, because Sarah has been one of my closest friends since childhood. She and Genny have been just like sisters to me for many years.

"What about Sarah?" I ask as we enter the house.

"She's going to call you dear. She wants to see you before you leave."

"Oh, that's nice," I say. Sarah and me used to do some crazy stuff. I'm glad my parents never found out about some of the dumb stuff we used to do I think and then, I smell a luscious aroma, coming from the kitchen. Now I can hardly wait to see what is on the menu for tonight. I could use a tight meal, because my mama is the best cook I know and I don't know, when I'll get another one like hers, after I'm gone again.

I'm waiting for the call to dinner as I take my clothes out of my luggage. I've been here several hours and old memories are starting to flood my brain. I remember the reason I left Lexington. My engagement to Scooter Davis didn't work out. We had been friends since the second grade, then we became good friends and then, we were an item all the way through high school. I had waited for scooter to get out of the armed forces and we were to be married as soon as he returned, but somehow that didn't work out, instead Scooter returned with a woman he was already married to, and didn't even bother to tell me. The next thing I knew, the phone in my house was ringing off the hook. Everyone was calling to tell me that scooter was back, and what's worse, that he had brought his new bride home with him. Naturally I was devastated and in a somewhat state of shock, but my parents and Sarah stood by me through my period of mourning, and I got through it.

"Come and get it." I here mama calling from the dining room.

I get downstairs and into the dining room, and I see that the table is full of all kinds of good food. Mama had really out done herself, she had cooked baked ham, turkey and stuffing, collard greens, potato salad, home made dinner rolls, macaroni and cheese, sweet potato pie and lots more.

"Ma, you didn't have to do all this for me."

"I didn't honey," she says, and then I hear this big sound coming from many voices saying "Surprise" and it was the voices of friends and relatives I hadn't seen in a long time coming out from everywhere. They were blowing party horns and I see my best friend Sarah and we grab each other and we hug and hug, then I spot another one of my good friends, Genny, and I grab her and we hug. At this point I'm so elated that my friends and family are here to greet me, and I kiss all my cousins and aunts and uncles. There were friends of my parents that I have known since childhood.

We all finally sit down to the table, but first daddy leads us in prayer. After that we all began to dig into the food, everyone talking and laughing. I felt like I was at home again and as if I had never gone away.

"You're one of those big city girls now," Uncle Jerry is saying to me.

"No, not really, I'm still a country girl," I say. Aunt Sharon and Uncle Jerry has just become the parent's of a new baby girl and she is making her presence known. Her loud crying has everyone looking in her direction. Aunt Sharon gets up from the table and takes the infant into another room so she can breast feed the baby. Personally I don't want kids, I think to myself. They are a pain in the butt. All that crying and getting up before day to feed them is not my idea of a good time. I love kids and all, but when I get through playing with them I want them to go home with their mother. Mama says I'll change my mind, but I know that I won't.

Sarah is sitting next to me, and she is saying something, but I can't hear what she is saying over all the noise in the house. Mama is playing her gospel music loud and I can't hear myself think. I can't think of anything to say right now. I just need to get some rest.

"Let's go out bowling after dinner," Sarah says to me.

"Sure. I can work off some of my tension," I say.

"Great. Genny do you want to come with us?" Sarah asks, as she wipes her mouth daintily with her napkin. Sarah always was the neat and tidy one among the three of us.

"Did you know that Scooter and his wife broke up already?" Genny asks me.

"No. Nobody told me."

"Yeah, I hear that he's saying that he made a mistake getting married. He says you are the only one he has ever loved and that he was just caught up in his loneliness when he got married."

"Really? Well it's way too late for him. I have something to tell you later," I say.

"Hurry and eat girl, I want to hear what you have to tell me," Genny says, hunching me with her shoulder. At this point, I'm trying to eat slow and enjoy every bit of all the food for as long as I can. This is so good I think, and now I remember what I've been missing. This food is delicious and I'm going to eat as much as I can, now while I have a chance, although I can't wait to tell Sarah about Johnny. I need to have her opinion on this one. She has never steered me wrong in the past. I trust her judgment.

Later, when we're in the car on the way to one of the local bowling alleys, I'm sitting in the front seat with Sarah and Genny is in the back. This is just like old times, Genny, Sarah and me, all together again.

"Come on Callie, tell us all about what's going on with you, since you left Lexington." Sarah says, with a hint of mischief in her voice.

"Yeah, spill it," Genny chimes in.

"Neither of you are going to believe this, but I'm engaged." I squeal, after not being able to give them the information they've been waiting to hear for almost half the night.

"What? Engaged," Sarah is saying as her mouth drops open.

"How did you manage that Callie? You've been gone, what, about two weeks now?" Genny asks and then belts out that little sarcastic laugh of hers.

"To whom in the world are you engaged to?" Sarah asks, putting emphasis on the "to".

"Well, I met him a few weeks ago. We just kind of fell in love and he asked me to marry him." I tell them as

I start to giggle a little, almost embarrassed that I hardly know Johnny.

"Who asked you to marry him Callie? Who is he?" Genny wanted to know, as we were about to pull into the parking lot of the bowling alley. Another car comes out of nowhere, pulls up and cuts us off, pulling ahead of us and then parking.

"That's Scooter Davis' car. I wonder what he's doing here," Genny drawls in that down home kind of Southern sarcasm.

"Never mind him, I want to know about this guy you met in New York City," Sarah says, while she's trying to fit into a small parking space with her long 1988 Lincoln Continental.

Now that we have finally stopped, I turn sideways in the front seat, so I can see Genny and Sarah at the same time. I don't want to miss any expressions on their faces when I tell them what happened and how I got engaged. They are both now eagerly awaiting the details of how I managed to find my new love. As I begin to tell them all about how we met, and what transpired after that, they are totally captivated by what I am saying. I must be a good storyteller, because they haven't interrupted me once. They both seem to be very intrigued by Johnny and when I show them my ring, that I've been hiding up until this point, I hear a gasp of awe from both of them.

"This is like some fairy tale," Sarah finally does interrupt me, not being able to keep quiet any longer.

"Yeah, Callie, how could you keep something as wonderful as this a secret? I mean, an actor from Hollywood and all. "Why haven't you told anyone?"

Genny asks me, as if I've kept a big secret from them that they feel I should have revealed before today.

I know you're not going to let a good catch like that get away," Sarah adds.

"Well, I haven't told you everything."

"Is there more?" Sarah chimes in with a look of total surprise on her face.

"I haven't told you about Pierre Debore, and that he wants me to come to Paris to model for his agency."

"What?" Genny yells, with an I can't believe this, expression on her face.

"Callie, you'd better be trying to keep up with that man in Hollywood. You know how desperate some women are these days," Sarah says as she looks into the mirror and moistens her eyebrows as if she's going to meet someone very soon, herself.

"I know," I say.

When we get inside the bowling alley, I see Scooter walking around with a drink in his hand covered by a white handkerchief. Everyone knows it's alcohol, so why is he hiding it like no one knows what is in the covered glass. He comes toward me and I try to avoid him, but I fail, because he is determined to get in my way.

"Hello Callie," he says to me.

"Hello Scooter." I greet him, rather stiffly. I don't want to get caught up in his webb again. One go around with Scooter is enough. Once dumped is one time too many, and why does he think I want to see him again after the humiliation I've gone through in this town, when he brought his bride home from the army, he was still engaged to me. He didn't even bother to break the engagement. He just showed up back here married to another woman. That's when I decided then and there that I would leave Lexington. His marriage didn't last a month. In my opinion, that's what he deserves.

"It's good to see you," he says.

"Nice to see you too," I lied. It's not nice to see his cheating behind, but I play it off.

Sarah and Genny are standing over by the bar. They look as if they are conferring with each other about something. I'm starting to feel a little embarrassed.

"I would like to apologize to you Callie."

"Save it Scooter. I really don't care anymore. See, I'm engaged to be married myself," I say showing him the ring on my finger. He's looking rather surprised as I flaunt the ring in his face. He never thought I would find someone this soon after he so blatantly scorned me.

"How about I pick you up tomorrow night? Just to talk, nothing more," he says, taking a sip of the contents of the glass, which was wrapped in the handkerchief.

"I really don't think that's a good idea Scooter. I'm sure my fiance wouldn't think that your suggestion was a good idea either," I say, as I'm gliding away from him.

"Come on Callie." I hear Sarah calling me.

"I know you're not going in that direction again," Genny says, loud enough for Scooter to hear what she is saying about him.

"You can count on that."

It was so much fun bowling with the girls again. We laughed and talked most of the evening as we bowled game after game. Scooter sat watching us from the barstool he sat on. He hardly took his eyes off me. I was hoping that his heart was breaking inside, just as he had caused my heart to break.

As we're sitting at a table and the girls are drinking beer, relaxing and they are telling me about their newfound boyfriends. They both seem to have gotten good men. They too are making plans for marriage. All three of us vowed we would be at each other's wedding no matter what. They also suggest that I fly out to meet Johnny as soon as possible. I am also wanting to go to him now and not wait another two weeks. I want to be with him now. I will call Pierre tomorrow and tell him I won't be coming to Paris. Pierre had given me until Sunday to make up my mind, and tomorrow is Sunday. I'm ready and willing to give up my big dream to be with Johnny, and now he is really all that matters to me.

It's late when I get home. The porch light has been left on for me. I get out of the car and wave to the girls. They wait for me to get into the house. I go inside and sneak up to my room in the dark. I really don't want to wake my parents, because I don't want to talk anymore tonight. I just want to think about how and when I'm going out to L. A. When I get in my room, there is a note on the bed. It's a note from Johnny. He must have called while I was out with the girls. He tells me to call him early in the morning, since he didn't get to talk to me tonight. He was just checking to see if I was all right.

I lay on the bed, thinking I want to talk to him now, but I don't want to wake him because he might have to do a shoot tomorrow or something. So I just lay here in the dark now hoping that my bubble doesn't burst and find me splattered all over the place, like when Scooter came home with his new bride, I felt like I exploded inside and there was nothing I could do at that moment in time to heal my broken heart, when everyone knows only God can heal a broken heart.

Tomorrow is Sunday and my parents will expect me to go to church with them, as I have had to do all of my life and just as I have sang in the choir all of my life, because I love to sing and I have a good voice and maybe I should be a singer some day.

The night went fast and it's early morning. It's time to call Johnny and maybe wake him up if he has to work today. I'm hoping he's already up. One thing I hate is waking someone up to talk to me. It seems they don't even know what you are saying; at least I know I'm that way when someone calls me, while I'm still asleep. I pick up the receiver and start to dial his number anyway, and it's not long before I hear the phone ringing. It was about the sixth ring, when I heard his voice on the other end of the line.

"Hello," he answers groggily.

"Johnny, it's me. I didn't wake you did I?" I ask, knowing full well that I did wake him.

"No. I'm awake. I tried to get you last night, but you wern't there."

"I went bowling with some girlfriends from my old high school," I say.

"I really miss you Callie. I want to get married as soon as possible."

"I miss you too. It won't be long before we're together."

"Have you told your parents about our getting married?"

"No, but I'm going to tell them today after church," I tell him.

"Well call me later and let me know what they think about it. I love you."

"I love you too. I'll call you later," I say, and then I hang up the phone. I didn't want to say good-bye. I hated saying goodbye. Goodbye seems so final. I never wanted to say goodbye to Johnny. I want him in my mind, heart and soul forever.

We sat close to the front when we got to the church. Reverend Patterson winked at me from the pulpit. He was smiling, showing his gladness that I had come to church today.

"We have one of our members here from New York with us today," Reverend Patterson was saying. "Come on up here Callie and lead a song with the choir."

I get up from my seat and go up to the choirs box and stand there. I didn't know what I would sing, and then I thought I would sing a song that was everybody's favorite. The choir would back me up as I sang. As I began to sing, I hit those high notes like never before, and I could see that my parents were as proud of me as ever. I always could sing, but it was never my favorite thing to do. The music played as I hit more of the high notes and then the low ones. People began to stand and clap their hands as I brought the house down. The choir never sang better, and I never sang better, as I sang and worshipped in my old church home.

Reverend Patterson preached today like I have never heard him preach before. It seemed like a real good day and I was happy to be apart of the wonderful service that had taken place this Sunday morning. People came up to me and shook my hand and welcomed me home for my short-lived visit. I was glad to be back in my old surroundings again, but my heart was somewhere else. My heart was in a place it had never been before, so that makes L. A., my new home, because home is where Johnny is. I know I'm going to love Los Angeles. I hope I run into some of my favorite movie stars. Johnny says they are all over the place. You see movie stars all the time in some of the most unexpected places. It sounds as if L. A. is a fun place to be and it will be like heaven to be there with Johnny.

Chapter 4

I can't wait to get on the plane. I'm in the airport and want to get to California as fast as possible. I'm pacing the floor waiting and the clock seems as if it refuses to hurry up just for me. I have a two-hour layover in Denver. It's probably going to drive me crazy. I've decided to surprise Johnny and come a week early. I can't stand being without him for another minute. My parents were just a little upset, when I left. I tried to explain to them the best I could, without telling them I was engaged. I never got around to that. It just would have prolonged things and I would have missed the morning flight. I'll tell them when I phone them from L.A.

Now it's five minutes to boarding time. I see that there is a commotion at the airline desk. I wonder what can be wrong, so I go up to the desk. The woman in front of me is having some kind of problem, but I can't determine just what it might be.

"Is something wrong?" I ask.

"Can I have your name?" The woman asks me without answering my question.

"My name is Callie Mason," I say, as the woman is now checking some kind of list.

"I'm sorry Ms Mason, but your reservation has been canceled because of over booking. It's not your fault, so the airline would like to make you an offer. If you stay over night, we will give you an airline ticket to any destination that this airline travels." She says quite proudly, as if I care about that now.

"Miss, I don't want another airline ticket, all I want is to get on this plane today," I say in a tone of anger that usually does not show up in me.

"This is the best I can do for you Ms Mason. There aren't enough seats on the plane."

"Then I'll sit on the floor."

"Passengers are not aloud to sit on the floor, Ms. Mason."

"I mean I'm desperate, so do something," I say now, as beads of sweat pop out on my forehead and roll down my face and into my mouth. Of all the things to happen when I'm almost desperate to get to Johnny. I can't wait to see him and tomorrow is not suitable in my opinion. What's wrong with these people? Don't they know this is one of the most important times in my life, and I don't want to make any waves with Johnny? He's expecting me today.

"Look, maybe I can help you," the woman says, noticing how desperate I am. She winks at me, with a twinkle in here eye. "One of the flight attendants called in sick just a little while ago, now maybe I can give you a quick course in being an attendant and you can still get to L.A. today."

What? I don't know anything about being no flight attendant," I say, almost in a rage.

"Let's go into the office. I'm going to give you some quick lessons and a uniform, and you'll do just fine I'm sure. This will save my friend and help you at the same time," she says, as she grabs me by the hand and we start to run toward a steel door.

This isn't happening, and I can't believe what this woman is doing and I don't know if I should do it, and what if I get caught. I could go to jail or something even more drastic. I can see the headlines now. "Fake flight attendant jailed for impersonating a real flight attendant." It would get back to Lexington and my parents would be so embarrassed and so would I. I would be too embarrassed to ever go back there again. All the neighbors would be talking, no the whole town would be talking, but I still follow her into an office that's located on the side of the ticket area.

"Here, put this on," she says as she gets the uniform out of the closet.

"I don't know what I'm suppose to do," I say nervously.

"All you have to do is serve the food. Follow the other flight attendant's cues. In other words, watch what they do and you do the same."

"Are you sure I can pull this off?"

"You'll be fine. Trust me," she says. Because I'm so desperate to see Johnny, I actually believe her. I can do this I'm saying over and over to myself.

I find myself running through the tunnel to the plane, trying to make it before the door closes. At this point no one knows I'm coming aboard and I have to make it before that door closes. I will never tell a single soul about what I'm about to do, if I live through this.

"Wait," I yell.

"Am I happy to see you," the flight attendant is saying, as she pulls me through the door. "I thought I would be the only one on board and would have to do all the serving alone."

"Well, don't worry. I'm here now," I say even more nervously, while looking around to check things out. She closes the door and now and I see everyone seated and I start to panic, because I don't even know what the procedure is and what do I do if something happens and we need oxygen or something and what If I don't know how to prepare the food, but hopefully the flight attendant will do it. Now all I have to do is look cool and vibrant at the same time, like I'm so full of life and not a worry in the world. That's the way most flight attendants look, as if the plane is flying on their confidence alone and that alone will cause the trip to be successful. Just make all the passengers feel like I have more confidence in this plane and the pilots then I do in anything else in the whole world during the three longest hours of my entire life.

Now that it's time to serve the food, I start down the aisle with the cart and I'm shaking as I try to serve the people in first class. The man is watching my quivering hand, as I serve him coffee and now I'm totally panic stricken, but somehow I get through it before too long and while the other flight attendant is serving, I quickly go to the kitchenette, where the food and drinks are and pour myself a glass of wine and gulp it down quickly before I pass out from sheer terror. It's nerve racking enough too be sitting at a height of thirty-five thousand feet, but standing and walking up and down the aisle trying to serve people is another story. I'm beginning now to have great respect for flight attendants. I see a woman who is holding her hand up trying to get my attention, but I try not to look in her direction, but finally I have to look and when I get to her, she wants me to pour her a glass of water, because that is all she wants to drink right now, so I pour her a glass of water and try to finish serving the others, and somehow I get through the ordeal of serving all the passengers that I was suppose to serve and now it's almost over.

I'm so happy that the plane is finally going to land. The pilot just announced that we would be landing in ten minutes. Somehow I want to laugh, but I feel like it's too soon. I have to get off this plane before I can laugh or cry whichever emotion is stronger when I set foot on the ground. I might even kiss the ground, because I will be so happy to be in the same city as Johnny and now it won't be long before I see him again, which seems like eternity since the last time I saw him. I want to feel his arms around me, and then I will feel safe and have the security that all of us women need from the men we love and I will return the gentleness and kindness that we women are suppose to portray in a relationship and much more of course.

I run outside of the building and get a taxi, that is sitting, across the walkway and I get in and tell the driver where I want to go, because Johnny had given me his address the day he left me in New York and I hid it safely in a secret compartment of my purse. I was always hiding things and then couldn't find them, but I was lucky I was able to find Johnny's address. Here I was in Los Angeles, "City of Angels." What a beautiful name I'm thinking, a beautiful name for a beautiful city. Johnny and I make such a beautiful couple and I've missed him every moment that we have been apart, although I didn't think I would, but I do.

I get out of the taxi in front of a very nice apartment building, and it says 233 Palmer, and I know I'm at the right place. When I get to the elevator I push the three for the third floor, and his apartment is number 312 and as I walk looking for the number, I finally see it and start to tremble inside. I feel like I'm shaking all over and then I get up the nerve to knock on the door.

When the door opens, Johnny is standing there before my very eyes. He is as handsome as ever with his grande physique and that luscious dimple in his chin and that gorgeous smile now turning more serious.

"Callie," he says to me, as if he is happily surprised. I throw my arms around him and he hugs me tight and then kisses me full on the mouth. Why didn't you tell me you were coming?" He chimes.

"Aren't you happy to see me?" I ask.

"Of course I am. I'm very happy to see you." He takes my bag because I only have one and the rest of my clothes are still in New York with Cynthia. She promised to send them as soon as I let her know I'm in California.

Once we get to his apartment, I'm surprised at how beautiful and neat he keeps it. We sit down at the table and he holds my hand and kisses it.

"I thought you might change your mind."

"I'll never change my mind about you," I say. At this point I'm looking deep into his eyes and he into mine. I feel the effect of the moment, as if time was standing still and I could almost hear the wind blowing as if it were rustling through trees and a stillness that only love can bring and make one feel alive and free in the atmosphere of sheer delight.

He has not let go of my hand since we sat down; he gets up still holding my hand and leads me toward the couch. We sit down and he kisses me with deep passion and I also kiss him with the same kind of deep emotion and love one can only give to the one who has the key to ones heart and my heart belongs to Johnny.

"Promise me you will never leave me Callie," he says, as he runs his hands through my hair that is so long and lustrous.

"I promise," I tell him, with great intensity.

"When do you want to get married?" He asks.

"When ever you like."

Later in the evening we go out for dinner in Johnny's sleek black Cadillac. He must be doing well, because he is living pretty high on the hog. I have the feeling that I'm not good enough for Johnny, because I really have not accomplished that much. Here I am twenty-five years old, I have no education past high school and I'm dreaming about becoming a model, which may or may not happen. As we ride down the streets of L.A., I'm holding his right hand while he drives with his left hand only taking his hand away from mine to turn corners and then his hand finds mine again. I don't have anything to offer Johnny and I don't know how long it will take for me to find work. I don't want him to think that I'm expecting him to take care of me.

"Is something wrong?" He asks.

"No, I'm fine. It's just that this town is so great and I'm with you and I'm just a bit overwhelmed."

"Well get ready to take off, because I'm going to make you the happiest woman in the world," he whispers.

This is like a dream I didn't want to wake up from, but to keep dreaming this same dream forever and ever, but we were pulling up to the restaurant now and it was fabulous. I wore my black sleek dress. It was the only one I brought with me. I hadn't brought that many clothes, but I made sure I had my going out dress for an occasion such as this. There were valets and water fountains outside the place and beautiful lights that decorated the building. I was in seventh heaven when I was with Johnny and with him is where I want to stay.

He pulls out my chair for me to sit down once we're inside and have been seated and then sits down across from me. We are still amazed at the fact that we are together and he is trying very hard to make the evening good and I'm trying to make him glad he chose me and not someone else. I know there must be tons of women Johnny could have, but I'm more than grateful that he has chosen me. I tell him while we wait for our food, that I want to powder my nose, and he smiles and tells me not to stay away too long. I assure him that I will not stay too long and that I could never again stay away from him, so not to worry I'm his from now on.

As I'm leaving the table, I see couples all around sitting and taking in the romantic atmosphere. I hear the music from the band playing lightly in the background. I feel like the luckiest woman on earth and when I enter the room, there are several women inside the ladies room.

They are also fixing their makeup and trying to look good for their husbands or boyfriends. I see one woman in particular. She is quite attractive.

"Do you have change for a five dollar bill?" A woman dressed in a sheik red low cut dress, asks me.

"No, I'm sorry I don't," I say, as I fumble in my purse for my makeup case.

"I have this terrible headache," the woman in the red dress is saying to me. She probably wants to get a couple of aspirin from the machine.

"I have something for a headache," I say, as I once again look in my purse, for the second time, for a bottle of aspirin.

"That's sweet of you," she says, as she takes the aspirin from me.

"Glad I can help," I reply.

I watch the woman take the aspirin and then leave the ladies room. I finish putting on my makeup which takes me about ten minutes. My whole idea is to look good for Johnny. Now that I feel my face looks as good as it can get, I also leave and start for the table where I left Johnny. When I see him, there is someone standing at the table talking to him. It looks like the same woman I gave the aspirin to, and as I get a few feet closer, I realize it is the same woman. I'm now wondering who she is and how does she know Johnny. As I get closer, Johnny sees me and waves to me. He is smiling as I sit down to the table.

"Callie, this is Sonia O'Neal," he says to me, looking as if he is proud to introduce me.

"I believe we met in the ladies room. Callie was nice enough to give me some aspirin for this awful headache," she says to Johnny.

"Oh, so you two have met already."

"Nice to formally meet you," I say. I have to admit; I'm feeling a little jealous at this point and now I'm wondering how does Johnny know this woman.

"Sonia is a co-worker of mine," Johnny informs me.

"Oh, are you an actress?" I ask. I notice that the woman is looking at Johnny with just a slight frown on her face.

"No, not exactly," she says.

"See you at work," Johnny says to Sonia.

"Both of you have a nice evening," she says to Johnny and me, and then starts across the room where she sits down with another woman who was much older.

I tried not to think about the woman as Johnny and I ate our dinner. He had a steak dinner and I had lobster. The candle lit table gave the serenity of quietness, that I longed for. I had not had a stable life since I left Lexington. Now I feel as if I belong to someone. I have purpose and meaning in my life. The handsome man sitting across from me is definitely from heaven. He constantly flirted with me as we ate. What a man, I'm thinking to myself. He keeps winking at me and smiling at me, giving me his almost undivided attention, except when he stopped to pay attention to his food. The small band was now playing the music to one of Whitney Houston's songs. I continue to eat and bask in the glory of it all.

It's late when we get back to Johnny's apartment or should I say our apartment, because we'll be married by this time next week, and Johnny goes in to take a shower before bed and I go into the half bath to take a shower and get ready for bed. Mama always says that a man won't respect you if you give up everything before marriage. I know that I won't make that mistake because; Johnny has agreed to wait because he knows how I feel about things such as sex, love and marriage. Johnny is such a good man because he is patient and willing to do things the way I want things done, about getting married and all. I want my parents to come the L. A., but they may not come this far and I'm not so sure I want them.

Johnny is on the phone when I get out of the shower. He is talking softly to someone. I don't know who. I'm a bit afraid to ask. I do have to trust the man I'm going to marry. If he wants me to know, he will tell me.

"Well, don't you smell good," he says.

"You smell pretty good yourself." His cologne is causing me to become aroused with the passion I feel for him, so I stay on the other side of the room for a while until I can regain my composure. Johnny sits on the sofa and stares at me, for a while. I'm very uncomfortable now and I smile back at him from across the room.

"Would you like some hot tea before bed?" I ask.

"No, I'm just satisfied being here with you," he says still staring at me from across the room.

"Yeah, me too," I say.

"This has been a very good evening," he says, as he puts his feet on the table in front of the sofa.

"I had a very nice time."

"Come over here and sit by me," he says, patting the cushion next to him. I really haven't gained control yet, because I feel as if I'm in a trance. I almost feel hypnotized from his overwhelming presence, but I do as he says and I go over and sit by him on the sofa.

"I have to leave pretty early in the morning for work. You know how it is with us actors, we have to be on set before dawn."

"Yes, of course."

"You make yourself right at home while I'm gone and I'll see you when I get in around six o'clock tomorrow evening."

"Okay," I whisper. He puts his arm around me and kisses me on the forehead. I kind of snuggle in his arms.

I must have slept right through the night, because when I awakened this morning, I was in my bed. The hands on the clock said 6:45a.m. and I knew I must have missed Johnny. He would already have left for work. I put my head back on my pillow and tried to figure out what it was I would do all day. My first thought was to look for a job, but I dismissed the idea and thought I would just have a day to myself. Maybe I would look around L.A. and get a feel for the city. I could do some shopping and get a nice dinner for Johnny when he gets home, I think to myself. Even though it was Barely February, it really wasn't that cold out at all, not like back in New York. I planned my day and one of the things I would do is call my parents, and make sure Cynthia had sent the remainder of my things. I feel as if I'm going to have a wonderful day. Dinner with Johnny tonight would make up for being alone today. In time, I would make new friends, get a job and best of all be Mrs. Johnny Parker.

I can hardly wait to get outside and when I do, I find a taxi and ask him to take me to the nearest shopping mall. In ten minutes, I'm there. I pay the driver get out of the taxi and start for the front doors. Once inside, the mall is very crowded and I see many strange faces and some very exotic looking people. I walk slowly looking at everything so as not to miss anything. There is so much to see and I also spot a grocery store. My money is still dwindling, so I figure I had better get the food and go back to the apartment. By the time I'm done shopping, it's almost noon. I have two grocery bags as I pass one of the bars in the mall, I happen to look into the dimly lit bar and see two figures sitting at a table. That man sitting there with that woman has a physique much like that of Johnny's. I look a little closer through the glass window and to my surprise, I realize it is Johnny. Who is that woman he's sitting with, and just as I get it across my brain, I recognize the woman from the restaurant last night. Yes, I can see clearly that it's Sonia O'Neal. She was the woman Johnny had introduced to me in the restaurant last night. I had a feeling that there was more to Sonia then just being a co-worker.

I watched the two of them for another ten minutes as they sat talking. I'm being careful not to be seen. My heart is racing and my knees are weak, and my hands are trembling, as I stand there almost glued to the glass window, as I continue to watch them. There must be some explanation for this rendezvous. I know Johnny loves me, or I'm pretty sure that he loves me. My mind is racing a mile a minute as I try to justify their meeting. He's taking a sip of his drink as she continues to talk. He is getting up from the table now and he's headed for the pay phone on the wall. Now I'm wondering if he's going to call me at the apartment, but he won't get me because I'm here in the mall watching him phone someone. I see Sonia light a cigarette and take a sip of her drink. Within a couple of minutes Johnny comes back and they both get up and go out a door on the other side of the bar. I also abruptly leave the mall, almost running and in disbelief.

Now that I'm back at the apartment, I almost collapse on the sofa. The trauma of what I have seen earlier almost has me paralyzed. Sweat is starting to pop out on my forehead and I'm still trembling from the shock of it all. I try to calm myself, and convince myself that it was all innocent, and Johnny would come home and explain everything. Never in a thousand years would I have expected to run into Johnny and see him in a bar with another woman. The woman I had already had suspicions about from our first meeting. This just could not be happening. I tell myself that I'm over reacting and that I'm letting my jealousy get the best of me, but deep down I'm not convinced.

Around two o'clock in the afternoon, the food is cooking in the oven and the house smells real good from the aroma of Cornish hen and stuffing. It has taken all my strength to do the cooking because of my insecurity of where I really stand with Johnny. I still haven't recovered from the shock of what took place earlier in the day. I try to put it out of my mind, but it just keeps coming back. To get my mind off things, I decide to call Cynthia and remind her to get my clothes to me as fast as possible, because I'm running out of things to wear. Somehow I find her number in my little address book and I start to dial her number. She is at home because it's her day off. As I begin to dial Cynthia's phone number, I think maybe I should tell her what has happened and maybe she can help me to make some sense of it all. The phone is ringing and

I'm still debating about telling her about my stumbling upon Johnny at the mall, in the bar.

"Hello."

"Hello. Cynthia, it's me," I say.

"Callie, how are you?"

"I don't know," I tell her, as I stand here trembling.

"What do you mean, you don't know?" Cynthia asks in that suspicious tone of hers.

"I Think Johnny is seeing another woman, but I'm not sure," I say, as I'm twisting my hair nervously, as I often do.

"Believe me, when a woman suspects her man is seeing another woman, it's probably true," she says.

"Well, it was a public place," I say.

"So there's probably a lot more going on behind closed doors. You need to stop making up excuses for him. When it comes to men, go with your first gut instinct, is what I always say."

"What should I do?" I ask.

"You probably should get the heck out of there," Cynthia says.

"Well don't forget to send my things and I have to go now," I say.

"Maybe I should hold off on sending your clothes until you find out what is going on with your little boyfriend," Cynthia says.

"Maybe you're right. I'll call you back when I find out what is going on." I hang up the phone feeling even worse than before. What if Cynthia is right?

How am I to find out if Johnny is seeing this Sonia woman? The only way to find out something is to follow the person. I will feel pretty terrible following Johnny, but I may feel worse later if I don't. I'm just so glad that dinner is finished, and I'll warm it up when Johnny gets home in the next couple of hours. I hope I will be able to act normal as if nothing has happened. I don't want to make him suspicious of me, by detecting something in my behavior. Johnny is very sensitive and will notice the slightest change in me if I act differently.

In the next hours I start to change for dinner, because Johnny will be getting in soon, I'm almost feeling numb from the experience at the mall. I try to tell myself that I'm being silly and that I should trust the man I'm to marry in less than a week, but that nagging pain in my chest, tells me that I am not able to trust him, because I have always heard from mama that love doesn't hurt. I'm feeling pain and right now I hurt. Even if there is nothing going on with Sonia and Johnny, why is he spending time with her in a bar in the middle of the day? There has to be some kind of connection between them. What ever it is between the two of them, I am certainly dedicated to finding out what that connection is all about.

When Johnny comes through the door, it is almost five o'clock and he kisses me on the cheek. I already have the food on the table and we each have our own Cornish hen and stuffing cooked in a small glasscooking dish that goes in the oven. The food looks very inviting. While he goes into the bathroom to wash up, I decide to light some candles, hoping the romanticism will get his mind off everything except me. I also put on my best perfume and my sleek black dress for the occasion. I just hope I'm not over dressed. Maybe I should have told Cynthia to send my clothes, but as usual, I find myself a bit confused as to what it is I want to do.

"How was your day?" Johnny asks as he puts his napkin in his lap.

"Fine," I say.

"Baby, we need to start making our wedding plans.

I mean, we haven't discussed it very much and we need to get out a few invitations and stuff like that," he says talking fast.

"Oh yes, I suppose you're right," I tell him and then clear my throat, because it feels as if something is stuck in it.

"This food is quite good Callie. I didn't know you were such a good cook."

"I learned to cook very early."

"Indeed you did," he says as he continues to dig into the food.

"Did you do anything interesting today other than cooking this delicious meal?" He asks.

"No. I got a few things at the grocery store, came back and made dinner," I say. I didn't exactly tell him what grocery store. I certainly was not going to mention that I had been to the mall and that I saw him there with Sonia.

"How about you? Did you have an interesting day?" I ask.

"No, not really. It was pretty much the same old boring routine," he says and I want to say, what about Sonia and your little escapade at the bar in the mall, but I just sit there dabbling at my food.

"What's wrong? Aren't you hungry?" He asks me putting down his fork.

"I guess I ate too much for lunch." Now he is looking at me strangely. I really don't know what to say, without giving myself away. If I say anything now, I will probably explode and everything will come gushing out of my mouth like a dam that has broken and all the water starts gushing over the edge of a waterfall or something. So I don't say anything at all.

Later I clear the table and wash the dishes. Johnny is watching the six o'clock news as he sits on the sofa with his feet up on the cocktail table. He is engrossed in what the newscaster is saying and I don't bother him, although I'm dying to ask him what he did for lunch today, but I'm afraid I may hear something I don't want to hear. If he says something other than what happened, I'm going to feel as if I will never be able to trust him again. If I don't ask him, I'll be forever in suspense, not knowing if he will tell the truth or tell a lie and I need to know if he will tell me the truth, but I won't ask him because too much is at stake here and I'm not ready to hear the truth or a lie.

When I finish the dishes I go in and sit on the sofa beside Johnny. He is still watching the news very intensely. I look to see what he is watching and I see men in FBI jackets running around like crazy with guns. It looks like some kind of hostage situation or something. Whatever is happening Johnny is very intrigued with the whole thing. I pretend to be interested in what he's watching and when I start to speak, he shushes me by putting his finger to his lips. I do as he says and stop talking so he can hear what is being said on the news.

"Did you see that? Those guys are some good agents," he says as he positions himself on the edge of the sofa to get a better look at what is going on.

"Oh, really," I say.

"Those guys need medals."

"I suppose." I'm really not interested in what is happening on television, my mind is so far from FBI agents; I couldn't even perceive what was going on. To me it looked like a bunch of guys running around playing Cowboys and Indians or something. Right now I need Johnny to give me some hint that we are a couple and that there's nothing between him and that Sonia woman. I have to admit she is attractive and that is what scares me so much. She may be trying to get her hooks into my man. Johnny tells me all the time that he loves me and I believe him. It's just that sometimes other women can be tempting and sexy when in a tight corner. She could get him off balance and he not know what hit him until it was over, although I believe that Johnny is a strong man and I do trust him, but I don't trust her at all.

"I'm sorry. Am I ignoring my sweetheart?" He says to me.

"No. I'm fine. Just sitting here in the room with you is good enough for me," I say.

"Come here." he says, but gets up and comes to where I'm sitting and puts his arm around my neck and pulls me to him. I lean my head on his chest and put my arm around his waist and squeezing him just a little. I feel comfortable now and my fears are almost gone, when the phone rings. Johnny picks up the phone and he seems to be talking in broken sentences. I can't really understand the conversation. I'm looking at him now as a frown comes across his face. It's at this point I'm wondering who and what has broken up our moment of intimacy. I want him to get off the phone so we can continue where we left off when the phone rang. You know, the part where he has me close to him, and I'm getting inpatient with whoever is on the other end of the line.

It's minutes later when Johnny finally does hang up the phone with a puzzled look on his face, and then he turns to me with that beautiful smile of his and touches my hair. I now know that he is getting ready to lower the boom, I just don't know what the boom is, but I'm sure that I'm about to find out.

"Honey, something important has come up at work and I'm going to have to go take care of it. We'll take up where we left off when I get back," he blurts out, while getting his jacket and cap, because there is a brisk coolness in the air tonight.

"When will you be home?" I ask.

"It shouldn't take long. You just sit here and relax and I'll be back before you know it." On that note he was out the door and gone and I just sat on the sofa almost in a daze and feeling just a little bit suspicious, and when I look up at the television, I see this white couple kissing after taking breath mints which doesn't make me feel any better. As I'm sitting here I realize that it's only a few days until we're to be married and I haven't made any plans, as to what it is we're going to do, because Johnny and me haven't really had the time to discuss it at length and I'm really starting to panic now, because I'm feeling really insecure. It seems that this is what I have been feeling most of the time lately, that not knowing kind of feeling, a feeling of dismay, and in a state of confusion. I know that I'm going to have to talk to someone about this limbo state I'm in and now I just have to figure out whom that someone will be.

Ten minutes later I find myself dialing Sarah's number in Lexington. She has always given me good advice in the past when we were growing up. She always seemed to really care about what it was I cared about in life and she was one of my best friends since we were very young. I'm still a bit hesitant as I dial, but I have to talk to somebody, or I'll just go crazy.

"Hello." I hear Sarah's voice.

"Sarah, hi. It's me Callie."

"Callie, how are you and where are you?" She asks.

"I'm here in L.A. with Johnny and I'm calling you because I need your help with something Sarah," I tell her with a little sniffle.

"You know I'll help you if I can Callie. What's up with you?"

"Well, It's Johnny, Sarah, I just don't know what is going on with him. He says he loves me, but there are some mysterious things going on with him."

"Like what?" Sarah asks.

"Well, like his suddenly leaving, because of some important work and earlier in the day, I happen to run up on him in a bar at the mall having lunch with a woman at a restaurant and it was the same woman he introduced to me earlier in the week."

"So you think something is up with that?" She asks.

"Well, yes I do Sarah. Don't you think it strange that he is having lunch with a woman he introduced to me, while we were out for dinner and now I find him having lunch with that same woman? We're supposed to be getting married in a few days and we really haven't made any plans and now I don't know if I should be making plans."

"Does your parents know you're getting married?"

"Not at all Sarah and please don't tell them. You know they would never agree with my decision. I'm supposed to be getting an education. You know how my folks are about that subject."

"Maybe you had better weigh everything out first, before you do anything."

"You could be right. I feel as if I'm moving too fast."

"Callie, make sure that this is really what you want to do and don't do what doesn't feel right," she says with concern in her voice.

We talk for a few more minutes and I promise Sarah that I will call her and let her know what it is that I am going to do, about marrying Johnny and all. She was really quite comforting and I felt as if someone was behind me whatever I decided to do. Sarah was one person that would always be on my side and wanted me to have what I wanted out of life. Not like my parents, who just wanted me to get a degree. It seemed as if that was the only thing they cared about and not caring much at all about my happiness.

I'm sitting on the sofa with the television on, but my mind is suspended in the air. I'm not actually thinking about anything, and the reason is, I just don't know what to think. The show that I'm watching, is drifting in and out. At times I catch a few words of what they are saying and then sink back into suspension. Maybe I'm going into some kind of depression. I certainly hope not. I'm not one for sitting around acting depressed and stuff like that. I tell myself I had better snap out of it because that mess just ain't for me. I'm going to go out and find work no matter what Johnny says. I'm not going to sit in this apartment all day playing stay at home wife. Besides I don't have anything to stay home for. It's not like Johnny and I have kids or anything, in that case I do think mothers should be with their children as much as possible during their formative years at the very least.

I was still awake when Johnny finally came home. I didn't bother to ask any questions. I figured I wouldn't get the right answers anyway. He fell asleep while watching the midnight news and I left him alone, not wanting to be a pest. I knew he was tired from whatever it was he had been doing that evening, but I couldn't sleep. I was trying to make up my mind about what it was I was going to do. Stay with Johnny and keep my mouth shut or do some way out thing, such as leave him in the middle of the night to never be found again. It might just be the thing to do, since he never bothered to explain where he was or what he had been doing all evening and what about Sonia. Who was she to Johnny? That is the question and I'm just going to have to find out what connections she has to the man I was engaged to be married to.

Chapter 5

It's nine-thirty a.m. and I'm on my way to Paris. I'm leaving Johnny because when I woke up this morning he had already left and things are not what I had expected them to be. I still love him a lot of course, but his not coming home until all hours, leaving after dinner, and being with that Sonia woman is all so ridiculous. I was on the phone by seven a.m. to Cynthia who told me Pierre had called to give me one more chance to become a fashion model with his agency. I phoned him right back at seven-thirty a.m. Los Angels time, and by nine a.m Pacific standard time, I find myself in flight to Paris by way of New York. I feel as if someone is tearing my heart out and somehow I can't believe all that has happened to me in a period of just 5 weeks. I've decided not to marry Johnny and fulfill my life's dream of becoming a model.

"What would you like to drink with your breakfast?" The flight attendant was saying. I didn't hear her at first because I was in la la land as usual.

"I'll have some orange juice," I say, as I look around and find that I'm the only black person on this flight. Very few of us ever think about traveling abroad. It's a good thing I took French in high school; it will most assuredly come in handy, when I do get there. I look around again and I see a woman who looks as if she is going to be sick while holding a bag to her mouth. I quickly turn my head now, because that's all I need to ruin my breakfast, is seeing some woman puking, while I'm eating my breakfast. I have a window seat and the man sitting next to me looks as if he is sick, and has not said one word to me since we took off from the airport in L.A. Of course we will have to change planes in New York City and Cynthia promised to meet me there during my layover and bring the clothes I left at her apartment. I'm refusing to let myself think about Johnny and I'm trying to be strong. I'm beginning to wonder if love will ever work out for me. As I stare out of the window, I see some clouds and land below that look like squared off plots of ground. I'm hoping that we get to New York soon, so I can really be on my way to Paris from J.F.K. Airport. Time seems to be going by so slowly, as I'm suspended in mid air with nothing to do but think and try not to think about Johnny.

I hear someone screaming, but I can't see above all the other heads. I'm stretching my neck now to see if I can see something. There are other passengers whispering and stretching also to see if they can detect something. I feel that something strange is happening, but I don't know what. Now, there is a disturbance in the flight attendant's area. Now I feel fear grip me like never before. Suddenly a man comes out from behind a curtain in the front of the plane and he is holding a gun. Now I'm terrified just as all the other passengers are from what I can tell. Passengers are beginning to scream and duck for cover. I feel as if my eyes are bulging out of my head. I see others with terrified looks on their faces also.

"Everybody shut up and don't do anything stupid if you want to live," I hear the man with the gun say in some kind of an accent. I can see the flight attendants seated at the front of the plane. They too look scared out of their wits. I hope he doesn't notice me, I'm thinking. I'm also thinking that I don't want to die. This just cannot be happening to me. All I want to do is get to Paris and start my modeling career and now I may never get there because some idiot is hijacking the plane. As I'm getting this all registered into my brain I hear a voice over the speaker.

"This is your pilot speaking, this plane is now being hijacked and we are now on our way to who knows where." As the pilot is finishing his message to the passengers, I feel the plane turning and I also see passengers gasping in disbelief. At this point I feel that there are at least two hijackers on board. I can hear someone crying.

"I thought I told everybody to shut up," the hijacker with the darker skin, and the big nose and beard, says again.

The man with the gun is dressed like an American, but his nationality is not recognizable and he also has sunglasses on his head and is coming down the aisle looking at all the passengers. I try not to look at him as he passes by my row. If my parents knew what trouble I was into now, I would never hear the end of it, that is, if I live. Oh God, I want to live. I want to live, I keep saying over and over in my mind.

"Everybody put your heads down now," the hijacker is saying, while he's waving his gun in the air and pointing it at people from time to time.

Callie Mason, how do you keep getting yourself into these things? If only I could just get to where I want to go for once, without being hijacked or something. I'm starting to feel angry now. This is just not fair. How can these people stop lives like this, just so they can go where they want to go without paying airfare? Oh boy, I might never see Johnny again, but I have to see him again, but if I'm dead I won't see him again, not in this life anyway. I must forget about Johnny now and concentrate on getting out of this mess we're all in. The man next to me is also frightened. He's looking at me now as if I can save him. I can't save myself right now.

The plane is starting to tip at the right wing. Passengers are now starting to scream again. I close my eyes real tight and a squeak sound comes out of my mouth. I hear a shot from in the front of the plane. This is now getting pretty serious I'm thinking. A few seconds later the plane is level again and flying with some steadiness. A baby is crying and the hijacker with the turban is looking at the woman who is holding her crying baby. I'm now holding my breath as to what he will do, if the baby doesn't stop. My nerves at this point is coming unglued and I start to shiver from fright while the plane starts to rock again from side to side, the baby still crying and that awful look on this man's face that's holding the gun gives me flash backs as to why I ever went to church in the first place and why daddy was such a good man of faith. I start to pray which should have been my first instinct, but I haven't been that faithful lately and now I just hope that it will do some good because I don't know the last time God has heard from me and now ain't that a shame, because I need some help up here.

"You, come," he is talking to me, as I look at him with a questioning look.

"You come here," he says again and yes, he is talking to me of all people on this plane.

I slowly start to get up out of my seat and then into the aisle and then start to walk slowly towards the man with the gun. When I get to the woman just in front of me I can see that she is also a black woman who is holding a bag and trying to throw up in the bag and I wish I had a bag so I could throw up too.

"What do you want with me?" I ask. Now he grabs me around the neck and puts the gun to my head now I'm getting just a little ticked off, because I don't have time for this mess and I just want to go to Paris and be a model until Johnny comes for me if he ever will I don't know.

I'm so angry at this point I Stomp the man's toes, slips out of his grip and then punch him in the eye as hard as I can, and now there are other men running towards us and they within seconds are all over the man and me and I'm trying to get out of the middle of their subduing the hijacker, and now two other men with guns head for the pilot's cabin and burst in while I'm still lying on the floor with the other men trying to get the hijacker off me. Thank God that didn't last long. I was about to have a serious heart attack or a stroke, thinking that I might not see Johnny again.

Later, I find out that the two men that stormed the pilot's cabin and took the other hijacker into custody were two off duty detectives on their way to New York. People are cheering me and the detectives and I just feel as If I could just parachute out of this plane and walk to New York. It is more peaceful if I could do just that. I am still shaking and now I'm crying tears because I feel as if I'm totally unbalanced and don't know what I want anymore after what just happened. I really don't want to be on another plane when I get off this one. I need time to think about what is going on with me and just what it is I should be doing in the first place.

Now that I'm off the plane in New York's LaGuardia Airport, there are reporters everywhere as we walk toward the terminal, I hear one of the passengers say out loud.

"That's the lady that attacked the hijacker. If it weren't for her we might still be on that plane headed for who knows where." The reporters start to rush me, as I trip while trying to make a run for it, but I'm not fast enough. One of the reporters grabs my coat and is hanging onto it for dear life.

"Miss, what is your name?" The reporter asks.

"Go away and leave me alone," I yell at a woman reporter.

"Hey lady what happened up there?" A man is now hanging onto the other side of my coat as I try to escape from both of them. Now I'm running at a gallop and the two reporters are running along holding onto my rain and shine coat as I desperately try to make a break. As I try to look behind me I can see other reporters trying to catch me as well. I just want to get inside the airport and try and calm down. There are just too many people running behind me, and what does this all-mean anyway. I'm just Callie Mason a nobody who just wants to be loved by somebody.

Once inside the airport I give up and start to try and answer some of the questions because by now they practically have me hog-tied with the belt from my coat. Once I sat down, they let go of me and took pen and pad in their hands in a writing position. I look up and as

I'm about to begin to answer one of the questions, I see Johnny running towards me looking quite serious. At this point I just give up, because I had left Johnny in L.A. this morning so I thought.

"My name is Callie Mason and yes I did punch one of the hijackers in the eye."

"Are you some kind of security agent?" The man reporter asked.

"No, I'm just a woman on my way... I stop in the middle of the sentence because Johnny is staring right at me.

"I'm staying in New York with a friend," I say.

"Were you frightened?" The woman asked.

"Wouldn't you be?" I ask her.

"Is that bruise on your face from the scuffle you had on the plane?"

"Yes, I guess it is," I say. I didn't know that I had a bruise on my face and I quickly take out my compact and open it up to look into the small mirror. Yes there is a bruise on my face.

The reporters ask me a few more questions and then move on to the flight attendants and pilots for more details of the hijacking. I look at Johnny wondering where in the world did he come from and how did he get here, as I slowly walk towards him.

"Why are you doing this?" He asks me looking me squarely in my face.

"I really don't think you need me right now Johnny," I say, and he takes me by my shoulders between both his hands and looks me in the eyes.

"Callie, I love you. We're getting married. Do you remember that, Callie?"

"Johnny admit it, you're just too busy for me. You don't need a wife, at least not now," I say looking back at him squarely in his eyes.

"Let's talk about this," he says, taking my arm and leading to a more quiet area.

"Johnny there is nothing else to talk about. We just haven't been connecting lately and I think that you might have started to resent me just a little."

"Why that's ridiculous. Why would I resent the woman I love?"

"No it is not," I say with force and now people are starting to stare at us.

"Look, I have to catch the next flight out of here to L.A. I'm suppose to be working and I hope you make up your mind and come back."

"How did you get here so quickly anyway?" I ask.

"Never mind that, I want you to come home with me. At least call me tonight and let me know what you really want to do. I have to go now."

I stand in the airport and watch him walk away. I must be crazy, but before I could think about it any further I see Cynthia coming in my direction. As soon as she is in hearing distance, she starts yelling.

"Johnny called me to try to find out why you were leaving him," she says for the whole world to hear about my business.

"I just saw him," I say feeling a little down and out now, not knowing if I should have run after Johnny and pledged my love for him.

"What did he say to you and where is he going?" Cynthia asks with disbelief in her eyes.

"Come on let's go," I say, pulling her along by her coat sleeve.

It's around six o'clock in the evening and I still haven't left for Paris. My day was so hectic; I just didn't feel like getting on another plane. Maybe Paris is just not in the plan for me. Cynthia was in shock when she found out I was on the plane that had been hijacked earlier in the day. She gave me a sedative and told me to lie down in the guest room. I welcomed the quietness of the hour. If only I could get my head on straight, maybe just maybe I could get going in life. Before I can turn over, I hear something on the television news station. I thought I heard my own name mentioned. I start to listen harder and then I get up and run into the living room where the television is sitting and there I am on the news being interviewed by the reporters after we finally landed in New York and I look as if I'm in total disarray.

"Come in here Cynthia," I yell.

"What is it?" She asks, as she darts into the living room.

"I'm on the news," I tell her, while my mouth is hanging open.

"I'll be. That's you all right. You look great," Cynthia says.

I'm going back to bed," I say.

As I'm lying on the bed, tears start to roll down my cheeks. I'm so lonely without Johnny, but he scares me when he doesn't come home at night and I see him with Sonia and he lies about some things. How can I trust him if he doesn't tell me the truth about his whereabouts. I don't even know where he works. All I know is that he leaves very early in the morning and comes home late at night. He says he loves me, like in the airport today and how did he get there so fast anyway and I just let him walk out of there without me. One of these days I'm going to get something right in this life. If only mama and daddy could see the mess I'm making of my life, or maybe they shouldn't see the mess I'm making because it would kill them to know that their little girl has gone bananas. I'm sure they haven't missed the evening news either. If I don't get it together soon I'm going to commit my self. The phone is ringing now interrupts my thought. I listen to it ring again. Now I can hear Cynthia answering the phone.

"Telephone Callie," I hear her say.

"Who is it?" I ask.

"It's important. You better get in here now."

I roll over and slowly get up from the bed. I hope it's not any reporters. I just want to forget about everything that has happened today. I really need some rest and who is it anyway? I hope mama and daddy hasn't seen the hijacking on the news.

"Hello."

"It's me Callie," Johnny says.

"What do you want?" I ask.

"Callie you could have been killed today. You need to be here with me. You need someone to look after you."

"You don't need me Johnny."

"You're wrong. I need you more than anything in the world,." he says, almost yelling.

"You hardly ever come home," I say.

"I'll soon be able to explain that, but right now, you'll have to trust me."

I'm hanging up now Johnny. I'm really very tired," I say.

Once back in bed, I begin to wonder even more if I was too hasty in leaving Johnny, but quickly dismissed the thought. My heart ached every time he came home late and I didn't know where he was or what he was doing. We didn't really spend that much time together and we were supposed to be getting married. Life was so simple when I was at home in Lexington, and living on the edge of town, where red dirt made it colorful and listening to the crickets at night gave me a sense of belonging. It was never this hard and I always had my parents to give me good advice. Now I was too ashamed to ask them any advice about Johnny and me. I want them to think that I can make it on my own and not have to call home for advice every other day. I know I need to be alone for a while. I need to sort out my mistakes and try not to make them again. My hopes and dreams are fading and if I don't act soon, they may never come to pass. It's so easy to get distracted and fall into traps that you are not expecting or even wanting to be engaged in and I'm feeling abused and misused concerning my new life away from home. My whole philosophy was that when someone loved you it was real and for keeps, but I'm finding out nothing in my life is real anymore and certainly not lasting.

When I wonder what life is all about, nothing in particular comes to mind. I must have been living in a glass bubble all of my life, protected by my parents and now that I'm in the real world, nothing is making sense to me at all. It's as if I'm traveling on a road to nowhere and hope that it will lead to somewhere. My thoughts are fragments of my imagination and as scattered as the wind. My confidence is withering and my dreams shattered. Now I must make up my mind and go in that direction, be persistent and pray that everything works out for the better.

I know tomorrow will be better and much more calm. I am aching for tomorrow to come so today will be over. My body is in New York, my heart is in Los Angeles with Johnny and my mind is in Paris. What a mixed up person I am. I've always been told to follow my heart and wait on my dreams to come true. Now I feel that it was a falsehood, because my heart has done nothing but get me into trouble. Maybe I should listen to my brain for a change. Life is not a bowl of cherries and I don't feel particularly self-sufficient right now, so I just hope that time will heal my wounds and I can go on and live my life. Johnny knows by now that I am not coming back to L.A. Yes, time will go on and will not wait for me.

A few days after speaking with Johnny, I'm on my way back to Lexington instead of Paris. Pierre has once again allowed me ten more days to get there. The plane is about to land at the airport. I just wanted to see my folks again before going to Paris. You would have thought that last plane ride would have scared me off, but here I am again flying among the blue skies and white clouds that look like white puffballs. The ground was still far below and I can't wait to see mama and daddy. I know they are always happy to see their daughter.

Now that the plane is finally landing, I'm just a bit nervous. They will be waiting for me at the gate. I see them as I enter the terminal and I throw my arms around mama first and then daddy. They are smiling and very happy to see me. My makeup is now smeared from the hugs and kisses they are giving me and we start for the exit of the terminal to the car. It looks as if it is going to rain and I hope so, because when I get to the house where I grew up, I'm going to my room and sleep for a very long time. The stress of the last six weeks has been phenomenal and I need to regroup so that I can go on.

When we get to the house, it is pouring down rain and all three of us make a beeline for the front door. Once inside I feel as if I had never left. It's home and it's cozy and the aroma of mama's cooking collard greens and candy yams and apple cobbler filled the whole house. I was hungry for some good home cooking.

"You just relax in your room honey. I'll call you when I'm finished with dinner," mama says as she gives me one of her famous smiles. She's known for her beautiful smile, although mama is only five feet two inches and I'm five feet nine inches, she never let me forget who the boss is, just because I'm seven inches taller than she, but I know I have to stay in line. I got my height from daddy who is at least six feet four.

Mama always did pamper me, just like daddy always did as well. They are such wonderful parents. I just can't grasp why it is that I can't have a relationship like theirs. My room is still decorated in the soft white that mama always kept it in. She said white was for the little angel of the house. Of course that was I. I sat on my soft bed covered in a linen white comforter, with pink lace. The same pictures were on the walls. It was filled with pictures of my high school fiends, especially Sarah and Genny and me. As I'm looking at the pictures, I start to remember some of the days back in high school when Scooter and me was a hot item and all the girls were jealous of us. Scooter was one of the best looking boys around and all the girls liked him, but he liked me best. I went to all the basket ball games, because Scooter was on the Varsity Team. I loved watching him dunking that ball into the hoop. It would go in as smooth as silk. None of the others on the team could shoot a ball into the hoop like Scooter. I would stand up and yell, "go Scooter go." Those good old days are over and I let out a deep sigh of regret.

We all sat down for dinner around six p.m. and when we finished, mama and daddy went to bed and I sat out on the porch swing. It had been a long day for my parents. Mama cooking all that food and then driving to the airport to get me. I imagine it was all they could take for one day, since they always got up before the chickens. The moon is full and the stars are shining very bright. It's a perfect night for romance, but I quickly dismissed the thought. Besides romance was not a part of my life these days. It seemed as if every man wanted to play me. I'm sitting here watching some of the neighbors a ways down the street. I know instantly that they are new to the area, because they would know who I was if they weren't. There is also a car driving slowly by, and I can't see who is in the car. The car stops and I get a little anxious, because I don't know who is in the car. I'm trying to make out the figure behind the steering wheel, but it's too dark to see inside.

After a couple of minutes a figure starts to get out. Now I'm really starting to feel anxious. I'm almost up off the swing and then I hear a man speaking.

"Hi Callie."

"Scooter is that you?" I ask as, I now begin to recognize his voice.

"Yeah, it's me," he says as if he's a little down and out.

I walk to the edge of the porch and stand there with my arms folded wondering what on earth is scooter doing here and how did he know I would be in town. I know news does travel fast in this town. He must have heard I was coming home for a visit.

He starts up the walk as I start down the steps into the yard. He looks as handsome as ever with his slim hard body that definitely had that athletic look with his crew cut. To my surprise he gives me a big bear hug and lifts me right off the ground. He seems happy to see me and to be quite honest, I'm happy to see him.

"What are you doing here?" I ask.

"Hoping to see you," he says, with a look of hope in his eyes.

"What makes you think I want to see you?"

"I was just hoping that you would. I know I've made a big mistake not marrying you and I was hoping that well, maybe we could be friends at least," he says, as he pulls at his nose like he always did when he was nervous.

"Nothing wrong with being friends," I say, because I can use the company.

"Come on Callie. Let's be real. You know I want to be more than just friends."

"Look Scooter, I'm really not interested in any kind of friendships with any of the male species right now," I say, with a little irritation in my tone of voice.

"Love never forgets, Callie. I have never forgotten you. Broken hearts never die you know. They just get stronger with each encounter and then they love again," he continues to say, as I admire his language of love. It must be something out of some poem book.

"I know love never forgets. I'll never forget what we had, but now my heart belongs to someone else," I say.

"If you give me a chance, I'll make it all up to you. Everything I did to you and everything he has done," he says, resting his arms on my shoulders. I'll make it all up to you." he says again, as he leans in for a kiss, but I'm quick and he gets me on the cheek.

Then I look into his eyes and I start to believe that he is sorry and wants to make it up to me. After all he was the first person I ever loved, and somehow I believe him when he says love never forgets. He kisses me lightly on the cheek again and then stands back. He is somehow waiting for an answer. He is waiting for me to say something, anything at all. My mind is racing at a hundred miles an hour and I don't want to brush him off and yet I'm afraid to give him any hope, so we just stand there in the moonlight looking at each other and hoping the other will break the silence and I can't stand it any longer, so I do the honors of breaking it first.

"Look Scooter, I just don't know what it is I'm feeling right now. I'm sort of on the rebound and anything can happen."

"I'll take that chance," he says, as he jumps right in to counter attack.

"I don't want to be hurt by you again, Scooter. One devastation per male is all that I allow. Do you understand?" I say.

"I won't hurt you Callie. Cross my heart," he says with a slight smile on his face.

I know that when one says cross my heart in Lexington, that nothing more convincing could be said. It was something we all said as kids growing up, and no one ever broke a promise when they said those words, so I had to believe him.

"Okay, while I'm here visiting my parents, we'll see what happens," I tell him with some relief, while I smile back at him and I can see my eyes twinkling in his beautiful eyes.

"Thank you," he says, putting his arms around me and planting a big kiss on my forehead.

"You are very welcome," I say.

For the next few days Scooter and I are always together. We go to the movies, out to the restaurant to eat, bowling, and I hardly have time to visit with my parents or Sarah and Genny. I must say that I am having a wonderful time and it's just what I need these days. Scooter's intense desire to recapture the love that was lost between us has heightened my zest for life. I have never felt better and I do hope it lasts. I can tell that he is having the time of his life as well and he is determined to keep what he once lost and now has found and we see each other everyday.

On this beautiful Saturday morning daddy wants me to spend time with him on the golf course. I tell him I will be down soon. He is eating breakfast and talking to mama and waiting for me to appear. He seems happy that I am going with him and I'm glad to be able to make him happy as he has made me happy since I was a very little girl, when I realized how parents can either be good parents or bad parents. I was blessed, to have gotten good parents.

"I'm ready," I say, as I enter the kitchen.

"Sit down and have some breakfast dear," mama so graciously tries to convince me.

"I'm still full from all that pizza Scooter and I ate at the movies last night."

"She can't fool me. She's trying to watch her figure," daddy says, teasing me.

I start to do deep knee bends right in the middle of the kitchen floor. Mama starts to laugh as she finishes up the morning dishes, which I feel I should have been washing them, myself. Mama hardly wants to let anyone in her kitchen. She says no one can clean it like she can and I never gave her any flack about it either.

"I'm just warming up for the golf game," I say. I always loved to make my parents laugh. They knew I was happy when I became silly and played around with them. My relationship with my parents has always been very unique. We were very good friends and I could tell them anything. There were many days when I cried on my mama's shoulder and she never seemed to mind and always listened and gave me good God given advice every time. I never felt rejection a day in my life and I knew that I was special to them. It just doesn't seem fair that every child can't have what I have and have always had, and that is loving parents. They have always identified with me and I with them despite the few times of opposition and my one time of shear defiance when I skipped school and went to the movies with Scooter.

When daddy and I get to the golf course it's as green as I last remember it to be. It seems as if it's greener than the last time I was here. It's so hot out here, daddy and me and a few others are the only ones out on the green.

I have some reservations concerning the hot sun blaring down, but daddy seems not to notice and has just swung at the ball and it's flying through the air towards the first hole. As I look up into the deep blue sky, suddenly I'm in the clouds with the ball. My mind has wondered to my new heart felt romance with Scooter, but even I know that Scooter does not make my heart go flip flop the way it does when I'm with Johnny. Scooter has saved me from the heart felt pain of not having Johnny as I now feel as if I owe him something, at least another chance, in which I know will probably lead to nowhere.

"Good going," I encourage daddy, as my mind comes back to earth leaving the deep blue sky up there where it belongs.

"I do believe I'm going to have a good game of golf today,." he chants.

"It certainly, most definitely looks that way," I say giving him a thumbs up sign.

We played most of the afternoon with the blazing hot sun glaring down on us. Daddy seemed not to notice, but I am just plain hot from the sun and humidity. I'm sweating bullets from my brow. I have to wipe my forehead at least fifty times in an hour. We're in our second hour and headed for the 9th hole. I pull my cap down more over my eyes to try and keep out the sun. Daddy is already ahead of me as we now walk across the green grass. I see daddy starting to sit down on the green and I think to myself that it's an odd thing for him to do, but didn't pay that much attention until I see him now lying on the green. This to me is much too strange, so I pick up my pace and then start to run towards him. I'm calling to him as I run in his direction and I start to panic and my heart is beating very fast. My stomach starts to feel queezy, because I know that something is terribly wrong. My legs start to feel rubbery under me as if I might fall into the grass. I'm panting very hard now from fear, anxiety and exhaustion. My mind races back to my childhood, when daddy has me on his lap and playing patty cakes with me. Now I see us at the beach and also going fishing together. It seems as if my whole life with him is now passing before my very eyes. It's like some kind of premonition.

"Daddy, daddy," I call out to him. He is trying to raise his arm but it falls limply down to the ground. I'm getting closer now but it seems as if I will never get to him as he's lying there and I can hear him gasping for air. I can see that he is in a lot of pain and has one hand over his chest as if that is where the pain is coming from. This can't be happening I'm saying to myself and my own heart feels heavy from the fear that I now face. This is a moment in time I never wanted to ever take place or be a part of in life. I notice the sun is setting and it's a dull orange and it looks so beautiful. When I reach him, I'm wiping tears from my eyes because I know deep down inside that it is time to shed tears and also time to mourn. His eyes are closed and I take his head in my lap as I sit on the ground and rock him as tears are streaming down my face. I don't say anything because I know he can't hear me. He can't hear me because he has left and gone to a better place. He always said not to cry, when he left, because he would be in heaven and that we would see each other again. Somehow I feel it is my fault. I should have stopped playing earlier and this wouldn't have happened. What is mama going to say? Will she blame me for this terrible tragedy?

Five days later the house is full of people by ten a.m. this morning, because friends and relatives are here for daddy's funeral. I am still in shock and Sarah and Genny, keep reassuring me that it was not my fault that daddy had a heart attack and died. As I'm sitting on the sofa with my dark dress on and my dark glasses, so no one can see how bad my eyes are swollen from continually crying day and night, I long for Johnny. The doctor had to give mama and me tranquillizers from the shock and pain of losing the most precious person to us both. My head is calm now and I just sit rigid on the sofa waiting to go to the church. People are all over the place and talking softly to one another. All of the church members are here. Some are still outside the house in the yard. I can't wait until this is over. The pain has been too sharp and dull all at the same time. I don't know if I can ever get over this loss.

I hear someone say that the limo's are here. I look at my watch and see that it is now 10:30a.m. I have dreaded this moment from the very beginning of this horrible nightmare. Scooter is here to ride in the limo with me. He has also been very supportive since this whole thing happened. The relatives on daddy's side of the family are large in number and some of them have to stay in a hotel, because although the house is big, it is not quite big enough for such a large group of people.

Once outside, Scooter helps me into the limo and others follow. There must be at least three limousines parked in front of the house. The others will have to go in their own cars or ride with someone because daddy's family is so big. Cynthia has flown in from New York and I am so happy that she came. She has also been strength for me during this time of bereavement and I'm eternally grateful to her. All my friends are here to support me, like Sarah and Genny my two best friends since grade school.

As we ride through the streets of Lexington, I see all the familiar places I used to go when I was growing up here. The skating rink where we all had so much fun together. We went every Friday night for years. Everyone knew everyone else and it was one big happy family. When we turn the corner I see my old high school. Yes, the place where I used to have so much fun with all my friends and the day I graduated, I was so happy I couldn't stop crying. The place where I was a cheerleader for the high school athletic teams. I can just see myself now jumping around on the gym floors doing the cheers and rooting for our high school team to kick butt. Those were the good old days to me now. I didn't know just how good they were until now.

When we get to the church where my father has been the pastor for many years until he retired. Tears are streaming down my face; Scooter is holding my hand with one of his and puts his other arm around my shoulder. We all file into the church, which is already packed with people. The family is lead to the front pews and I am right behind mama and one of the deacons who is helping mama to stand on her feet. As we sit down I hear them singing the old Negro spiritual, "Precious Lord" and I feel as if a vice is locked around my heart and squeezing it tight. The pain is unbearable. "Why Lord, why did this have to happen now?" I ask Him. I don't hear anything, but I didn't expect to, because daddy always told me that God never makes mistakes.

Mama is crying and so are a lot of daddy's relatives, my aunts, uncles, cousins and others are wiping away tears from their eyes. Now the choir breaks out with "Oh Happy Day," another great song for all occasions, and a great going home song. I'm sitting on the front pew next to mama and Scooter next to me. He is giving me such great support through this whole thing. It also helps a lot to know that all my best friends are here to support me too, but not Johnny. He is not here for me. I need him here for me.

Just as I get these thoughts out, I look around to see that a large crowd is here and there is standing room only. Many are in the corridor and I can see some standing on the church steps because just now the door opened and I almost faint. It's Johnny he did come. I see him sit down in the back of the church. Cynthia must have given him the news about daddy. I can hardly understand what the man up front is saying. It's like I'm almost in a dream and can't wake up. My thoughts are scattered and aimless. I don't know what to think. I'm still looking at him and I can see that he sees me. I finally turn around as to not make a disturbance. People will wonder what it is I'm looking at now. I can't believe he's really here. Now I can't wait for the service to be over. I don't hear a word that is being said. My mind is off in space. The assistant Pastor is bringing the eulogy and I notice that I am shaking all over. Scooter squeezes my hand to try to calm me down, but the pain of my loss and the excitement of Johnny sitting in the back are all too much for me. I can't stop shaking, because it's almost time for the family to go up to where daddy is and give him their last words and say goodbye. It will soon be time for me to go up to daddy and tell him that I have always loved him and always will love him, even in death.

As Scooter takes me by the hand and help me up from the pew, I feel as if my legs won't carry me. He holds me tight around my waist as I try not to look up and see any faces. Once we get to the casket, I almost faint and Scooter has to hold me up. Tears are streaming down my face, and I can't get any words out of my mouth. I can hear mama crying softly in back of me where she is sitting on the front pew. Now I can hear the choir singing, "I'll fly away." They continue to sing, one bright morning, when this life is over I'll fly away. I can't take it any more and I turn to go back to sit down and when I look up I see Johnny standing at the door in the back of the church with a very odd look on his face. For a moment I can see that we have eye contact and then I drop my eyes and continue walking to my seat on the pew.

When the service is over and as the family procession is in the aisle and leaving our seats to go to the graveyard, Scooter puts his arm around my shoulder. I look right into Johnny's eyes again, as he's watching me leave the church. I just want to run to him and throw my arms around him and tell him how much I still love him, but I don't want to embarrass myself and everyone else by doing that now. He suddenly takes his eyes off me and looks the other way. I know he has figured out who Scooter is and now I feel more pain.

As we're getting into the limo, I look back to see if I can see Johnny and maybe explain something to him, but I don't see him and now I'm being slightly pushed to get into the limo. Hopefully he'll be here when I get back or maybe I'll see him at the gravesite. I don't want to let him get away before I can talk to him. He came all this way to be here with me and he sees me with Scooter. How dumb can I get? I might as well realize that Johnny is the only man I want, but can I have him and will he have me now? That is a question that remains to be seen.

The graveside ceremony is almost over, thank God. I don't know how much more of this I can stand in one days time. As I look behind me now I see Johnny and several other men dressed in dark suits leaning against a sheik black car. His hands are in his pockets and he looks as if he is looking right at me. I stare for a moment and then I try to concentrate on what the preacher is saying. I now hear everyone saying Amen. I'm glad it's over. Goodbye daddy I say in my heart, goodbye, but not forever. I'll see you in heaven I say to myself.

As we start for the limos and cars to go back to the church to eat and fellowship with friends and loved ones, I look in Johnny's direction. I see him and the other men start to get into the black cars. Now I break away and start running for the car. The car is taking off slowly. I start to run faster. "Johnny, Johnny stop," I call after him, but the car picks up speed, as it heads for the cemetery gates and into the street. I'm still running and yelling "stop" but the car doesn't stop and then it is out of view. I fall on my knees and cover my face with my hands. I'm totally lost without any direction. The pain swells up in me and I feel as if I am going to burst. Then I feel a hand on my arm. I look up and Scooter takes my arm and helps me up off the ground.

As we head back for the church I'm stunned and devastated. Scooter can see that I'm almost in a state of shock.

"Don't worry about him. Callie," Scooter says, trying to comfort me.

"I'm not worried," I say, in a very soft voice.

"He's not good enough for you."

At this point I say nothing. Maybe I'm not good enough for him, I think to myself. He came all this way and now I'm two timing him with Scooter. I may never see him again.

How stupid can I be. I must get him back and never let him go. Scooter will hate me forever, I just know he will, but Scooter is here now and Johnny is not. I let him get away. I probably drove him away with my selfishness. I just know I can't live without him. Scooter now takes me by the hand and leads me to the waiting limousine, that will take us back to the house, where everyone will have an extended gathering and eat and talk and act as if this is the best day of their lives. You know how when someone dies, everyone gets together and eat and drink and get drunk and all that. I'm in the mood for a drink myself and drinking is something I don't usually do, but to lose the two men in your life that you love all in the same week is a little bit too much to bear, at least it is for me. I suppose it would be too much for anyone. It's too much for me.

Chapter 6

We finished breakfast and decided to get some air on the boat deck. Yes, Sarah and Genny and I are on a cruise. We are cruising the Caribbean, because they felt I needed some time to relax. They are such good friends. The ocean liner is luxurious and I have to admit that I do feel a lot better. We are on our second day of our seven-day cruise and I have been able to let go of a lot of frustration and pain. I promised Pierre again that I would come to Paris right after the cruise and he understands my pain. It seems that I am always in pain and there is not much I can do about it either. I'm looking forward to the show and dinner tonight. The food is so good on this ship and I'm going to eat and eat until I can't eat anymore.

"This is so beautiful, isn't it?" I ask?

"Yes it is, but I wished you felt as beautiful. Sarah says, looking at me sideways. "You look as if you have just lost your best friend and here you are on this lovely ship with your two best friends. Now what's up with that." She asks me point blank?

"I feel great," I say, knowing that I'm not convincing anyone.

"You feel great?" Genny asks?

"You could have fooled me," Sarah says, laying her head back on the lounge chair.

"You two are hallucinating," I say, although I know they are right. I must look like a limp dishrag or something, because that's the way I'm feeling inside. I'm trying hard to have a good time, but I can't imagine what a good time is anymore. I am looking forward to the show tonight. Maybe that will give me a booster shot, at least I hope so. I'm on this cruise and feel as if I have nothing to look forward to in life. Life is a drag. I know there's got to be more to it then this. Sitting on this ship with two of my best friends and don't know what to do next. This is the pit all right. Someday, I just might have a little happiness, but when in the world will that be? Right now, it seems to be a long way off.

"Maybe we can find someone to cheer her up tonight," Sarah says, now crossing her legs and looking up at the sky with that smirk on her face.

"Yeah, I hope we can do something for her," Genny says, sarcastically.

"You guys are some real friends alright. I'm fine and I don't need any cheering up," I say, trying to look real happy and smiling a pasted smile on my face.

"Yeah, right," Genny says, as she rolls her eyes in dismay.

"What's wrong with you guys. Can't you see I'm having a good time?" I say.

Genny and Sarah just look at each other and roll their eyes. They know I'm lying and I am not very convincing at this point, although I wish I could be so they would just stop talking.

For the next hour we just lay there on the boat deck not saying anything else. Each one of us with our own thoughts. The sun is blaring down, and I don't want to get too much of a tan, because my beautiful skin is just the right shade of tan to begin with, and I don't want to get too dark on this cruise. It seems that black folk don't want to be too dark and white folk don't want to be too white. Why can't we just all except ourselves for what God made us to be and let it go at that, but then life would be too simple and uninteresting to say the least. And I do hope I will have a good time tonight at the concert and show, but I'm not getting my hopes up either.

It's later in the evening and we are all now in the room getting ready for the big event tonight. This is my first cruise and I have to admit it is a very fun place to be. The food is good and there are so many things to do, and now I'm trying to find the right dress to wear to the concert and don't know why, but I am starting to get into this cruise after all I'm thinking as I pull out my favorite black dress with the V-neck and when I put the diamond pin in the bottom of the V that I got for my eighteenth birthday, it just sets the dress right off. I always feel good when I wear this dress, because I feel that I look my very best and that's when I act my best.

We're sitting at the best table in the room. Not too close and not too far from the stage. I can tell that Genny and Sarah are a little nervous. They are anxious to see some fine man walk through the door. Me, I'm just here to have a good time, and it's about time I had a good time, after all the loss I have sustained just so very recently. My spirits are lifting and I intend to have a good time no matter what. I may never get this chance to be on a cruise again, who knows, this could be my first and last cruise, so I better make the best of it while I have a chance.

"Oh my goodness. Who are those fine men coming in the door?" Sarah Asks.

"You are right about that, they are fine," Genny says, starting to fan her self with the table napkin and crossing her legs like she is in church or something.

I knew it wouldn't be long before Genny and Sarah would spot some men. They were just talented that way. It was as if they could smell them coming into a room before they ever saw them, but I am used to these flirtatious girls. I'm glad I'm not as flirtatious as they are. I just don't know what gets into them when they see a man, and he really don't have to be that fine either. As a matter of fact, I remember when they both had some pretty ugly men. But you couldn't tell neither one of them that. They were so stuck on them.

"What are you having to drink Callie?" Genny asks me.

"I'll have some lemonade," I say.

"Lemonade." Sarah chirps. Who has lemonade on a cruise at nine o'clock at night in the middle of the ocean on a cruise at a concert?" She asks, looking at me as if she is defining how dumb I am or something.

"I do," I say sternly.

"Well you help yourself girl, cause I'm having something just a little bit stronger than that," Sarah says, while looking at the liquor menu and Genny trying to look at it at the same time.

The evening is getting off to a good start. The music is good and they have all the best rhythm and blues singers around. Some of the told time ones who I think are the best are here and the room is full of magic. Sarah and Genny have been invited to another table with the gentlemen that came in earlier in the evening and seem to be having a good time. Frankly, I'm glad they are there and I'm here alone. I don't have to pretend now, and I don't have to look a certain way when they are not around. I can just be myself, whatever that is for the moment.

"Are you sitting alone?"

I'm startled and I turn to see who is speaking to me. I look up and there is this indescribable man standing next to me as he pulls out a chair and starts to sit down. I can hardly get any words out before he is already seated and staring me right in the face. He is tall and lean and wearing a Taylor made suite that must have cost at least five hundred dollars and wearing a gold watch on his left wrist and a gold men's bracelet on his right wrist. He had exquisite teeth that could be seem through his bright smile. His hair was elegantly cut and waved from front to back. I thought I must have been dreaming, because I have never seen anyone so well groomed and as beautiful as he, well except for Johnny, but I can't think about him now. I'm so startled that I start to tremble and hope that the man is not noticing how nervous I am.

"Uh, no, that is, no one is sitting here," I say, stuttering my words.

"Well that's good, because there is no place else I'd rather be sitting right now," he says pulling out a chair to sit down next to me. My mind starts to wonder back to daddy's funeral and how I lost Johnny and didn't get to talk with him. I remember how sad mama was that day daddy had died and left her all alone. They had been together almost thirty-five years. They had been married ten years when I was born. Having older parents, turned out to be an advantage to me. I was spoiled rotten, if you can call that an advantage. Scooter is probably wondering what is happening with the two of us, because I didn't even tell him I was going on this cruise with Sarah and Genny, but I assume he will get the news from mama, when he comes to call on me and here I am on this Grande ship with my two closest friends and a very handsome man sitting across from me and I can't figure out if he is real or a figment of my imagination. Things haven't seemed real since daddy died and somehow I can't distinguish imagination from reality.

"You seem as if you're off in space somewhere," the man says to me, as he lights a cigarette.

"Oh, I'm sorry. I just lost my father and I'm just a little bit disoriented," I reply, hoping to get some kind of sympathy.

"I'm sorry to hear that. Is there any thing I can do?"

"No thank you. I'm handling it."

"Are you sure?" I mean if there is anything I can do, just tell me."

"You're very kind," I say, being just a little irritated by his insisting on being at my table in the first place. I don't know him and he doesn't know me, so why is he here anyway. I have lots of things to think about and I don't trust myself either. Surely he will get the hint and drift along to some other woman's table, at least that's what I'm hoping he will do. This is not the time for me to meet new people, when my head is all mixed up and I'm tormented with guilt and thoughts of Johnny. Why doesn't he go away. Maybe tomorrow, but not today. I've been on the rebound for the second time in a little of no time. It wasn't that long ago Scooter went into the armed forces and before he left, he gave me an engagement ring that was so very beautiful and before I could show it off good, I hear he has married someone he met in the armed forces. He must have thought that she was better than me. I mean, I'm just a country girl and when he met a big city girl, he couldn't even come back to me. He didn't even send me a letter. I had to hear about his marriage to someone else through the grapevine. Now here is a stranger sitting across from me trying to seduce me and I can't even feel his presence. I don't even see him as a person. He's some kind of object to me. He doesn't look like Johnny and he's not Johnny.

"Hey, are you in there?" He says to me, while I'm still in the middle of my daydream.

"Would you like something to drink?" He asks with a very concerned look on his face.

"No thank you. I'm fine." I really just can't believe this is happening. Here I am sitting here feeling comfortable for once in who knows how long and now here comes this fine man to my table and wants to buy me a drink. No this is not happening to me again. I could very well fall for the man. He is just too good looking, especially at a time when I'm on the rebound.

"Who are you?" I ask.

"I'm Paul Hayes, and you? What's your name?"

"I'm Callie Mason," I say, as I'm looking off into space somewhere. I can't tell if I'm flattered or annoyed.

I'm feeling as if men scare me these days. I don't know if I should take the drink or run for the nearest exit. I keep sitting here anyway, trying to think of something to say. I don't want to appear too unfriendly, after all he may be a nice gentleman and I could sure use the company.

"So, what brings you on this cruise?" He asks, while he's lights another cigarette.

"My friends thought I needed some time out," I tell him, trying to impress him at the same time.

"Well, I'm glad you decided to take the time out, because I'm beginning to appreciate this trip," he says, with a smile that displays his shiny white teeth that he must have just had polished.

"It is beginning to get more interesting all the time," I say, as I'm fidgeting with my earring.

"Would you like to dance?" He asks me, as if he's quite confident that I'll except.

"Sure. Why not?"

We get up from the table and he takes my hand and leads me to the dance floor. The music is slow and moody and I kind of relax into his arms. I'm feeling the mood and I think Paul feels it too. I look over at the table where Sarah and Genny are sitting with the two men and I see both of them nodding their heads in approval. He is starting to pull me a little closer, but I resist just a little. I don't want to give him any ideas. After all he could be married and I'm not one for getting involved with a married man, because I have heard of too many bad endings for women who thought that the married man they were with would leave their wives for them. How stupid could they be anyway. Women need to stick to having their own man and not a man that belongs to someone else. I have a real pet peeve about that and maybe I had better ask him before we get too acquainted on this ship and besides I'm on the rebound for the second time.

After the dance ended, we went back to the table. Genny and Sarah were still talking with the other gentlemen and seemed to still be having a good time. The crowd was getting thicker and the large room was very packed with all kinds of people that were laughing and talking and having what seemed to be a good time. I have to admit that I also am having a good time, but I think I'm afraid to really let go and let laughter and happiness invade my shattered emotions. This is a quick picker upper and I had better take advantage of it while I can.

"So, are you on this cruise alone?" I ask, nervously.

"I sure am," he says, and then he leans back in his chair.

"You must have left your wife and kids at home," I tell him.

"No, I don't have a wife and kids," he says, smiling as if he knows something about me that I don't know, and even if he thinks he does, I'm sure that he probably does not know what he may think he knows.

"Well, that's nice to know. I don't like pushing in on other people's territory," I say, as I'm crossing my legs in agreement with the answer. He can see that I'm relieved and that now I might be able to relax and try and have a good time.

"How about yourself?" He asks

"What about myself?" I ask as, if I don't know what he is talking about.

"Are you involved or married?" He asks.

"No, I am not and that's for sure," I say.

"You sound as if you've just been jilted," he chuckles, just a little to make it sound light.

"Well, you could be right about that." I tell him as I'm nervously shifting myself in the chair.

The rest of the evening is going very well. Paul and I are having the time of our lives. He is making me laugh and that's something I have not been able to do for quite some time now. He has such a nice personality and has given me many compliments throughout the night. He is a person that is kind and understanding and he avoids questions that might seem to pry into my life. He is making me conscious of the fact that life goes on. I have a lot to look back on, but tonight is one night I can forget the most horrendous time of my life, when I lost daddy and Johnny practically all at the same time.

At about midnight Paul is seeing me to my cabin. He is sheik and handsome and all the things a woman would want in a man. He takes my hand and kisses it as he spreads that beautiful smile across his face. I smile back and then I go inside my cabin. When I get inside, I flop down on the bed. I feel as if I'm in a whirl wind. I can't get my thoughts together. I feel as if I'm drifting in space and have no direction. I lay back on the bed and shortly feel myself falling into dreamland.

We're in our fifth day of the seven day cruise and Paul and I have been seeing a lot of each other. We meet for breakfast lunch and dinner. The girls say that I have abandoned them, although they are having a lot of fun themselves with the men they met the other night at the concert. This cruise has proved to be just what I needed. I have certainly come out of my depression and feel that life is still worth living. It's funny how one day life seems so bleak and the next day it is the most beautiful thing to be alive. People who commit suicide are just one day away from daylight. One day away from having a glorious life, and then they end it all too soon, before the light comes shining through. The light always comes shining through, if we would just wait. Just wait for first light.

Someone is knocking on my cabin door. I can hear Sarah on the other side calling to me. I don't know if I really want to be bothered right now. I'm just lying here thinking and am not in the mood for being disturbed, but I decide to get up and open the door. Sarah is standing in front of me in her bathing suit with a towel wrapped around her waist glaring at me as if I'm some kind of traitor.

All the times she and Genny abandoned me when they ran up on some good looking dudes, and now they act as if I've done something wrong, because I've been spending a lot of time with Paul on this cruise and ain't that pretty much why we're here in the first place. I mean to run upon some fine men, as if they haven't been occupied themselves with those men from the concert the other night.

"Just a minute," I say, as I'm opening the door.

"And what are you up to?" Sarah asks, while standing there with her hands on her hips

"I'm not up to anything," I taunt, sarcastically.

"Oh yes you are," she says, as she glares at me.

"Sarah, I'm really busy right now and I don't have time to stand here and argue with you."

"Your right about that. Get your swim suit. You're coming on the deck with Genny and me," Sarah says, bursting into the room and looking for my suit, while I stand there with my mouth open.

"Well of all the nerve," I say.

"Don't I though," she says, handing the swim suit to me to put on, and to keep down the fuss, I go ahead and put it on and soon I'm following her to the deck where Genny is already waiting for us.

"Hi," I say, as I flop down on the lounge chair.

"Well look who has finally joined us," Genny says, with a big smile on her face.

"Yes, she has graced us with her presence," Sarah laughs, quite sarcastically.

"Cut the drama, besides you two haven't exactly been all that available either," I say.

"Yeah, but Callie, at least we still realize that we're on a cruise with you," Genny chimes in.

"Have it your way," I say as, I pick up a magazine that is lying on a table beside my chair and start to page through it. The first thing I see is a picture of a man and woman lying on a beach somewhere in the Caribbean. It makes me feel kind of left out, but I start to relax, as I cover my face with the magazine from the slightly blowing wind and the blaring sun is saturating my brain waves into believing that I am in a fairy tale sort of dream that I wish could go on forever, but I know that I will have to face reality for what it's worth in less than seventy-two hours. The magic of this voyage is none other than superficial and my whole body and soul will soon feel the pangs of the real world not very long from this very moment.

An hour later I'm still lying next to my two best friends, who seem to be relaxing as well. We're not talking, but each engulfed in our own thoughts. I don't know what I would do without the two of them. They have always been there for me. We're like the Three

Musketeers. You know that, all for one, and one for all kind of thing, being bound together even in our absence of one another, we are always still together in spirit. I feel really blessed to have them. My life will be better for it.

My mind now drifts to mama. I should give her a call. She has been through a lot, losing daddy and all and I want to always be there for her. I'll call her after dinner tonight, that way I know she will be home and in a restful mood. I don't want nothing to happen to mama. She's all I got left who understands me and knows everything about me. Being my mother, I guess she would know everything about me. I can depend on her expertise advise and her understanding of me being her daughter. She knows every time just what I need and don't need, although she has never mentioned the fact that I have been pretty irresponsible lately when it comes to men, I guess she figures that life and experience is the best teacher. When I was growing up, mama always came to the rescue, but now she seems worn and possibly still in shock from daddy dying so suddenly. She looked frail as if the life had just been sucked out of her. Her soul mate was gone, and that meant a part of her has died as well. She has lots of family and friends who will help her through this time of bereavement and she has me, right now I'd better get ready because at seven p.m. Paul is escorting me to dinner.

I quickly look into the mirror to see if there are any last minute details I need to attend to. My makeup is on just right, and my new dress I bought in the ship's boutique is stunning. I have to give it to myself, I look fabulous. Well most models do look that way, which brings to mind that Pierre is still waiting in Paris for me and I now promise myself that I am going to Paris right after the cruise and will stop procrastinating on every decision I make. I really want to be a model more than anything on this earth. Since I left home it seems as if I have done everything but accommodate Pierre in his offer of making me a super model. I've been sidetracked and bamboozled by life. My Heart keeps getting in the way and my soul longs for that one special person, but that's what happens to a lot of young girls. Their heart and soul keeps getting in the way, destroying their dreams and then they wind up without a dream at all because that man is sometimes like a leach and have sucked the blood right out of them. The blood is life all by itself and we women have got to stop going fishing and catching nothing but blood suckers. That's how I see it anyway.

I believe Paul is knocking on my cabin door. I've been so caught up in self indulgence that I hadn't noticed that someone was out there. I hope he is not getting upset and thinking I'm playing games with him. You know how guys are when their ego is involved. They get real edgy and their self esteem starts to shrink down to nothing. That's why we women have to keep boosting it.

"Just a minute," I say, as I go toward the door to open it.

When I open the door, Paul is standing there looking very elegant as always. He has a bouquet of roses and quickly gives them to me as he slightly bows. I have to admit I'm surprised at this gesture, but delighted all the same. I take the flowers and proceed to the bathroom to put the flowers into the vase and then put water in to keep them fresh. I start to arrange them and stop to admire them.

"Let's go, or we'll be late for dinner," Paul calls to me from the other room.

"I'm coming." I pick up my small hand purse from off the bed and walk over to him and take his arm. He politely smiles and we head for the restaurant, where he had made reservations for our own little private dinner. Sarah and Genny would be going to the buffet tonight. They told me earlier that they didn't have a date for dinner before the entertainment show that is to begin around nine p.m.

We are making small chit chat as we stroll through the ship's corridors. I'm feeling quite enchanted by now, but something inside me is holding back. The fear of being hurt is still lurking deep down inside my soul. I hate people who kill the soul, that causes a gut wrenching pain that is so unbearable one wishes one could just die and get it over with, but I'm a survivor and I am going to survive all the loss I have sustained in the past few weeks.

"Well Ms. Callie Mason, you sure look heavenly tonight."

"You mean I look like a Barbie doll or something."

"You read my mind. That's exactly what I was thinking."

"You're a real charmer, you know."

"If I could charm you, I would be most happy."

By now we're entering the restaurant and I begin to smell the sweet aroma of delicious food. I'm trying to keep my figure in tact for my modeling career, but I guess it's alright to splurge just a little while on this magnificent adventure. I can't remember when I have had such a good time and I know that soon it will end, because nothing lasts forever, only your soul lasts forever.

As we're eating I'm thinking the food is exquisite and so is my date. We haven't said a lot because we're both enjoying the food so much. Paul stops from time to time as he's wiping his mouth with his napkin to say something funny that makes me laugh, and then we start to eat again. I love lobster and of course that's what I'm having with some crab cakes on the side. Paul is having steak and lobster, and we both had a very large salad. The table is set very tastefully and we are enjoying each others company very much. From time to time, I'm feeling a nagging ache inside my stomach, but recently, I have learned to ignore it. I also forgot to call mama last night, but I'll be sure I give her a call before I go to bed tonight, because I will be up late packing as tomorrow is our last day on board and I don't want to be packing at the last minute like I always do.

As we continue to eat with the band playing softly for us, I start to remember when I met Johnny back in New York in early January. I met him in the hotel and we both got on the elevator. I knew the moment I saw him that he was the man I wanted to marry. I had never seen him before in my life, but somehow I knew he was the one for me. It all seemed as if things were going to work out for awhile, but then things didn't work out and now I don't know where in the world he is. I guess love and marriage is not for me. Life is not dealing me a very good hand these days, but I've got to keep playing the game. Daddy always told me that life was what you make of it, and I believe daddy. I see daddy's face in my mind's eye. I will never forget his face.

"Hey, where are you, in orbit somewhere?" Paul Asks.

"Oh, I'm sorry. You know, I just drifted for a moment, but I'm back."

"I'm glad to hear that. I hope you are enjoying yourself."

"Oh yes, I am enjoying myself very much indeed." "Callie, it seems as if something is bothering you." "No, really, I'm fine."

He could have cut me with a butter knife. My skin is so tender, and I'm wearing my feelings all over my sleeves, that is if I had any sleeves to this dress, which I don't. Paul isn't stupid and he knows that there is something on my mind, but I think he is afraid to ask me directly just what is bothering me. I didn't know I was still this bad off. I was feeling confident about myself up until now. How could I possibly be thinking about Johnny, when this gorgeous man is here having dinner with me, but I try to blow it off and start to now act really interested in the band and tell him how good the music is, that the band is playing, and I'm embarrassed that he knows I was not really with him, but off in dream land someplace. I hope I never see Johnny again. I will never allow him to hurt me like he has again either. I hope something bad happens to him. No, I don't hope anything bad happens to him. How could I even think such a thing, but it's not that I don't think he deserves for something bad to happen to him.

"I'd like to ask you something."

"What is it?" I ask.

"Do you think I might have a chance to win your heart?" Paul asks me point blank.

"I don't know if I can answer that question."

"Why not?"

"I just don't feel that I'm ready to answer that honestly."

"Well when you think you can, let me know," he says, as he lights a cigarette.

We talked further and listened to the music and tried to enjoy ourselves, but I think that the rest of the evening went down hill from that moment on and it wasn't long after that Paul walked me back to my cabin. I think he is peeved about the fact that I couldn't answer his question and I really don't blame him. He deserves better than that. Any woman would give their life savings for a man like Paul.

Today is our last day on the ship. I'm almost glad to be going home. Sarah, Genny and I are walking on the deck in our swim suits, covered by our white Terri cloth short robes. We are laughing and talking about everything that has happened since we took the cruise. We will certainly have a lot to talk about over the next years to come. Sarah and Genny did some wild stuff, so they say, like gambling in the casino. I never knew they were gambling, because they know I don't approve of it and they surely didn't even try to ask me to join them, because they knew I wouldn't.

It's a little cool as we continue to walk the deck, watching all the different people engaged in the boat deck activities. Some are swimming, others are playing shuffleboard, and others just walking and talking or looking over the rail at the ocean. The air feels good and I'm satisfied with the trip.

"What's that noise?" Genny asks.

"What noise?"

"That noise. Sarah do you hear it?"

"Hear what?" Sarah chimes in.

"What are you talking about?" I ask Genny.

"Look at that up in the sky."

"What is it?" Genny asks

"It looks like some kind of flying object," I say.

"You're right Sarah says."

I continue to look up into the sky, covering my eyes with my hand for shade so I can see better. The sound is getting louder and louder as it nears the ship. I keep looking into the sky trying to make out exactly what the object is. What ever it is, it's causing a huge gust of wind upon the ship. Other people are looking up now, trying to figure out just what is happening. The wind is getting stronger and stronger as the object that now looks like a helicopter nears the ship. People are trying to hold onto their sun hats, as sun dresses flair up with women trying to hold them down. Our Terri cloth robes are blowing from the continuous huge gust of wind from the helicopter. We kind of huddle together in order to keep from being blown away.

"What the devil is happening?" Sarah asks.

"Why is that helicopter coming right at this ship?" Genny asks.

I'm still staring in amazement, as I'm trying to hold onto Genny and Sarah. Our hair is flying all over the place and I just got mine done in the beauty salon yesterday afternoon, which cost me a hundred dollars and now it's all over my head and Sarah and Genny's weave looks as if it's about to come right off their heads as we continue to huddle together to keep the wind out of our faces as the helicopter get closer. It looks as if it's coming right for the ship, but it couldn't because this is not a military ship, it's a cruise ship for God's sake.

"It's coming right at us." Genny says.

"It looks like it's getter lower." Sarah tries to shout over the loud sound of the chopper.

"We'd better get away from this area. It looks as if it's going to land right on this ship." I say.

"Come on." Genny says as she tries to pull Sarah and I away from the area.

"The wind is getting stronger and it's hard to move." I say as we try to walk in a different direction and now the ships captain is in view with his binoculars and looking up, as he tries to see who is aboard the helicopter. He puts the bull horn to his mouth and yells for the helicopter to move away from the boat, but the helicopter just hovers over by the pool, while passengers are scurrying to get away from the loud sound of the helicopter. Genny, Sarah and I are still huddled, as I turn around to look towards the big bird. Now I can plainly see that it has large letters that Spell out FBI.

"These are FBI Agents," I say.

"Are you sure?" Sarah asks.

"There are large white letters that spell FBI." I say, as I'm trying to cover my ears from the loud sound of the object. At this point I can see that the helicopter has actually landed on our ship, and A man in a dark blue wind breaker has gotten out of the vehicle and headed towards us. Genny and Sarah break free and start to run towards the other end of the ship, and as I turn to make sure that someone is not calling to me, I start to make out the figure in the dark blue wind breaker and dark blue cache pants, with FBI letters on the front of the jacket. As the man gets closer and closer, I make out the figure. It's Johnny!

"Johnny, is that you?"

"Yeah, it's me."

"What are you doing on this ship for heaven sake?" "I came to find you Callie."

"What's all this FBI business? Are you an FBI Agent?" I ask, with my mouth now hanging open, as he grabs my arms to make me look at him. I am in shock and don't know what on earth to do next. I just stand there gaping at him.

"I had to find you Callie. I want to apologize. I want you back in my life."

"Johnny, I'm on a cruise in the middle of the ocean. Couldn't you have waited until I was done with my vacation?" The wind is still blowing like crazy from the helicopter and blowing us both so hard, I think that his clothes and my robe might come right off our bodies. "What are you doing with the FBI. You're not FBI are you Johnny?"

"Yes, I am, but I couldn't tell you that, because I have been on a very secret mission."

"You're an Agent, but you couldn't tell me? That's just not right Johnny," I say and glancing up, I see Genny running after her hair piece that must have blown off her head.

"I'll explain it later," he says

"Explain, and I'm not going to be in the country after this cruise. I'm going to Paris."

"Callie, please call me in California before you go. I have to talk to you and explain everything, but now I'm going to have to get off this ship."

"I'll call you, but just go. They're going to throw me off this thing," I say, as I hear the captain of the ship shouting over the bull horn for the helicopter to leave or they're going to call the authorities, which they probably already have.

"You'd better go Johnny. The Captain is going to call someone."

"I am the authorities," he says. "Just to keep from disturbing the other passengers any longer, I will leave now, but I'm not going to let you get away Callie," he says, as he heads for the big bird that is still hovering over the deck by the pool, and I'm still dazed, and a little embarrassed, I just stand here and watch him board the helicopter and take off up into the sky and it's not long before he is clean out of sight, and I start to run to my cabin.

I'm in a state of panic and confusion as I get nearer to the door of my room. My heart is breaking, because I didn't realize that I still was in love with Johnny until now, I have tried to suppress the feeling, but now I know, that my heart belongs to him and no one else.

As I lay on the bed, tears start to fall and I wished that I could have gotten on that helicopter and left with him, but I'm still afraid of him. I'm afraid he will hurt me over and over again. I know that I don't truly trust him, because of all the deception, and I don't know if I can really forgive him for taking me through all this and not telling me that he was a government agent making me wonder all the time what he was doing and what he was up to. I still don't know what that Sonia woman has to do with him, and I'm not sure I want to know.

I hear someone at the door. I quickly get up, run into the bathroom and run cold water on my eyes to keep anyone from knowing that I've been crying. I dry my face and go towards the cabin door to open it, still in my swim suit and Terri cloth robe, I answer the door.

"Callie, are you alright and what was that all about girl?" Genny asks.

"I really don't know and I don't want to discuss it right now."

"Was that Johnny?" She asks, looking at me as if to say you better give me an answer.

"Yes, it was Johnny."

"Well what did he want? I mean if anyone approaches the ship on a helicopter, it must have been awfully important," she says, as she sits down on the bed beside me looking bewildered.

"I told you I really don't want to talk about it now. I'll see you at dinner."

"All right. You sure you're Okay?" She asks, as she walks towards the door and opens it.

"I'm fine," I say, and gently close the door in her face.

I cant believe this is happening, just as I'm doing so well and having such a good time on board the ship, meeting Paul and having such a relaxing vacation and now this. Johnny never ceases to amaze me and if this is the kind of life I'm going to live with him as an agent, I don't know if I can handle it, but my heart longs for the man I know will never be trained or tamed by any woman. I am very distraught and confused right now. I keep trying to live my life without him and he shows up unannounced and looking so handsome and is so gentle spoken, that it makes my heart turn flips inside my body and feeling as if I'm going to hyperventilate. Either I put up with him, or I've got to break it off for good. I can't go on feeling so insecure in this so-called relationship with him.

Suddenly someone startles me at the door. I don't want to see anyone at this particular time. I can't seem to get my thoughts together. My hair is still wind blown all over my head and I now wonder if Genny ever caught up with her weave that flew right off her head, and the last time I saw her, she was chasing it at a very fast sprint, up on the deck when the helicopter was kicking up so much wind, but now I hear another knock at the door, and decide to answer it. Things can't get any worse at this point, since nothing has gone the way I've wanted it to since I left home.

"Who is it?"

"It's me, Paul."

"Just a minute," I say, as I'm trying to push my hair down into place and tightening my robe.

I open the door and find him standing there, looking a little sheepish. I feel that he really doesn't know what to say, but I try and break the ice with him, so he won't feel too embarrassed.

"Hi Paul," I say, trying to act normal as if nothing has happened.

"Callie was that you up on deck with the FBI fellow, and what was that all about anyway?"

"I won't lie to you Paul. The fellow up on deck was my fiance. He's trying to get back with me and I just don't know what it is I'm doing right now."

"Well Callie, you know that I have feelings for you, even though we haven't known each other for that long, but I know what I want when I see it," he says.

"You're a good man Paul, but I'm as I told you, sort of on the rebound right now."

"I know you told me that, but I didn't think the guy would come fly over the ship in a helicopter, he says, as he is shaking his head side to side. I just hope that you will give me some thought, before you make up your mind to go back with him, that's all."

"Paul I don't want to lead you on and we will probably never see each other again. I'm leaving for Paris as soon as the cruise is over, and that will be in less than twenty-four hours. I wish you the best in life Paul. I really do." I say, as I now realize that I had not even invited Paul in as we stood there talking, me with my hand still on the door knob and him standing outside the cabin door.

"Goodbye Callie," he says, and abruptly turns and heads down the corridor.

I'm kind of relieved now that he is gone. I just don't know what is wrong with me. I don't even know myself anymore or what it is I want. Paul is one handsome fellow, but there is just no chance that we could ever make a couple. I still have Paris on my mind and yes, maybe Johnny as well is on my mind and I'm so mixed up, I don't know what to do, and now someone else is at the door and

I don't want to answer it. What if it's Paul again. I hope not, but I can't let the door go unanswered, because my curiosity is too overwhelming.

"Who is it?" I call out.

"It's us Callie. Open the door."

"Hold your horses," I say, to Genny and Sarah through the door.

I really am going to have to explain this whole thing again to Genny and Sarah. They're not going to let me get away without an explanation. They will drill me until they get everything they want to know right out of me, so I'm just going to give them the information they want, so they will let me get some rest and think out this whole bazaar afternoon.

"Come in Girls," I tort, holding the door open for them to enter.

"Well," Sarah says, as she and Genny sit on the bed, waiting to hear the story.

"Well what?" I say, putting my hands in my robe pocket and almost daring them to say another word about the incident on deck with Johnny. Even though I don't really want to answer, Genny and Sarah are doing just what I thought they would do. They are glaring as if I owe them an explanation, and in a way I do, because Genny's hair did get blown away by the wind the chopper stirred up. I'm going to stay in my room until we get off the ship, because I'm too embarrassed to face the other passengers.

"You know what Callie? Let's have it," Sarah Says, pulling down her sunglasses to look me in the eye while Genny is folding her arms in agreement.

It was over an hour, before they left. They were quite satisfied when they left my cabin, because I have told them everything they wanted to know about Johnny and me. They wanted to know how I felt about him now and if I wanted to continue seeing Paul after the trip was over. I explained to them that there would be nothing between Paul and myself and as far as Johnny was concerned, I just didn't know what to do about that, but I did tell them that I would be continuing on to Paris as soon as possible and that I would keep in touch with the both of them. After all I left home to become a model and a model I will be, if it is the last thing I do. My dream since I was a little girl, was about to finally come true. I will miss all those I love, being so far from home and all, but that's what a model has to do to make it big in the business, and Paris is where every model would like to start. I have that chance and I'm going to take it as soon as I get off this ship.

Chapter 7

The flight to Paris has been a long one. I'm so glad to finally be on the ground. I'm waiting for Pierre's chauffeur to pick me up at the front of the airport. I'm quite chilled, as I pull the collar of my fur coat up closer around by neck. My leather gloves aren't as warm as I would like them to be, but it's better than not having any on at all. I'm feeling a little insecure, because I didn't see any other black people around. I did see one on the plane, but he never said a word to me. I'm also feeling a bit of culture shock right now and hope that I will adjust to France very soon. I can't believe I'm really here. It's like nothing I have ever seen before. The buildings look very foreign to me. Everything looks a lot different from back home in the United States. Mama saw me off from the airport in Lexington, and no, I didn't call Johnny before I left as he had asked me too. I just know I would have never gotten to Paris if I had called him before I left. He would have talked me out of it. I know I still love him, but he hurt me bad and now I'm afraid he'll hurt me again. I can not bear that kind of pain again. I must do all I can to escape the pain that kills the soul and breaks the heart. I know that only God can heal a broken heart.

I must have been standing here at least twenty minutes, before I see this long black limousine pull up in front of me. The chauffeur is looking around as if he is trying to find someone. I keep looking at him, hoping he is the one Pierre has sent for me, because it's getting even colder now and I just want to get somewhere, take a hot shower, and relax from the long flight over the ocean. I must admit I was just a little nervous flying over all that water for such a long period of time, but thank goodness I made it in one piece.

"Are you Mademoiselle Callie Mason?" The man asks me in a deep French accent, after rolling down the window to the limousine and sticking his head out.

"Qui Qui," I say, in the French language, that I learned in high school and my final Grade had been a "D."

As I'm riding in back of the limousine, I see many brick French looking buildings. The shock of being in a different country is starting to sink into my psyche and fear is welling up in me. I really don't know Pierre, but it's too late to think about that now, I'm already here in Paris and the driver is not speaking to me at all and I can't think of anything to say to him either. I'm riding in a very luxurious limo with a small television, a wet bar, and plush leather seats that you can sink down in and relax with ease. Now this is what I'm talking about, living life to the fullest and living an extravagant and happy life with lots of money. That's right money, and that's why I'm here. Pour l'argent. (For the money). Yes, my French is coming back to me now. I just hope the French people can understand me.

It's not long before we're pulling up to this large Graystone building that sort of looks like a mini castle or something. This must be Pierre's home. The estate is large as we drive through the gate and around a long drive that curves into a circle. The landscape is beautiful and there are statues near a small man made waterfall. Now I see a man dressed in a black suit and white shirt who appears to be the butler. He is coming towards the limo as we stop at a rear door. Yes, he is coming in our direction. He looks very stiff and poised all at the same time. It looks as if he's been trained to look that way. I'll bet he has never done any hard labor a day in his life and I'll bet Pierre pays him very well.

"Bonjour, Bonjour."

I now spot Pierre running out of his place of abode and waving frantically as he makes his way to the limo. The chauffeur is now opening my door and I start to get out to greet Pierre as well. He is smiling from ear to ear and is motioning for me to get out.

"It is so good to see you my dear. I thought you would never get here," he says, panting heavily from the long run down the driveway.

"I'm happy to be here," I say, as I get out of the limo.

"You must be tired my dear. How was your trip?"

"Very good," I say, as Pierre lends me his arm and leads me to one of the entrances.

When we get inside, the place is as beautiful as I had imagined. There are exquisite paintings by some of the most famous artists, lovely crystal nick knacks all around with lavish rugs of royal colors, and mahogany furniture and lustrous chandeliers hanging in all the rooms, with marble floors and a large fireplace with gold accessories in one of the sitting rooms. I am a bit taken aback at the luxury of this well decorated home.

"My butler will show you to your room and we'll meet down here for dinner in two hours," Pierre says, to me as he looks at his watch and scurries away.

"I'll be ready," I say, as I start to feel hunger pains in the pit of my stomach and wonder if I can hold out for two more hours. To bad I didn't fill my purse with candy bars or something. I am quite hungry at this point in time and my stomach feels as if it's in knots as we start to climb the staircase to the second floor. My legs feel as if they are going to fall off if we don't hurry up and get up these stairs. The butler is leading me to a room that is down a long hallway and around a corner from the stairs. I'm hoping I'm not too far from everyone. This place is huge and a little scary, although I will have to get used to it, because Pierre insists that I stay here with him and his wife who is now off on some kind of safari in Africa and won't be back for two weeks.

Once inside my lovely room, I fall on the bed and close my eyes. I just lay here while my mind starts to wonder. I want to get up, but my tired body is starting to feel jet lag and I just keep laying here as my mind starts to wonder, and I can't stop it from wondering. I start to see daddy and how he looked at the funeral. I begin to feel what I felt that day, when the one man I loved so much lay a corpse. He was a good friend to me and a good daddy too and he would never hurt me like I have been hurt these past months. I see mama in her pain and all the people that came to the house afterwards and we all sat down and ate lots of food and my relatives drank lots of liquor outside in the back yard, so mama wouldn't see them and how I wanted to take a drink of that vodka they were drinking, cause maybe it would have made me feel better. I needed to feel better that day. I thought that awful ache would never leave me, but some how I have managed to let it die down, but the pain from my relationship with Johnny, that didn't work, it made me even sicker. The time Johnny didn't come home for three days and he never did explain his where abouts and about that Sonia woman. He didn't even apologize to me on the ship, after he disrupted the cruise and everyone topside with all that wind and noise from the chopper and then I find out that he is a FBI agent. He never even tried to explain anything about it and then flew off into the sky just like he came and he wanted me to call him. I don't think so. It has been too much pain to bear, but the good Lord said he wouldn't put no more on us than we can bear and now I feel so sleepy that I'm starting to drift and can't seem to think anymore because...

It's an hour before I awake and see that I must get ready for dinner. I didn't mean to sleep so long, as a matter of fact, I didn't mean to sleep at all. I hope no one has come to the door, while I was snoozing and probably having the same dream I always have. That reoccurring dream of Johnny always leaving me and I can't find him and I keep searching throughout the whole dream and I just can not find him anywhere, but he feels so close to me as if I can reach out and touch him, but he's nowhere to be found. It's been almost a year since I first met Johnny in that hotel in New York. It was my meeting him that intercepted by dream to become a model and it was all for nothing. I don't know if I will ever see him again.

The phone is ringing and the red button is flashing, as I stand there amazed wondering if I should pick up the receiver. It must be for me, because the red light is announcing itself so I can answer it.

"Hello?" I ask, into the receiver. My hello is more like a question instead of an answer.

"Honey is that you?" My mother asks.

"Mother. What a nice surprise it is to hear your voice. Are you O.K.?" I ask, while trying to get out of my clothes and trying to find something in the bags that were brought to my room, most likely while I was asleep.

"I'm so happy you made it alright. You are all right aren't you Callie?" She asks, in that tone that says you had better tell me the truth kind of tone.

"Yes, I'm fine mother," I say, in a light tone of voice so she will believe what I'm saying.

"I'm calling to see if you are alright and also I want to tell you that, that Cynthia from New York, well she keeps calling for you and wants me to give her your number where your are, but I told her I would let you know she called and that you would contact her." She says, all in one breath.

"Thanks for letting me know mother. Do you have any idea what it is she wants? Is she sick or in some kind of trouble?" I ask, her in my most concerned voice, because I am concerned.

"Well, she says, that Johnny keeps calling her and wants your number. I guess he doesn't know how to get in contact with you, and by the way Scooter keeps calling too. She says.

"Mother I don't want either of them to have my number here in Paris. I have a lot to do in getting ready for runway training and I'll be busy for long hours each day," I told her what Pierre had told me on the phone, before I got here. He let me know that this would be no picnic, which is going to take a lot of hard work. I can't let Scooter or Johnny interfere with my career now. I'm just too close. Too close to being the model that I've always dreamed about when me and Sarah and Genny were kids and I used to dress up in my mothers clothes and pretend that the porch was the runway and me switching across the porch, while my little fanny was moving up and down with every step I took. Mama would look out the screen door and tell me to cool my little fanny down, or she would get the switch after me. Sarah and Genny would laugh because I would get caught twisting my fanny like I saw the models do on TV.

"If you say so dear. I won't give them your number, but I will tell Cynthia that you will contact her as soon as possible," she says, in her most pleasant voice.

"Goodbye mama. I love you and I'll see you soon," I say.

"Goodbye dear and take care of yourself."

After mama hung up the phone I stood there holding the receiver for a moment. I would have to call Cynthia, but what would I tell her to say to Johnny. I know he must be furious by now, but I gave him every chance. I even put my life on hold for that fly by night of a man. He is just too unstable in his life and career to have a loving and doting wife at home. He's always so tired he sure ain't much in the romance department very often, but I do remember those times when he was good and rested and even Don Juan didn't have nothing on Johnny, but those times were few and far between. His work was always between us. The work I knew nothing about until just a few days ago. He's an FBI agent. I just can't get over that mess. How could he keep something like that a secret from me?

Dinner was delicious and now I'm in my room feeling a little lonely. Pierre and some of the other models he employs were here to meet me and I can tell that Danielle didn't seem to care for me at all. I don't even know her and she's already giving me the evil eye. She also lives with Pierre and his wife and I'll be right here in the same house with that witch. I wonder what kind of woman is Pierre's wife anyway. I will find out soon enough, in fact as soon as she gets back from her safari. Why would a woman who is lavished in everything want to go on a safari anyway? She must be awfully bored with Pierre or something. I can't imagine me leaving a house like this to go on some stupid safari. Just leave it to the rich and famous, because they all are just a bit eccentric if you ask me. When I get rich, I'm going to make sure I stay the same. Mama always said that money was the root of all evil, and if mama is still around, I had better not let any money go to my head, because mama will probably thump me up side my pretty head if she gets a chance. No, money is not going to change me. I'm not going to forget where I came from and that's Louisville, a town with red dirt and dusty roads and sometimes no sidewalk to walk on, just the dirt roads. Although I do have to admit, I am a little vein at times, but that's what it takes to become a model anyway. If I didn't think I was pretty and be just a bit vain, I wouldn't be model material. It takes a vain and confident woman to walk down that runway and maybe sometimes showing most of all she's got and I did say most, because mama would kill me if I ever stripped butt naked. Everybody in Lexington would never let us live it down. Frankly, I think Pierre is going to find that I'm a different kind of model, one who will not be open for suggestion to compromise my morals.

It must be five a.m. and I hear the maid in the hallway ringing the bell. She does this every morning for breakfast if and to basically wake us up. This morning I'm finding it hard to get up, because by now I know that breakfast will be just a boiled egg and a glass of juice and a piece of toast. Pierre has us all on a very strict diet. This is one reason why he likes his models to stay with him, so he can starve us all to death. I must admit, I'm just a bit famished since I'm been here this past week, but staying slim goes with the territory, but if it causes me to start to have an eating disorder, it's goodbye modeling career, because nothing is worth it if it's going to put my life in danger. I do love myself that much, and anyway, there are all sorts of beautiful women in the world and a lot of them look pretty darn good, even if they are a size ten or twelve now days they want you to be a size two. I bet I won't kill myself to be a two, as tall as I am, I need some nourishment to keep me going. I mean that's just common sense, even if I have to sneak and eat. I ain't ready to die.

"Callie, are you up sleepy head?" Danielle says, as she's knocking on my bedroom door.

"I am very much awake. I'll see you downstairs." I call out to her and what does she want anyway. She is not my mama. Who does she think she is knocking on my door this time of the morning? She doesn't tell me when to get up. This is going to be one interesting situation with this person. I can feel she is going to be the thorn in my side if I don't just kick her behind first.

After showering and getting dressed I'm on my way down to have breakfast. I'm just a few minutes late, but hopefully no one will notice. Pierre usually gets to the table late so at least he won't know that I'm not on time and when I get to the table, I'm right. Everyone is here except for Pierre, so that means we will have to wait a few more minutes to eat, because we can't start without him. It's one of the rules. He wants to make sure we're not eating too much.

As soon as Pierre walks into the room we all let out a sigh of relief because we know it won't be long before we eat our boiled egg, piece of toast and juice that will have to carry us the rest of the day, until supper, when we get a piece of broiled chicken and a baked potato and a glass of wine. The wine helps me to relax after a long day of high stepping and switching my behind during practice. Our next show is tomorrow night, but it will be the first one for me. There will be photographers taking loads of pictures and lots of people gazing at me as I strut my stuff. I can't wait to strut my stuff.

"Okay, you can eat now ladies," Pierre says, while placing his napkin on his lap. Eat all your food you don't want to get hungry before dinner," he knows we'll all be starved by dinnertime. He's using psychology on us, trying to make out as if we're getting enough to eat for the next twelve to fifteen hours.

"Pierre, one of us was late for breakfast this morning. I hate to be a tattle tail, but it was Ms. Congeniality over there," she laughs, as she points in my direction.

"I wasn't that late. Only a few minutes," I say, trying to clear my throat because it's as if I got a frog in there somewhere.

"Now ladies we are not going to get catty this early in the morning, now are we," Pierre says, as he picks up his knife and fork to cut his egg. "Lets just all have breakfast like civilized human beings."

I'm very civilized. It's that witch Danielle, that looks like she's from the Yukon mountains that's the uncivilized one and I'm really going to have a talk with her real soon.

Breakfast is eaten in complete silence because of the tension in the air. The air is so thick you can cut it with a knife. I don't know if I will want to eat very many breakfasts with this Danielle person.

She's probably jealous that Pierre has brought me here to live as well. She must have thought that she was the only special person of all the girls and now that I'm here, she feels threatened, but that's her problem not mine, because I intend to be the best runway model ever. They will know my name everywhere. It will be a household word. I will make mama proud of me if it's the last thing I do.

Daddy will be looking down from heaven and will be proud of his little girl too.

While we're practicing our own stylish walk for the show tomorrow night, I begin to sweat bullets. Over and over, Pierre has us walking and walking until he thinks we have it perfect and none of us have it right yet. We have been in Pierre's own private studio with a homemade runway for the last ten hours. I am aching all over and my feet hurt so badly and I'm hungry and want to just rest for a while if Pierre would just give us a break. I feel as if I've lost ten pounds just today after all this walking and swinging our hips, cause we must have walked at least twenty miles today. I feel as if my hip is out of its socket. Maybe if I swing the other hip, it might throw the dislocated hip back into place. I keep walking as we all keep walking one in front of the other continuously doing the same walk over and over again, while Pierre's taps his cane on the wood floor with smoke coming out of his pipe like a chimney stack.

"Callie put some heart and soul into it," shouts Pierre, as he's looking at me with his pipe hanging out of his mouth and walking towards me. "You know how they say in America how you people have soul. Show me that Callie. Show me some soul," he shouts again and fanning his hand in the air. Oh no he didn't say that. No he didn't say that to you Callie. I began stepping high and swinging it. I can't let the sisters down. I've got to work it now. Work it Callie I say in my head. Work it girl.

"Now you stepping," Pierre says, with a big smile on his face as he walks beside me. "Now you walk like the beautiful stallion that you are." Pierre motions for the others to keep walking so he can see if they are up to his standards. Thank goodness I've finally got it the way he wants it. My feet are killing me and now I find myself thinking about how I will get some extra food and hide it in my purse. Maybe Danielle doesn't feel like she's better than I am now. Maybe she will just leave me alone now, but I really can't convince myself of that, because it's probably not going to happen anytime soon.

On the way back to Pierre's house, we are riding down a street full of nightclubs. Young people are out on the street just hanging outside the clubs and talking, while others look to be doing more than that. I close my eyes and try to remember what Johnny looks like. His image is not coming easy. I keep trying and I think I almost see him outlined in my mind, but then I lose it. I can't even remember his face anymore. I can just get part of it. I can't get the full picture. This makes me angry because I want to picture how he looks, but I can't. I just can't remember. We've been apart too much and we were not together that long. I wonder if he is thinking about me at this very moment in time. I wonder if he still loves me, that is if he ever did love me. I have to think about him now, because tomorrow is the fashion show and I won't have time to think about him. No, not tomorrow.

I come back to reality to find that we are pulling into the driveway of Pierre's home. The butler is already out of the house to escort us in. He is running to open the car door. I hope he doesn't fall and break a leg or something. He is so loyal to Pierre as loyal as anyone can be to another person. As soon as he gets to the car and opens the door, I jump out quickly to avoid any conversation. I just want to get to my room because it is so late and I'm dead tired and my feet feel as if they've gotten numb and I can't feel them very well. These twelve and fifteen hour days are starting to wear me completely out. I want to be a model, but is all this really necessary and the fact that we hardly get anything to eat is disgusting. I like being thin, but I don't want to become anorexic either. I heard Danielle in the bathroom regurgitating just last night. She probably wants to be thin for tomorrow evening for the fashion show. I don't want to resort to that kind of behavior just to stay in the modeling business. I love myself too much for that and if Pierre starts to think that I'm getting too fat, then I will just quit. It's not worth dying for.

After I'm all settled in the bed I start to feel a bit nauseated. This is not normal for me to feel nausea. I have a strong stomach and I don't know what could possibly be wrong, so I get up again and go to my little refrigerator I have in my room and get out some soda that no one knows I have of course and pour some into a cup and drink it all and then lye back down on the bed. As soon as I lye down, the phone rings. Who could be calling me at this time of the night? Pierre is going to be furious. I hope he hasn't heard the ringing. I quickly pick up the phone to keep it from ringing again.

"Hello. Hello."

"Hello Callie. It's me Johnny."

"Johnny," I say, in complete surprise. "How did you get this number?"

"I called your mother. She gave me the number and why didn't you call me Callie? You could have let me know where you were."

"I didn't think we had anything to talk about Johnny."

"How can you say that? I landed a helicopter on your cruise ship Callie. Did you think that I just happened by? I came to find you in the middle of the ocean. It must mean something."

"It does Johnny, it means you're crazy and you didn't even tell me that you were an FBI agent. I feel as though I can't trust you."

"You know you can trust me Callie. It's just that I couldn't tell you because I was on a top-secret mission and I didn't need you to ask questions that I would not answer."

"So now what. What do you want from me?"

"I want you back in my life. It's as simple as that."

"No it isn't. It's not that simple. I'm here in Paris doing what I've always wanted to do. I gave up this chance twice for you and you let me down. You were out late every night and you didn't even bother to tell me where you were or if you were even coming back and you never did explain that Sonia woman."

"She's one of the agents. I couldn't tell you that then. I wanted you to trust me. I hoped that you would trust me and not leave me."

"Come to California the first chance you get so we can talk this over face to face Callie."

"No. I'm not coming there. I'm busy with my career Johnny and don't call me again," I say, and then slam the receiver down. How dare he call me now. I'm not going to let him ruin this for me. Not now when I'm so close to becoming a super model. Pierre says he has no doubt that I will become a super model if he has anything to do with it. Why doesn't he just leave me alone? I don't want to be hurt anymore. First Scooter and now Johnny. I trusted him when I first met him. I put my career on hold for him. I might have even given it up all together if he had just loved me, but instead, I hardly ever saw him and then I find out he's a government agent when he lands a chopper on my vacation cruise ship. I don't know how I can ever trust him again. I don't want to be back in his little apartment in L.A. waiting for him and playing guessing games about where he is or when he's coming home. No, no, no, I hear myself screaming in my head.

There is so much commotion in this dressing room. It's time for me to go out on the runway. I'm number seven and I can see the number seven flashing on and off like a neon sign. My makeup is being put on by one of the makeup artists as I look in the mirror at myself I find that I look stunning. I'm wearing a sheik black low cut dress with slits up both sides and a very expensive diamond necklace. I want the makeup artist to hurry. I'm anxious to get out there. I only have five minutes to finish dressing when my number starts flashing. It will be my first runway walk and I want to be out there at exactly the precise moment I should be there. I look over at the other black model. She looks so exotic compared to myself. She has these large slanted eyes and long neck. I look good, but there is really nothing exotic about me. I just hope the crowd likes me. That will be more than I could ever ask for.

"Let's go Callie," Pierre says, as he looks me up and down. "It's time to blow them away."

"I'm coming," I say, pushing past the man who is doing my makeup and almost tripping over my dress. I just hope Pierre wasn't noticing. I need to calm down. Take a deep breath Callie and relax I tell myself.

One minute later I'm on that runway strutting my stuff. I can see flash bulbs going off in the darkness. The lights are so bright on the walkway, as I'm walking and where the crowd is seated is total darkness. I can't see anyone out there, just the flashes of light from the cameras. I can hear some cheering from the crowd. I do believe they like me. I hear more cheers as I start my walk back. I feel like a star. I get a glimpse of Pierre standing behind the curtains to the right of me looking very proud. It's almost over. I'm almost back now and just have about ten more steps before I go behind the curtain. Finally I'm there. I take a deep breath as I get back into the dressing room. It was more nerve racking then I thought it would be. They are already waiting for me to get into another lovely dress and I will have to start the walk all over again, but it's Okay because, now I'm living my dream.

No one can stop me now. I am on my way to where I've wanted to be my whole life. When I was back in Lexington I always strutted down the street. Mama would tell me to stop twisting my butt so much. But I was practicing for when I would become a famous model. I must have practiced for a good twenty years, ever since I was five years old.

Sunday morning is the only morning we get to sleep late. It's seven a.m. and I'm starting to wake up. I opened one eye to see the digital clock on the table next to my bed that so boldly tells me it is eight o'clock in the morning. I rolled over and tried to go back to sleep again. I certainly don't want to get up this early. My stomach is making weird sounds because I'm so famished, but I've learned to ignore it. I think I've lost at least ten pounds the two months I've been here. Pierre's wife is home from her safari and all she and Pierre does is argue all the time about all the money she spends. The room is dark and my eyes are very heavy. The modeling business is hard work and long hours. My body feels stiff and sore all over. I really want to make it in this business, but I must try harder. I've come too far. I must not fail. This means too much to me and I will never forgive myself if I fail. The only thing that makes me so sick right now is the wall of ice between Danielle and myself. She will never like me and there is nothing I can do about it. She rats on me every chance she gets, and Pierre is noticing that something is very wrong between the two of us, but I won't worry about that now. There is just too much at stake to worry about a jealous sick woman like Danielle. She has no real reason to have a beef with me, and I will continue to ignore her.

I have been here in Paris for quite some time. I can't believe that I have lasted this long. We've been doing fashion show after fashion show and I have to admit. I am an expert and one reason is that I have walked that invisible runway since I was five years old, so it didn't take much for me to master a modeling career. Pierre is very proud of me and he wants me to further my career to the world's top model. I haven't talked to any friends or relatives for over a month. I do miss all the people I love. My heart longs for someone to love me. Yes, I need it. Now that I've made it as a model, I'm feeling very empty. I have no one to share my fame and fortune with. Last week I was quoted as being one of the best black models in the business. Yes, I'm proud of myself, but I feel a void in my life that I know for sure that I can't fill on my own. The love I need is the love I can't have. I will never get over Johnny it seems, and my pride is to strong to break, for that love I need so badly. I really have to get to the kitchen and find something to eat. My bones are starting to show. At least I don't look anorexic yet, but how long will it take before I am just that. In my opinion, it's just a matter of time before my diagnosis of anorexia will manifest it's ugly head.

When I get to the kitchen I see Danielle sitting at the table reading the newspaper. She gives me one of her cold hard looks and then starts to read the newspaper again. I just waltz over to the refrigerator to see if there is any fruit. I can feel her cold eyes on me as I stand there with my back to her. I am so angry now I just want to tell her off. She just won't stop her mess with me. She has gotten on my very last nerve and I want her to get off it right now.

"Is something wrong with you? You keep staring at me as if you might attack me," I tell her as I turn around to look at her. Is there something I can do for you?" I say as nasty as I can.

"Yeah, you can do something for me," she says. "You can get out of this kitchen. I was here first and I really don't want your company," she says, in her deepest French accent.

"You don't own this kitchen my dear," I say, as I slam the refrigerator door and walk over to the sink to get me a glass of water, and while I'm standing there letting the water run so it will get cold, I feel her steely cold eyes on my back.

"I might not own it, but I'll be here longer than you will."

"Listen Miss stuff, I'd be here forever too if I had a personality like yours, cause ain't no man going to have a sarcastic, stubborn mule like you anyway. With that last statement I made, I felt a thud on my back. No she didn't hit me. I quickly turned around and tried to slap her into next week. Then it was on, cause I then grabbed her hair and threw her to the floor and straddled her and start to laugh hysterically, as I see her looking so helpless. The great Danielle thrown to the ground by her rival, Callie Mason. This is all so ludicrous. The whole thing is crazy and I feel a little crazy as I'm starting to pinch her nose and she is kicking wildly to try and get me off her.

"What is going on here?" Pierre says, as he's entering the room. "Callie will you please get off of Danielle this very moment," he says, looking very flustered and waving his pipe in the air.

"Of course Pierre. I will certainly get off the lovely Danielle," I say, as I attempt to get up off her. Her face is beet red and I know she is feeling embarrassed.

"Go, Go Callie to your room and you too Danielle.

I want to talk to both of you later."

"Yes, I'll be in my room. I say closing my robe that had come undone. Danielle just ran out of the room screaming obscenities at the top of her voice. I felt pretty good myself. She deserved it.

When I get to my room, I realize that my hunger has increased and now I'm stuck in here until Pierre calls for a conference. This is bad. I need food and now I get an idea to just go into the bathroom with my glass and try to drink as much water as I can before I faint. After I drink three glasses of water, I sit down in front of the television. With nothing else to do, I turn it on to the news channel. I also pick up yesterday's newspaper as well and start to read some of the headlines. As I continue to read, suddenly there is a news flash. I begin to hear something about espionage, a set up and FBI agents. I look up from the newspaper to see a very large picture of Johnny on my television screen. I am so shocked; I throw down the paper and stretch my neck forward in order to hear what the newscaster is saying. My eyes feel as if they are going to pop right out of their sockets. The reporter is saying that this man on the screen has been shot and is in the hospital in Los Angeles under tight security. I can't believe my eyes and ears. This can't be. Johnny's been shot? It was as if I was asking myself this question and I just heard it with my own ears. Now my heart is starting to pound and I'm starting to feel faint. The picture of Johnny is larger than life, while the newscaster goes on to say that he is under arrest. Why would he be under arrest? I know Johnny would never ever do anything that was against the law, so there must be some terrible mistake that has been made. I'm starting to feel even more faint and the room is starting to spin and my head feels very light and then...

When I awake. Pierre and his wife are standing over me and the maid is fanning me and trying to give me water at the same time. I can barely see them and soon my vision becomes clearer.

Pierre is starting to pace the floor while his "lovely Butterfly," as he calls her, is rambling on and on in French and I don't know a word she is saying, because she is talking so fast. She reminded me of a glittery fluttery butterfly. That must be the reason Pierre calls her that.

"Are you all right my dear?" She asks, while she is almost in a state of panic.

"I think so. Yes, I'm fine. I just need to sit up," I say, as I'm trying to get my feet off the bed.

"What happened to you," Pierre asks, with large drops of sweat rolling off his face.

"Nothing. I guess I'm just hungry," I say.

"Go and get her food," he says to the maid, and she scurries away as fast as she can.

"I'll be fine. I just need to be alone now."

"Well if you say so," Pierre's wife says, as she fans herself with the same fan the maid was fanning me with when I awoke.

"Come dear. Callie wants to be alone," she says.

"Once you eat, you'll be fine," Pierre says, as he closes the door behind them.

As soon as they're gone, I jump up and start to get my luggage out of the closet. I must get to Los Angeles to find Johnny. I know he needs me now. I will never forgive myself if something bad happens to him. Well, if something worse happens to him. Something bad has already happened. Johnny must be feeling all-alone at a time like this. Your friends always leave you when you need them the most, I'm thinking as I begin to pull stuff out of the dresser drawers and throw them into each piece of luggage. I don't have any time to waste. I must call the airport to find out when I can get the next thing smoking. Time is of the essence.

"Can I come in?" I hear the maid say, on the other side of the door.

"Yes, come in please. Put the tray on the table and go."

"Are you going some place?" She asks, noticing the luggage almost full and very unkemptly packed, while I'm giving her the eye to get herself out of the room.

"Okay, I'm leaving."

"I must tell Pierre that you are packing your things."

"I don't care what you tell him, Just get out of here."

It hasn't been two minutes before I hear another knock at the door. I can hear Pierre and his wife talking French to each other. I shouldn't let them in right now, I've got to finish packing all this stuff before I miss the plane. The flight I booked leaves in two hours and I've got to get to the airport right away. I don't have one minute to waste. Johnny needs me and I've got to get to him. Pierre and his wife are starting to pound on the door. I just keep furiously packing my things. I've got to call a taxi now, If I'm going to get to the airport on time. They are still beating on the door while I'm dialing the number to the taxi company. The phone keeps ringing and ringing. Why don't they answer?

"I need a taxi right away." I say frantically to the dispatcher, after someone says hello and I suddenly knock the telephone onto the floor, because I'm so nervous.

After I give the man the information and I confirm my flight. I start to eat the food on the tray. I'm stuffing it down as quickly as I can. It's no telling when I'll have time to get another meal. I drink all of the apple juice and start to gobble up the sweet roll. I've already finished the bacon, eggs and toast. Why couldn't we have this kind of meal at least once a week. Pierre wouldn't let us have much more than boiled eggs and toast for the whole day and a salad and apple juice at night. I'm starting to feel strength come into my body. I'm going to need it for the trip.

Ten minutes later I hear the taxi outside blowing the horn. I grab the three bags as best I can and head towards the door, almost forgetting that Pierre and his wife are still out there, so I open the door and try to push past them, and once I'm past them I walk as fast as I can down the stairs with the luggage, while Pierre and his wife are screaming at me to tell them what it is I am doing and where in the world am I going.

"I'm sorry Pierre, I have to leave. There is an emergency and I have to go now."

"You can't go now. You have three shows tomorrow. I know you have not forgotten this."

"I'll get in touch soon," I say, as I'm going through the door to the outside of the house. When the taxi driver sees me, he quickly rushes to help me with the bags, as Pierre, as his "Lovely Butterfly" are shouting to me to come back, but I'm going to Johnny. I'm never coming back. None of this has made any sense to me anyhow. I'm weak and frail from over work and Lack of food and sleep. I don't think that this is the dream that I have dreamed my whole life long. My dream only had good things in it. Not starvation and confinement. I love Paris. It is so beautiful and full of elegance, but my heart is with Johnny, although I appreciate everything that Pierre has done for me I must go to the man I love. I just hope he doesn't die before I get there. I will never forgive myself. I've got plenty of money in the bank. I've saved up quite a nest egg since I've been here, so I won't go hungry. Not anymore. I'm going to eat all the food I want from now on, cause I really need to put on a few pounds to this puny body that I've always been so mindful to take care of. In fact, I have always been one to finish all of my vegetables. My parents never had to make me eat my veggies. I've always wanted a healthy body and now I'm going to have to fix it, because now it's broken. I hope that Johnny doesn't mind that I'm ten pounds lighter. I hope he's conscience enough to know that I'm there. My love for him will keep him alive. I've just got to get to him. I've got to let him know that I'm there for him. He has some kind of power over me that I just can't explain, not even to myself and I can't do a thing about it either. He has my heart and he's not going to give it back, but I can live with that.

Chapter 8

I've already checked into the Bonaventure and now on my way to the hospital where Johnny is being heavily guarded. I don't know how I'm going to see him, so I'm going to have to think of a good plan. There will be men on the outside of his door keeping watch. I don't know why I just didn't stay with him. I guess I just didn't know how much me means to me and now I might just lose him. I've got to find a way to get into his room without being seen or maybe disguising myself as a nurse. Yes, that's what I'll do. I'll find a nurses uniform and pretend that I'm his nurse.

I get into the elevator with several people. They're all staring at the wall of the elevator. I'm starting to shake, because I know it won't be long before I see him, that is if I can pull off my disguise. It seems as if the elevator will never reach the seventh floor. I checked at the front desk below and found out that his room number is seven-seventeen. I'm very impatient and fidgeting with my hair. These people must think I'm crazy, I must look a fright, as I tend to bite my lower lip and fidget with my hair when I nervous. No one seems to be noticing me, which is good, but you never know who is watching. A man is starting to notice me now. I must stop being noticeable. I don't want to draw any attention to myself. I want to be as inconspicuous as possible while I'm in this place.

It seemed as if the elevator would never reach the seventh floor, but it has and I'm scared to death, as I step out into the corridor. I look both ways to see if I can find a guard outside of a door. I don't see anyone, so that means I'm going to have to search for his room number. It will be just a shame if I come all this way and can't get to see him. I know he needs me. I really don't know what kind of condition he is in. I wonder if he will even know me, or be conscious enough to speak to me, but I hope I will soon find out. It looks as if the room numbers are going backwards and it's going to be hard to cover this floor without being seen. I don't want anyone to remember me, so I pull out shades to cover my eyes and pull my hair close to my face to cover as much of it as I can. I feel as if I'm in the movies and on some kind of secret mission or something and in a way, that's exactly what I'm on, some kind of secret mission.

As soon as I spot the room numbers that is the category with Johnny's room, I begin to walk slowly. As I continue to walk, I realize that it must be around that corner wall ahead of me. I can stand there and peek around to see if anyone is standing outside his door. Now, I'm able to spot a utility room, and I'm hoping maybe, just maybe I can find a uniform of some sort in there, but first, I've got to check around that wall. As I begin to walk very softly to the edge of the wall I can hear women's voices near by. I stop and start to fix my hair and pull out my makeup mirror to appear to be primping before seeing a patient. As they go past me almost not noticing me, I then carefully take a sneak peek around the corner of the wall. I can see a man sitting in a chair reading a magazine. He must be Johnny's guard. He is dressed in a three piece suit and look as if he is yawning. I quickly turn and go back to the utility room, go inside and close the door after me. I find a light switch in the dark and turn on the light. My adrenaline is rushing to my head and I feel as if I'm on a high. As I'm rummaging through things in the room, I happen to see just what I'm looking for, a nurses uniform. I quickly start to pull off my clothes and start to dress myself in the nurse's outfit, hat and all. I don't see any white shoes, so I'm going to have to wear the black ones I have on. I hope the guard won't notice that I'm not completely suited as a nurse. I should take off this lipstick I'm thinking, so I begin to take out some Kleenex and begin to rub my lips hard with the soft stuff to try and get it off.

Before I leave the little room, I pat down my hair and smooth out the almost wrinkled white dress. My heart is thumping at a hundred miles a minute. I'm excited and scared all at the same time. My heart always thumps when I'm near Johnny and I'm just about to see him again. If we could just get it together and stop all the bickering. We can't seem to come to terms about anything. Even though I love him and I believe he loves me, we need some serious help, but now I've got to get into his room without being suspected of being a fraud. My heart is still racing as I open the door to leave the small room and I'm trying very hard to stop my teeth from clacking together I'm so afraid. What if he doesn't want to see me. After all I did reject him when he floated onto the cruise ship in the chopper. He has done everything to try and win me back and I just pushed him aside. I hope he will forgive me.

Slowly, I walk up to the man seated outside Johnny's room. I'm standing there with a stethoscope around my neck to make me look legitimate. My knees are almost knocking together, and that's pretty hard to do, since I'm so thin now, thanks to Pierre and the gang. As I start to say something to the man, he looks up at me curiously and tips his hat as a gesture of recognizing my presence. I start to stutter out some words that didn't make sense.

"My medicine is to the patient. I mean, I have medicine I have to give to my patient," I say, trying to correct my first statement and stumbling over his large foot.

"Go on in," the man says leaning back over to brush the mark off his foot I made while stumbling over it. Now that I'm in the room, I see Johnny lying there with his eyes shut. I hope he's alright and just asleep. I walk closer to the bed and peep over into his face. Suddenly his eyes open and I'm startled, but I can see that he knows who I am and that I'm not really one of the nurses.

"Callie is that you? How did you get in here and what's that you're wearing?" Then he answers his own question. You're wearing a nurse's uniform Callie. What's going on?"

"I had to pose as a nurse Johnny, or they wouldn't have let me in."

"Who wouldn't have let you in."

"Your guard. He's sitting outside the door guarding you. Didn't you know you were being detained in your room by a guard?"

"I've been under anesthesia. I'm just waking up from surgery. I got hit in the shoulder and in my left side."

"Thank God you're alive," I whisper, leaning over to give him a kiss on the cheek.

"I thought you were in Paris."

"I was, but I'm here for you Johnny. I don't ever want to leave you again. Look what happens when I leave you to take care of yourself. You get shot. Who did this to you anyway?" I continue to whisper, as to not let the man outside the door hear what I was saying.

"I've been set up. There are men out there who is trying to kill me Callie. You've got to get me out of here or I might not see tomorrow," he says, as he is trying to sit up.

"Lye down. You need your rest. I'll figure out something."

"I hope so, but I'm so weak, I don't know how you're going to do this alone."

"Trust me. You just be awake around midnight. I'll be back to get you," I say, leaning down to give him another kiss.

"Callie."

"What is it Johnny?"

"Be careful. Just be very careful."

"Don't you worry. I will be back to get you. I won't let anyone hurt you again, ever."

As I leave his room, I start mumbling nurse's jargon. Something about blood pressure and pulse and heart rate. I want the man to believe I'm a nurse, because I've got to come back to get him. The more the man thinks I'm a real nurse, the easier it will be to get back into the room tonight. I just hope they don't change guards on me. That might make it a little bit tougher to get in and get Johnny out, but I've got to first come up with a plan and I hope Johnny doesn't take a sleeping pill from the real nurse.

As I'm riding back to the hotel in the taxi, I begin to think about how I first met Johnny. This romance has certainly has been more like a whirlwind, than anything I've ever known about other peoples relationships. My head is spinning once again and now, I've gotten into something I never dreamed would happen to a poor little girl from Lexington. I'm going to get myself in trouble with the law. I can't let those men who are trying to kill him get to him. I'll have to hope and pray that they don't get to him before I do. I've got six hours to come up with the plan, get it organized and then execute it. Johnny may be right. I might need to get some help, but who can help me. I don't know anyone here in Los Angeles, or maybe I do know someone. If Sonia was Johnny's partner, hopefully, just maybe she doesn't want anything to happen to him, and if she was more than just a partner, she certainly wouldn't want anything to happen to him. I've got to talk to her, find out just what all she does know about this whole thing. Yes, I'll call her right away. I have her number right in my address and number book. I made sure of it, when I thought she and Johnny were more than friends. Her number will come in handy after all. I just hope she will talk to me.

It took me almost and hour to get to the hotel and then call Sonia. The phone keeps ringing and I pray she answers it. I'll let it ring just a bit longer, maybe she is in the shower and can't get to the phone quick enough. She's got to pick up.

I finally hear a click. Someone has picked up the receiver.

"Sonia is that you? I ask, as if I know her.

"Who is this?"

"I know you don't really know me, but I'm Johnny's friend Callie."

"So, what do you want with me?"

"I need to talk to you, I say, falling down on my knees in front of the sofa.

"If you want me to help you get back with your boyfriend, I'm not the one," she says rather sarcastically. "I hear you broke his heart. I really don't like you lady. He's my partner and I care what happens to him."

"Did you know he is in the hospital from gun shot wounds?" I ask, a little sarcastically as well.

"What do you mean. I just got back into town and no one has told me anything. Is he alright?"

"Yes and no. He says he might not last the night, because some people out there are trying to kill him for sure. I need your help. I've got to get him out of the hospital and into hiding someplace. Please Sonia I need your help. Do it for Johnny."

"I have an idea who it is that wants him out of the way," she says, as if she's thinking about something I know nothing about. "He's right Callie. He can't stay in the hospital. He's a sitting target. Where are you anyway?"

"I'm at the Bonaventure."

"Stay tight. I'll be right over and maybe we can come up with a plan to help Johnny."

"Thanks Sonia. You don't know what this means to me."

"I'm doing this for Johnny. He'd do the same for me," she says, and then the phone went dead.

"I'm pacing the floor waiting for Sonia to get here. I feel I at least have her support now. This is some very deep mess Johnny is in and I will just die if anything happens to him. I now know that I want to spend the rest of my life with him and could kick myself for not realizing it sooner. I have got to be the most naive person on the face of the earth, but it will be unto death do us part, before I ever let him out of my sight again. A man like him doesn't come along every day nor does one come along every ten thousand days. He was sent to me and I didn't appreciate him. He had even asked me to marry me, but no, I have to pursue my fantasies. Become a model and all that stuff. I'm the one who jerked him around and now I'm paying for it, when it all could have been so simple, I had to rock the boat and now it has tipped over. I'm helpless and don't know what to do, but I'll think of something.

It was a whole hour before Sonia gets to my hotel room. She is dressed boyish style as she always does whenever I used to see her with Johnny. I told her to make herself comfortable, while I made us some coffee, compliments of the Bonaventure Hotel. She seemed to be very worried when she got to my room. I think she knows something that I don't know. I feel her tenseness from the other room as I'm fixing the coffee. I hope she takes it black, because I don't have any creamer or sugar left.

"Here. I hope you like it. It's black. No cream or sugar left around here," I say, handing her a cup of steaming hot coffee. My hands are trembling as I hand it to her and she notices that I'm scared.

"Don't worry. We'll figure this thing out, but we don't have much time, if I know what I think I know," she says, taking a sip of the hot coffee. I'm sure she must have burned her tongue, but if she did, she didn't let on.

"What is it Sonia? I get the feeling that you know a lot about what has happened."

"Callie, Johnny is in a lot of trouble, if it's who I think it is, that wants to get rid of him, he needs all the help he can get. You see, last week Johnny exposed some agents that was laundering money, and now I think the ones that have not been caught, are out to do him in."

"Do you know who they are and can you help me get him out of that hospital?"

"Yes, and this is how we're going to do it. I did some heavy thinking on the way over here and I've come up with this plan." As she begins to tell me what the plan is, I just sit there nodding my head to let her know that I understood the plan and that I was willing to do what she said.

It took about half an hour for her to get it all out. She told me that helping Johnny, we would be cramping the style of some very powerful people and that ours lives also will be in danger. I just said, let's do it, and now it's about 8:00 o'clock in the evening. I'm suppose to be back to the hospital around midnight. That's what I told Johnny before I left, and I know that he will be waiting for me to appear around that time. We only have four hours to get the plan rolling and get him out I know he's smart enough not to take the sleeping pill they will try to make him take around nine o'clock tonight. That's what they usually do in the hospital. Come around and give you a sleeping pill so you won't bother them for the rest of the night, with one exception, when they want to wake you up out of your sleep to do whatever it is they do to you at two in the morning.

"Let's go get him," Sonia says, waking me out of a stupor. I do declare. I have never been so scared in all my life. I'm just a country girl from Kentucky. I don't know anything about this big city crime stuff, such as a hit out on folks and money laundering. This mess sounds like a really heavy caper or something, but I'll do anything to get Johnny to safety. His life is in Sonia and my hands and we won't let him down.

We're back at the hospital in less than twenty minutes. Sonia parks her black jaguar at the front entrance. I get out and head for the seventh floor. I'm trying to walk steady. I haven't had any rest since I got here this afternoon and I'm suffering from jet lag. I'm starting to sweat. My teeth are starting to chatter as if I got the flu and having chills. I keep walking fast towards the elevator and catch it just as the door is about to close, I stick my hand in to open it up. The people inside are looking as if they are annoyed with me. I punch the seven button and move to the back of the elevator. I don't want to be noticed and I'm also the last to get off, because everyone else's floor is below the floor I get off on.

It seems forever before I hear the ping sound of the elevator alerting me, that it's time to exit. I hurry out and head straight for Johnny's room. Being that it almost midnight, I go into the utility room to find some different shoes. I'm in luck. I find a pair that fit me just right. I put on the stethoscope find a clip board and I'm out the door, looking to the right and left of me to see if any one is watching. I don't see anyone yet. The nurse's station happens to be around the corner from his room, so it makes it a little easier to stay out of the way of the real nurses. I already have the dress on from earlier in the day. I haven't changed since I was here the first time. Now, I have to get past the guard.

When I get to where the guard is, I start to talk to him. I try to feel him out to see what he's about. He listens for a while and before I go into Johnny's room, I ask him if he would like a cup of coffee, because it looks as if he's getting sleepy.

"That would be nice of you to get me a cup," he says.

"We always keep a hot pot of coffee at the nurse's station," I tell him, and putting on a very fake smile, while opening the door to Johnny's room. When I get inside, I can see that he is asleep.

"Johnny, wake up," I whisper, as I'm shaking him just a little.

"Callie. You're here. I'm just a bit groggy. They had to give me something for the pain."

"Don't talk. You need your strength. We've got to get you out of town."

"I don't have any clothes. They took them away." "Oh, this is a problem. Wait here."

"Where are you going Callie? Don't leave me here."

"Don't worry. I will never leave you again, Johnny."

Once back into the corridor. I went as fast as I could to the coffee machine next to the utility room that is pretty much isolated from the other rooms. I put the money into the vending machine and nothing comes out. I tried beating on it. Still nothing. Then I kicked it and a cup came down and coffee came pouring out. The cup is now too full and I have to pour some into the holes below the spout. I reach into the dress I stole this afternoon and pulled out some sleeping pills. I put two into the coffee, stirred it up with a plastic spoon I found on the floor and headed back to Johnny's room.

"Here is your coffee," I say, smiling. "This will surely wake you up."

"Thanks. I am getting a bit sleepy," the guard says. As I happen to look over my shoulder, I see Sonia peeking from around the corner. I'm surprised to see her and glad all at the same time, because I don't know how I'm going to get Johnny up and down the stairwell alone and when I get back inside his room, he is sitting up, but looking very weak and tired. I wink at him and he smiles that beautiful smile showing all thirty-two of those even teeth.

"I thought you'd never get here," he says, a bit groggily. He is pretty doped up and is going to be hard to handle. I don't know if he can help me out at all. The chart on the wall says that the nurse was just in to check on him and is not due back for at least an hour.

"Don't you have any clothes at all to put on? I don't know what to do. Well, maybe I do. Don't worry, I'll get you some clothes," I assure him. "Be right back."

When I leave the room, I find that the guard is already asleep. I motion for Sonia to come were I am. We both take a hold of the sleeping mans arms and drag him into Johnny's room and begin to undress him as he's lying on the floor. The sleeping pills were double strength.

"Sonia, what are you doing here?" Johnny asks her.

"I'm here to save you. What else? I'm your partner ain't I and partners look out for each other. So shut your mouth. I've got work to do."

"As you say, but I'm really glad you're here to help me."

"We've got to hurry Sonia," I tell her. We still have to get Johnny dressed in these clothes."

"He won't wake up will he?" Sonia asks me.

"He's out. I put some pretty potent stuff in his coffee. He won't wake up. He'll sleep like a baby for at least two hours."

"Who is that?" Johnny asks me.

"He's the man guarding your door. I put some sleeping pills into his coffee."

"Johnny, we've got to get you out of here fast, and you've got to help us. I know you're probably in pain, but you have to try and walk, once we get you dressed," Sonia says, as she begins to put the shirt on him. One arm is in a sling and the shirt will have to go over it and just one arm will be in and the arm that is in the sling will have to go over the sling. I'm starting to put the man's pants on Johnny. It seems to be taking forever to get them on, since he can't move around on the bed very well. He's groggy and can barely help me get them on him.

"Raise up a little Johnny, so I can pull your pants all the way up."

He seems to be drifting out again. He's got to stay awake to get him down the stairs and out of the hospital.

"Wake up Johnny," I whisper, and he slowly opens his eyes and shuts them again.

"Wake up. You're an FBI agent. This is no time for sleeping," Sonia says, while patting his face with the water from the ice pitcher. Johnny opens his eyes and tries to get out of bed.

Now that we have him dressed we get him up and into a chair, while we drag the sleeping guard into the bathroom and then we take the pillows and put them under the sheet, as if there is someone in bed, and I'm starting to get the feeling as if we're in some kind of movie or just having a bad dream, but I'm not dreaming and I'm not in a movie. This is the real deal. Mama would faint if she had any idea about what I'm doing. I remember once when mama's brother had just gotten out of prison and came to visit us. Mama never stop preaching to him the whole time he was at our house about obeying the laws of the land. Poor uncle Billie, never did get a moment of peace the whole two weeks he was at our house and one morning we all woke up and he was gone. Daddy said mama preached him right out of the house and I could see that daddy wasn't too sad about him leaving. I felt sorry for Uncle Billie. He always did treat me special and he taught me how to shoot marbles. I don't know where he got them, cause hardly anybody sells marbles anymore.

"Come on Callie. Help me get Johnny on his feet. We've got to get out of here now."

"Good Idea," I tort. I have to admit I'm getting just a bit impatient. I want Johnny out of here now.

"Lets go Johnny," I say, as I help Sonia pull him to his feet.

"Steady as she goes," Sonia says, to Johnny, as she holds onto the back of his injured shoulder.

"Try to take a step," I say, hoping he can walk.

"That's it," says Sonia. "One step at a time."

"You can do it Johnny. We're almost to the door Johnny," I say.

Once into the hospital corridor, Sonia and I are on each side of Johnny. I have his arm around my shoulder and Sonia is holding the back of him to try and keep him steady. We're almost to the exit door, just a short ways from his room and then I start to wonder how are we going to get him down the stairs. Will he be able to hold himself up on the stairs. What if he can't. Then what, but we've got to try. There is just no other way we can get him out, if he can't stand up. He's just too big of a man to carry. He's got to hold himself up.

"You're doing good Johnny," I tell him.

"Just a little more and we're to the stairs," Sonia says, breathing rather hard at this point. You'd think she was in better shape, being a FBI agent and all. If she gets caught helping Johnny, her life won't amount to a hill of beans either. She's taking a big chance by helping us. I'm learning to appreciate her now. I could never have gotten this far without her. She's a pretty decent person. I can see why Johnny thinks so much of her. Being partners, she had his back and he had hers, and she still has his back. I guess they have a bond that will last forever, just as my love for him will last for eternity. I'm still just a bit jealous, but it's a good kind of jealousy. Now I know that they are just partners. They will be partners for life.

Some how we make it down the stairs and into Sonia's Lincoln. I find out that she took the jaguar parked it and rented a Cadillac with a fake name, as agents sometimes do to keep anonymous. Johnny is lying down in the back seat. I can hear him moan from time to time. Sonia is taking us to a motel just outside L.A. She's says it's very secluded and there are hardly any patrons that visit it. I just wish we could hurry and get there. Johnny needs to be able to stretch out comfortably. He's very tall and we couldn't get his legs up onto the seat of the sedan. We could barely get him into the back seat of the car.

"How much longer before we get there?" I ask.

"Not long." But Callie, I want to tell you something. I want you to rest at the motel for twenty four hours, so Johnny can get his strength up and then, I want you to drive him to Atlanta. He has friends there. They're retired FBI agents who think the world of him. They will help you. I've got the addresses here in my coat pocket."

"You've thought of everything Sonia. How can I ever thank you?"

"You can thank me by keeping Johnny and yourself alive," she says, smiling at me.

"Remember, you can't contact me anymore after tonight. My phones will be tapped for sure. This is the last contact we will be able to have, until his friends in Atlanta clear him."

"You think they can clear him and find the bad guys?" I ask hopefully.

"Believe me. They will do anything for Johnny. He's like the son they never had."

"I'll never forget you for this Sonia."

"Please. I need you to forget me. You must never mention my name to anyone ever. When this is all over, we'll all go out and celebrate. Just keep you and Johnny safe. He's wounded and is depending solely on you. I put some soda and food on ice in the trunk, so you won't have to stop too often. There's also a can of gasoline and a first aid kit too. You'll have to give Johnny a shot for pain in about an hour, or the pain alone will kill him. It's all in the trunk of the car."

"I don't know how to give a shot," I say frantically.

"I'll show you when we get him in the room. After that, he's in your hands Callie. You've got to take good care of him. Bathe him in cold water once every two hours to keep the fever down. Give him the antibiotics, and shoot him the morphine every four hours."

Once we get Johnny into the room and onto the bed, Sonia gives me a map and points out the way to Atlanta. After giving Johnny his shot, she gives me a big hug and then she is gone. She already had a parked car at the motel to get back to town. She thought of everything. Now it's up to me. I have to get him to Atlanta if it's the last thing I do, but I hope it won't be the last thing I do. Johnny and me have a lot of living to catch up on and I've got to make sure we do it. When I was in love with Scooter and he came back from the armed forces married to another woman, I thought I would never love another man the way I loved Scooter. My heart was broken into a million pieces. I thought I would never recover from that devastating event, but now I have Johnny back and I'll be a monkey's uncle, before I ever let him get away from me again and I'm not ashamed to say so. If we women don't hold on to our men and forget about our pride, we will always be left out and living alone because there are too many women out there who will strip their pride naked to be with the one they love.

Johnny is beginning to move a little. The pain must be waking him up. His eyes are still closed, but I can tell he is conscience. I start to run to the bathroom, where I put the first aid kit Sonia gave me. I start to fumble around trying to remember exactly what to do in order to give him his shot of morphine. I can hear him start to moan. He must be feeling a lot of pain because when I get to the side of the bed, I can see it in his eyes.

"I'm going to give you something for the pain," I tell him. "Trust me. I know what I'm doing." I say, to make him believe that I know how to administer his shot.

"Where are we?"

"I'll explain everything after I give you this and don't talk so much, you'll need your strength to travel," I say, noticing that he is looking very confused about this whole ordeal and is wincing from the injection I'm giving him.

"Look, tomorrow we're headed for Atlanta. Sonia says your friends there will help us. She has already contacted them and they know we're coming, so you've got to rest now."

"I'm glad you're here Callie. I don't ever want to lose you. You mean everything to me."

"Don't worry. I won't let you lose me ever again." I give him a kiss on the forehead. I just hope he gets better soon. He doesn't look good. He wasn't out of surgery no more than six hours when I seen him the first time and when we left the hospital he had only been there a good 13 hours all together, but I had no choice but to get him out of there. His life is in danger from his own colleagues who set him up, and now I'm involved in a federal case with him. But Johnny is innocent of any wrong doing and I have to help him. I have no choice because he needs me. I just hope he doesn't get an infection or any other complications. I didn't want to have to move him so soon after surgery, but they were going to kill him if I didn't. They're the ones who have done wrong, but I'm feeling like I'm the one that's wrong, breaking the law and helping an alleged suspect escape and now we're both fugitives from the law. He's so helpless and I won't leave him no matter what.

"Where are you?" He asks me. "I don't know if I can make it. I feel lousy."

"I'm right here Johnny and you are going to make it. You'll feel better tomorrow, so try and get some rest. I'm right here beside you." I say, as I climb onto the bed beside him. "I'm right here Johnny." I stroke his head softly, as I start to think about how much has happened in the last year. I was just a bratty kid when I left home almost a year ago, and on my way to New York City to become this fabulous model and since then, I've had to grow up fast. I never new being grown up and on my own, brought so much responsibility with it, and I never dreamed I would be in this much trouble. It will be Christmas in a few weeks and Johnny and I will probably be in Atlanta. I won't get to see any of my relatives or friends this year, but I'll be with Johnny and that's all that counts. Nothing else really matters to me. He is truly my soul mate for now and forever.

Johnny slept well last night. I continued to put cold water on him most of the night to keep any fever away, and now we're on our way to Atlanta in Sonia's Luxury Cadillac. Johnny sleeps most of the time in the back seat, but he's much more coherent and alert today. We have at least several days to ride ahead of us, and I'm going to have to stop and rest more than once, because I can't drive it alone. I loathe the fact that Johnny has to ride so long, but we can't take any chances being seen on any commercial transportation. We should hit Las Vegas in about ten hours. We can spend the night there for sure. Johnny insisted that we go right through Las Vegas and not by pass it. I don't know why, I figure he knows something that I don't, so that's the route I headed in. It won't be long now before I will have to stop and get some hot soup into Johnny. He's got to get some kind of nourishment soon. He hasn't eaten in hours. It reminds me of the time when daddy was sick and he wouldn't eat or drink anything for days and he got so dehydrated he almost died and mama started making him drink her homemade hot chicken broth whether he liked it or not and it wasn't long before he got well. Daddy never did forgive mama for forcing that chicken broth down his throat, but mama said she didn't care if he stayed mad for the rest of his life, because if she hadn't done just that, daddy would have died for sure. Of course he finally forgave her and even thanked her for doing what he wouldn't do.

"Where are we?" Johnny asks, as I drift back to the present.

"We're about thirty miles from Las Vegas."

"When you get there, head for the strip," he says.

"Alright, I will Johnny. You just relax while I stop at this restaurant and get you some hot soup," I reply, as if I'm not going to take no for an answer."

"Right," he says, as he tries to straighten up in the back seat.

"Stay put and don't move around too much,." I say, after stopping in front of one of the chain restaurants. "I'll be right back. You've got to have something to stick to your bones."

"I'm not going anywhere," he says, trying to laugh off the fact that he couldn't go anywhere if he wanted to. "And by the way, bring me some milk. It always settles my stomach."

"What ever you want your majesty," I say, turning around and giving him a big smile. I'm acting as if everything is fine, but I'm really petrified concerning the fact that I don't have a prognosis on him. I don't know for sure if he's not bleeding internally, or some other God awful thing might be wrong with him. He should be in the care of a doctor, but that's impossible right now. I'll just have to pray that he's healing as he should and there will be no complications. So far, so good. I just hope that it stays that way. God please don't let anything happen to Johnny. I can't live without him now. I never should have left him, but what is done is done and I've got to stop blaming myself. This would have happened whether I was with him or not. I don't have anything to do with what is going on, I try to convince myself. I must keep emotionally sound, because he is totally dependent on me for his life.

It seems as if I've been standing in this line forever. I keep looking out of the restaurant window to make sure nothing is happening to Johnny.

"Miss, could you hurry it up and take my order please. I have a sick person in the car and I need to get some hot soup as quickly as possible."

"I'm sorry to hear that lady. You can cut in front of me," the nice man, said kindly.

"Thank you very much," I tell the man, who has stepped back to let me in front of him.

I finally got the soup and a small carton of milk for Johnny and I also got me a burger and some fries. It seemed to take forever. I didn't want to leave Johnny for a minute. I got in the back seat of the car and fed it to him. He dozed off again as soon as he finished, but before he did, he insisted that I wake him once we're in Las Vegas and on the strip. I asked him if he wanted to go gambling or something and what's all this about Vegas. He didn't say anything, but just said to let him know when we were there. I agreed to do so.

I drove for another forty minutes before we reached the city limits of Sin City. Once on the strip, I thought it was time to wake Johnny. I could hear the even sound of his breathing assuring me that he was asleep. I didn't want to disturb his rest, but he insisted that I wake him at this point.

"Johnny are you awake?" I only had to call him once. I remember that he is a very light sleeper, maybe it's that FBI training that teaches him to practically sleep with one eye open.

"Yeah, I'm awake. Are we on the strip yet?"

"We're here."

"Go down to the next block and turn right," he almost commands, after sitting up as straight as he can to see exactly where we were.

"Where are we going?"

"Just do like I say."

"Alright Johnny. Whatever you say." I look into the rear view mirror to make sure he's not delusional or some stuff like that.

I do as Johnny says and turn right at the next block. I drive slowly, and then I see a row of wedding chapels. I can't believe people get married here like this. I even see a drive up chapel a little ways up the street.

"Callie, do you see a sign that says Drive through Chapel?"

"Yes, I see it."

"Well, If you'll marry me, pull up to chapel window."

"Are you asking me to marry you? Are you sure you're not feverish?"

"I know what I'm doing Callie, just answer the question."

"Yes, yes I'll marry you."

"Well, let's do it."

I'm now in total shock and bliss all at the same time. Johnny wants to marry me at the drive up chapel in Las Vegas Nevada. I'm going to be his wife. I am so elated, I can hardly control myself.

"You're sure aren't you Johnny. Are you up to this? I mean physically up to this."

"I am baby. I'm so up to this."

I pull up to the drive up wedding chapel and ring the bell. Shortly a fat bald head man comes out to the window. He's still dressed in his pajamas and carrying a bible and some paper and a pen.

"Do you want to get married?" He asks, in a deep solemn voice.

"Yes, we do," I say, as I'm smiling from ear to ear.

"What are your names and where is your husband to be?" The fat man asks me, looking into the front seat of the car.

"I'm back here," Johnny says, rather weakly.

"Oh, I see. What ever suits you."

"Just get on with it. We don't have all night," Johnny says, from the back seat of the car.

"Do you take this woman. By the way what are your names?"

"Callie and Johnny," I mumble, quickly. I still can't believe what's happening.

"Do you take this man to be your lawfully wedded husband and do you take this woman to be your lawfully wedded wife?" The man is saying, as he is peering over the top of his glasses.

"I do," I say happily.

"I do," Johnny says, and then coughs to clear his throat.

"I now pronounce you man and wife. Sign here and that will be seventy-five dollars in cash," he clearly states, with no expression, and I'm just so elated and taken aback at the same time, as I hand the man the money and he hands me the license for me and Johnny to sign, but I'm going to have to sign it for Johnny, but that's alright, because now I'm a married woman.

"We'd better rest here for the night Callie. I can't stand it in this back seat much longer."

"Where should we stay?"

"How about the honey moon suite at the MGM," he says, knowing that he is making me the happiest woman in the world. He is so sweet even with his gun shot wounds and as sick as he is, he has made me so happy, and now I have a husband. The man I've waited for all my life. Mama will be floored when I tell her about how we were married. It's the best Christmas present I could ever have gotten. I've got to get him to the hotel fast so he can rest. The back seat of the car is not comfortable for him in his condition and I've got to figure out how I will get him out of the car and to our honeymoon suite. We can't raise any suspicion, because I know there must be a man hunt out for us. We can't stay here long either. We've got to get to his friends in Atlanta. That's the only protection we have, but tonight before I go to sleep. I'm going to say my prayers the way I was taught. I have to say a prayer for Johnny, and me because right now, we need all the help we can get. I don't see the light at the end of the tunnel. That light seems to be so far away. I hope we find it soon.

Chapter 9

We finally made it to Atlanta. It took us two more days, after our two day stay in Vegas. Johnny is looking good and feeling a whole lot better. I have to admit I took dog gone good care of my man. I gave him his antibiotics, pain killers, bathed him down in cold water regularly and changed his bandages often. I stayed up with him most of the night, just watching him to make sure he was still breathing. I told him he better not die on me now, because we just got married and that just would not be fair to me if he died, after all the trouble we both went through to be together. He assured me that he would not die, at least not for the next 50 years or so. I was glad he was confident about living. The only thing is, we're both fugitives on the run. Johnny, because of some agents setting him up and busting him and me for aiding and abetting an alleged felon. It's all over the news here in Atlanta. That's why I had to get Johnny and me some disguises so we could sneak into the hotel without being noticed. Life has certainly dealt us some bad blows, but we have each other and that's what makes it special. At this point, I can't make it without him and he can't make it without me.

We're staying at one of the more affluent hotels, hoping that this would be one of the last places they will be looking for us. I suppose they will be looking in some sleazy motels, but staying in one of the most luxurious Hotels in Atlanta hopefully will throw the police off. We've got to locate his friends.

"I think I'm getting hungry. Call down and get some food sent up here Callie. You look famished too. Have you been taking care of yourself. You're looking very thin," He comments.

"Sure. I'm fine. I just haven't had much time to eat."

"Well, just make sure you order some bread with the meals. You can use something to fatten you up a little."

"Alright. I'll order some bread.

"Get some milk with that order too."

"I don't like milk."

"Well get some anyway." He is looking at me as if I've committed some terrible sin.

"So, now that you're feeling better and we're married, you're giving orders. Is that it?"

"No, that is not it. I just want to see you healthy that's all. Besides, I'm the boss."

"So you're the boss."

"You got it my love," he says, because it's hard for him to talk.

"You can be my boss anytime."

It was a full hour before we got our food. We ordered so much, that it took that long for the hotel restaurant to get it ready and bring it to our room. It's the first real meal I've had in months and Johnny was starving too. It had been days that he's had only soup and juice. I had steak and lobster, and Johnny had two steaks and lobster with bread and butter and a quart of beer. I don't drink alcohol, so I had twenty ounces of Pepsi. By the time we finished, we were so full we both fell asleep and when I awakened and looked at the clock, we'd been asleep for three hours. I guess we're both tired from this whole ordeal and Johnny is still sleeping and I'm going to let him sleep a while longer before I wake him up. He is still weak from his wounds, but at least he's a lot stronger than when we started this trip. I am so happy to be his wife until I can't stop smiling to myself every time I think about it, the way we got married and all. It was the biggest surprise of my life. I still don't have a real ring, but Johnny is going to get me one as soon as possible, he says. And some day we're going to have a real wedding too. If only things were different. If only we could get out of this trouble we're in. It's going to take some doings and a lot of praying to get us out of this extremely difficult situation. Now that I'm Mrs. Johnny Parker, It's death do us part all the way. I will follow him to the ends of the earth.

I didn't intend to wake Johnny, but the ringing of the phone did wake him. I'm really afraid to answer it. I don't know who it could be. No one knows where we are, or at least no one is suppose to know where we are.

"Hello," I say, very timidly, and then I see Johnny open his eyes, and then turn to look at me.

"I'm calling complements of the hotel. We're giving away prizes in the Lounge. Every Friday is ladies night and we give away free drinks to all the ladies and prizes up to five hundred dollars," the man behind the voice says.

"Who is it Callie?" Johnny asks, as he sits up on the bed wincing from pain.

"It's somebody from the hotel. They say it's ladies night with free prizes."

"Tell them thank you and we'll be right down."

"Really. We're going down to the lounge?" I ask, looking at him with a very big surprised look on my face, while he attempts to go into the bath room, and I'm thinking he's not strong enough yet to go gallivanting around the hotel, and besides we are hiding from the law

"Yes, we are. I'm taking my wife out for the night. Nobody knows we're here and we are on our honeymoon you know."

"I know, but do you think it's safe? We are all over the news if I remember correctly."

"We'll get a nice secluded table and enjoy our honeymoon, just to two of us."

"I hope you know what you're doing, but don't get me wrong, I'd love to spend the evening with my new husband, while he dances with me and tells me how much he loves me."

"Then help me shower and dress, I'm still a little disabled you know."

"It will be my pleasure my king. I am at your slightest command."

Johnny and I are showered, dressed and got ready to go down to the lounge. He's walking pretty well on his own. He's healing fast and I'm glad to see him almost looking like his old self again. I must be careful to watch him though, because he tires easily. I really don't want him to go down to the lounge, but he wants to take me out for an evening and I can't deny him this very sweet gesture he is making, just to make me happy, but as quiet as it's kept,

I can enjoy Johnny where ever we are. It doesn't matter to me, just as long as we're together.

Now that we're in our own little cozy booth in the lounge. I'm starting to relax just a little. Johnny is right, we've been under so much strain, and a night out should do us both some good. To our surprise, there are several big names here to sing their latest love songs. I'm sitting as close to Johnny as I can. You couldn't get a tooth pick between us. He is so tall and handsome, some of these wild chicks here in Atlanta might want to challenge me for my man, so I'm keeping a tight rein on him just to let the others know who he's with, still the fear of being found out keeps nagging at me. What if someone recognizes us and calls the police? We've got to clear Johnny before we're found. We've got to get in touch with his friends, so they can help us, but earlier when Johnny called the number to one of his friends, the line was disconnected. Johnny says we're going to have to search for them. This is a big city. How in the world will we ever find them.

"Callie, are you back from space?" Johnny asks.

"Oh, I was just wondering how long it's going to take to find your friends, that's all."

"Stop worrying. I have connections here and I'll probably find them within forty-eight hours."

"I hope so."

"Until then, let's see if I can stand up long enough to dance to this romantic slow song."

"I'd be delighted," I say, and I was even more delighted when I realized that one of my favorite singers was on stage, singing one of his latest love songs.

"Do you know who that is, Johnny."

"Yeah, I know who it is and do you know who this is?" He says, pointing to himself.

"Of course I do. I'm dancing with the most wonderful man in the entire world."

"I thought you did," he says, smiling that beautiful smile that lights up my world.

As we continue to slow dance, I can feel that Johnny's shirt is wet from perspiration. He's not suppose to be perspiring like this. I checked with a doctor about gun shot wounds. At this stage he should be done with the sweats, unless he's starting to relapse. It's been almost ten days since I took him out of the hospital with Sonia's help and I've done everything I was suppose to do in nursing him back to health, but something is definitely wrong.

"Johnny, are you Okay?" I ask, with concern in my voice.

"Sure. I just probably need to sit down for awhile," he says as he starts to lead me off the dance floor.

"I told you this might not be such a good idea. It's going to take more convalescing before you'll be strong again," I say, as we sit down in the booth.

"Hey waiter. Give me a shot of brandy," he calls to the man, dressed in a black tuxedo.

"You don't need that Johnny. You're still on medication. You won't be off your antibiotics for another two weeks," I say, with a little of annoyance in my voice.

"One won't hurt me. In fact it just might help." He shoots back, with some returned annoyance in his voice as well.

"Are we having our first fight since we've been married?"

"No, we're just having a disagreement."

"I'm serious. You're perspiring like a sweat hog. We should go back to our room."

Suddenly Johnny starts to look as if he sees someone he knows. I can tell by the expression on his face that something is wrong. I know that look. I've seen it many times before, and when he gets that look, the fun and games are over and now I'm starting to get scared.

"What is it? Is something wrong, Johnny?" I ask, looking in the direction Johnny is looking in.

"It's an agent I used to work with. I don't know why he's here. He could be looking for us."

"How does he know we're here? Nobody should know where we are. We haven't told anyone a thing." I say as I'm trying to scoot down in the booth to keep from being seen.

"It's not an easy thing to escape the agency. We'd better get out of here. I don't think he's seen us yet, but it won't be long before he does," Johnny says, grabbing my hand as we scoot out of the booth and head for the nearest exit. By the time we get to the elevator, to go up to the eighth floor, the man comes out of the lounge, then Johnny grabs my hand again and we head for the exit stairwell.

On our way up the stairs I can see that Johnny seems to look ill. I put his arm around my shoulder, so I can help him up the stairs. We're going as fast as I can with him bearing much of his weight on me as we try to reach the second floor, and then try to take the elevator the rest of the way to the eighth floor. If we don't hurry, Johnny just might pass out. I told him we should stay in the room, because he's not well enough to move around so much, but he wouldn't listen to me. I know he wanted to make me happy, but if he passes out before we get to our room, we're through. I don't know who the man was that spooked Johnny, but I know he must be dangerous. Why didn't he listen to me in the first place. Now this task of getting him to the room is going to be a hard one. I can barely hold him up. If I can just get him to the elevator, We've got a good chance of not being seen by the man.

"Come on Johnny. You can make it. We're almost to the second floor."

"I'm sorry Callie. I should have listened to you. I'm going to make it. Don't worry. I won't pass out on you."

a few minutes later we're inside the room. Johnny practically falls on the bed. I run to the bathroom to get cold water to put on him. He looks as if he's about to go unconscious and now I'm almost terrified that he may be too ill for me to take care of him. He may need a doctor. Why didn't I get him a doctor in the beginning, when we took him from the hospital. I thought I took such good care of him and now it seems that he may be ill beyond my care. Now what should I do. We can't be caught in a hospital now, or we'll surely be found out and thrown in jail. Johnny is too sick to go to jail. We've got to lay low in this room until he's well enough for sure.

It's midnight and I'm still putting cold water on Johnny to take the fever down. He's conscious now and talking about incidents I have no knowledge of. I don't know what he's rambling about. He said something about a gun and newspaper and bed. I can't exactly understand what it is he means by all of it, but I'm so tired I can hardly keep my eyes open. I'd better put the wet towel down for a little while so I can take a nap. Just a very small nap is all

I need and then I can watch Johnny. He'll probably sleep the rest of the night. I'll get up soon and check on him.

I finally wake up and it's five o'clock in the morning. I jump up to get cold water for Johnny, but to discover he is not on the bed. I frantically look in the bathroom and he's not there. Oh my stars. Where is he? I hope he hasn't left without me. I sit on the bed with my head in my hands, and now I begin to cry crocodile tears. I guess it's time for a good cry after all that's happened. He wouldn't leave me here alone, would he? I know he wouldn't leave me. He's too much of a gentleman for that. Just as I'm starting to really feel sorry for myself, Johnny comes through the door.

"Where on earth have you been?" I ask

"I had some business to take care of."

"You could have at least let me know you were going out."

"If I had, you would have tried to stop me."

"I thought you were having a set back from your wounds."

"I must have had a bad reaction to the alcohol and the medication," he says.

"Don't ever scare me like this again. I thought you had left me."

"Why would you think a thing like that. We're one now remember."

"Yeah, we're one," I say smiling, and throwing my arms around his neck and hugging him tight.

"We'll stay here a couple of days and then we have to leave this hotel. I'm not exactly sure what that agent was doing here, but I know he's used as a sniper."

"He's a hit man?" I ask, raising my voice in fright.

"You said it. That's why I went out to get us some protection."

"What do you mean, some protection?"

"This is what I mean," he says, as he pulls out an automatic weapon.

"Where did you get that?" I ask, with my mouth hanging open.

"You forget I have connections here."

"Well, I hope you don't have to use it. That thing could hurt somebody.

"Tomorrow we go over to Stone Mountain to meet with Jimmy and Sly, the two retired agents I told you about. They're good friends of mine. They'll help me find the men who set me up and put two slugs into me."

It was almost noon when we left the hotel. Johnny refused to let me drive. He says he's as good as new. I begged to differ with him, but as usual he won the argument, because I learned that it doesn't pay to argue with Johnny and I've never been the arguing kind to start with, so it's works out just fine. I'm afraid though that if we don't find a good hideout, we're going to get caught. Thank goodness Johnny has recuperated from his wounds. Now he's in charge and that's a good thing. Some women don't want their man to take charge, but I'm not one of them. When we used to visit Aunt Sally and Uncle Joe, Aunt Sally bossed uncle Joe all the time and one time when uncle Joe didn't come home until the next morning, aunt Sally stayed up all night cutting up all his clothes and then when he came through the door, she hit him over the head with a tea kettle and he had two big knots on his head for a long time and all the men teased him at the factory where he worked. I want Johnny to take charge and be the man, because, if I tried to boss him like Aunt Sally did Uncle Joe, he would leave me for sure. I won't try to take Johnny's manhood from him, not that he would even let me, anyway.

"I think we're being followed." Johnny says to me as he's checking the rear view mirror.

"What should we do?" I ask, while turning to look out the back window.

"Keep looking straight Callie. Don't let on that we suspect anything."

"Okay." I duck down in the car. I'm thinking that they might start shooting at us at any time. I hope it's not the sniper we saw in the lounge last night, or we're finished. Snipers never miss, so I'm told. I'm not in the mood for dodging bullets today. I just need one day of peace, that's all.

"That's just a little to obvious Callie, you ducking down in the seat. You're suppose to not do anything as bogus as ducking down in the seat. Now, they probably know we're on to them."

"I'm sorry. I'm just not used to being followed by snipers. You're used to this stuff."

"Who said it was snipers?" Johnny asks me.

"Well who else would it be?"

"I don't know, but I intend to lose them," he says.

As Johnny attempts to weave in and out between cars as a strategy in trying to lose the two men in the car that is following us, I'm holding on for dear life as Johnny speeds up even more and I'm swaying from side to side and horns are honking at us, and some are giving us the sign language. The car following us is weaving in and out as well and is keeping up with us, although I don't know how. When Johnny takes a sharp left around a corner, we almost hit a bus and Johnny swerves just in time to miss it. No this is not happening. I'm not suited for this extremely dangerous activity. Oh my God we're going to hit a semi.

"Johnny please slow down. I'm scared."

"I'm going to take an off ramp. We're sure to lose them then."

As we go on the off ramp, Johnny drives faster around a corner and drives into a kind of garage, and we jump out of car and pull the large garage door down.

"Are we safe?" I ask.

"For the time being. I've got to get to Jimmy and Sly. They'll know who those guys were, that were trying to run us off the road. Trust me Callie. We're going to get out of this alive. You believe me don't you?"

"I believe whatever you say."

Thirty minutes later, we're driving around in Stone Mountain, trying to find the street where one of Johnny's Friends live. We're driving slowly as people are standing around and looking at us. I have the feeling they know we don't live here. I can see why they call it Stone Mountain. The mountain is huge with large carvings into the mountain. It's a black community. I didn't know there would be so many black people here. We should feel right at home, but I don't. As we drive slowly turning off one road to another looking for Jimmy's house, there are cold eyes staring at us as if we had better watch our step. People are out on their porches even though it's winter here and not long before Christmas, the weather is not really cold and many people are out on the streets. I feel as if we're monkeys in a zoo and we're behind the glass cages with humans looking in at us. I have my hands in my pockets and then I pull my coat collar up around my face, as I try to hide my face, and then put my hands back in my pockets. The cold stares are giving me chills

"There it is. That's the house there," he says, while I let out a very relieved sigh.

"I hope someone is home. I'm tired and hungry, after that wild chase back there," I say, and rolling my eyes as if I never, and I really have never…

"Callie, I hope you're not sorry you married me and got into all this trouble," Johnny says, apologetically.

"Of course not. Where you go, I go," I say, smiling and rubbing his face gently. "But we do have to clear you and get us out of this set up."

"Jimmy and Sly will help us with that," he says, as he's stroking my long hair to the ends.

"I certainly hope so. I'm getting tired of this James Bond fiasco.

Just as I finished my last syllable, a man came out onto the porch of the house we are sitting in front of. He's a medium height man with a mustache and a dark complexion. I'm thinking is this Johnny's friend and if it is, he doesn't look like much of a FBI man to me. I wonder if he can really help us. I was expecting to see a tall muscular man similar to Johnny, but this man looks like a scrawny little mouse.

"Johnny, tell me this is not the man you've been talking about."

"Yeah, that's Jimmy, alright," he says to me.

"He doesn't look like a retired FBI man Johnny," I say, sarcastically.

"Jimmy was one of the best."

"He's so scrawny, he looks sick or something," I say, looking at the man from under my sunglasses, while Johnny gives me a peck on the cheek and tells me not to worry.

"I'd better go meet him," Johnny says to me.

When Johnny gets out of the car to meet the man on the large veranda, I stay in the car with my hands clenched into fists. I'm so scared we're not going to get out of this alive. I keep looking as Johnny and the man shake hands. The man is smiling and patting Johnny on his good shoulder. I'm looking at Johnny and thinking what a tall handsome man I have. They keep talking and now another man is joining them on the porch, and I'm wondering who is man number two. The three men continue to talk and not long after the second man came outside, all three of them went into the house. Now I'm really worried, because I don't know what's happening now. There is a man hunt out for us and a reward, so how can we trust these men not to turn us in for the reward. I hope Johnny hurries up and comes out to tell me what on earth is going on, after all, I'm in this trick bag just as much as he is.

After Johnny is in the house for a good ten minutes, he appears on the veranda and motions for me to come inside. I look into the rear view mirror to check my hair and put on lip stick, before getting out of the car, and when I get onto the porch, Johnny takes me by the hand and attempts to lead me inside. I pull back slightly, because I want to talk to him before we get inside the large mansion, with a brick wall surrounding it.

"Johnny, this just doesn't feel right. What did you talk about in there?" I ask.

"I'll tell you later. Right now, lets go inside," he said.

"Okay, but I want to know everything later," I say, looking at him sternly.

"Do I ever keep anything from you?" He asks me.

"No, but there's always a first time for everything," I said, trying to keep it light.

"Come on baby. We're in good hands now. These are very good friends of mine."

"If you say so."

After going into the house. I see the two men that were on the veranda with Johnny and a woman sitting on the couch with flaming read hair and long red fingernails, dressed in a black leather pants suit. Johnny leads me to a large comfortable looking arm chair and gently nudges me into it. I'm just sitting here, while he goes over to the two men standing by the window. They continue to talk for several minutes. I can here them speaking in a low monotone voice, but can't understand what it is they are saying. One man takes out a cigarette and Johnny pulls out his lighter and lights it for the man. I believe that this man is Jimmy and the other slightly taller man with the bald head must be Sly. I'm now looking at the woman with the flaming red hair and red nails. She's acting as if she doesn't even know I'm in the room, so I oblige her by doing the same thing, acting as if she is not in the room. The house is decorated exquisitely. It's a marvelous house with large rooms downstairs, and a beautiful staircase that leads upstairs. I'm debating with myself as to if the woman on the couch is the wife of one of the men or is she just a hooker or something, because of the way she's dressed. I'm beginning to think that Johnny's friends aren't as wholesome as I thought they'd be. It looks as if there is some shady business going on here, but at this point, I don't know what the devil it is.

Johnny is coming towards me now. I certainly hope he has good news. About something, or about anything for that matter. I just want to get out of here. I just like it when Johnny and I are alone. We've hardly had a honeymoon at all. We're on the run from the law, and I'm scared all the time that something is going to happen to Johnny. I'm not so worried about myself as I am for him. I don't know how he's going to get the guy that set him up. They are the ones selling drugs and laundering money and Johnny is being accused of doing it instead of the real ones. What could they possibly have been talking about. Hopefully, they've come up with a plan to get us out of this nightmare. Neither one of us deserves this kind of thing to happen to us. There must be tons of innocent people incarcerated and set up by more richer and powerful people. They always said that money talks. I'm beginning to thing that it does more than talk. It also walks. Money can set a lot of things in motion, that just plain talk could never do and it's also the root of all evil according to the good book.

"You Okay, baby?" Johnny asks, after coming over to where I'm sitting.

"I'm alright," I say, as I'm looking into his eyes for some kind of clue that everything is going to work out just fine.

I want you to stay here with Jimmy's woman. The guys and me have got to take care of some serious business," he rambles on, as he gives me a big kiss on the mouth.

"But, I thought you were going to explain some things to me. I think I have a right to know what is going on Johnny. I'm in this mess just as much as you are," I said, with some anger in my voice.

"And I'm going to get us out of this," he whispers softly.

"What business are you guys up to?" I whisper back, because I don't want the others to know what I'm saying to Johnny and Johnny squats down in front of the chair I'm sitting in and then takes my hand and kisses it.

"We've got to go into Atlanta and buy some more automatic weapons. The guys behind setting me up, are very dangerous and Jimmy, Sly and myself have got to be prepared for what's to come. Those men who tried to run us off the road are not playing tidily winks. They are dead serious about getting me before I can get the evidence I need to nail them."

"Is it safe for me to be here with Miss Flaming Fire over there?" I ask, looking in the woman's direction.

"As safe as can be. Miss Flaming Fire over there is Jimmy's woman, but she's also one of the top women agents around. She's one of the top marksmen in the business, or should I say markswomen."

"Well I'm certainly glad to here it, but hurry back. I don't want to be here without you." I say, taking his hand and kissing the back of it softly.

"Be back in a flash my love," he says, smiling that big beautiful smile that shows all thirty-two pearly whites, and with that, he stood up and started for the door, where the other men were already standing waiting on him to depart for Metro Atlanta and he was still somewhat weak from his wounds, which made him a little slower than he normally would be, which made me almost frantic with worry.

"See you when you get back."

Hours have passed, since Johnny and the other two men left. The red headed woman hasn't said anything to me. I'm getting the feeling that there is more to her than meets the eye. I'm determined not to say anything to her either, after all I'm the guest here, and she has shown me no hospitality and I'm not one for begging anyone to talk to me. In my opinion, she should show me some courtesy, but it looks as if neither one of us will break the ice, so my mind travels back to my home town. I was so protected and loved when I was growing up. I used to get mad at my parents when they wouldn't let me stay out late like some of the other kids did. I thought they were being mean to me, but now I know that it was because they loved me and wanted to keep me safe. The reason I'm thinking about that now, is because I don't feel safe anymore. At least not now. I almost wish I was back in my little bedroom in my parents house all snug and warm in my bed with all my stuffed animals all around to keep me company, and even wishing I was back at school with all the black kids calling me white girl, because I always tried to use perfect English, and didn't take to slang at all. It's just lately, since being away from home I've started to use some Ebonics. I noticed that Johnny's friends use a lot of slang language, but when I think about it, it might be some type of code they use to keep others from knowing what they are talking about.

It's been three hours now that Johnny's been gone with those men, and suddenly I notice that the woman on the couch has been looking at me. Every time I look at her, she quickly turns away. She does this several mores times and I'm really getting disturbed my her actions. If she keeps this up, I'm going to think that she likes women or some stuff like that. I ain't about that and she better stop looking at me funny.

"Is something wrong?" I ask, the woman, with some concern in my voice.

"Ain't nothing wrong. I just wonder how you and Johnny are going to get out of this," she says. He's up against some pretty mean boys. They're so corrupt, they got the top dogs scared, and you two are on the most wanted list. I hope you know that," she says, in a sinister manner.

"What's it to you? Don't nobody need your help anyway. Johnny and I can take care of us," I say, with a nasty tone.

"How long you and Johnny been married?" She asks me.

"Nunya," I say flippantly.

"Did you know that Johnny and I was together, before Jimmy and me?"

"You're a liar," I tort.

"When he gets back, ask him," she says, with a hateful smirk on her face.

"I don't have to, because I know your lying," I say

"Whatever," she says, as she starts to file her long red nails.

"You can dream all you want. You wish you could have been with Johnny. Besides Jimmy is your man, so what are you even mentioning mine for, even if you had been together before me. You ain't never going to get the chance to be with him again," I say, sticking my tongue out at her.

"You want to bet on that," she says.

"Look lady. You're talking about my husband and the conversation stops now," I tell her, looking her right in the eye balls and just as I pull my tongue back into my mouth, Johnny and the others come through the door and Johnny comes right over to me.

"We know who set me up," he says.

"What are you going to do?" I ask, getting up out of the chair I've been glued to ever since he left the house earlier.

"We're going to get them. We have to make them confess to clear me."

"Johnny how long are we going to be here? I don't like this place."

"We've got to stay here Callie. We'll be safe here with Jimmy and Sly. Besides they're going to be working with me in executing a plan to capture and detain the bad guys for questioning."

"What ever you say, but the sooner we get out of here the better," I say, in a most disappointing way. I'm disappointed and I can imagine that mama is in shock, with all that has been happening with me. I suppose the whole of Lexington is in an uproar by now. Me being on the most wanted list and my face plastered all over the TV. news. I've got to call mama to let her know I'm Okay. I hope I don't give my poor mama a heart attack. I will never forgive myself if mama dies behind all this mess. The wonderful daughter she raised is no more. Now I'm an alleged fugitive from justice, but unjustly, because Johnny hasn't done anything and if he hasn't done anything, then neither have I. Oh, if I can just convince myself of that, but I have to believe it or I won't have any hope left. I don't want to go to prison and I don't want Johnny to go to prison either, so I'm going to have to wait this thing out and if we die, we die together. I can't live without the man who feeds my very soul. I won't live without him.

The rest of the day went by fast. It is late and everyone is still up. It must be past midnight, and Johnny and the others are still talking at a table in the kitchen. It must take a lot of planning, because they've been at that table for four hours now. I don't know where it is we're suppose to sleep. No one has told us, where we can retire for the night. There is plenty of room in this large house and it appears that most of the bedrooms are upstairs, although I haven't seen the whole house. I'm still stuck to this arm chair, because I'm so darn uncomfortable in this house. It seems as if Johnny is so busy with the plan, he's hardly had time to talk with me all day. I feel a little abandoned, but I hope I'm not being selfish, when our lives are on the line here. I feel safer here than I did in the hotel, because this beautiful house has a brick wall around it. It must have been built for some high tech security reasons, but just the same, I'm glad it's there and the Doberman Pinscher out in the yard are also a real asset for security purposes. These retired guys are living the life, except for the fact that they don't know that they are retired. They can't let go of the agency. In their own way they feel that they have to continue to be a part of it. But for Johnny and me, it's a good thing that these men are our allies.

It's two a.m. in the morning and Johnny and I have just got into the room they gave us to sleep in. I found out that no one sleeps in this house until meetings are over and guards are posted. I personally don't care what the rules are, just as long as it keeps us safe. As I look over onto the night stand. I see a telephone. I've got to call mama to let her know I'm alright for now anyway. She still doesn't know that Johnny and I are married either.

"Johnny, do you suppose I can call mama now. She needs to know that I'm alright, and I want to break the good news about our getting married and all."

"Sure. Go ahead. You're mama needs to know that you're safe, but I'm not so sure she's is going to want to wish her new son-in-law best wishes, after all, I'm the one who has you in all this trouble."

"You couldn't have gotten me in this Johnny if I hadn't wanted to be in it. I love you and that's all that counts and besides, you're innocent."

"You're wonderful Callie. Although I do feel a bit guilty for letting you get involved."

"Well don't. I'm grown enough to know what it is I'm doing and I believe that justice will prevail in the end."

"I wish I was as optimistic as you are. We're dealing with corrupt federal agents."

"I just believe that the good Lord will help us, because we're innocent," I say.

"I'm really not a religious kind of person Callie. I just know that if Johnny doesn't take care of Johnny, no one else will, and now I have you to take care of, and I'm going to do just that," he says, giving me a big hug.

"I'd better call mama while it's heavy on my mind. I hope everything is Okay with her."

"Yeah, go ahead. She's probably sick with worry," Johnny says running his fingers through his thick beautiful hair. Johnny has what black folk call good hair. It's black and thick and naturally curly. I can't wait until we have kids and they all turn out with hair like Johnny's and now I've got to call mama.

As I'm dialing the eleven numbers that it takes to call her at home, my hand is trembling. I will fall apart if she cries and sounds as if she worried to death about me in this situation. Johnny went back downstairs to give me some privacy, and I don't think he wants to hear what mama and me have to say. He feels responsible for my being sought after by the law, no matter how much I tell him that it was my own decision to do what I did, and that was helping him to escape from the hospital. If I hadn't, he would be in jail awaiting a trial and would never have been able to clear his name. I'm responsible for my own actions. He is not to blame for something I would have done anyway. I've seen too many innocent people take the rap for something they didn't do and my Johnny shouldn't have to be one of them.

"Hello," I say, when mama picks up the receiver after the third ring.

"Callie is that you? I've been so worried about you and all your friends are calling and they're all worried too. What in heavens name is going on Callie? You're all over the news and in all the newspapers. Are you all right?" She asks, just about all in one breath.

"I'm fine mama. I just had to call you to let you know that I'm alright., for now anyway."

"What does that mean, for now anyway, Callie.

You are going to be all right aren't you?"

"Yes mama, and by the way, I got married."

"You got married? To who?"

"You remember I told you about Johnny don't you? We got married a week ago."

"That's right. That's the guy who got you into this mess. He's all over the news too," she says, in not so nice a tone, but I assured her that Johnny didn't make me do anything I didn't want to do.

"Mama, Johnny is a very good man and he didn't do anything. He's been set up by some of the other agents he worked with in the past. I love him mama and he loves me. Tell Sarah and Genny not to worry about me. I'll see you and them as soon as I can, but I've got to go now. Love you."

After I hung up the phone, I feel a lot better that mama's knows everything and trusts my judgment. It kind of gives me the strength I need to go on. Mama doesn't approve of what I'm doing, but she believes that I know what I have to do for me. Only time will tell if I'm right, but deep down inside me I know I'm right. Loving Johnny has been the most right I have ever done in my life.

One half hour after I hung up with mama, Johnny came back up to the room. He didn't ask me what mama said, and I didn't tell him anything about our conversation, he just turned on the TV. to the news channel and as usual for the past few weeks have seen our faces in living color on the TV. screen. After listening for a couple of minutes, he turns if off angrily. I don't say anything, because I can see that he is in no mood for talking, I just go into the private bathroom in our bedroom to take a shower. I can hardly relax anymore, but this hot shower should help me sleep tonight along with a couple of sleeping pills. My mind and body is stressed and I can feel the stress that Johnny is going through. Maybe I'll give him a nice back rub later, that is if he will let me. It seems he doesn't want me to touch him lately. I guess he is just too worried to relax, but worrying every minute is not going to help us at all. He needs sleep and he needs rest. I don't know how he's making it, with his wounds, but he has made great progress since he got shot, it's just that he needs to rest to keep up his strength.

When I come out of the shower, Johnny has fallen asleep on the bed. I'm a bit disappointed that we didn't have time to discuss the plans that were made concerning what, where and when they were going to make their move to snatch the guys that knew who set him up, so I guess I'll just have to wait until morning when he's had some sleep. I dare not wake him. He definitely needs the rest. Suddenly I remember a movie I saw once where this couple was hiding out from the law, because the leading character in the movie had been set up and they were running away from the authorities like Johnny and me, but they didn't make it. They were shot and killed by the sheriff and his deputies and didn't even have a chance to surrender. I can only pray that vwe don't end up the same way. My confidence is starting to fade just a little, but tomorrow I know I'll feel better. I can feel the sleeping pill start to take effect and suddenly I don't care anymore. I just want to get some sleep, because I am so tired and must ask Johnny about him and Jimmy's woman. She must be lying about being with Johnny, but I'll think about that tomorrow.

This morning, I awake to Johnny shaking me.

"Wake up sleepy head," he says, giving me that big smile of his.

"Look who's talking," I said, yawning and stretching all at the same time.

"Get up, get dressed, we have to talk," he says, slapping me on my behind after I turned on my side to try and get another little nap before getting up. I wanted to talk last night and he fell asleep on me with all his clothes on and I had to undress him and put some cover over him so he wouldn't get cold. I knew if he got cold he would wake up, it would ruin his sleep and then he wouldn't be in a good mood today, and I wouldn't be able to find out just what in tar nation is going on here. He's up and as far as I can tell, he's in a good mood, but I just want to sleep just a little while longer. Just ten more minutes would do me a lot of good, but I can see that's out of the question, when Johnny is standing over me waiting for me to get out of bed.

"What's the hurry. We've got all day," I say, trying to pull the covers over my head, while Johnny is now at the foot of the bed tickling my feet. I start to laugh and try to get my feet away from him, but he manages to keep up with my kicking, finding the bottom of my feet every time, and now I'm almost hysterical from his tickling me. I'm so exhausted from this whole thing, I jump out of bed and run for the bathroom and lock the door.

Once inside the bathroom, I splash cold water on my face. I can still see the steam in the mirror, where Johnny must have taken a shower earlier, while I was asleep. I find my tooth brush in the cabinet, where I left it last night and after putting tooth paste on it, I begin to brush away.

"Hurry up out of there. I told you I have to talk about something," he says, through the bathroom door, as I begin to rinse my mouth with water and start to gargle with mouth wash.

"Sounds like you're drowning in there," he calls out to me.

"I'll be out soon, I say, while taking the brush to brush my hair into place. I don't want to let myself go, now that I'm married like so many women do. I want to look good for Johnny every moment of the day and night. I don't ever want him to see me with a frizzy head and no makeup on. I will just die if he ever saw me that way, because he keeps himself so well groomed, from head to toe, I'm going to have to do the same for him.

Once out of the bathroom, he gives he a luscious kiss. I've been waiting for some attention for quite some time now. Being on the run puts a damper on ones love life. The main thing on our minds is staying out of jail and staying alive, thanks to his friends Jimmy and Sly, we're safe for now. This place is so heavily guarded no one can get inside the wall without being shot or mauled by the pinchers. The only thing is, I don't know why Jimmy and Sly have to have this much protection, but right now, I really appreciate the tight security that they have here. No telling what all Jimmy and Sly ain't into.

"How about I take you out to a club tonight," Johnny says, pulling me down onto his lap.

"Are you sure that's safe?" I ask.

"If you cut your hair and dye it auburn, no one will be the wiser," he says, pinching my nose just a little playfully.

"You want me to cut my hair?" I say, looking at him causatively.

"You need to change your appearance anyway, so as to throw off anyone who might have seen us on the news," He says, while tightening his arms around my waist.

"You're probably right. I'll dye it right away, but I don't have any dye."

"Just ask Carmen. I know she's got some dye around here somewhere. I know she wasn't born with flaming red hair."

"You want me to dye my hair that horrible color? If that's the case. The answer is no," I say.

"I'm sure she has other colors," he says.

"And how would you know that?" I ask, wanting to find out how much he knows about Jimmy's woman. I really wanted to ask him if she and he had been together like she said, but I figure this is not the right time for that now. I have his attention and I don't want to spoil it with talking about that wench, who is obviously jealous of me and Johnny's being married. I guess she wishes that Jimmy would marry her, and what's up with that anyway. Why don't he marry her? They've been together for years, so Johnny says, but I'm not going to worry about them now. I have to get as much of Johnny's attention as I can, while I can.

"Have you looked at her head. I know she wasn't born with that hair," he says, while laughing just a little, trying not to show his real disgust for her hair.

"Yes. I think her hair is rather cute," I say, trying not to let on that I simply loathe the woman.

"I'm sure you're probably the only one that thinks so. Looking at her hair makes my eyes hurt," he says.

"Well you better not talk about my hair after I dye it."

"You'll look good if your hair is purple."

"I'm glad you think so," I say, rubbing his head the way he likes me to and then we are so absorbed into each other, it's as if time stands still, and there is no one else in the world but the two of us and that's the way I like it most, having that secluded feeling of being on an island where no one can get to us and we can't see anyone but each other. We have to take these stolen moments when they come, because when we come back to reality, it's a hard and dangerous world we come back to, and that's why the fantasy land that we've created for ourselves, helps us to keep in tune with each other and to keep our sanity. It's our love that makes us strong.

It's after nine p.m., when we get into the long black limousine. Johnny, Jimmy, Sly, Carmen, Jimmy's woman and myself are headed for the night life in Atlanta. I'm wearing my fur coat with one of Carmen's skimpy dresses underneath it. I also have auburn hair and my hair is cut much shorter than it was this morning when I woke up. I kind of like my new look. I can see that Johnny likes it to. We're suppose to be going out on the town to one of Atlanta's most glamorous night clubs. I can deal with that, since we have not really celebrated our wedding, Johnny feels that this will be a way officially having a kind of wedding get together. I know he feels bad about the fact, that we have not been able to be alone and be on a honeymoon, just the two of us, but just as long as he's safe and I'm safe, I don't have any real qualms about it. I'm just happy that he is happy with me and that he is happy being with his friends for a fun time. Fun is a word that Johnny doesn't know much about, but I'll teach him to loosen up and enjoy life when the time comes.

When we get to the club, the valet comes around and opens the door for us. He also parks the limousine for us too. I have never been to a place like this before.

It must be nice to enjoy this kind of service as a part of ones lifestyle. Someday Johnny and I will live a luxurious lifestyle like his friends, Jimmy and Sly. I just don't know where they get all this money. I have heard that Atlanta is a good place for blacks to get ahead, so they probably know people with lots of money and that's probably how they got their money. I've always heard, it's not what you know, but who you know, and these guys must know some pretty wealthy people.

We get to a table that's for two and Johnny pulls out the chair for me, Jimmy, Carmen and Sly go to another table. The lights are dim, a live band is playing and the table is lit up with one candle. It's got to be the most romantic place I have ever seen. There are soft red and blue lights and beautiful royal blues, reds and purple wall colors with a dance floor in the middle of the room. I have never seen such elegance. The people were dressed in the finest of clothes, with the women in lovely sheik night dresses and the men in Taylor made suits that matched shirt and tie. There was a long bar on one side of the room that was made of plush black leather. It was definitely a place for Atlanta's elite population, because each chair at the tables were also made of plush black leather. I feel as if I'm queen for a night. Johnny is holding my hands in his large soft elegant hands and looking deeply into my eyes as the band is playing a soft melody, with the piano as the lead instrument. I wish this night would never end, but don't we all know nothing lasts forever. Another day will break with the dawn and it will be another day that Johnny and I will fear for our lives.

It wasn't long before Johnny and I were dancing to the soft slow music that the band was playing. The piano lead was just a glorious kind of sound. The sky was visible through the glass ceiling of the club, where you can see the stars brightly shining in the darkness of the night, as Johnny is holding me tight and whispering words of love in my ear. What a night to remember. I will always remember it being a very special night in our lives, and Jimmy Carmen and Sly seemed to be enjoying themselves at the other booth behind ours. I appreciate the fact that they are leaving Johnny and me to ourselves, so we can enjoy being on our honeymoon. We've had three hours of heavenly bliss together.

As the night progresses, I'm aware of some odd changes In mood by first Johnny and then the others. Sly has called Johnny into a corner, and Jimmy has now joined them, leaving Carmen at their both alone. The three men talk for a good ten minutes, and I can see that something is wrong. Johnny has taken one hand out of his pants pocket and is now running it through his curly hair. Jimmy and Sly are now looking at something or someone on the other side of the room. This is a sign that something is not like it's suppose to be, but what could it be. I quickly scope around the room to see if I can see anything that looks suspicious, but I can't distinguish anything out of the ordinary, except Johnny is now coming towards me at a fast pace. I quickly pick up my purse to be ready if something is wrong. When he gets to the booth where I am, he stands there with his back to the crowd as if to shield me from something. I look into his eyes, which tells me that something is definitely wrong.

"Jimmy has spotted one of the guys that he knows set him up in L.A. I want you to get up slowly and move around in front of me and walk casually to the door." He says calmly, and frightened, I do as he says. When we reach the front door of the club, I can see Jimmy, Carmen and Sly have already gotten the limo and are waiting inside. Johnny takes me by the arm and we go towards the car and just as we reach it, there are gun shots. Johnny quickly opens the door and shoves me inside and then gets in himself.

"What was that?" I ask almost in a state of shock, but no one would answer me.

"Was that them?" Johnny asks the others, while looking out the back window and pushing me down lower in the seat.

"That's them." Jimmy says, as he's driving like a bat out of hell and turning corners on two wheels.

"Johnny, what's happening?" I ask, in a very scared little voice.

"It's the pigs that set me up. It's three of them and they're right behind us."

"We've got to get back to the estate and barricade ourselves in case there a shoot out?" Sly tells everyone, and now I'm really scared. I never counted on this much action in my marriage when I was growing up in Lexington. I never in my wildest dreams thought I'd ever be in anything like this.

"Johnny," I say, wanting him to tell me what in the world was going on.

"Don't worry Callie. Everything is going to be alright," he says to me, as he is now almost covering me with his body down in the seat of the limousine.

"They're catching up," sly says, as he pulls out a sawed off shotgun.

"Drive man," Sly says, to Jimmy."

"What do you think I'm doing Sly? I've got the pedal to the floor man," Jimmy says, roughly.

"You got your gun Johnny?" Sly asks, from the front of the limo.

"Yeah, I got my piece," Johnny says, reaching into the inside of his coat and pulling out what looked to be a magnum 45, and the reason I know is because daddy had a gun collection and he taught me the names of about ten types of guns. Daddy loved his collection and he loved to hunt.

"Lose them jokers," Sly says to Jimmy.

"If you don't like my driving, then you drive," Jimmy says to sly, with a hint of real annoyance in his voice.

All of a sudden gun shots ring out from the car behind us, and Johnny is practically smothering me, trying to keep me down out of gun range. The next thing I know Sly and Carmen both are shooting back at the car behind us and the car swerves almost off the road. The streets are full of people as we're weaving in and out through traffic, and people are blowing their horns at us in disgust, as we continue down the streets of Atlanta, I also notice that now the police are after us, but the next thing I see is that the car behind us has turned off to the left and is now out of sight.

"Now the cops are on us," Jimmy says.

"Lose'um and fast," Johnny says to Jimmy.

"No one got hurt, did they?" Jimmy asks

"We're all alive and kicking," Johnny says to Jimmy, while letting me up from that awkward position he put me in a few minutes ago. He would have taken a bullet for me. Now I know he loves me, as if I didn't already know that.

a few minutes later we lose the cops and are headed to Stone Mountain to the estate. Sly says we're going to have to barricade ourselves in and keep watch all night, in case those men who were following us decide to pay us all a visit, but that there is little chance once we make it back that they will be able to come close enough to us, with all the security around the whole place.

"Step on it Jimmy. These guys ain't playing. I just hope we've lost them for good," Johnny says, with a bit of authority in his tone.

"Those are the guys that did the laundering, sold the drugs and stole drug money and set you up. With you alive to bust them, they think they'd better take you out before that happens." Says Jimmy, as he takes another sharp turn, and Sly is still pointing the sawed off shotgun out the window just in case they catch up to us. But you know what Johnny, crooked agents always get caught."

It's almost two a.m. when we get to the large wall where the gate will open with a code from the inside of the car to let us through. When the car enters the garage, we all get out in a hurry and go through the secret panel door, that leads into the basement corridor. Johnny, Sly and Jimmy, go up stairs to check around and leave Carmen and me in the basement. We're there for about fifteen minutes before they call for us to come upstairs and once upstairs, the three men scramble around to get more guns out of the gun case to load them, as we pull all the blinds and draw the drapes closed. We continue to move quickly around the house as if something is about to happen. I'm starting to wonder if they all know something that I don't know. As my mind wonders a bit, a light comes on. The truth is, they know that the men will come and they are preparing for a gun battle right from the house. Jimmy makes sure that the dogs are out on the grounds, and turns off all night lights surrounding the place. This is just too weird for words. It's a good thing that this house is secluded from other near by houses, because this way others won't get in the way of flying bullets. Johnny is giving me a quick lesson on how to use one of the semi-automatics. He wants me to be able to defend myself if need be. This is got to be right out of some movie, I just don't know how this one will end.

After getting ready, moving furniture, locking all doors, putting some of his men outside the house with walkie-talkies, they're ready. I'm behind a marble desk from the office with Johnny. We just sit and wait for exactly what, nobody knows. They're just being prepared for the worst.

"We're going to get out of this, Callie," Johnny reassures me, as he strokes my curly auburn hair and then kisses me on the cheek. I wouldn't think this was exactly the time for romance, but we don't know if we'll see each other again after tonight. At least that's what I'm thinking as my teeth start to chatter and my hands tremble.

"I love you Johnny," I say, with my teeth clicking together, and I can hardly get the words out.

"We'll make it, Callie. I promise you we will," he says, looking deeply into my eyes.

"I trust you," I say, with a half smile on my face, because Johnny has to know that I believe in him, or he might lose confidence in himself and then if that happens, we're dead meat. At least that's the way I calculate the situation.

After an hour and a half, we're still waiting. I'm getting so tired and sleepy, but none of us can sleep or are allowed to sleep. Every few minutes, the men take turns going outside to see if all the men stationed outside are still there. Each time they come back, everything is well on the outside so far. I am not ready to die now. My life has just began with Johnny and now it might be over before the night is over, but right now, I'm saying my prayers to God to save our lives. I promise God if you will just keep us all safe and get Johnny and me out of this, I'm going to go to church every Sunday. Please God, I promise and cross my heart and hope to die God, if I don't do it. Amen.

Just as I get the last words out, I hear gun shots. All the men run for the edge of the window to look out from behind the drapes. Jimmy is on the walkie talkie, trying to verify what is happening outside the house.

"They're out there somewhere. Let's go Johnny, Let's go Sly," Jimmy says, as the three men leave out the side door that leads to the pool area. I continue to huddle behind the marble desk and Carmen makes her way to me behind the desk, that I'm stuck behind like I'm stuck like molasses.

"Are you Okay?" Carmen asks.

"Yeah, I'm Okay," I say, still trembling.

"I just wanted to let you know that I lied about Johnny and me. You didn't say anything to him about it did you?" She asks, as she checks her gun for ammunition.

"No, I didn't mention it to him," I whisper and just then, I hear many gun shots ring out.

"Oh my God," I cry out.

"Keep quiet. You don't want to give away our position," Carmen whispers back to me.

"What is happening?" I ask.

"Don't worry. They're some of the best agents in the business. She says as she gets up to look out of the corner of the window with her gun in her hand.

Thirty seconds went by without any gun fire. Now it's like, all hell has broken loose. I can hear gun fire in rounds consistently. I run to the window to look out and all I can see is pitch blackness. Suddenly, I hear a loud noise back by the side door. It's as if someone is trying to get through it.

"Someone is breaking into the side door," I say to Carmen, and I pick up the semi-automatic to aim it in the direction of the side door, and Carmen comes toward me with her gun aimed at the door also. We can hear more shots outside. It sounds like the Fourth of July out there and we can see the fire from the guns briefly lighting up in the darkness.

Suddenly, we see all three men come through the side door, looking as if they are returning from a long hard battle.

"Johnny take the women and get out of here now," Jimmy yells to Johnny.

"I'm not going to leave you guys here like this," Johnny says firmly.

"The police will be here soon and you've got to get Callie out of here and take Carmen with you. She can get on a plane somewhere. Just Go. Sly and I can always say we got into it with some drug king pins or something, you know they want revenge for bustin'um or something, but you'll go to prison if they catch you here," Jimmy says, looking out of the curtain again.

Suddenly we hear sirens in the distance, and Carmen and I head for the garage door.

"We've got to go Johnny," I say, tugging on his arm. We can't stay."

Sly and Jimmy come over to Johnny and they all three embrace as if it might be the last time they see each other alive. The three men hate to part now that they are back together again, but it must be this way, for everyone's sake.

"Let's go Johnny,." Carmen said, in order to break up the men's embrace.

"Alright. We're out of here," Johnny says, and he starts toward the door where we are already waiting that leads to the garage where the Caddy is parked.

"We'll get'um for you Johnny. We won't rest until they're caught and your name cleared," Jimmy yells to Johnny, just as he's about to go out the door, and Johnny turns and looks at his two friends and then close the door behind us as we enter the garage.

All three of us get into the black Caddy, with Johnny and me in the front seat and Carmen in the back seat. In two seconds we're out of the garage and down to the gate. The gate magically opens and we're out onto the dark street, which looks more like a road to me than a street, and police cars are passing us on their way to where we just left. I don't know how long I can go on like this, but I guess it's better than sitting in jail. I just hope we escape without losing our lives, because we're on the run again. It was nice to be held up in a house like the one we were in, but it would be even better if we had a house like that and we weren't fugitives from the law.

It sounds like more gun shots in the distance. I hope the guys are alright. The police must be there by now. It's a good thing we left, because Johnny would never be able to clear his name sitting behind bars and people lying at his trial and that's exactly what would happen. They would lie to keep Johnny out of their way, so they could continue doing their dirty work, pretending to be honorable agents. Well if Johnny, and his friends have anything to say about it, they won't get that chance, and I'll never blame Johnny for any of this and when it's all over, we're going to be the happiest couple in the world, that is until we have some little Johnny's running around the house.

"Carmen, you Okay?" Johnny asks.

"I'm fine, just get us out of town in a hurry," she says, still looking out the window to see if we're being followed.

"What a night," I say, letting out a relieved sigh.

"Yeah, and I hope we don't have anymore of these, but I'm worried about Jimmy and Sly and the other guys," Johnny says.

"Don't worry about them. They have big connections in the police department. Let's just hope those men that came after us get caught and don't come back to get Jimmy and Sly, but if they did, they'd be up against more than they can handle. So don't worry," Carmen says, as she lights up a cigarette and slumps down in the back seat of the car.

"I need a nap," I say, laying my head back on the head rest.

"Go ahead baby. Try to get some rest. I got it," Johnny says, talking about he's good to go for driving while I sleep.

"I think I'll take a snooze myself," Carmen says, as she puts out her cigarette.

"Both of you get some rest, so you can take over for me in a few hours." Johnny says as he heads for Interstate 65, and none of us know where we're going to wind up. I do know this, that I don't want to go to anybody's jail. I need to do what it takes, to stay alive, but if going to jail means that I'm going to live, then I guess then, I would make that choice when the time came. I wonder if Johnny has anything at all in his mind about what it is we're doing and where in the world are we going now, because we need to hide out for awhile and lay low until we get our plan laid out smoothly. We need to get it all together and stick to the plan, and what is Carmen going to do. She can't stay with us because she's in enough trouble to last her for a long while, if she's caught with us.

I feel as if I'm drifting now off to sleep. I trust Johnny's driving, so it will be a good sleep for me. If the car stops, I know I will wake up. I can only sleep in a moving vehicle if it stops I'm definitely going to be alert as to what is the reason the car is stopping. I hope we don't stop soon. One day this will be over, and Johnny and I can lead a normal life. I know he's innocent and him and his friends will prove it. I'll go anywhere with Johnny for a long as I have to. Sometimes bad things just happen to good people and Johnny is good people. He didn't do those things that those other agents said he did. It was actually them that did the crimes and put it on my Johnny, and now he has to run for his life, and since I'm involved and we're married now, I have to run for my life too. This makes me miss daddy too, because he would tell me what I should do, but I don't know if I would do it, if it meant losing Johnny or giving him up, but if I could talk to him, I could tell him to pray for our safety. I was raised to live a good and disciplined life, with daddy being a pastor of his church since before I was born, but somehow since leaving home, nothing has turned out the way I've wanted it to, my heart has been broken and now somewhat repaired and my soul has been tormented from being separated from the spiritual inspiration that I've known since the day I was born. The joy I used to feel, because I knew I was doing what was right, but now I have lost my relationship with my creator. I've lost my first love. I was raised to go to church and serve God and I was happy then, but somewhere along this road, I have lost my way.

I slept for hours, when I woke up, Carmen was driving, Johnny was in the back seat asleep, and we were pulling into the parking area of Savannah Georgia's airport. I can't imagine what we are doing here, but I find that I don't ask as many questions as I used to. I just go along with the program.

"This is where I get off. I'm flying back to Atlanta. Jimmy told me to make sure you two were out of Atlanta and on your way to a good hide out." Carmen says as she parks the car.

"Thanks for everything," I say, and then lean over and give her a hug.

"Jimmy says to take this cell phone so he can keep in contact, but first find a good hotel somewhere and he'll contact Johnny as soon as he and Sly figure out their next plan for catching those guys that's trying to kill Johnny," she sighs, and then hands me the cell phone and a wad of money.

"Take care of yourself," I tell her, feeling as if we just lost our best friend.

"Hey, you two do the same," she sort of chuckles, as she gets out of the car.

Just as she entered the building, Johnny began to stir in the back seat. He sits up and stretches a bit before looking around him, not knowing where we are. He starts to get out of the car and finds his way behind the wheel of the car, and looking at me as if I owe him some explanation.

"Well, where are we and where is Carmen? She didn't run out on us did she?" He asks as he's getting out of his black leather jacket to make himself comfortable for driving.

"I'm afraid so, but she left Jimmy's cell phone and some extra cash, so he can contact us and keep us informed of the progress they're making in finding those guys, and to keep check on us to make sure we're safe," I say, trying to get it all out as quickly as I can to fill him in on the plan. Johnny likes to be in control and when he thinks he's losing it, he can get just a little impatient and a little scary too. He is just too big of a man to want to get him upset. Being six feet five inches gives a man a lot of advantages, like no one wants to see anyone of that stature lose their temper. That can't be a very pretty sight. Fortunately I've never had the privilege.

"Where did you say we were, again?" He asks, looking about him.

"I didn't, but we're in Savannah Georgia," I tell him, looking into his face to see what expression he would have behind that information I just gave to him.

"Sounds as good as any other town. I think we'll hold up here for awhile, find us a good hotel and make more plans for staying alive," he says, while looking into the rear view mirror. He's always checking his surroundings. I guess that's part of his FBI training, which also makes me feel a little more secure then if I was with just any old body.

"Sounds good to me. My body longs for a good hot shower and bed with fresh sheets," I said, laying back on the seat as if nothing is wrong in my life. I just feel so happy when I'm with Johnny, nothing can make me feel bad, not even the fact that we are in trouble up to our eyeballs. As long as we're together nothing can defeat us. We are going to get this thing straightened out somehow. It has to be that way, or our lives won't be worth a plug Nichol. Maybe this time Johnny and I can spend some real time together, because we don't have much to do at this point, but to wait for Jimmy and Sly to get the job done for us. At this point we're too hot to be seen anytime soon. This might give me a chance to know Johnny just a tad bit more. Even though I love him to death, I don't know as much about him as I would like to at this point in time. Maybe I'm just in too much of a hurry to get on with it, because relationships do take a lot of time to develop in the right way.

It's the afternoon, before we find the place that's a good three star hotel and also a bit secluded in between a grove of trees that you can't see from the road. It's the perfect place to hide for now, as we pull up to the front of the hotel, after driving through the trees that led to this very nice secluded place. Somehow, I feel like a two ton weight has been lifted off my back. I can almost breath freely and now I can probably relax for a while. Johnny and I put on our disguises, before going inside to get a room. We are still being heavily hunted, so we put on our disguises in case someone has seen the news and might recognize our true selves. When will this charade ever be over with?" I hope it's soon.

Before we get out of the car, I put on my long blonde wig, believe it or not and Johnny puts on a thick mustache, a cowboy hat and sunglasses. We do look totally different with our disguises on us. We go into the hotel to the service desk to get a room. Johnny and I both are looking around to see if anyone seems to recognize us, which I think that would be hard to do considering the fact that we are well disguised.

"Can I help you?" The man behind the desk asks the two of us, looking from Johnny to me, and from me to Johnny.

"We'd like a suite?" Johnny says, to my surprise.

"Are you sure? Our suites are two hundred and fifty dollars a night."

"I said I wanted a suite, didn't I?" Johnny asks the man, while pulling a big roll of money.

"Of course. We have a wonderful suite for you and the lady," the man says, smiling from ear to ear after seeing the large amount of money Johnny laid on the service counter.

"Here's the money, now where do I sign?" Johnny asked, with a touch of anger in his voice.

"Just fill these few lines out here and sign please," the man said, a little nervously.

"Can we have the keys now?" Johnny asks the man, while holding out his hand.

"Yes, of course. Have a pleasant stay sir," the man says, as he hands the keys to Johnny.

Once inside the suite, I quickly get out of my clothes and head for the shower. Johnny wants me to hurry, so he can shower and take a nap. He is dead tired from all that has happened and trying to heal from his wounds, which he hasn't been able to really rest and recuperate as he should. I'm just happy that we're in an out of the way place, which should give us some peace of mind for awhile. Hopefully we can clear our minds and enjoy each other for a change since being married only a few weeks ago. I am Mrs. Johnny Parker now, and I wouldn't trade that for the world.

Once we're both settled on the bed, Johnny calls for room service. He orders us a very lavish dinner and a bottle of wine. The television is on and it's just a couple of minutes away from the news, when the cell phone Johnny has so Jimmy and Sly can inform him of any progress, suddenly rings.

"Hello." Johnny answers with caution.

"Johnny, this is Sly. Jimmy says that I should check up on you. Are you two OK.?" He says on the other end of the phone and I can hear every word he is saying.

"Yep, we're just chilling at the moment. What's the scoop?"

"Well, after you guys left, the police showed up and those guys that tried to blow us away were long gone by the time the police got here. They asked us some questions about all the shooting, but Jimmy convinced them that the men came to his house to make the trouble, so being ex-agents and all they took his word for it."

"Is Carmen back there yet? You do know that she left us here in Savannah and took a flight out of here," Johnny says, as he listens for good news.

"Yeah, Carmen got back just a while ago. She's fine. Jimmy thinks he can get a go between to find out who those guys are, although we have a good idea, we're not sure yet. Jimmy says when he catches up to them, he'll make'um talk so you can get out of this mess," he says to Johnny.

"Thanks for everything Sly and tell Jimmy I owe him big time."

"You know us Johnny. We'll take care of everything for you. Stay low and wait for our call," Sly says, to Johnny and then hangs up the phone.

"Is everything alright?" I ask Johnny as I'm holding my breath.

"Yes, everything is fine for now. Try and relax. We have a long road ahead of us Callie," Johnny says, to me as he turns the television up so we can hear the news.

"Do we have to look at our mugs plastered all over the television screen Johnny? I'm really tired of looking at us. Those pictures are horrible. They make us look like some kind of hardened criminals or something. I know I don't look that bad," I say, as Johnny continues to look without taking his eyes off the television screen.

"Quiet," he whispers, as he continues to stare at the television screen.

"Look. You see that man right there," he says, pointing to a couple of agents on TV. Those are the guys we saw in Atlanta in the nightclub. Those must be the same guys that came to Jimmy's house that night. Those must be the guys that set me up for sure," he says, getting off the bed and beginning to pace back and forth.

"I'd better call Sly back and tell him what I just figured out."

"You don't have the number, or do you?" I ask hoping that he somehow knows it by memory.

"You're right. I don't have his number. Hopefully, he'll call back soon. He's got to get those guys, or I may have to do it myself."

"You can't risk being caught," I say, a little timidly.

"If they don't get them within a week or so, I'm going after them Callie."

"I hope it doesn't come to that, but if it does, I'll be right there beside you Johnny."

"That's sweet of you my love, but this is not the kind of job you need to be involved in."

"Well, I wish that Jimmy and Sly find them soon. I don't want to lose you now," I say, putting my head in my hands. Suddenly this is all becoming bigger than life. I used to think that I was the fragile dainty type, but now, it seems as if I've recruited myself into something far above my wildest dreams could ever take me, but it's all very real. Johnny and I are in a lot of trouble. I just hope that mama isn't worrying too much. I tried to comfort her when we spoke last. I think she believes that I had nothing to do with most of it, but the truth is I'm in way over my head, and Johnny, well this is his life. The life he's lived for the past seven years. It's seems that it's like a game to him. May the best player win, but can anyone win now? I just don't know.

When the food finally got to the room, I practically grabbed the food out of the young man's hands, threw him the fifty dollar bill and closed the door in his face. He was well compensated for bringing the food up to our room. The meals only cost thirty dollars and he had a twenty dollar tip.

I couldn't wait to sink my teeth into some real food. I ordered southern fried chicken with mashed potatoes and gravy with biscuits, and Johnny ordered fried cat fish with cold slaw and he washed his down with a mug of beer. I just had a soda to go with my meal, which is my favorite drink. We watched some stupid show on television. and before I knew what was happening, Johnny and I both drifted off into dreamland, because it had been days since we'd had a good nights sleep.'

It is two a.m. and Johnny and I are both up in the middle of the night. It seems that we went to sleep so early and now we can't sleep and since we can't sleep, we've discussed just what it is we're going to do here in Savannah Georgia. Johnny says we should find an apartment and get jobs. It won't be long before the money runs out. It seems as if no one really pays too much attention to anyone else around here, and we feel it's a good place to be for now. I can't imagine where we're going to find work and even if we do, we're going to have to stay in our disguises even while we're working.

After talking several hours, about what it is we're going to be doing here, we're both very tired once again. I try to stay up while watching one of the old time movies, when movies were movies, I find myself crying at the end of a very dramatic romantic kind of movie, that I wish there were more of these kind around. I love the kind of movies you can watch with your whole family and not feel embarrassed in front of your husband, mother, or children, which I plan to have some day. I just don't know when that day will be. Having children just seems to be the spiritual thing to do. I want as many as we can possibly afford, because we've got to have some little Callie's and little Johnny's running around the place that we decide to make our home.

It's so nice, just lying in Johnny's arms and listening to him plan our lives. He stops from time to time to ask me if I agree with him, and I say yes, because whatever Johnny wants, I want as well. He's such a gentle man. He's the kind of man I've been looking for most of my life. I thought that I would be with Scooter forever, until he came home from the armed forces already married. I thought I would never get over it. I was so embarrassed, because the whole town was talking about it and they all felt so sorry for me, and I would hardly come out of the house for days at a time, and when I did, I tired to hide my face with a head scarf, so people wouldn't stop me to give me their condolences, like somebody died or something, which is exactly how I felt, because I had so much grief built up inside of me and there was nowhere for it to go. There was no way for me to get rid of the pain I felt, except when I went to church on Sundays and I would pray that God would take that awful feeling away from me, and after about four Sundays, I felt a whole lot better. Today I have the greatest gift of all and that gift is Johnny. I never thought I would ever love anyone again, but I got a second chance at love.

Chapter 11

Johnny and I have moved out of the hotel and have gotten an apartment. Were both working in our disguises and getting along pretty well. Its the weekend, Saturday as a matter of fact, so Johnny and I are both home today. Johnny is being somewhat impatient about not being able to get to the guys who set him up. I have to do all I can to keep him from going after them himself. He says he will give it a couple of more weeks, if we last that long without getting caught, to see if Jimmy and Sly can find them and if that doesn't happen, he's back in the game of hunting them down himself. I personally hope that he never has to do that, because if he does, I'm in it with him all the way. I'm going to be just as involved in getting them as he is. He's not leaving me behind.

"Callie, hand me a towel," Johnny calls from the bathroom.

"Okay, I'm looking in the towel closet for some clean ones."

"How about we go to the state fair later this evening," he says, once I'm in the bathroom and handing him a towel, so he can get out of the shower.

"Sounds good to me. We need to do something fun for a change." I tell him, as he steps out of the shower with the towel rapped around his waist.

"Good, then that's what we'll do, go out and have some fun."

"What time are we going? I think I'll wear my new outfit", I say, speaking of the spring dress with the little jacket to match.

"We'll probably go around six o'clock this evening," he says, running his fingers through my hair, that I just got curled earlier this morning at the beauty salon. I don't know if I'm going to go there again, because she kept me under that hot drier for so long, I thought she was trying to cook my scalp. I finally had to turn off the drier myself, while she was gossiping so much, she must have forgotten all about me under that thing. The one thing I hate most is going to the salon. It is very painstaking for me. I'm really used to mama doing my hair, because she did fix it just about my whole life and she never burned me with the hot iron like you get burned at the beauty salon and they make out like it's your fault you got burned. You didn't hold your head still enough or you must have been nodding and your head dipped for a moment, but that's just to keep the blame off themselves, is what I say about it.

I'm going to read for the rest of the day and just relax until it's time to go to the fair. I remember when we used to go to the state fair right outside Metropolis Illinois. I used to be quite amazed at the mud wrestlers and the women wrestlers too. I had never really seen anything like that before, so it was quite interesting to me at the time. I was just a kid then, but now I don't care too much for the sport, since my favorite wrestler doesn't wrestle anymore. He got married and then he kind of left the scene for a while, but sometimes you might see him on some wrestling show, but not like you used to, for one thing he's a little up in age now and rich, so I don't see the sense in it now anyway, with all that money and a pretty wife at home. He's paid his dues to the sport of wrestling.

The cell phone rings while Johnny is in the kitchen fixing us something to eat. He cooks better than I do, so he doesn't mind doing the cooking, when we're not eating out. The time I made some chicken and dumplings, the dumplings was so gummy and sticky and the chicken wasn't all the way done, and the cornbread was so dry, me and Johnny both almost choked to death on it, and later that night Johnny was real sick, but tried to play it off as if it was something else that made him sick, but I knew it was the chicken and dumplings, and after that, he never let me cook again. We either go out to eat, or Johnny cooks for us, and I really don't mind, because I was so ashamed when I did cook and he got sick, I felt so bad for him, so I'm going to take cooking lessons before I cook again.

When I pick up the cell phone that's been ringing, while I'm thinking about my cooking, I find that Sly is on the other end. He sounds anxious to talk with Johnny. He sounds as if something could be wrong. What now? All this has got to end soon, or I'm going to have a nervous break down.

"Johnny, it's the cell phone. It's for you. It's Sly."

"Tell him to hold on and I'll be right there," he yells from the kitchen.

Johnny soon comes out of the kitchen I hand him the cell phone and he wipes his hands on the apron he has on. He has a worried look on his face, and that's something I rarely see, is Johnny looking worried. He is always so confident about everything and this causes me some concern as he takes the phone that I'm extending to him.

"Yeah. It's me," Johnny says into the cell phone, as he continues to talk, I can see beads of sweat starting to break out on his face. I can see that something is wrong as he starts pacing back and forth. Johnny and Sly talk for another five minutes and it appears that the conversation is getting more and more serious. I'm getting very impatient to hear what it is the two men are saying. I hope it's not as urgent as it seems, by the look on Johnny's face, I know that it is, and It will be just a couple of minutes before they end their conversation and Johnny will tell me what the problem is about.

"Johnny, what's wrong?" I said, as soon as he gets off the cell phone with Sly.

"Something serious has happened to Carmen."

"What. What's happened to her?" I ask frantically.

"They say the guys that's after me, kidnapped her and are holding her to make an exchange for me." He says, as he pounds his fist on the wall and luckily he didn't put a hole in it.

"How did they get her?" I ask, now very upset that this has happened to Carmen and that Johnny is going to be the skate goat and I know he won't stop at not finding the men that has Carmen.

"Sly says they got her coming out of a grocery store in Atlanta. But, he says for me to lye low, it's no sense in both of us getting taken by those thugs. I'm going to give it a couple of days and then I'm going to join Jimmy and Sly in trying to get Carmen back. But tonight, we're going out to the fair just as I promised," he says, looking at me through teary glazed eyes.

"I understand," I say, but I don't know how we're going to enjoy ourselves with all that has happened with Carmen and the fact that they want to make a trade, Johnny for Carmen is now the ultimate straw that breaks the camels back as far as I'm concerned. This thing is going from bad to worse and there is not a thing I can do about it, and I'm hoping that they get Carmen back soon. I don't want it to come down to them having to trade Johnny in to get Carmen back.

It's hard for us to really enjoy the rest of the afternoon. I'm trying to continue reading and Johnny is just very quiet sitting in front of the television. We haven't said much since the phone call from Sly. I suppose there isn't too much to say at a time like this. I feel that Johnny thinks it is his fault that this is happening to Carmen, but I say that the real culprits are the ones that's tearing up all of our lives for no good reason. Johnny and I haven't had a descent time together since we got married over a month ago now. Nobody is deserving of what these greedy men have put us through. I'm going to do my best to make it up to Johnny somehow, although I know it's not my fault, being Johnny's wife automatically makes me the one to have to make it better for him. I have to show him all the love that I can in a time like this. I'm doing my best, I just hope that Johnny will accept my love for him during this very awful and trying time. He has been pretty standoffish towards me some of the time and other times he willingly accepts my love and tells me how much he appreciates my loyalty.

"Callie, are you ready to go?" He calls to me, from the living room where he has been sitting in front of the television for hours, although I don't believe that he has really been watching it.

"Yes, I'm ready," I call back to Johnny with a little voice that says I don't want to show any authority in it, because this is not the time to be too pushy about anything.

"Let's go then," he calls back, with a little annoyance in his voice.

It doesn't take me long to finish getting ready. I don't want to stir anything up. I want to go out and have a good time with my new husband. We need a chance to enjoy each other. I'm happy that we're going to the fair. Maybe we can do some laughing for a change, but I'm feeling something about Johnny I hope I'm wrong about. I'll have to see what happens and I hope I'm dead wrong. Life is too short to spend it running and if I know Johnny like I think I know him, he's not going to let anyone get the best of him.

Even though it's early spring, I should have brought a heavier jacket for the night air. As we walk through the fair grounds, Johnny gives me his leather jacket. He has on a long sleeve shirt and swears to me that he is not chilled at all. He says it's my frail body that is causing me to be so cold all the time and insists on fattening me up some. I really wouldn't mind putting on a few pounds, since leaving Paris, my eating habits there have tried to stick with me, but Johnny is definitely helping me to work on changing that part of my life.

The fair grounds are getting even more crowded with people as we continue to stroll. The different rides are tempting to me. I haven't been in the bumper cars since I was fifteen. They always were my favorite ride. The large Ferris wheels are as scary to me as they always have been. The sound of music and carnival ride sounds, are beginning to be a familiar sound to my ears. All of the surroundings are bringing back good memories from when I went to the fair with Sarah and Genny. We always went everywhere together. I really do miss them and I know they are pulling for Johnny and me. I bet they thought I would never have wound up in this predicament. No, not in a million years, but I have and I don't regret being with Johnny for one minute. He means all-of the world to me.

"Let's get some cotton candy," I chirp, hoping I sound happy.

"Good Idea. I haven't had cotton candy since I was a kid," he says, laughing just a little, as we go over to where the cotton candy is being sold. There are lots of people in front of us waiting to get their daily dose of sugar, just as we are, hoping that the line goes rather quickly. I can just taste it melting in my mouth as we hold hands and looking at each other as if there is no one else in the world.

"I think I'll have a large cotton candy," Johnny says, like a little kid, but tonight we're both going to be kids and have fun like any other kid out here on the fair grounds.

"Make mine a small one," I responded.

"We should go on the Ferris wheel. We can see the whole town from up there," he says, pointing to the large object that takes you way up high and down again.

"That should be fun. Let's do it," I laugh teasingly, just a wee bit.

"Oh, so you think you're tough do you. I'll bet that you scream the whole time we're riding," he says, with a twinkle in his eye.

"We'll see who does the screaming," I say, slapping him on the arm.

A few minutes later we have our cotton candy and we're walking around for just a bit before we get on the Ferris wheel. We're enjoying looking at all the different people because we don't know them from Adam and that's what makes it so nice. No one knows who we are and we don't have to hide. The air is starting to warm up from the big bond fire outside the grounds and it makes for a very romantic atmosphere, because Johnny leans down and kisses me on the lips with cotton candy sticking from his lips to mine.

When we're done eating, we go towards the tall ride and wait in line for our tickets. We don't mind the wait, because we know it will be fun to act like a kid again. I don't ever remember feeling this happy before in my entire life. Me and Johnny together at the fair, makes me feel so heavenly. Together we can conquer the world if we can just get the chance to live normal healthy lives. Our love for each other will take us through this dilemma and all the obstacles that will ever come our way.

Once we're secured into our seat on the Ferris wheel, I start to feel a rush of fright coming over me. I don't want Johnny to know that, to my own surprise, I'm pretty scared to go up so high on this old thing that looks like it's seen it's last days and maybe in the age range of one hundred years old. I hadn't noticed how old this old thing looked before I got on.

"You Okay?" Johnny asks.

"Yeah, I'm fine," I say, with a weak voice.

"Come on. It's going to be fun." Johnny says, trying to make me feel better about this ride.

"Whee," I say, trying to fool Johnny into thinking I'm excited about the whole thing.

"Up we go." he says, as the Ferris wheel starts moving.

By the time we get to the top everyone on the ride was screaming. It went to the top so fast, I could hardly catch my breath and I thought I was going to be sick, then all of a sudden we're going down so fast, it must be going about fifty miles per hour or better. Johnny is trying to keep his cool, but starts to yell like all the rest of us, when we start to go back up so fast again.

"I thought you were so brave," I yell loud, so Johnny can hear me.

"I'm getting too old for this," he yells back at me.

"Oh, I can't take it anymore," I scream and laughing all at the same time and thinking that this is more fun than I thought it would be.

Now we're going down again and Johnny and I are holding on to each other for dear life. We're both screaming to the top of our lungs at this point and enjoying every moment of it. Somehow, I know that this night will end and we'll be back to the real world, but until then, we're having the time of our lives and can't wait to get on more rides, play all the games and eat more food. I have a real taste for a chilidog with lots of cheese.

"Let's play the game where you throw the darts at the balloons to win a prize." I love that game and it's so hard to win at any of them, but I still like to play them.

"Whatever you like my queen."

"Thank you my king."

"This way to the game of your dreams."

As we're walking through the crowd, it's dark out, but it's lit up with the activities, as if it's some kind of festival with pretty colored lights and magnificent florescent lights, as me and Johnny make it through the crowd there are other couples holding hands and small children holding onto their parent's hands and literally dragging them to different rides and when we stop to get a chili dog, we get to sit down at a small table with two chairs to eat our food and drink a soda. I'm surprised Johnny is drinking a soda and not having a beer, which is always his favorite drink.

As we continue to eat and watch the crowd, a man on stilts walks by and there are clowns running along behind him. The stars are so bright in the sky, which makes it a perfect evening for love.

"I hope you are having a good time my dear."

"I most certainly am enjoying myself with my new husband."

"My love for my new wife is far beyond the farthest star in the sky."

"We must be the happiest couple in the world at this very moment," I whisper in his ear.

"That we are my sweet," he says, taking my hand and kissing it gently.

As we sit there looking up into the sky and holding hands, I notice something strange as I turn to look at Johnny. He is aware that I'm looking at something and then he turns and looks in the same direction that I'm looking in. When he sees what I see, the expression on his face turns to ice and I know that what I see, is the danger he sees. He sits still almost frozen with eyes fixed on the two men moving slowly through the crowd and getting closer to us.

"Lets' move," he says, taking my hand and leading me very quickly up out of our seats and into the vast crowd, that is suppose to swallow us up from any harm or danger.

"Who are those men?" I ask, while still in flight.

"Those are the guys that's after me," he says, while practically dragging me through the crowd.

"I thought they were looking at us suspiciously," I said, almost out of breath.

As we're running through the masses, Johnny still has me by the hand and we're weaving and dodging in and out of the crowd, and then all of a sudden I find that we're running toward this canvas tent on the edge of the fair grounds. The next thing I know, we're inside the tent. There are lots of people inside the tent, and there seems to be a man up front that is preaching to the crowd about hell and damnation.

"You don't want to go there. It's hot in hell," the preacher is saying to the people, who are sitting in folding chairs and listening intently to what the man is saying.

Johnny and I slide into two of the chairs close to the front and sit there hoping that the men don't come in and find us.

"Sit very still Callie and don't turn around."

"Are they here?" I ask under my breath, too afraid to speak any louder.

"Yes. They're in the back looking through the crowd."

"Have they spotted us?"

"No. They're still looking," he says, without moving his lips.

The man preaching is now aware that the two men are in under the tent and beckons for them to come up front.

"Come up here young man. I can see you need the salvation of God."

The two men stare at each other and then leave the tent to our surprise, but Johnny and I sit still in our seats with a crowd of people surrounding us in a way that we could very well not have been seen, but two minutes later the preacher is preaching more about hell and is starting to invite the people up to the alter as he put it, to get saved. As the people start to move out of their seats, we spot the two men coming back in under the tent, and just as we spot them, Johnny takes my hand and he leads to the front with all the crowd behind us coming up and surrounding us as we are right in front of the preacher and stooping down some, so that the men won't see us.

"Do you want to be saved tonight from your sins and find peace and love in God?" The man asks and then all the others say yes, they want to be saved.

I want whatever is going to bring some peace to me and Johnny. Being raised as a preachers daughter, I was taught all about living the good life, but somewhere along the line, I've lost my way. I do want peace and joy back in my life. I want to do what's right, but I don't know how to get there anymore.

Johnny and I are in so much trouble, and it must be God, that we're still alive.

The preacher is telling everyone to pray the prayer to be saved. Johnny is standing there, but looking around from time to time to see if the men are still in the tent. The crowd is pretty much hiding us from the men that's after us. We're standing up close to the preacher and the rest of the crowd that came up to the alter is behind us. I'm hoping that we are unable to be seen in the crowd and the men don't spot us. We used to go to tent meetings all the time, when I was a girl and the preacher would scare me so bad, I said I would never go to another one again in my life and here I am in a tent meeting and the evangelist preacher is saying that I'm going to hell if I don't repent. What could it hurt if I say the prayer and repent of my wrong doings. No one will ever know, and who knows, God just might help me and Johnny out of this whole mess, so I say the prayer with the rest of the crowd, not out loud but in my mind. Johnny is standing next to me, but he is too interested in the men, that are after us looking around continuously to make sure we haven't been detected in the vast crowd that had to come to alter to be saved. The main thing is now, how do we get out of here and back to the apartment without being caught by these killers who are out to get us.

As soon as we're done saying the sinners prayer and getting saved, and it was no play thing to me, I really want God to save me and Johnny out of this horrific calamity we're in, and we go back to sit down with the biggest portion of the crowd in front of us. After sitting down, we sort of scoot down in our seats again trying not to be noticed. There is only one way out of the tent, and that's the way we came in and the way the men came in, who might be standing outside waiting for us to exit the canvas covering. Johnny is squeezing my hand as we sit there, trying not to look as if anything is wrong, and I can tell that the wheels in Johnny's head are turning fast to figure out how we will get out without being seen.

When it's all over, the masses start to file out of the tent's opening. Johnny takes my hand again and we go in another direction. I'm wondering what he is up to.

"We're taking a different way out," he says to me, while pulling me in another direction from the one the crowd is taking.

"I think the men must still be out there," I say.

"That's why we're going to crawl out from the back of the tent," he says to me, as he's pulling me along behind him.

"I'm going to get my new outfit all dirty." I just got this beautiful dress and jacket to match and now I'm going to filthy it up by crawling under the tent, where there is nothing but red clay dirt. It certainly reminds me of home, where there is nothing but red dirt for miles. I remember it well.

"It's that or die. You want to save your dress or your life?" He says to me, pulling me even harder now, as if I might resist. Even Johnny knows I have a stubborn streak in me.

"I think I want to live," I assure him, as I pick up my pace.

Once out of the tent, I'm right about my dress. It's practically ruined with red clay dirt and we're running now towards the car to get away as fast as we can. I can hardly keep up with Johnny who still has me by the hand and dragging me behind him as fast as my legs can carry me. The car is at least within sight now, which hopefully we'll be inside soon and away from the fair. How those men found out we were at the fair is going to have to be figured out, so they can't find us again, although now they know we're in the area, we may have to quit our jobs and lay low to keep them from finding us again. Somehow we're going to have to make them think we are no longer in Savannah. I know Johnny will think of something. He always does.

After we safely make it back to our little apartment, we both almost collapse onto the bed. We lye on the bed side by side trying to get our breath and to get some of the tension to recede. We lye there saying nothing, but I can see that Johnny is engaged in some very deep thinking.

"Well, we made it out of that one," he sighs, as he's looking up at the ceiling.

"That was a close one." I sigh, as I'm looking up at the ceiling as well.

"Now I suppose we have to lay low. We can't go back to our jobs, or they'll find us for sure."

"What should we do?" I ask.

"I don't know yet, but whatever we do, we're not leaving the apartment except for going out for food and other necessities."

"Do you suppose Carmen is all right? You don't think they've hurt her do you?" I'm really concerned about Carmen at this point. We haven't heard from Jimmy or Sly concerning her and I think Johnny is worried too.

"Carmen has plenty of good survival skills. I just hope she uses them right. She could possibly talk them into letting her live if she can convince them that they need her."

It's been a week since we went to the fair. Johnny and I haven't been doing anything, but holding up in the apartment watching television, for any news about how close the police and the other agents are to finding us, and so far they have no clue as to where we are, and we've been eating lots of pizza and Johnny has been drinking lots of beer, to wash the pizza down. Frankly, I think he just likes the stuff. He has beer with every meal and then when he's not eating, he drinks it. I tell him that we're different now, and he claims he'll quit the beer after today.

I'm also bored stiff from sitting around all day with little or nothing to do. The weather is nice and it's really too nice to be sitting in the apartment. I'll probably take a nap to try and pass the time away, I'm so bored, I'm almost lethargic.

"I'm going to go out and get some stuff, Callie. I'll be back in a little while."

"Don't take too long. I'll get worried."

"Looks like you're sleepy. Take a nap and by the time you wake up, I'll be back."

"Maybe I will take a little one."

"What do you want me to bring you?"

"Bring me some soda and some chips."

"Will do."

As Johnny leaves the apartment, I can feel myself being even more tired and sleepy. It's probably all the stress that has built up in me that's making me suddenly so tired. I want to stay awake until Johnny returns, so that I know he's all right, but the tiredness is getting the better of me. I know mama, Sarah and Genny must be worried about me. They know I'm a survivor, but they are probably praying that I do survive this mass situation I've gotten into. I feel kind of light headed or like I'm spaced out or something. I might be going crazy for all I know, but until I wake up, I won't worry about that. Right now all I need is sleep.

When I awaken I look at the clock. It's been several hours since Johnny left and he's not back yet from the store. I jump up and look out the window to see if I can see him coming or, if I can see the car. I don't see him or the car. At this point I start to panic. Where is he and what could have happened to him. I hope he hasn't been caught by the police or killed by those corrupt agents, I'm thinking as I begin to pace back and forth. I probably need to turn to the news channel and see, if there has been any new developments in our case, or really to see if Johnny has been caught. As I turn the television. on, I start to switch channels quickly trying to get to the right channel as fast as possible. My patience is very short at this moment. I have to know where Johnny is, but I truly hope he has not been discovered and I don't remember if he had on his disguise or not.

After making several local calls, I'm really worried now. How could this be happening? How could he just disappear like this. I have to get a hold on myself, I'm trembling and shaking all over. I can't live without Johnny. He's all I have. He's my husband and I want him with me, not in some prison or dead. He doesn't deserve this, because he's innocent and It's just not fair, and now suddenly I have this knowing feeling that Johnny has done what I'd hoped he wouldn't do. I'm beginning to think that he has gone to Atlanta to help Jimmy and Sly get Carmen back, or he just might have gone after those guys that framed him to clear his name and get us out of this mess. He could not have done this without me. If he's gone to Atlanta, how could he have gone without me. He's probably trying to make sure that I'm safe and not get me involved in such a dangerous mission.

A few minutes later, I find the answer to it all. Johnny has left me a note on the refrigerator, telling me that he has gone to Atlanta to help Jimmy and Sly find Carmen. He says that he just can't sit by and let this happen without him being there to help. He feels he is the blame for Carmen getting caught by those bad agents and that he feels that he is responsible for helping his friends find Carmen. Well he's not leaving me behind either. He should have known that I would not sit still and just wait until this was over. I'm going to Atlanta too. As soon as I gather a few things I'm going to hit the road.

When I get to the rent-a-car service, I rent and maroon Chrysler to get me to where I'm going. The man is giving me the papers to sign, so I sign them and I'm out the door to where the car is parked.

I get in and then realize I don't know how to get to Atlanta, so I run back in to see if I can get a map.

"Do you have any maps?" I ask the man behind the counter, who just rented me the car.

"Sure. That'll be six dollars."

"Don't you have any maps that are a little cheaper than six dollars?" I ask the man, in my most annoyed tone of voice.

"No, I'm sorry we don't."

"Alright. Give it to me," I say, throwing the money on the counter and grabbing the map and practically running out the door, because I left the motor of the car running and all I need now is for someone to steal the car I just rented and haven't even used yet. The way my luck has been going, it wouldn't surprise me in the least bit. All my life, it seems as if I've had to work twice as hard for things, when other people could just have things to just fall into their laps. Why is all this happening to me. Lord only knows why I'm destined to live life the hard way. Before I left Lexington I had lived a good and comfortable life at home with my parents. Now since, I left home almost a year and a half ago, my life has taken so many twists and turns, sometimes I don't know whether I'm coming or going, but right now, I'm going after my man and nothing can stop me from that.

Once inside the car, I laid the map out on the front seat, trying to find the route from Savannah to Atlanta. It doesn't take me long to see which route to take. I've always been good at reading maps. As long as I have a map, I'm in good shape, and when I get there I'm going to have a fit on Johnny's behind for leaving me alone like this to worry about him. Men are such unpredictable creatures. You think you know them and bam, you find out you don't know them the way you think you did at all. I'm going to have to punish Johnny for this one. If I don't, he'll pick up and do this anytime he feels like it. He's got to know that this is a no-no. Mama was right. You've got to train'um or they'll walk right over you. At this point, it looks like I'm the one being trained, not the other way around.

From what I can tell from the map, it's only going to take me a few hours to get to Atlanta. I figure I can handle that. I'm almost to the interstate that will take me there. I can see the sign that says Atlanta Georgia. As I'm making my way to the highway, I remember that I have the cell phone in my purse, that Jimmy gave to Johnny. It has to have a call back number on it. I'll call it as soon as I get a chance to see if I can reach them. How lucky can I get, although my luck hasn't been running so good lately, well almost never this good and after looking at the gas hand, I'm going to have to stop at that station just up ahead before I actually get on my way. I hate stopping for gas. I wish I had checked to gauge earlier. I'm so ready to get on that highway. Johnny should have known I wouldn't wait and that I would try to find him.

As I pull up to the pump for gas, I carefully put on my red wig. I don't want to be recognized, which is another reason Johnny should not have left me. Now, if I get caught by the police, which is something that just crossed my mind. I'm so in a hurry to find Johnny, I almost forgot I have to be very careful about getting caught myself. The station looks empty enough. I can probably get the gas without a lot of people to see me. I will just get some chips and soda, like I told Johnny to bring me and he didn't show up and is now probably in Atlanta by this time, which is a good time to call the number to Jimmy's house, that I found on the caller I.D. system.

"Hello," the man says, after I call the number and the voice sounds like Sly's voice.

"Hello. This is Callie. Is Johnny with you and Jimmy. He told me that he was going to Atlanta?"

"Yeah, he's here. I'll put him on."

"Hello Callie. I thought I told you to stay home and wait for me," Johnny says harshly to me and I don't know why, because he's the one that's in the wrong. Of all the nerve.

"I can't believe you did this Johnny. Leaving me in Savannah alone."

"Me and the boys are on to something and I need you to stay out of sight until I get back."

"I'm on my way there Johnny," I say, as I start to pump the gas into the car.

"What do you mean, you're on your way, Callie?"

"Just as I said. I'm on my way to Atlanta now."

"Are you sure you know the way?" He asks, now knowing that I'm not going to take no for an answer.

"I have a map and I'm on my way there now, as soon as I finish pumping this gas."

"How are you getting here?"

"I have a car."

"I rented one. Now what's the address? You never should have left me here in the first place," I say, with some anger in my tone of voice.

"It's 2356 North Silver Stone Drive. And Callie, I'm sorry for leaving you. You're right. I should have talked this out with you, but I thought you would wait for me to get back"

"You're not leaving me Johnny. We're in this thing together," I say, wishing I could just give him one big swat up side his head for doing this to me.

"Just get here quickly, because me and the guys have something to do in a few hours, and I need you to be here and in a safe place before we do what we have to do," he says, now letting me know in his own tone of voice that he is serious about what he has to do and he doesn't want me interfering with the plan by my being late.

When I get to Atlanta later in the evening, I can't believe the many freeways I'm going to have to conquer. I'm going to first have to get off and find someone who can point me to Stone Mountain. This looks pretty confusing to me. All the crisis cross highways is giving me a headache. I'd better get there before Johnny's deadline or I'm going to be in trouble with all the guys. They've probably got a lead as to where they can find Carmen and if I mess that up. They're all going to string me up.

After stopping at a convenience store, I get the directions I need to get to Stone Mountain. I drink my soda and eat my chips as I'm trying to drive. Atlanta is something to see. I've never seen so many black folk in one place before. It's large and spread out and very green with tall trees that seems to reach to the sky. It's as if nature has been very well preserved in this part of the country. I take off my red wig as I continue to drive. I hate wearing that thing. It makes my head so hot and sweaty. I just like my own hair. I just want my good life back again. I'm going to let Johnny have it when I see him. He had better never do this again. Here we are wanted fugitives and he leaves me out to fend for myself. Now he says he's sorry. He will have to start thinking before acting, now that he is married.

As I drive up to the large walled fence around the property, I'm relieved that I made it safely to the house where Jimmy, Sly and his men live. I can see a camera looking right at me as I drive up to the gate to ring for entrance. I ring and immediately the gate opens and

I drive up the winding driveway to the large secluded house surrounded by gigantic trees. I can also see Johnny standing on the luxurious spacious veranda, waiting for me as I wind my way slowly up to the mansion. I tell myself that I'm going to be calm and loving when I get to where Johnny is standing. I continue my way up the drive and slowly stop the car close to the veranda. Johnny comes toward me, as I get out of the car.

"Why did you leave me like that?" I yell at him.

"I didn't want to put you in any danger, Callie," he says to me trying to keep a calm demeanor.

"I was in danger without you," I continue yelling at him.

"I don't have time for this now," he says, turning to go into the house.

"You better have time. I'm in this just like you are Johnny," I say, running behind him and striking him in the middle of his back.

"What's wrong with you? We've got to find Carmen, after all she put her life on the line for us. Remember?" He says as he's holding my arms to keep me from striking him.

"That's no excuse for leaving me." I tell him now trying to kick him, because he's holding my arms too tightly for me to hit him.

"What's all the racket out here?" Sly says, after appearing onto the veranda and looking surprised to see me.

"Ask your buddy here," I say, still trying to break Johnny's grip on my arms.

"What have you done to the pretty lady?" Sly smiles at Johnny, as if it's some kind of joke between the two of them.

"I've got it under control," Johnny says to Sly.

Johnny practically drags me into the house, up the stairs and into one of the bedrooms. I start to cry, because I'm feeling as if I'm obsolete to Johnny right now.

"You're a spoiled brat, but it's all good, because I'm the one that spoiled you," he says, taking me in his arms and kissing me passionately.

I almost try to break free, but I don't and kiss him back. I'm never going to let him out of my sight again. At least not while we're wanted fugitives. I almost went crazy with worry about him and he didn't even tell me he was leaving. He just left me a note. That is not acceptable to me and I think he knows not to do anything like this again.

"You could have been stopped by the police or anything. You had me worried sick," he says, while brushing away the tears from my eyes.

"Well you had me worried too, you know. So worried I had to come find you," I said, as I now go to sit on the bed, because I'm exhausted from all the worry and driving.

"I won't ever leave you again," Johnny says, as he sits beside me and takes my hands in his hands, and kissing me on the forehead, as he often does.

Later that evening I find out from Johnny that they know where Carmen is being held. Some undercover agents have tipped them off. The plan is to bust in at an unexpected time and try to rescue Carmen. They know that she's still alive, they just don't know what condition she's in. I not thrilled about what is about to take place, but I know there is nothing that will stop them from rescuing their fellow agent and Jimmy's woman. I still find it hard to forgive her for telling me that she and Johnny had been together, and then later confessing that she had lied about the whole thing. From what I can gather, she's being held at some warehouse in Atlanta, not far from the club we had patronized the last time we were here. Jimmy is totally irate and swears to kill those guys that's holding her there. The one name I keep hearing is Cortez. It seems that he is the one who's behind this whole set up. He's the one who is running the ring that all the corrupt agents are involved in. He's also the one who set Johnny up and tried to have him killed. Cortez knows that Johnny, Jimmy, Carmen and Sly all worked together in the past, before Jimmy and Sly retired. He knows he's going to have to make a deal with the men, to keep them from killing him. That's why he's holding Carmen, so he can bargain her to try and get his own life spared. He knows that Jimmy and Sly will get him for what they've done to Johnny.

Around twelve-thirty a.m., I awake to voices in the hallway. Johnny is not on the bed beside me. Soon the door opens and I can see Johnny standing there in the doorway talking to Sly and then he enters the bedroom, where I am sitting up, waiting to hear from him exactly what is going on. He goes over to the window and lights a cigarette and then he suddenly puts it out, without taking a draw off it. I'm wondering what's up with that. He knows I'm waiting for an explanation. He slowly puts his lighter back into his pants pocket and turns towards me.

"We're going after Carmen tonight. Jimmy and Sly have gotten an inside tip as to her whereabouts. We're not sure of what kind of physical state she's in, but we're going to be leaving within the next fifteen minutes."

"Then, I'm going with you," I manage to get out, hoping that Johnny won't deny me my efforts in helping to bring back Carmen.

"No. You have to stay here where you'll be safe. I couldn't bare it if anything happened to you. My life would surely be over if anything happened to you."

"I won't be in the way. I promise. I can be of help. I can possibly go in ahead of you guys. Pretending I'm lost, or pretending that I'm a prostitute or something. Think it over. I can probably pave the way for the rest of you. You've got to let me try. I won't let you go without me," I insist.

"You might have something. Let me talk it over with the guys and see what they have to say about it. Are you sure you want to do this Callie?" He asks, looking me straight in the eye as if he's trying to find any hint of fear or uncertainty.

"Yes, I'm sure."

"Wait here," he said, as he goes toward the door and goes into the hallway, and while he's out there I can over hear him and the others discussing a plan, but I can't quite understand what it is they are saying about me and if they will let me do this. Johnny knows that if my mind is made up, he might as well let me do it. He's afraid I might just show up on my own.

Once he's done talking with the guys and he's back in the bedroom, where I'm anxiously waiting, he comes over and sits on the bed beside me.

"The guys have a plan. They've agreed to let you go and the plan is, you're to go into the warehouse and pretend that you're lost and just stumbled in off the street. You tell them that you're lost and don't know exactly where you are. You'll be wearing your disguise, in case they've been watching the news. We don't want them to know who you are. If they discover who you are, we're dead Callie. Are you sure this is what you want to do?"

"Yes. Where you go, I'm go," I say sternly, trying to be as convincing as I can, that I know what I'm doing.

"We'll go over the plan again once we're in the van. You'll have a wire on you, so we can hear what is going on and you're going to say something that will signal us to come in. You've got to be able to stay in long enough to find out where Carmen is being held. When you feel it's right for us to bust in, you'll give us a phrase such as..."

"Such as, I just broke a nail. How about that?" I ask.

"Sounds good. When you want us to bust in, you say, I just broke a nail, and Callie, be careful, he says, stroking my face gently. I don't want to lose you."

"Don't worry. That ain't going to happen."

Once inside the van, they wire me up and go over the plan as we travel to Atlanta. I can tell the guys are more nervous then I am. I keep assuring them that I can do it, and they give me a forty-five magnum, strapped under my blouse and a bullet proof vest, which all of it is covered with a black long length leather coat and I'm also wearing silk pants for moving around easily in case I have to run for my life, and some black knee top boots, with rubber souls with crevasses to help me to be a little more sure footed, to keep from easily falling down. This whole scene is right out of some movie or something. When I left home to become a model, I had no idea where fate would lead me, but surely I never thought it would take a path like this one. I love Johnny so much, that whatever he's in, I'm in and believe me, at this point, we're in over our heads. If the police don't catch us, the bad agents might do us in, although I'm thinking positive right now, because if I don't, I might not be thinking anything on God's green earth again.

Forty minutes after leaving the house, we're inside Atlanta and sitting a quarter of a mile away from the warehouse, where Carmen is supposedly being held hostage. I'm starting to get a little nervous now that the time is near for me to exit the van where Johnny and the others will be waiting and listening for their cue to storm the warehouse. Johnny is looking at me to see if there are any signs of me wanting to back out of this extremely dangerous and curious predicament. I look back at him with a steady gaze to assure him that I'm alright with the plan. We've gone over and over the plan all the way here. Just as I'm about to step out of the van to become an imposter, Johnny takes my hand and kisses it and Jimmy and Sly, and the others seemingly lower their heads as if they almost know I'm not coming back alive. I have to do this, if it will soften things for the guys to break in and get both Carmen and me out safely.

Five minutes later I'm knocking on the large panel door to the warehouse. I don't know what I will meet when someone comes to answer the door. My knees are knocking together as I try to keep my composure. Nothing is happening and this is making me even more nervous and just as I'm about to give up, a small opening in the door slides back and I hear a man's voice.

"Who is it and what do you want?" The voice asks gruffly.

"I'm lost and don't know where I am," I say, with a weak voice.

"Just a minute," the man says.

I'm standing here with the wire on my person, and a small earphone to hear any instructions that Johnny and the guys want to give me. Up until now I hear nothing. This means that I'm to continue with the plan. I can see the moon shining on the river in the darkness. It's like a florescent light beaming down on the river. It seems like forever, since the man told me to wait. I just hope I can pull this off without getting us all killed. I have to get to where Carmen is so I can inform the guys as to how to get in and how to get to Carmen, once they're inside. It's going to take a lot of skill on their part to get past the men and get to Carmen and take her out.

The door opens, and all at once I find I'm being snatched inside by my coat collar. My feet are almost off the floor. The man is big and burley looking with some facial hair that is trimmed neatly around the top of his upper lip and his chin.

"Callie, are you Okay?" I hear Johnny's voice in my ear- piece.

"Okay, Okay, there's no need for all this," I say, trying to signal to Johnny that I'm still good, so far. The man still has me by the collar and pulling me down the entrance way into a large space, where I can see other men sitting around a table all dressed in expensive looking suits, who seem to be playing some sort of card game.

"What did you find Sam?" One of the men asked the big burley man.

"It's a woman, Mr. Cortez." The man says, still holding onto my collar.

"Bring her over here, so I can get a look," the man Called Cortez is saying, while I start to remember that Johnny and the others seem to think it was a man named Cortez, that set Johnny up in the first place and the man that they are trying to catch, so that this man Cortez, can clear Johnny.

The big guy named Sam, pushes me towards the table, where the men are sitting and once I'm in full view of the man Cortez, he looks up at me.

"What are you doing here?" He asks me, as he takes a puff off his cigar.

"I'm lost," I say, with a tremble in my voice.

"What are you doing way out here? There's no reason for you to be out this far," he said, flipping the ash from his cigar into an ashtray.

"I told you, I'm lost. I don't know how I wound up here. I must have taken a wrong turn. I'm not familiar with the area," I say, wishing that, I am convincing the man named Cortez, that I'm lost.

The other men at the table are just sitting there with cards in their hands waiting for this Cortez man to get through with me, so that they can continue the game. I'm starting to shake pretty bad now, but not to the point that I will lose control. I'm surprised that they haven't tried to search me. They must pretty much believe my story, after all, who on earth would dare attempt to intrude on these men. They have to be very confident of themselves, to overlook such a detail as frisking me.

"Take her in the back," Cortez says, to the big man named Sam.

"Let's go lady," the man says, to me giving me another nudge towards a hallway that leads to another part of the warehouse.

"Where are you taking me?" I ask the man named Sam.

"Shut up and keep walking" he says.

"Callie, keep cool we hear you. Maybe you can find out exactly where Carmen is located?" Johnny says into my ear- piece. I just wish I could say something to him to let him and the others know the lay out of the building, but first I have to see where it is they are taking me and if I can find Carmen.

"Why are you taking me down this hallway? Where does this lead to?" I say, trying to give out as much information as I can at this stage.

"It might lead to your destruction, if you don't shut up, or I might just turn you over to Nick," the man says nastily.

"Be quiet Callie and see where you're going, then try to give us more information," I hear Johnny saying in my ear.

Soon the man Sam opens a door to a small room and pushes me inside. Now I'm alone and don't know what to do next. I'm going to have to talk to the guys to find out just what to do, because now, I'm incapacitated. I feel knots in my stomach and now I'm really starting to get scared, because I don't know what they have in mind for me. I thought I would be able to talk them into trusting me a little better, so that Johnny and the others could storm the place, but now it looks as if it's going to take a lot more to finding Carmen and getting her out and myself as well. I might have bitten off more than I can chew, at least for the moment. It could be that Carmen is not even here at this warehouse. She's got to be here, or we're all going down a one way street.

"Johnny, they've put me in a room. There's not much I can do now."

"How many are here?" He asks, in into my ear.

"It's six of them. Four are at the table playing cards and another one is the man who opened the door and put me in this room and there's one more, but I don't know where he is. I just keep hearing them talking about Nick. I don't know if he's with Carmen or exactly where he is."

"We're going to have to come in if you don't find her in the next thirty minutes. We can't take the chance of anything happening to you," Johnny says firmly.

"Just give me some time. I'll think of something," I say, back into my mouth piece that's on the inside of my collar, that I was afraid would come loose and I wouldn't be able to talk to the guys.

"You got thirty minutes Callie, or else we're coming in. I know you're in a room down the hallway."

"I've got to locate Carmen first. She's got to be in another room near by. I'm going to make a scene to get the man back here. That way, if Carmen is here, she can let me know that she hears me," I say, back to Johnny.

As soon as I'm done talking to Johnny, I start to beat on the door and yelling for someone to let me out. Two minutes have gone by according to my watch, and no one has shown up yet. I start to beat on the door some more. I'm yelling louder than I did the last time. If Carmen is near by, she will surely know that I'm here. I'm sure she will recognize my voice and know that Jimmy and the others are on to where she is being held.

"Let me out of here," I yell as loudly as I possibly can, but still no one comes, but now I hear some tapping on the wall. Someone is tapping on the wall. It must be Carmen. She must know that I'm in the next room. She really has recognized my voice.

"Johnny, someone is tapping on the wall. It must be Carmen," I say, with excitement.

"Tap back on the wall and see what happens. Carmen knows Morse code," he said.

"I don't know any codes," I say, frustrated.

"I'm going to tell you how you tap out her name, and if it's her, she will tap back," he says eagerly, and now he's telling the others in the van what is going on.

Johnny tells me how to tap out Carmen's name and then I hear tapping back. I don't understand it so I tell it to Johnny, and he says that what she has tapped back is, yes I'm Carmen. Now we are all ecstatic and just a little bit anxious.

"Okay, now we know she's there. I want you to lay low now, because in just a few minutes we're coming in after the both of you," Johnny says, with a voice, that says don't even try to talk me out of it, because the time is now.

"Callie, don't forget your weapon. Use it if you have to" he says, and then I hear a click, meaning all conversation is over. They're coming in.

As I'm beginning to perspire, I'm wiping my brow with my hand to keep the sweat out of my eyes. I need to see clearly for what is about to happen. I open my blouse to make it easier to reach my weapon if I need it and I probably will need it before it's over. At least Carmen knows we're here to get her, and I'm sure on the other side of the wall, she's preparing for something to happen as well. Johnny feels that it's his fault that she's been kidnapped. I haven't been able to do much, but we do know that Carmen is here and I know where she is, so it helps for Johnny and the others to come and get us, and I'm getting more scared by the second waiting for Johnny and the guys to bust in.

Thirty seconds later, I hear a lot of noise. It seems as if the door has been busted down, and I can here yelling and gunfire. I can hear Johnny, and Jimmy telling the men to get on the floor, while I can yet hear someone running down the hallway. We still don't know where the man they call Nick is located in the building. I can hear more yelling. Soon someone busts into the room where I am and it's not Johnny or the others. It must be that man called Nick. He is grabbing onto me and using me as a human shield as he makes his way towards another exit.

"Let her go." hear Johnny yell.

"Get Carmen," I hear Jimmy yell to Sly.

"Don't come any closer," the man who has me shielding himself, tells Johnny.

"Let her go. This is between you and me man," Johnny says, inching himself closer and now I can see that he has his gun in his hand.

"You want me to shoot her?" He yells back.

"You don't have to do that."

"Then you'd better back off," he says, as I'm getting an idea in my head. I kick the man in the shin, he lets go of me and I fall to the floor. Now Johnny has a clear shot at him and he takes it. The man falls on top of me as I'm lying on the floor, and Johnny runs to me and pulls the man off me. We both start down the hallway slowly not knowing where any of the men are at this time.

"Shhh," Johnny says, as he walks in front of me to shield me.

We're moving closer to the room where Carmen is and I motion to Johnny that the next room we approach will be the one Carmen is in. He nods his head and when we get in front of the door, Johnny stands back and then boom, he kicks the door open, and when he does, someone in the room is shooting at us. Johnny quickly pushes me to the floor and fires back at whoever it is, that's shooting at us. Johnny ducks inside the room, and I can hear another commotion in the large room where the men were playing cards. There's more gunfire up in that room as well.

I'm still lying on the floor in front of the dark room where Johnny has just slipped into. There is more gunfire and I hear someone say, I'm hit, then I see Carmen run out of the room and hit the floor beside me.

"Where's Jimmy?" She asks.

"I don't know." I say.

Now there is more gunfire coming from the room just in front of us, and then I see Johnny coming out of the room in one piece, with part of his sleeve torn off of his jacket, that says, he must have been in some kind of physical confrontation while he was inside the room.

"We've got to find Jimmy and the others and get out of here. There's no telling how many are on the way." He says almost out of breath, as he pulls both of us to our feet and we head down the darkened hallway to see if we can find Jimmy and the others and get out while we have a chance.

"You two go to the van fast, then pull around to the door. Leave the van door open so we can get in as fast as possible. I've got to go see what's happening with the other guys."

"Alright," Carmen and I both say, and then we run for the door and once outside, we run like we're some kind of track stars. I never knew I could run so fast.

Once inside the van, Carmen and I wait. We have both eyes on the doorway hoping to see our men come out of that door. My stomach feels as if it's in knots again. Johnny has got to come out of that door. I can't lose him now, and I'm sure that Carmen is just as scared as I am waiting to see Jimmy come out as well. Now we both look at each other not knowing what to do or say so we don't say anything. The wait is getting too much to bear when we hear more gunfire.

"We'd better pull around to the door now," I say, as I'm getting behind the wheel of the van.

"Good idea," Carmen says, in a very low voice.

"Carmen, is something wrong?" I ask, because I detect that something is not quite right.

"They shot me about a half hour before you came. I think they thought I was dead," she says.

"Oh my God," I scream, when I see all the blood that is covering her body, as I'm driving to the entrance of the warehouse. My hands get all clammy and I'm starting to perspire heavily, as I'm making my way to the door, where Johnny and the others are suppose to come out.

Two minutes have gone by and we haven't heard anything. I can see two cars coming from the other direction. There are men inside the vehicle in dark suits.

"Oh no. There's more of them coming," I yell as, I'm praying for them to come out of the building. Come out. Come out. Come out. I keep saying in my mind, and then I see them. All of them are racing for the van door that has been left open for them. Please make it I say in my mind. The two cars are getting closer and Johnny and the men are almost to the van, and finally when they're all in, I let out a deep sigh.

"Drive," Johnny yells, to me as I put the accelerator to the floor, and the tires make a squealing sound and I can see dust flying from behind the van through the rearview mirror.

As we speed away from the warehouse, the cars behind us have spotted us and are coming after us.

"She's been shot," I say.

"What," Jimmy says, as he tries to find out where Carmen has been hit.

"We've got to get her help quick. She says she was shot about thirty minutes before she knew we were there," I say.

"Oh no," Johnny says, as he drops his head down.

"Go Callie. Get us back to the Mountain as fast as possible," Jimmy says, looking as if he just might keel over himself if anything else happens to Carmen.

"Are they still behind us?" Jimmy asks Sly.

"We've got to lose them. I'll drive. Callie, slide out of the drivers seat and let me have it," Johnny says, as he's making the maneuver.

"Thank God," I say, as I'm moving out and letting Johnny in behind the wheel of the van.

"They're shooting at us. Drive this thing Johnny," Jimmy says, almost crying because Carmen has been shot and bleeding profusely.

"Sly, are you and the guys Okay?" Jimmy asks the others.

"Yeah, we're alright and we're all here," Sly says to Jimmy.

It's not long before we lose the car that's following us and we head for the house in Stone Mountain. Jimmy has already called a doctor to meet us there when we get there. I'm sitting in the seat next to Johnny as he drives the van fast enough, but not too fast to get stopped by the police or else we're all done for. I'm so thankful that Johnny and the others are o.k., and now we've got to get Carmen to the house before she bleeds to death. I don't want Johnny to feel it's his fault for what happened to Carmen. Johnny doesn't deserve any of this. He is innocent and I'm innocent, but I'm in more trouble for helping him then he is. I don't know how I got my black behind into all this mess, but the heart of a woman is as high as a mountain and as deep as the deepest valley, when it comes to her man. She will walk the dessert, if it means she will be by his side. I would have never forgiven myself, if I hadn't come to Johnny in this curious time of need. Daddy always said look before you leap, but I have totally disregarded his advice and leaped into this most dangerous situation without a second thought. Love really is stronger than death, which is what the bible says.

When Scooter and I was sweethearts we did everything together too, but Scooter never did have any money. He didn't even have two dimes to rub together when we were out on a date and I usually wound up paying for everything, and Johnny won't let me pay for anything. I was so in love, so I thought at the time, I hardly paid attention to the fact that Scooter didn't really have anything to offer me and that, it's the guy who should foot most of the dating monies, if he really cares enough about you. By Scooter marrying someone else, after he had promised to marry me, shows me that, he didn't really have the love for me that I would have required of him. I mean, it's only right that he take some of the responsibility if not all of it. I guess the old way is out and the new way is in, but in my opinion, how else are you going to tell if the guy is serious about you or not. If a guy truly loves you, he will want to take the lead in the relationship and do the pursuing and the paying. I like the old way best, because without it, somehow it takes away from the respect and glory of the woman that should protect the man's honor and chivalry.

Chapter 12

It's good to be back at our apartment in Savannah. Jimmy called Johnny this morning to tell us that Carmen is recuperating nicely. Johnny somehow feels good about the fact that he was involved in getting Carmen back alive, because he still blames himself for her being kidnapped. We're just hanging out in the apartment and being quiet. Each of us in our own little world, and just grateful to still be alive. We're still being sought after by the police and we don't know how much longer we can evade them. We're just happy to be together and not in jail, although at this point, we feel that it's just a matter of time before we find jail our home, if we don't find Cortez and make him confess. We heard that Cortez got away, back when we got Carmen out of the warehouse in Atlanta, but Johnny and the guys are not giving up finding him.

We haven't gone back to our jobs. We feel it's too risky now. Cortez will also be looking for us now. He will be trying to get us before we get him so I've been pretty bored since we came back here to Savannah and we're also happy to be out of Atlanta. I'm real hungry today because there is no food in the apartment and Johnny and me are going out to buy groceries a little later. We both are almost numb from our experience in Atlanta. I think our minds and bodies are still in shock.

"What time we going to get something to eat?" Johnny calls from the kitchen while, looking inside the refrigerator with nothing in it.

"As soon as I freshen up," I call back to him. I know we have to go out and get something to eat and we have to put on our disguises, which I hate more than anything. At first it wasn't so bad because, we were just being chased by the police and now because, we've been free so long, I'm used to being that way and hate the disguises. Why are we in so much trouble when we didn't even do anything. Johnny is innocent. He's the one who's paying by having to run from something he hasn't done. I'm sick and tired of that stupid wig and I hate Johnny's fake mustache that's plastered all over his top lip. He's so handsome he still looks good fake mustache and all.

"I'm ready," I call out to him

"Be right there," he calls back to me.

As we ride to the grocery store that's across town, we listen to the radio and laugh at some of the lyrics of the songs. It's a nice day and summer is just around the corner. Spring is one of my favorite seasons. The other one is Fall. Johnny and me have been married for almost six months now. I love him more every day. He really is one of the finer kind of men, or should I say one of the finer kind of wanted men. I can hardly believe that, Johnny and I are on the most wanted list. This whole thing is crazy, but I'm sticking by my man, because I know he's innocent.

Once inside the grocery store, Johnny and I move slowly through the aisles and keep our heads down. We don't want to be recognized. Our disguises have worked so far. I just hope our luck doesn't run out. As we continue down the aisle, I see someone I think I know.

"Johnny, isn't that the man from the tent meeting that preached that night we went to the fair?" I ask him, with urgency in my voice.

"Yes, I think that's him," Johnny says.

"Let's go down the other aisle so we don't run into him. Remember we promised him that we'd come to his church on Randolph Street and we haven't made it there yet."

"He doesn't remember us."

"Well it looks like we're going to find out, because here he comes," I said, trying to hide my face as we start to walk faster like we're in a hurry.

"Young man, young woman," the preacher man calls to us."

"Yes," I answer the man.

"It's so nice to see the both of you again. I've been waiting to see you in church," he says, as he takes off his black hat.

"Yes, well we've been out of town. We just recently got back," Johnny says.

"Well then, I hope to see you at church this Sunday," he says to the both of us.

"Yes, we'll be there," Johnny says, as he's trying to move past the man.

"Oh, by the way, are the two of you working? I see you're out in the middle of the day, because if you're not, the parish has an opening for a couple to live and work on the grounds and you two look like such a nice young couple. If you're interested, stop by the church office tomorrow. My name is Reverend Karl Jones," he says, extending his hand out to us one at a time.

We're Johnny and Callie and we'll give it some thought," Johnny says, as he pulls my sleeve to keep me moving along, because we're really anxious to get away from the man.

"We'll give it some thought," Johnny says, as he continues to pulls my sleeve to keep moving past the man, while I'm looking back trying to give the man a descent goodbye and being just a little embarrassed at the way Johnny is pulling me down the aisle. People always know when you're trying to brush them off, especially in a grocery store, cause mama used to do that all the time when she saw some of the old church members who didn't go to our church anymore, mama would always try to avoid them and she would drag me quickly down another aisle trying to keep from running into the members who left the congregation and started attending another church.

"The man is going to think we're trying to get away from him," I tell Johnny, trying to make it sound as if I really don't care, but I do.

"We can't waste time talking to people. We have to get our stuff and get back to the apartment. We are wanted people you know," Johnny says, reminding me that we're fugitives. I guess I'm just so happy because I'm Johnny's wife, I forget most of the time that we are hiding out from the law, not to mention those jackals that set Johnny up and now want to kill us both. This is not the dream I had when I was a little girl. I had hoped that my prince charming would come along, but I would have never guessed it would be this kind of deal. I said for better or worse and that's just what I meant. I will stay with Johnny no matter what. We never did have a lot of divorce in our family. My parents always taught me that marriage is for life. We can't just jump in and out whenever we feel like it. We make a vow to God, but sometimes we're just plain lying to God, because some know from the beginning if it don't suit them, they're gone. Daddy always taught me, that it's better to never make a vow to God, then to break a vow.

"You're right Johnny. We'd better get back to the apartment."

As we leave the grocery store Johnny's cell phone rings. That means it's probably Jimmy. I hope nothing is wrong. Maybe he's just checking in with us to make sure we're Okay. I feel myself getting a little nervous, even though I'm trying to convince myself that it's probably nothing at all. Time is beginning to wear on both me and Johnny from living in this mud pool of life. At this point we have got to be at the bottom of the pool.

"What's up, Jimmy?" I hear Johnny saying into the cell phone.

"What? How do you know?" Is all I can hear from Johnny's end of the phone.

"What is it?" I ask almost in a panic.

"Got you. Thanks Jimmy." Johnny is saying, and then gets off the phone.

"We can't go back to the apartment," he says to me, looking strangely as he checks our surroundings

"What? Why not?" I ask as, I start to tremble.

"Cortez is on to where we are and we just can't go back Callie," Johnny says, putting his free arm around my shoulder and hugging me close to him.

"What are we going to do? We don't have much money left and we have no place else to go."

"Wait a minute. Remember the offer Reverend Jones gave us?"

"Yes, what about it?"

"We're going to take him up on his offer," Johnny says, putting the groceries into the back seat of the car before getting into the drivers- seat.

"But all my clothes and personal things are at the apartment," I say, sheepishly trying not to aggravate Johnny at a time of distress.

"We can't go back Callie and that's final. Cortez and his blood- thirsty hounds are too close for comfort. We have to leave whatever is there. Don't worry, we'll get more clothes. We can replace clothes, Callie," he says stroking my hair, in his oh so caring manner, that made me fall for him in the first place.

"We're going to live in a living quarters behind the church, as two parishioners. This ought to be good. Well, let's pay the Reverend Jones a visit," I say, as I scoot down in the front seat of the car. I need to rest my head for awhile. We seem to be on an adventure that just keeps on going on. Leave it to Johnny to take the Reverend up on his offer. The animosity I have for Cortez and his mad dogs is starting to mount up. Now we're out of a home and all our belongings, because we can't go back. We've been discovered by Cortez and now we're going to find the Reverend and accept his offer of working for him. This is going to be a real experience. Of course we'll be expected to attend church services every week, but when in Rome do as the Romans do.

Two hours later, we've found the Reverend and his church on Sycamore Street in Savannah. He has given us a place to stay. We will live in the Pastor's quarters, that is connected to the church. The Reverend Jones has his own little mansion in a more elaborate part of town. Johnny and I will run the place, such as taking care of the property, mowing the lawn, cleaning the church and we're staying here free, as long as we come to church regularly. The Reverend Jones didn't forget that we had come up to accept the Lord in our lives during the tent meeting and now, we'll be expected to act accordingly. Johnny says that Cortez and his men will never think about looking for us here. It just so happens that today is Saturday and tomorrow is Sunday. We will be at church tomorrow morning at eleven a.m. for Sunday morning service. It's been awhile since I've been to church. Daddy would roll over in his grave if he knew that all those years of bringing me up in his church, that I haven't even seen a church in over a year. Things just have led me in a different direction.

When we got up this morning, we were surprised ourselves at where we were waking up. Suddenly we're church goers, which isn't a bad thing, but certainly a bit strange, considering that we're wanted Felons. I always sleep late on Sunday and so does Johnny, when we have some free time from eluding the police, but not this Sunday, because we're due in church in exactly forty minutes. We couldn't have asked for a better hide out. We just play the game with Reverend Jones, although he doesn't know that we're just using him and the church for a hide out.

"Hurry up out of the bathroom, Johnny. I have to get ready too you know," I say, as I'm trying to rummage through the Sunday go to meeting clothes, Reverend Jones" wife gave me to wear. If it were up to me, I wouldn't wear any of this stuff, but right now I don't have a choice. I'm much taller then she is, and I'm thinking that this dress is going to hit me just above my knee-caps, but so what, I don't know these people anyway, so who cares. In a few weeks we're out of here and we won't see these people again, at least that's Johnny's plan.

"Now who's taking too long?" I hear Johnny call to me, as I'm putting on my make up.

"I'll be right out sugar," I call back to him, as I hear him pacing back and forth across the floor, as if he's going to his own wedding, which reminds me that we're due a wedding sometime in the future being that, we did have a drive up wedding in Vegas and until we have the whole shebang, with me wearing a wedding dress and a big diamond on my finger and our friends and relatives, we feel that we've missed something sacred. At least that's the way I feel. I'm really not sure if Johnny gives a care whether we have a wedding or not, but I'm sure I can convince him.

We go out the side door and around to the front of the church. We come inside with a crowd of others who have gotten there at the same time we entered the church. I'm a bit squeamish, as I hold Johnny's hand and we find a pew close to the front of the pulpit. It's part of the bargain that we attend church, while we make our living working around the church and also we get our room and board. It's a good deal and a good way to establish ourselves in the community. There are quite a few members, that have now come in and sat down. I turn to look at a lot of strange faces and deep down, I'm glad we don't know anyone at all. Johnny is straight and rigid beside me and he looks so good in his gray and black pin striped suit. He must be the best looking man in the place, but Johnny is always the best looking man wherever we go. I'm dressed in a light pink summer dress with a low-neck line that shows off my figure to the tee. Thank God I've put on seven pounds. If I had stayed with Pierre, I would be so skinny I'm not sure anyone would be able to see me. Johnny says he likes me with some meat on my bones.

Service is about to begin. There are ministers sitting up in the pulpit, but Pastor Jones has not come into the sanctuary as of yet. A man stands up with a bald head and mustache and a suit that looks two sizes too small and starts to pray the opening prayer. He starts to sweat half way through the prayer and keeps wiping his brow with a white handkerchief and he belts out the words, with his voice sounding like he has gravel in his throat. He starts to unbutton his suit coat as he continues to pray, with his large jaws vibrating to each and every word that comes out of his mouth. The rest of the congregation is saying amen, after every two or three sentences of the prayer in agreement. There is no air conditioning, so by now I'm starting to feel hot and I take one of the fans, that's placed into a small pocket on the back of the pew in front of me. I'm fanning away and I keep hoping that the man will end the prayer, because he keeps saying the same thing over and over, with that gravel tone in his voice. Johnny is still sitting up tall and straight next to me and he's as cool as a cucumber as always. It seems as if nothing bothers Johnny, but deep down in side he's got a heart of gold, the kind that makes a woman love her man to the greatest extent of the word love.

When the man finishes praying the choir get up to sing a song. I hope they don't sing one of those sad songs we always here at funerals. I'll just die if they do and now one of the ladies comes out front to lead the song.

"This ought to be good," I say, as I hunch Johnny in the side.

"Well it ain't over until the fat lady sings," he says, smiling at me.

When they start to sing, I can hardly believe my ears. The choir is singing one of everybody's favorite songs, Oh Happy Day. They're singing it to a fast beat and before I know It, I'm clapping my hands and moving from side to side to the beat. The woman can sing. This Sunday morning reminds me of so many Sunday mornings I had to be at church, because daddy was the pastor. I don't know how I've strayed so far away. I just hope that God will forgive me of the sins I've committed and that he will help me and Johnny out of the mess we're in. Johnny is still sitting quiet next to me with his eyes closed, as if he is meditating or sleeping. I don't know which one he's doing, meditating or sleeping, but anyone can see that he is all man.

After that very inspirational song, Pastor Jones comes in and sits down. The petite woman with a blue suite on gets up to read the announcements, for the coming church events. There is going to be a church picnic soon. I haven't been to one of those in a long time. She said a lot of other stuff that I can't remember, but I always remember when someone is talking about eating. I've noticed that Johnny hasn't been drinking any beer lately. He probably doesn't want to get caught with any beer, or he knows we're out of here.

Pastor Jones gets up now and sings one of the old church favorites and the choir start's to back him up. Pastor Jones has a very nice voice. He sings one of my favorite songs, "Because He lives." I always cry when I hear that song. As the tears stream down my face, Johnny reaches into his pocket and gives me his handkerchief for me to blow my nose and wipe my tears. As I do this, he puts his arm around my shoulders to comfort me and when I'm done crying, I give the handkerchief back to Johnny and he sticks it back into his pants pocket. I'm always so emotional when I'm in church and now I feel guilty that I haven't been to church for so long.

"Are you allright?" He asks me, as he pats me on the opposite shoulder, because he has his arm around me.

"Uh huh," I answer him, because I'm too emotional to speak words now.

Once Pastor Jones gets into his sermon, I've recovered from my moment of emotional trauma. I'm listening to him and hanging on his every word. Somehow I'm beginning to find some peace within me, that I have not known since I left home over a year ago. Maybe what I've been searching for has been with me all along. I'm beginning to feel as If I'm connecting with God again. I'm starting to feel a peace that is so deep inside me, that I don't ever want to let it go again.

At the end of the sermon, Reverend Jones is telling the congregation that Johnny and I are new members of Mount Zion Tabernacle. It's the first time I heard the name of the church.

"Come up here and take the right hand of fellowship," Reverend Jones motions for Johnny and me to come up in front of the church.

"Johnny, wake up, Johnny," I say, as I'm trying not to seem obvious that I'm prodding Johnny to get up and walk.

"What is it?" He asks me, and looking around at the same time.

"Follow me," I tell him, through my clenched teeth like a ventriloquist. Lord, if he doesn't follow me up in front, I'm going to be too embarrassed, because since Johnny had been asleep, he doesn't know exactly why I'm telling him to follow me and this could lead to something, but he's got to trust me for what I'm telling him, because now I'm getting up and I can see that he is going to get up with me and I let out a short sigh of relief. There is nothing more embarrassing then to be embarrassed in church, and if he hadn't gotten up, then he would have been embarrassed too and I don't want my Johnny embarrassed for nothing, besides I would never live it down.

As we stand before the whole church, the congregation gets up and gives us a standing ovation. I'm holding Johnny's hand and I'm hoping he doesn't notice how sweaty it is in his hand.

"These are our new members," Reverend Jones says to the congregation.

"Hallelujah," One woman yelled out, and the next thing I know is, that Reverend Jones and many of the other members break out into a dance to the beat of the jubilant music that the organ player is playing on the organ. Johnny and me stand there and then suddenly Johnny yells out.

"Hallelujah," He says, to my very own surprise and then I'm so happy that I yell out.

"Hallelujah." I smile at Johnny and we're all so happy and I feel so good, like a two ton weight has just been lifted off me.

Outside after church, many members came up to shake our hands. We actually feel as if we belong to something. These months of running from the law, has lowered our self- esteem and our moral. This is just what Johnny and I need. A family to belong to. I don't know when it was the last time that we felt so good. I believe that God has heard me and have forgiven us our sins.

"Welcome to Mount Zion Tabernacle," Reverend Jones says, to us as we're standing on the steps of the church and talking to others.

"Thank you Reverend," we both say at the same time.

"Johnny can I talk to you for a moment in private," the Reverend Jones says to Johnny.

"Of course Reverend Jones," Johnny says, as he steps aside with the Reverend Jones looking so good in his pin striped suit. And as they stand there talking, I can see Johnny nodding his head up and down. He seems to be agreeing with the Reverend Jones, in whatever it is they are discussing and I know Johnny will fill me in as soon as we're back in our living quarters of the church.

"You're going to love our church," a very short woman says to me in passing.

"Thank you. I'm sure," I say back to her, as I'm waiting for Johnny to finish speaking with the Reverend Jones.

Once back in our cubbyhole, Johnny fills me in, just as I knew he would about the conversation he had with the reverend. Johnny says that the reverend wants to take him under his wing and make him his assistant pastor. He says the reverend sees great potential in him and that God has revealed to him that Johnny is to be his right hand man in the running of the church. Of course this is a complete surprise to both of us, since the good reverend doesn't know that me and Johnny are fugitives from justice, which makes me wonder if he knows what he's talking about, by making Johnny his assistant, when we could both very well wind up incarcerated. Me and Johnny are having a life changing experience that we both don't quite understand yet. We just know that it feels awfully good to be in good standing with the Lord and have a whole congregation for your brothers and sisters and a pastor who we've found favor with. It's like we're different people and as if we are not the same people that we once were and surely not the same people that the law is looking for.

Several Months Later

It's a Monday and Johnny and I are in the front yard of the church mowing the lawn. We're taking turns riding the mower and now I'm watering the flowers that surround the building. Johnny and I are so happy and now I talk to mama from a phone booth in the next county twice a month. It's a hot July day and I'm perspiring as I'm trying to fix some the red and yellow roses that are beginning to droop over, because they are so tall. I'm going to have to find some sticks to hold them up. I love gardening I find to my amazement, since we've had to take care of the church grounds, I've found something in gardening that releases all frustration inside of me and that frustration tries to come, when I think about being caught by the police. It helps me to become one with nature and nature is the closest thing to being next to God himself.

As soon as I'm done with the flowers, I go around to the front of the church and I see that Johnny is still mowing the grass. I get closer to him, so I can ask him if he needs something to drink, because it's awfully hot out here today. As I approach him, I can see a police car with the big letters Sheriff on the side of the car, moving slowly down the street towards us. Naturally my heart rate picks up tremendously as I move more towards Johnny and when I get up next to him, I put my arm around his waist and smile up at him. He is standing very still as we stand there waiting for the police car to pass by us, but instead the car stops. We continue standing there, hoping that he will leave. We both can see that he is talking on his car phone. I know Johnny can feel me trembling, as we wait for something to happen and then suddenly the policeman gets out of the car and comes towards us.

"Hello folks."

"Hello," we both say in unison.

"It's a mighty find day out today," he says in a slow southern drawl, that is so famous here in the southern part of the country.

"Yes, it is," Johnny says, going over and extending his hand to the policeman, as I'm standing almost frozen like a block of ice.

"Have you two seen any young boys around here today? One of the residents in the neighborhood called me, so I'm checking it out. It seems that there has been some vandalism to a house near here."

"No. We haven't seen anyone at all that fits that description," Johnny says, very calmly to the policeman, as he sticks his hands into his pants pockets and leans back on his heels as he usually does, when he wants to look confident. He always looks so debonair when he does that.

"Well if you see anyone, give me a call at the station and I'll be right out," he says, tipping his hat, as he turns and goes towards the police car. Johnny and I are smiling and standing with our arms around each other as the policeman drives away slowly and then he picks us speed and soon he is out of sight. It's as if time had stood still and we were in the twilight zone. A feeling that comes to rob you of your very soul.

"That was close," Johnny says to me, as we now leave the mower and head for the living quarters to get some cold lemonade for our dry mouths, after this close encounter with the law. I didn't even know that they had black Sheriffs down here. I guess things have changed.

"Too close for comfort. I was shaking like a leaf on a tree."

"Yeah, that's why I held on tight to you, to try and hold you steady when the Sheriff came up to us. I was quite uneasy myself, but my training in the FBI taught me to never show any emotions around anyone of authority. They will suspect you for something, even if they don't know what it is they suspect you of."

"What are we going to do Johnny? How long can we go on like this?"

"For as long as we have to, Callie. Until we find out how to nail Cortez and Jimmy and Sly thinks it will be soon now."

"It seems as if it's taking forever to get Cortez. Are they sure they can do it?"

"I have a lot of faith in them. They'll get the job done. Don't worry."

"I love you Johnny and I trust your judgment."

"Thank you Callie. It makes a man feel good to know that his woman trusts him with her life. I won't let you down. I promise you, that we will have the life that we've dreamed about."

"I know we will, Johnny," I say, as I walk over to him and we embrace.

At the end of the day, Johnny and I are both so exhausted from working around the grounds of the church, we just kind of fall onto the bed and before we know it, we must both have fallen asleep very quickly, because it's 10:30 at night when I finally awaken to the telephone ringing. I don't have the faintest idea who it could be at this hour of the night.

"Johnny wake up. The phone is ringing"

"Answer it," he says, in a sleepy muffled voice.

"I'm afraid. It might be bad news."

"Give it to me," he mumbles and I pick up the receiver and hand it to him.

"Yeah," he spits out, after taking the cordless from me.

"What? When did this happen?" Johnny responds, and now he is beginning to sit up in bed.

"I'm very sorry to hear this? How did it happen?" He says, now looking at me as I start to sit up beside him, anxious to hear what has happened, that is making him have such a concerned look on his face, and a look that was definitely not familiar to me.

"Right. Will do," Johnny says and then putting the cordless down.

"What's happened?" I ask in fear of what the answer would be.

"Sly has been killed. They don't know exactly what has happened, but Jimmy believes that Cortez is at the bottom of it and Jimmy is determined now more then ever to get him," Johnny tells me, as he puts his head in his hands, while sitting on the side of the bed. Johnny and Sly along with Jimmy had been partners from way back, when they first went to FBI training some nine years ago. I know that there is nothing I can say at this time that will make him feel better. He is going to have to grieve just as if he'd lost a brother or something.

"Are you going to Atlanta?" I ask, not wanting to hear the wrong answer.

"No. Jimmy says it's better for me to lye low. He says that they may have killed Sly in order to smoke me out and get me too and that I'm to stay away from Atlanta."

"I'm sorry Johnny. Sly was a good guy," I say, as I put his head on my shoulder and stroke his black silky curly hair, that I love so much to run my fingers through. I hate that this has happened to Sly, but deep down inside, I'm glad it's not Johnny, although Sly might have died because of Johnny. I just hope that this will make Jimmy so mad, that he'll go after that Cortez animal and get him to confess that he set Johnny up. I don't know what it's like to live a normal life anymore. I just know that being in church makes me feel clean and loved, and something, I hope I will be able to do with a clean slate someday soon. I'm not going to say anything, because I know that Johnny is very grieved in his heart, that Sly is gone and there is nothing I can say that will comfort him at this time. Life can be a dog, especially at the least moment that you expect it, something tragic will happen. Look at the way daddy died when we were out together having a great time, father and daughter. He has a heart attack and dies right there on the green. I still feel guilty, that it's my fault he died. There should have been something I could have done if I had been a nurse. How would I have known that daddy would die so suddenly, as if I would have known in advance, that daddy would have an attack, when I was a girl, so I would then go to nursing school or become a doctor because I would be ready for that day on the green. Hardly not. Life just doesn't work that way, although I wished at that moment it did.

Johnny has been pacing the floor most of the night. He's doing all he can to stop himself from going to Atlanta against the advice of Jimmy. I'm also pumping him with advice to stay away. He's like a caged animal that can't get out of his cage. I'm trying to comfort him. I know he wants to say his good byes to Sly at his funeral, but it's just not the smart thing to do. I loathe that jackal Cortez. He's the lowest of the lowest. He's lower than a snake in the grass. Someday he'll get his just due and I want to be there to see him get it. I'll have to repent for my evil thoughts, but not tonight.

"Johnny, baby you should get some sleep," I try to tell him, in the softest voice I can muster up. I don't want to push his button at a time like this, because nothing is worse than seeing a big man like Johnny get irate.

"Go to sleep Callie. I have some thinking to do."

"Goodnight." The word comes out of my mouth, as I turn my back to Johnny and he continues pacing the floor, but I know that I'm in for a long night, because there is no way I can sleep with him in this grief stricken condition. I'll just pretend that I'm sleeping, so he can think that he can grieve alone. He wants to be alone with his thoughts and I can understand his feelings.

The last few days have been like being in hell. Johnny is tormenting himself and me about Sly's death and I've been trying to comfort him to no avail. He just won't be comforted. Tomorrow is Sunday and he's to preach his first sermon at the church and Monday is the day of Sly's funeral. I keep praying that Johnny just realizes that he can't go. The whole congregation is waiting to hear Johnny's first sermon, but with this in the way, I'm wondering if he can pull it off. All the people at the church love us and they especially love Johnny. He's so personable, one just can't help loving him. And just yesterday, Reverend Jones says that he is going to Florida for at least a year, because of health reasons and that he want's Johnny to take over the church until he returns, that is, if Johnny proves himself tomorrow, but neither Reverend Jones or myself have any doubts about Johnny preaching well during service tomorrow. Reverend Jones has heard Johnny preach in private and he says that he's a natural born preacher.

I can't believe the way our lives have turned out. We ran to the church because we didn't have anywhere else to go and now we're going to be leading the whole congregation. God does work in mysterious ways and that's the truth. Now my job is to keep Johnny away from Atlanta on Monday. All the talking I've been doing to Johnny to convince him that Jimmy is right, he should not attend Sly's funeral, seems to be going in one ear and out the other. He's not saying much, but I can tell that my talking isn't really convincing him. He's going to have to come to that decision on his own. He is not one, that let's others make up his mind for him. He's definitely his own man. Not even I can tell Johnny what to do, if he makes up his mind to do different, that's the way it's going to be.

Johnny did an excellent job with his sermon this morning just as we knew he would. Reverend Jones is as proud of him as I am. I didn't realize that Johnny was really into God until just recently. He tells me, that when he said the sinners prayer that night at the tent meeting, he really meant it and that's funny because when I said the prayer that night, I really meant it too. I can't believe how our lives have changed for the better and how happy we've become since coming here. There is still something standing in the way of our complete happiness and that's being citizens in good standing with the law. This is a dream that still has to come true. A dream when it comes true, will make for our perfection of happiness. That's what I'm talking about, perfect happiness with Johnny Parker.

"Johnny, why are you getting up so early? It's four o'clock in the morning," I say, after waking up to the sound of the alarm clock and Johnny knocking it on to the floor, while trying to turn it off.

"Nothing baby. Go back to sleep," he says, as he goes into the bathroom and while he's in there, I can hear him washing his face and I'm wondering why he would want to wash his face so early in the morning. No, he can't be doing what I think he's doing. He is going to defy Jimmy and me and go to Atlanta anyway. I know Johnny is not that dumb. He wouldn't do anything that would jeopardize his safety, because he knows that I need him here on earth to take care of me. He knows how irresponsible I am and without him, I'm a lost cause.

"Johnny what are you doing in there?" I ask curiously, while now starting to sit up in the bed with my eyes glued on the door, waiting for it to open.

"I thought I told you to go back to sleep," he says, in a not so nice tone of voice.

"I would if I knew what you were up to," I say, back in a not so nice tone of voice to him.

I'm not getting any response now, which means that I've irritated him and he doesn't want to say anything else to me now. I guess I'm just going to have to wait until he comes out and see.

You guessed it. We're on our way to Atlanta to attend Sly's funeral. I tried to talk Johnny out of it and so did Sly, but Sly is waiting for us to get there, so Johnny can be one of the Paul Bearers and for Johnny, it will be like old times to be there with Jimmy and the boys. Nothing was going to keep Johnny from going to Atlanta and we'll stay in Stone Mountain at Jimmy's as usual. It would have been a miracle if we could have talked Johnny out of going. I knew that from the start, but I had hoped that he would be reasonable and not go to Sly's funeral.

"It's hot and I'm thirsty. When can we get something to drink?" I ask Johnny, who is quiet and in his own little world, as he drives down the highway, with his long slender body down in a relaxed kind of position, as he keeps his eyes directly on the highway.

"I've got some soda on ice in the trunk. We don't have time to make any stops," he says, patting me on my thigh and then pointing to the back of the car in the direction of the trunk.

"Well if we could stop for a minute, I could get us one out of the cooler."

"We'll stop as soon as I can find a ramp. We don't want to stop on the highway, because we could draw suspicion to ourselves."

"All right," I say, folding my arms and almost pouting. Johnny has hardly said a word to me all day and I'm just a little ticked about it. I don't know why he has to keep me on ice too.

It's about ten minutes later, before we get off the highway to stop and get some sodas out of the trunk of the car. We stopped at a station and we sit inside the car, drinking the soda to try and cool off a bit. I know Johnny is anxious to get to Jimmy's house, but I'm so dry in my mouth I just couldn't stand it any longer. The sun is blaring down on us as we're both sweating and our clothes are visibly wet with perspiration. I never did like summer, even when I was a girl I hated when summer rolled around. I'm a Spring and Fall kind of girl. Even though I was born in the Southern part of the country, I never really adjusted to that kind of heat. On the other hand, Johnny loves hot weather. He was born and raised in California and he loves the heat. I just want to get to Atlanta and get some rest, while Johnny, Jimmy and the others take care of the funeral arrangements for Sly. Jimmy's house is so luxurious, until I can't complain about having to stay there. Johnny would have felt like a traitor if he hadn't made up his mind to be there. He just couldn't miss saying his good byes to Sly. They've been close him and Jimmy for a long time and have formed a bond, while working together as agents.

"Has your thirst been quenched?" He asks me, as he turned up the bottle of soda and gulps down the last of it.

"Yes. I'm quenched."

"Let's roll," he says, as he starts the motor to pull out of the station.

"Wait. I forgot. I have to go to the bathroom," I say, a little timidly and hoping that Johnny doesn't blow his top.

"Women," he says, as he pulls back up towards the entrance of the service station.

"I'll be right back."

When I get back to the car, after going to the ladies room in the station, Johnny still has the motor running. I get in and he looks at me as if he's just a bit irritated. Men don't hardly ever want to stop on the highway. They just want to keep going until they get there and they think that us women are pests when it comes to traveling. I mean, who can travel for hours and not want to stop to go to the bathroom. It's a part of traveling and especially when traveling with a woman. She has to stop to check herself in the mirror, if nothing else.

When we finally get to Jimmy's house, it's dusk. There are people in the yard, on the large veranda and lot's more inside the house. Jimmy was careful not to let any working agents attend the funeral. He made it a private one. Only the people that belonged to his and Johnny's circle was there. They all know that we're wanted by the law, but they wouldn't dare cross Jimmy or Johnny. When we go to the funeral, we'll be wearing our disguises in case someone slips through, but Jimmy and his men are usually so sharp, no one can get past their security. There are lots of men in dark suits all over the place. Jimmy took Johnny aside with the other men as soon as we arrived. I'm going to the room that we had the last time we were here to get some sleep. I'm so tired from the ride and from Johnny's silence, I could cry. It seems as if he's shutting me out and I can't stand not to be his immediate focus.

"Can I bring you anything Madame?" The butler says, after peeping in on me, as I start to take off my shoes to lye down.

"I'd like some lemonade on the rocks," I tell him, as I sit in the rocker rubbing my feet.

"It will be right up Madame," he says, as he shuts the door behind him. It must be nice to have butlers and maids. When you come to Jimmy's house, all his guests get the royal treatment. I'm going to try to relax in the comfort and the heavy security of the Estate. I feel safe for the moment. No one can get to us inside these grounds. I just want Johnny and me to have a big house and several children to run around the house and be financially stable. Now Johnny has lost his career with the FBI because some bad agents want to do bad things and then put the blame on another descent agent like my Johnny, but justice will prevail in the end. I'm sure of it.

"Hey baby," Johnny greets me, as he comes through the bedroom door. "I've got some pretty good news. The guys want me to preach Sly's funeral. I told them that we're church going people now and that I'm an assistant to the pastor in Savannah." He now smiles and waiting for me to give him a rub on the head or some verbal praise.

"Sly would like that," I say, as I take his hand to sit him down beside me on the bed. "No one would be a better person than you Johnny. I'm so proud of you."

"Yeah, I think Sly would like me to do it too. We've been close friends for a long time, him and Jimmy and me.

I love those guys like they were my own brothers, but they always thought of me the son they never had."

"I know you do, I say, patting his hand that's locked in mind and then I take his hand and kiss it, while looking deep into the eyes of the man I love.

"I don't know what I would do without you Callie. You're the best thing that has ever happened to me and I'm a very grateful person because of you."

"I didn't do so bad myself. You're the man I've always dreamed about, since I was little and wishing on a star and when I learned better, I prayed for you Johnny and you are here."

He takes me in his arms and holds me so tightly, that I feel I'm being hugged by a bear. It's the tightest he's ever held me, as if he never want to let me go. I feel the same way. I don't ever want to lose Johnny. I would never be able to duplicate him again. When God made Johnny, he broke the mold. I'm a fugitive of the law, and yet I'm the luckiest person on earth.

Suddenly there's a knock on the door. I go to the door and open it and find that the butler has two lemonades and two sweet rolls on a sliver dish. I am starved, so I don't waste any time closing the door behind the butler and sitting down to devour the food. Johnny waves his hand at me to eat all I want, because he must not be as hungry as I am, so I take the liberty of eating both rolls and drinking one and a half glasses of lemonade.

"Do you want to come downstairs with me? Everyone is gathering into the family room to socialize and let everyone catch up on the details of the funeral."

"Sure," I say, because I'm curious about what all is going on with the fellows and what they're up to. There is always something brewing with the fellows, I mean they are always up to something. I'll just pretend not to be watching and find out all the juicy details. There are so many people staying here for the funeral. All the men that's dressed in dark suits and their wives and girlfriends. This is going to be an interesting experience. I can just feel it in my bones. Of course I feel badly for Sly's family. He was a nice guy in my opinion. He was very respectful to me and he loved Johnny until death. I wish I could see Genny and Sarah. I miss them terribly and I know that they worry about me, but I don't want to get them into any of this. I can't wait until me and Johnny are cleared and I can see my friends and family again. I know that they miss me too.

We're all sitting in the family room. Johnny is sitting on the arm of the large cushion chair I'm sitting in. Some of the men are talking together and some of the women are talking together and some of the women are sitting with the men, like me and Johnny are sitting together. The liquor is flowing heavily, but Johnny and I aren't engaging in that part of the festivities. We hardly feel comfortable anymore around that sort of thing. Our lives have changed drastically for the better. We both are finding that we are continually changing for the better and we like the way it feels. The comforting feeling that we're in tune with the way God wants us to live. It gives both of us great satisfaction and a sense of security.

"Shut up Tony," the woman dressed in the red mini dress and short mink coat is yelling, as she tries to pull her arm away from the man and spills the drink she has in the other hand.

"Take it easy Cora. You're making a spectacle of yourself," the man named Tony is saying, as he continues to try to calm her down.

"I told you not to be flirting around all these women Tony. I'm not going to stand for you to disrespect me this way. Do you hear me," she yells, for all to hear.

Everyone who is in the room are now turning around to see just what is happening with the two who are having a lovers spat. Johnny looks at me and I look at him and the other men that were in a huddle talking. They turn to inspect the situation and then resume their conversation again. Jimmy has just entered the room and is walking over to the two lovebirds. He probably wants to resolve the situation before it gets out of hand, because now the woman is crying and her mascara is running down both sides of her face and she tries to wipe it away with her hand.

Jimmy has come between the two that are fighting and has his arms around both the woman and the man. He seems to be handling the situation quite well, because the woman is starting to smile. The man called Tony is looking very seriously at Jimmy as if Jimmy might be schooling him on how to treat a lady. I'm glad my Johnny doesn't need teaching on how to treat his woman. He's an expert at handling me.

Once everything is back under control, Johnny and I are talking about our new plans at the church, once we're done here and back in Savannah, we're going to live our lives as if nothing spectacular is going on. We're going to wait to see what revelation will unfold in helping us in our most unusual situation. The right thing to do, would be to give ourselves up, but we can't do that, until the guys find Cortez and make him confess, that he set Johnny up and that he's the drug dealing and money laundering and not Johnny. Jimmy says they're on to something and it won't take long to get Cortez right where they want him.

An hour later, as Johnny and me are walking on the veranda, we hear another argument that has ensued. We stop and listen as Johnny shushes me up with his finger vertically over his lips. We stand very still behind some lovely trimmed bushes, as we perk our ears to listen.

"Wait a minute Jimmy. Sly told me that if something happens to him, that he wants to be buried in our hometown in Memphis and I'm here to see that it happens that way," Sly's brother is telling Jimmy, outside the house on the grounds near where we are standing.

"Sly told me different and he's going to be buried in Stone Mountain where he has lived for the past ten years," Jimmy shoots back, with authority in his voice.

"I can't believe that you would fight me on this Jimmy. I am Sly's brother you know and how are we going to visit the grave. We'll have to come all the way from Memphis."

"It's not that far and that's the end of it. If you were paying for the funeral, you could have more to say about it, but you're not. So that's that," Jimmy says, throwing down his cigarette butt and mashing it under his foot and walks off toward the house. Sly's brother slowly takes off behind him, shaking his head from side to side.

"Let's go back into the house, where there's air conditioning. It's hotter than hell out here," Johnny says, taking my arm and leading me towards the door that's off the veranda.

"Why does everyone fight at a time like this?" I ask Johnny, as I wipe the sweat from my brow.

"Everyone is on edge, I guess. A lot of people loved Sly," Johnny says, as he pulls off his tee shirt and wipes the sweat off his body. "Later, I'm going to take a cold shower before I crash."

"Me too. It will make us both feel better," I say, as I touch the smooth Carmel skin on his back.

I'm going upstairs to get a clean shirt. I'll be right back down," he says to me.

When I look up to find out where the rumbling noise is coming from, I see two women pulling hair and scratching as they go at each other something fierce. I can't imagine what is going on wrong now, and then I recognize that it's Cora, the woman that was just fighting with her husband, earlier.

"What the..." Johnny says, as he goes over to where the fight is going on.

Now the two women are rolling on the floor and still have their hands locked into each other's hair. Others in the room are jumping back out of the way to keep from being hit by falling lamps and to keep from spilling their drinks. Everyone is now fixed on the two women tussling on the floor.

"What is going on here?" Jimmy says, as he rushed over to stop the women.

Before long, Jimmy and Johnny has separated the two women, who are still hurling slanderous names at each other and the man Tony, is nowhere in sight.

"Why don't we all get some food into our stomachs, so we all can sober up a bit," Jimmy says, as

he rings for the chef and when the chef comes into the room, he is looking around in amazement.

"We need food," Jimmy says, to the chef.

"Coming right up," the chef says, as he quickly leaves the room.

It seems that Cora and the other woman were fighting over Tony. Tony must have been flirting with the woman and got caught by Cora. The men that do all this flirting when they have a woman is just not showing the woman they love any respect. I have strong feeling about men who disrespect their women. That's why I picked Johnny. He would never disrespect me in our relationship.

I'm not getting the rest I thought I would get. It's after 10:00p.m. and everyone that's at the house, is still up and there are no signs of anyone going to bed. I hope this is not going to be an all night gathering, because if it is, I won't be involved. I've got to get some rest, or I feel as if I'm going to have a nervous breakdown. My body has been abused for many months now. First, I was being starved to death by Pierre, and then since we've been on the run, I very rarely get much sleep. The best sleep I've had is, since we came to work with Reverend Jones and it's been so peaceful being at the church.

"I'll be right back. I'm going to put on another shirt," Johnny says to me, as he heads up the stairs to the room we're occupying.

"I'll wait down here for you," I say, because I don't want to miss any of the excitement that may erupt at any moment. The two women have been separated and are now recuperating from their little bout in separate rooms of the house. Jimmy is having a talk with Tony, the object of the two women's affections, in a remote corner of the room. I can see Jimmy making hand gestures as he talks to Tony. I'm just going to find a chair and sit down until Johnny gets back from upstairs. I can't believe all of this that's happening, but I can assure you, that it is quite interesting. When I was in mourning over daddy, I can vouch for the fact, that when one has lost a loved one, there is nothing funny about it. I guess I should feel more compassion for the people who have lost their best friend and a close relative, but Johnny and me are in so much trouble, I hardly have no feelings for anyone else's problems. I know that this may be selfish of me, but these people will go on with their lives and Johnny and me well, we could very well wind up in jail for the rest of our lives.

"This is going to be a long night," Johnny says to me, when he gets back down to the family room, where everyone is still gathered.

"Why do you say that?" I ask him, as he helps me out of the soft cushioned chair and let's me sit on his lap the way he always does, when there are not enough seats to go around.

"Jimmy just told me as I was on my way back down here, that there could be trouble tonight. He has just gotten word that Cortez and his men may try to crash in on us, while we're in mourning for Sly. I just hope that, they're not that stupid. Jimmy and the boys have all kinds of automatic weapons, and rifles on the premises. They would be crazy to come anywhere near here."

"Well, this is dangerous, isn't it?" I ask with a frown on my face.

"Let's just say, that I hope it doesn't happen," Johnny says, as he strokes my long black hair.

Suddenly there is a loud bang coming from another part of the house. My mind is racing. I can't imagine what is going on now. It sounds as if something fell. I hope no one is hurt.

"What the devil is that Johnny?" I ask, as others in the room with drinks in their hands turn to look in the direction of the other part of the house, with puzzled looks on their faces.

"Let's go take a look," Johnny says, as he slightly pushes me up, so he can get up from the chair we're sitting in together.

"Nothing else can surprise me anymore. Let's go see what's up now," I say, taking his hand for confidence. At this point, anything could be happening.

When we get to the large dinning room area, there are two men and two women arguing about something. I have no idea what it is they are arguing about, but it's a pretty bad one.

"I'm taking Sly's things home to Memphis," the woman was saying.

"Who is that, Johnny?"

"It's Sly's sister, her husband, his brother and his wife. It seems that they're not in agreement about who is getting Sly's personal things from the house. It looks like his sister is getting first dibbs on his things, with a little opposition from her brother."

We could very well see that there was a table that had been overturned, and also a lamp lying on the floor. It looks like someone had stopped them from fighting, before they could get it going. One of the men that was on the grounds had the sisters husband in a headlock.

"Turn me lose man," he told the man, that had him in a headlock.

"Are you going to calm down, or what?" The man asked.

"I'm cool," he told him.

"Yaw'll ain't gettin nuttin, cause yaw'll ain't never done nuttin to deserve nuttin?" Sly's brother says to his sister and brother-in-law. Besides, I was closer to Sly then any of you was."

"I want his gold watch. He promised me that watch," his sister said, speaking a little more articulate then her brother.

"Over my dead body," Sly's brother told his sister.

"You are going to be resting with Sly, if you don't shut your trap," his sister screamed at him.

By now, Johnny and me are almost in a state of unexpected shock. If one more thing happens this night, I don't know what I'm going to do, but I still can't resist not missing a dog gone thing.

"That's cold. You can see she didn't care nuttin about Sly," the brother says to the man, who is trying to stop the whole thing.

Then suddenly Sly's sister's husband pushes his brother-in-law. He pushed him so hard that Sly's brother flies across the room and into another table knocking the table over and then slipped to the floor, so now Jimmy's man and Sly's brother-in-law are engaging in a fist fight. Then Johnny rushes in to stop the two men.

"Johnny, be careful," I scream, while I'm backing up towards the doorway.

Johnny grabs Sly's brother-in-law in the collar and back him into the wall.

"I can handle it," Jimmy's man says to Johnny.

"It doesn't look like you're handling anything," Johnny said back to the man.

"Come on Johnny. Let's get out of here," I say, as I run over and start tugging at Johnny's shirtsleeve.

"You're right baby. This isn't worth my time."

I find myself exhausted when Johnny and I get back to our room. I am truly upset now that Johnny had that little confrontation with Jimmy's man. Thank goodness that the Funeral is tomorrow. Then we can get out of here. I never suspected that this much confusion would exist among family and friends. Just leave it up to someone to die and all hell breaks lose. You would think that they would have a little more respect for Sly then this kind of behavior. I don't intend to go to anymore of Johnny's friend's funerals. I'll make sure I'm sick, or say I have a broken leg or something. These are some violent people, not to mention that Cortez and his dogs might crash the place.

"Johnny, I don't think we're safe here."

"I'm beginning to wonder about that myself. You'd think people would be a little more civilized at a time like this, but leave it up to some dummies to bust up some peace."

"Let's just get some rest and I hope we get through the night in one piece. Tomorrow is going to be a full day," I say, as I start to take off my shoes and then my skirt and blouse.

"Yeah, I'm really looking forward to it," Johnny says, as he starts to undress. "We can still make it a good night you know," he says winking at me.

It's not even six a.m. and I'm wide awake. Johnny is still sleeping beside me. He must really be exhausted after all that happened last night. I'm sure he went to sleep with a smile on his face, because I sure did. This is going to be a long day and I don't want to disturb Johnny any sooner that I have to. We'll probably be leaving for Savannah right after the funeral. Personally, I can't wait to get back to our little haven behind the church. Everything seems so real and clean there. I'm happy that Johnny and I have excepted Jesus as our savior. I felt as if I had just breathed fresh air for the first time in ages. I'm full of joy in my heart, because of my conversion. I just know that God is going to work out this mess we're in. I just know it.

"Honey, you awake? Johnny says, after I've been so careful not to disturb him.

"I didn't mean to wake you," I say, putting my finger to my lips and then on his.

He pulls me back into his arms and we just lay there. I think we both hate to face the day. We are just not in the mood for any more arguing and fighting among ourselves. We draw strength from each other before we face today's music. I wonder which cords are they going to strike during this sad occasion. Johnny is just as anxious to get back to Savannah as I am, in the sanctity of our new found world. It won't be long before everyone else is awake and there will most likely be mayhem in the camp.

"We have to talk," Johnny announces, as he turns over to face me on my side of the bed.

"What do we need to talk about?"

"We both need to call Reverend Jones and tell him what is going on with us."

"Are you sure we should do this Johnny? Maybe Jimmy and the others will find Cortez, make him confess and no one at the church will be the wiser. I don't want to spoil our relationship with the congregation."

"If they find out and we haven't told them, it will be ruined for sure. I know Reverend Jones will not turn his back on us, and he can tell us the right thing to do."

"You're right as usual," I say, as I'm already beginning to shake with fear of exposing ourselves to the people that love and trust us in the congregation. Sometimes black folk find it hard to forgive other black folk, because they want to see you down anyhow. You know that crab in a barrel syndrome. They'll be talking about, we came there like we were somebody and deceived Reverend Jones and all that, although we didn't plan on getting saved for real, but we did and we want to live according to the bible for the rest of our days. Mama will be so happy that I found the Lord again.

"I'll give him a call right now," Johnny says, as he picks up the receiver next to the bed.

It's a few minutes before he's done dialing and I'm almost embarrassed at what the good reverend will think of us now. He has made Johnny his assistant and now he's going to be mad and tell us he never wants to see us again. I'm sure of it, that's why I've covered my head with the sheet to protect me from the world and what Reverend Jones is going to say to Johnny. I mean, how could he ever forgive us for impersonating ourselves as descent people and now he's going to find out that we're fugitives.

"Hello. Can I speak with Reverend Jones," Johnny says politely.

The rest of the conversation was one that I couldn't hear. I'm going to have to wait until Johnny is done talking, before I will know exactly what Reverend Jones has to say about the predicament me and Johnny are in. I can't tell by looking at Johnny's face what they are talking about. I just hear Johnny telling him the story. I don't have a clue as to what the reverend's initial response will be. I just keep praying that he at least won't hate us for what we've done to him. After all, it isn't every day that a Pastor has fugitives as his assistants in the church. This is the longest conversation I have had the experience of almost listening to. It keeps going on with our story. I need to know what is being said on the other end of the phone. It won't be long now. I can tell that it's about to end.

"What did he say?" I ask, as soon as Johnny hung up the receiver.

"What I thought he would say."

"And what is that?" I say, almost sarcastically, because Johnny knows I'm boiling over with curiosity to know what the end of my fate will be.

"He says that we need to give ourselves up and that he and the church will stand behind us, because he believes me, when I tell him that we're innocent. He says do what is right and Justice will prevail in the end," Johnny says, a little on the somber side.

"Johnny, I'm scared," I say, scooting down in the bed again and pulling the sheet over my head.

"The reverend is right, Callie. We have to give our selves up right after the funeral. We can't go on living like this. We both know it's the right thing to do and besides, we still have hope that Jimmy will find Cortez and make him confess to this whole thing. He's just got to find him."

Later in the morning the house is extremely busy. All the stay over guests are up getting breakfast and getting ready for the funeral. My heart has sunk down into my shoes. I can't believe that I will be in jail by the end of the day. This is certainly not my idea of having a good time. Mama must be worried sick by now, but before the day is over, she will surely know where I am, because the media is going to eat this thing up, but most importantly I have to be strong for Johnny's sake. He's the one facing the biggest charges and I'm going to do just that.

"Why don't you run down and get us something to eat and bring it back up."

"What is it you want to eat?" I ask him, as I'm putting my silk robe on over my silk pajamas.

"Whatever you can find. I'm starved."

"I guess so. You haven't eaten much of anything since we got here," I say.

"Well get yourself something, because you haven't eaten that much yourself," he says, with that you need to do what I say kind of look on his face.

"Be right back," I say as, I slide into my house slippers.

While I'm down in the kitchen. I see all kinds of people that I didn't see the day before. Sly must have had a lot of friends and relatives. I never saw so many folk in one house in my life. There is a buffet spread out on the table with plenty of breakfast food. It looks as if they have eggs, sausage, bacon, molasses, biscuits, gravy, fried chicken, ham toast and waffles, sweet rolls with juice, coffee, and milk to drink. Jimmy must be filthy rich to be able to accommodate all of these people. This house must have cost a fortune. This is the kind of house I want me and Johnny to have some day.

"Tell Johnny I want to go over some things with him before we go," Jimmy says, as he puts his hand on my shoulder.

"Sure thing Jimmy," I say to him, as I give his hand a pat in a gesture to comfort him.

It's twelve noon when the Limousines arrive. Johnny and I are in the one with Jimmy and Carmen and some of Jimmy's men. I sit as close to Johnny as I can, because we're all pretty tightly packed in.

Everyone in the dark suites and women dressed in black with black veils, women I don't know at all. Jimmy's been too busy being a great host to everyone and time has not been allotted to introduce everyone to everyone else. I know Johnny and that's enough for me. Where he goes, I go. It seems that all the limousine occupants have shifted into the mourning mode. Just last night there was drinking, partying, fighting, you name it, it happened or almost happened.

By the time we pull up in front of the funeral home, all four limousines, carrying family parked directly in front. Now everybody is filing out of the black cars and being directed to get into a double line to enter the building. I'm still holding onto Johnny for dear life. He is quite calm to be doing his first funeral. I'll be sitting right up front to give him support. Sam and four others are surrounding Jimmy, Carmen, and Johnny and me. They're bodyguards for us. We've gotten a bit spoiled hanging around Jimmy. We better enjoy it, after the funeral we're going to jail.

I have this gut wrenching feeling, knowing that I'm probably going to be in jail before dark, but the worst of it is, I'm going to be separated from Johnny.

"How you holding up, Johnny?" I ask him, as I lock my arm in his arm, and we file into the funeral home, that's so jammed packed, there is no standing room left.

"I'm fine, but what about you? I know this is a very hard day for you for more reasons then one, but we'll get through this Callie, I promise," he says, as we go to the front of the place. The worst is now we have to look at Sly lying there a corpse, for the next couple of hours. I always did hate these kinds of events. People are acting civilized for the first time, since we came to town. Everyone has on their best mourning faces. Johnny sits me down next to him, in the front row. It's only a few minutes until it begins and I have to sit here the whole time, looking right at Sly lying there in his most expensive suit, with a look of peace on his face. Johnny gets to go up and face the crowd. Lucky him. I look around and there are some very interesting dressed women, with hats and more men in dark pin striped suits. The place is packed with people of all colors and ages.

It looks now as if someone is going to sing. This very short round looking woman goes to the microphone and looks around, as she adjusts it to her liking. Everyone is quiet, waiting for her to belt out Precious Lord. The most favorite song, that is sung at every black funeral in America. I think that everyone knows that the family will get tore up and that makes for a good funeral. I don't know why it can't be a good funeral if no one cries, but it's just a black tradition that's on it's way out.

As soon as she has finished singing, the whole place is practically crying, just as I predicted. She must have sung this song more sadly then anyone ever has in the history of the song. Even Johnny is wiping away a few tears. I pull out my handkerchief and give it to Johnny. Someone on the other side of the room is comforting Jimmy and Sly's sister and brother. I hate this mess. I just want it to be over. It seems that I'm doing more things that I hate lately, then I ever have in my whole life.

Ushers are fanning folk now, who have almost passed out from grief. A woman is now coming up to read the obituary and talk about what a wonderful guy Sly Slocum was and how he's in heaven now, even if he never did live a life according to the bible, in their opinion he's in heaven anyway. I liked Sly, but I'm ready to go out of here. All these people have made it even more hot in here and I'm just plain sweating from the heat and all these people packed in here like sardines, which causes me to start fanning and then I fan Johnny for a brief moment, so he can cool off a little, before he has to do the eulogy and then all the family and friends that want to say something about Sly means, this could take forever. If it doesn't end soon, I'm going to have to go out for air. It would be nice to have some fresh air and a cool drink of water. Air and water are taken so for granted, but now, I'd give a hundred dollars for either or both. If only daddy could see me now. No one could ever have told him in a million years that his little Callie would make such a mess of her life, sitting at a funeral and one hour away from being incarcerated, with who knows what kind of sentence after trial.

Johnny is almost half way through the eulogy. I know, because I helped him write it. I'm so hot and Sweaty, I can feel sweat running down my back underneath my dress. The south has some of the hottest and most humid summers, that's why I swore that I would not live in this much heat when I got grown. New York was where I wanted to be. Up there with the changes in the weather, that makes it tolerable to live there. Yeah, my dreams have all been interrupted by my undying love for Johnny and now my undying love for the Lord.

An hour later, we're finally leaving the funeral home. Johnny did an excellent job and I'm so proud of him. We all file back into the black limousines and head for the cemetery. Johnny has been silent since we got into the vehicle. Everyone is quiet. I can see relief on all the faces in the limousine. I've laid my head on Johnny's shoulder as we ride through the City of Atlanta. I see people on the streets that are homeless as we take some of the ride through the ghetto. I see playgrounds filled with kids of all ages. I see pregnant women walking and carrying bags of groceries, and empty lots and kids playing in the street and fire hydrants, with water gushing out. There are small stores and taverns and barbershops with the candy striped neon signs. This may be the last time I will get to look at a community with people living their lives. I feel that Johnny is feeling guilty for letting me help him. If he had it to do over again, I don't think he would let me near him. If he had it to do over again, he would not have let me take him from the hospital, when Cortez and his men shot him and left him for dead.

Once at the gravesite, cars are lined up all along the roadside. There must be three hundred people at least here to say their last good byes to Sly. Johnny has found a chair for me to sit in along with the family. He is about to start with the gravesite ceremony. Many others are standing around with heads bowed, waiting to be led in prayer, when suddenly I see some men in long coats walking towards where we are gathered. I feel as if I'm frozen stiff with fear. They look like some kind of plainclothes police officers. I can't believe this. They can't be coming for us. No one knows where we are, especially not out here at this graveyard. I can see Johnny stiffen as he looks in their direction. He looks as if he might know them. Oh God please don't let this be what I think it is.

The men walk right up to Johnny, tells him to put his hands behind his back, hand cuffs him and reads him his rights. He's looking directly at me and the other people there are sighing and gasping in unbelief. Jimmy has stood up now and is headed towards us along with Sam and a few others. We just have to go peaceably. There is no need to make a scene here and now.

"You have the right to remain silent. You have the right to an attorney," the man dressed in a long coat and hat said, as he read Johnny his rights.

"Callie Mason, will you please show yourself," the other man dressed in a white trench coat yelled out, as he took a step forward looking into the crowd.

"I'm here," I say, standing up and looking at Johnny for a sign of comfort and he winks at me in agreement, that I've done the right thing, by coming forward without any resistance.

"You could have at least had the decency to wait until he was finished with the prayer. This is a sacred time," Jimmy says angrily at the man, who is now pushing Johnny away from where he was standing, with the bible that has now fallen to the ground.

"What kind of men are you?" Carmen yelled out and it was the first time I had really noticed her, as she had been in her room most of the time, still recuperating from her wounds. Jimmy's men were starting to move in closer to the two men.

"There's no need for any further violence. Everyone keep calm," Johnny says to Jimmy and his men, and the detectives start to draw their weapons from inside their coats.

"Don't worry Johnny. We're going to get you and Callie out of this, if it's the last thing we do," Jimmy says to Johnny, with two clenched fists, that were ready to fight for his fellow comrade.

As the man put the handcuffs on me, Johnny clenched his teeth and then spit at the man. People were whispering and murmuring among themselves and making a path for the men to take me and Johnny to the car that was waiting. It was the longest walk of my life, knowing that my freedom has just ended and so has Johnny's. There are no words to describe how I feel, but I'm trying to remain calm for Johnny's sake, because I don't want him to feel my pain, although I feel his. We may never be together again. At this point the answer is in the wind. If I never see him again after this day, I have no regrets of what I've done. I know he is innocent and that's what really counts in my heart. I love Johnny more than when I first met him and that love will never end, as long as I have breath to breathe. The only regret that I do have, is that I might have done wrong in the eyes of God. I will never let go of what me and Johnny have and someday we will be the better for it.

Johnny and I are sitting side by side in the back of the police car. We just look at each other and we have not said a word. We are both handcuffed to a bar on either side of the back seat. We knew this day would come and there just is nothing to say now. We will get an attorney of course. Reverend Jones said he would do that for us and stick by us through this whole mess. We couldn't have found a better friend then the reverend. He still has faith in us, which makes us feel, that we are worth the trouble, that he is going to go through to help us out of this dilemma, which is putting it lightly.

Chapter 14

We've been in jail for the past two months and tomorrow is our trial. I have only seen Johnny in the Courtroom at our arraignment and hearings. I've missed him so much. Being in jail is got to be the most degrading thing that can happen to a descent person. Sometimes bad things happen to good people. Johnny is good people and he in no way deserves what has happened to him. Our attorney is Scott Terrell, a new attorney that has been retained for us by Jimmy. He's paying for all of our legal fees and Reverend Jones and the church in Savannah is sticking by us through it all. Reverend Jones sends us boxes of goodies and says he's praying for us to be acquitted. Of course I pray every day and night that Johnny keeps safe and that someone on the inside doesn't get to him, because Cortez, in his opinion is better off if Johnny is dead.

I've been picked on by some of the women in jail. They think I'm scared of them, but I just try to act in a Christian manner. They want to get me into fights and make it hard for me, but I also have some friends who keep the bad ones away from me by just one look. Big Mable has befriended me and always wants me to read the bible to her, because she can't read worth nothing and she says it, always looking as if she's ashamed of it, by putting her head down. Mable, is what I call her, has helped me stay safe from the other women who are jealous of my slim body and my all around good looks. Mable says that I'm the daughter she never had. She's been locked up for the past seventeen years for murder, which she said she had nothing to do with, but was convicted by an eye witness, who claims she was the one that robbed a small grocery store in East L.A. and then murdered the old man who was the owner. She says it was late at night when the old woman happened to be driving by in her car, and identified her as the robber. She said that she was nowhere near the store, but was not believed, because she had a prior record of shoplifting. It seems that now days if you make one mistake and even if you change and many do change on their own, you're labeled for the rest of your life and may never work again. To me this is ridiculous. Everyone has done something wrong. They just haven't been caught at it. Johnny is innocent and is in double jeopardy with the law wanting to put him away for something he hasn't done, and this Cortez, who is in pursuit to take Johnny's life. He didn't really have a choice, but to run, that is if he wanted to live and because I love him, I had no choice but to help him to escape.

My little world has been in a cell with a very timid kind of woman, who has been incarcerated for embezzling money from her company. In her opinion, it was a technical accounting error and she doesn't know where the money is. She believes that someone caught the error and took advantage of the situation and confiscated the money for themselves. It could be any one of the two hundred employees that work in that company. I feel sorry for most of the women here. Some are in for writing bad checks, thinking they could put the money in the bank before the check was actually processed. They needed milk for their babies and food for their children, while the men go free.

Since our trial begins tomorrow, I really need to concentrate on what is going to happen to me and Johnny. He sends me messages through our attorney and he still pledges his undying love for me and I send him the same message. Reverend Jones will be there and has chartered two buses for the congregation to also be present at the trial. He has been there for us through this whole thing, as soon as he found out about it from Johnny. My mother is coming with Genny and Sarah to also be present at the trial. Johnny has a brother and sister-in-law who is coming to be here with him. There will be agents testifying against Johnny who are connected with Cortez, and Jimmy swears by his dead mother that he will get Cortez before this trial is over and make him confess. Johnny is still angry with himself for letting me help him and getting myself so deeply involved, but I assure him as often as possible, that I would have done it, without his permission, because Sonia was willing and determined to get him out as much as I was determined to free him. Sonia will be testifying in Johnny's behalf, which is one good thing we have to look forward to. She knows the inner workings of the corrupt agents and she can give plenty of information that will support Johnny's testimony. Sonia has turned out to be one of Johnny's best friends. When I first saw them together in that restaurant last year, when I first came to L. A., I thought she was his woman on the side.

How wrong I was to think that about Sonia. She's risked an awful lot to help Johnny and me, and the fact that she helped him escape will never be told by me or by Johnny and there weren't any other witnesses. Besides we need her unspotted and unblemished record as an agent to testify in Johnny's behalf. And if she couldn't testify, we would never give away our secret to anyone ever. We won't even discuss it among ourselves.

It isn't even daybreak and I'm wide awake. I can't sleep any longer, being that today is the first day of the trial. I'm just lying here wondering what Johnny is doing, wondering if he's awake yet and if he's lying there in his cell thinking about me. The trial will last approximately a week, so our attorney Scott Terrell says. This is going to be some very long days, but it will be better than sitting in this cell the whole day. This is got to be a nightmare without Johnny being near me. The attorney is bringing me clothes that Sarah and Genny picked out and mama gave them to the attorney to bring to me to dress in before the trial starts. I'm glad mama and Sarah and Genny are going to be there.

"Parker, it's time to get showered and dressed," the matron says to me, as she starts to unlock the door and take me down the hall, where the showers are located. It sounded funny to have her call me Parker. I've never had the chance to use my married name, since me and Johnny were married.

"This early?"

"There's lots of preparation to leaving the cell and it's going to take a couple of hours to get everything in order, before we take you to the court house," she says in a monotone voice.

"My attorney is coming with my clothes. I need to be able to get them from him."

"If they get here in time."

Other inmates are watching me, as we walk through the cellblock. They're probably wishing it was their day in court. Some of them have been here and never arraigned for bail. They don't know when they're going to get a hearing or trial and get out of here.

"Hurry up. We don't have much time," the matron says, as she gives me a little shove into the shower room. I mean I can walk into the shower without a push, I'm not so deaf and dumb, that she has to give me that much of a hint as to what to do.

I start to shower and turn the water on as hot as I can stand it to be. I must want to wash off all of this stale smell that comes with the cell I'm in. The shower feels so good. It's not often they give us a chance to shower, only if you're going to court or being transferred or something. I take my time as I close my eyes and try to see Johnny's face. The soap makes me feel so clean again. I just want it to last for as long as I want it to.

"It's time to come out. Come out now," the matron says to me, with a stern voice.

"I'm coming," I yell back, as I start to dry off as quickly as I can with the towel.

When I get back to my cell, Attorney Terrell is waiting for me. I now realize that this is going to be the end or a new beginning of my life with Johnny, according to the outcome of the trial.

"I see you brought my clothes."

"Yes. How are you holding up?" He asks me, as he tries to look at me without emotion.

"I'm surviving. How is Johnny doing?"

"He's all right. He's worried about you though."

"I'll be fine, as long as I can see Johnny."

"Before the trial, I want to go over some things with both of you. When they bring you to the courthouse, I'll tell them I need to meet with the two of you in a room privately, before the trial starts."

"Should we be worried?"

"Well, you'll find out soon enough. I need the both of you together on this."

"I'll be right over," I say, in a no caring kind of way.

They decided to walk me through the tunnel that leads to the courthouse. Two Matrons and one police officer escorting me, as if I'm some kind of maniac criminal. I am quite insulted by this whole thing. Who do these people think they are treating me like this. My hands are handcuffed behind my back, which makes it hard to walk and breathe at the same time.

How much longer do we have to go?"

"Shut up. You'll be there when you get there," one of the matrons said to me, with a scowl on her that made her look like a pig in the face.

"I'm just asking because my stomach is cramping."

"What else is new?" the other matron said.

The tunnel is so long and scary, you think that you will never get to the other end. Every sound we make, there is an echo that follows. I need to see Johnny and fast, or I don't know if I'm going to make it through this awful time in our lives. God, help us. We need all the help we can get, with all the charges we have against us. Johnny is charged with money laundering and selling a controlled substance, and escaping and evading the law. My charges are helping a detainee to escape and harboring a fugitive. This is right out of some horror film. Little old me from Lexington, Kentucky. Right out of the south, being naive and not knowing much about the world and finding myself in a world of trouble, with the man I love, in as much or more trouble then I'm in and we don't have the slightest idea of how it's going to turn out. I may never see Johnny again, after the trial. God only knows. If and when we get out of this mess, Johnny and I won't have two nickels to rub together to start a new life.

When we finally did get to the courthouse, which seemed likes hours instead of minutes, I was taken to a small room to wait with one of the matrons in there with me. A little while later, Scott Terrell our attorney and armed guards came in with Johnny. I wanted to run to him and throw my arms around him, but we couldn't touch each other, with two armed guards standing there along with the matron. The attorney now takes the two guards into the corner to confer with them and soon after that, the two guards and the matron leaves to stand guard at the door, as me, Johnny and our attorney sits down at the table. I look across the table at Johnny and he winks at me, without that beautiful smile, that he usually has on his face. He reached across the table and takes my hands in his hands and holds them tightly. I just look into his eyes, and his eyes are apologetic, as he looks deep into mine.

"We'll get out of this Callie. We've got a good attorney and we've got good people praying for us. I know that justice will prevail and I want you to keep the faith."

"I believe what you believe," I tell him. "You're innocent and no matter what happens, this should have never even have happened to us and we will win."

"I'm glad the two of you have confidence in me, but we've still got a long road ahead of us in order to beat this rap. Now the reason I wanted to talk to you together is this, if by any remote chance that we begin to lose this case, would either of you want to plea bargain, or would you want to remain with the not guilty plea no matter what? The reason I'm asking is, I need to know this in order to know where I'm headed during the trial in the event, something damaging comes to light. I will ask you again at that time, should this happen, but I need to know how strongly you feel from the beginning about your plea."

"I assure you, that we will maintain our innocence throughout the trial," Johnny tells Attorney Terrell without flinching. I've got friends who will come through for me, one way or the other."

"You mean this thing with your friend Jimmy and Cortez?"

"Yes. Jimmy will find Cortez now that we don't have much time left."

"Well, he'd better make it quick. The trial only lasts five days and will end on Friday afternoon." Attorney Terrell tells us. "Today they will pick the jury and both of you will have a say in who to keep and who to disengage from the jury. Go by your gut instinct. I will also be watching carefully to see who needs to go and who I feel should stay on the jury. These people will be from all walks of life and our job is to pick the ones that will be most sympathetic to our situation. Although we don't know who that could be, until we ask the preliminary questions of the prospective jurors."

"Whatever happens, I want you to do everything you can to get Callie completely out of this, even if it makes it bad for me. I don't want Callie going to prison. Do you understand?" Johnny tells the man, with a bit of anger and sorrow in his tone.

"I understand, but hopefully it won't come to that, Mr. Parker," the attorney says, as he loosens the tie around his neck. "I'm here to save both of you."

"Johnny don't worry about me. Whatever happens, I'm going to be all right."

Johnny gets up from the table and comes around it to me. I stand up and he holds me tight. I want to cry more for him then for myself, but I keep back the tears and tell him how much I love him and he tells me the same, as he stokes my hair like he always have in the past.

"It's time to go. I'll call the guards in," Attorney Terrell says, getting up from his chair.

Johnny kisses me hard as if it might be the last time he will ever kiss me again. I'm more concerned about Johnny. He'll be crushed if anything bad happens to me. I want him to know that I'll be all right, whatever happens, but I'm not sure, if I've convinced him.

The day is as long as Attorney Terrell said it would be. Picking the jury was long and tedious work. It so happens that all three of us, Attorney Terrell, Johnny and me agreed wholeheartedly on which jurors to keep and which ones to discard. Personally, I think we're in for the fight of our lives. That evil looking prosecutor, well he looks at us as if he knows he's going to nail us to the wall. He looks as if he knows something that we don't know, but Attorney Terrell says not to worry about him, that he's just trying to intimidate us into possibly changing our plea. Our attorney feels that we have as good a chance to win as the other side. There is no evidence to link Johnny to any of the charges. There's some inside dirty work going on, that has him in this fix in the first place and the attorney is going to have to establish the facts, that there is no credible evidence surrounding this case that connects Johnny to any of the drug and laundering charges.

When the day is almost finished, we feel that we have the right jury for the trial. All three of us are happy about the outcome of the day. Johnny has more of a spark in his eyes and I, well I just have hope deep inside of me. I will be happy tomorrow when the trial starts, because I will get to see all the people that loves us. Mama, Sarah and Genny will be there, along with Reverend Jones and some of the congregation from the church, and some of Johnny's family. I've missed all of them so much, although I've never met any of Johnny's family.

"I'll see you tomorrow baby," Johnny says to me, as the guard takes him back to jail. I smile at him as he's taken away down a long corridor, that leads to the tunnel in, which I too will soon take, back to the cell I now live in, but hopefully not for long.

Back in my cell, I couldn't be more miserable. Now that I've seen Johnny and then had to leave him, I break down and start to cry uncontrollably. They've put me in solitary now, so no one can see, that I'm almost sickened by this whole ordeal. I've held up until now, but I don't know if I'm going to be able to keep myself under control, with the thought of being separated from Johnny for a lot of years to come, or even any year. We've never had a chance to have a real marriage and have a little house and kids and all that good stuff, that may never happen. The prosecutor is as evil as Dracula himself. He's probably his incarnate. I feel as if a heavy cloud has been engulfed all around me. I try to cheer myself up, but it's no use. The tragedy of it all has taken an enormous toll on my emotions. I feel as if I'm a broken woman, I can't let Johnny see that I've been severely weakened by this. I have to remain seemingly strong for his sake.

It has been a very long four days and today is the last day of the trial. Our attorney doesn't know exactly which way it's going to go. At the end of the day, the jury will deliberate. We're sitting here at the table with our attorney. Johnny has been keeping my spirits up all day. He's been winking and giving me the thumbs up sign, but I don't know why he's so confident today. We get a chance to talk during recesses, and that has meant a lot to both of us. The prosecuting attorney is using every trick in the book, to throw at our attorney, but he's pretty much hitting the ball back into the prosecutors court every time. I also get to talk with my family, Genny, Sarah, Johnny's friends and his sister and her husband, as well as reverend Jones and some of the congregation that came to support us. I will be glad when the whole thing is over. At this point, we can't say for sure who's winning. We're on thin ice, and that's for sure.

It's almost noon and it's the best time of all. Johnny and I get to eat lunch together in a small room off the courtroom. In case we don't get to see each other after today, they've allowed us to have this time together. Our attorney has brought us in some Fillet Minion, a baked potato, a salad, some broccoli and soda and for dessert, some apple pie, which is Johnny's favorite. We eat fast and then we talk and hug each other tightly, because it might be the last time. Reverend Jones says, when we get out of this and he's being very optimistic at this time in the trial, that Johnny and I can come back to Savannah Georgia and pick up where we left off. Johnny being his assistant and we can continue to live in the house that is connected to the church.

"When we get out of this Callie, I'm going to take you on a very expensive honey moon."

"First, I want us to get married in a church with all our friends and relatives there. I know we got married in Vegas at the drive up window at the chapel, but I want a big wedding."

"Your every wish is my command. You shall have a huge wedding."

"Make sure you eat all your food. I want you to have strength to combat this turmoil."

"Yeah, I might not have fillet minion for a long time," I say, as I'm cutting my meat.

"Johnny, Callie, we have just got some great news. Jimmy and some of your friends have just brought in Cortez. He's confessed that he set Johnny up," Attorney Terrell says, as he's coming into the little room, where we're still eating.

"He did it. I knew he'd get those dogs," Johnny says, jumping up and down like Rocky.

"You mean we're going to be acquitted?" I ask, almost choking on my food.

"I'm meeting with the D.A. in five minutes. I'm going to try to get the case thrown out."

"Oh my God," I say, almost gasping for air.

"How soon can we get out of here?" Johnny asks, still prancing around like a wild stallion.

"As soon as we get back into the Courtroom, Attorney Terrell says, as he is leaving out of the room to talk with the District Attorney.

Johnny and I run into each other's arms and hug and kiss and hug and kiss some more. I'm still in shock. I can't believe that Cortez has confessed to setting Johnny up and in hours we could be free. Jimmy came through for us like he said he would. I imagine Jimmy used every tactic in the book to get him to confess. It was getting down to the wire and Jimmy must have made a drastic move to capture Cortez and it worked.

Now we sit back down and hold hands across the table. Neither of us can grasp fully what had just happened. We can't wait to get back into the courtroom to see the final act of this sensational drama. My family and Johnny's family and our friends are all going to be in for a wonderful surprise. Reverend Jones was right. He said that justice would prevail. I'm so elated and yet still in shock.

"We're going to do all those things we just talked about, Callie."

"Johnny, this means we might be together this very night."

Forty minutes later we were back in the courtroom. All the evidence was presented by our attorney and he of course called Cortez to the stand and he confessed to the whole thing, but not before he had made a plea bargain with the District Attorney and it was no time after his confession, that the judge through out the whole case and ordered that Cortez be taken into custody instead.

Everyone is cheering and hugging each other and mama is crying and so is Sarah and Genny and Reverend Jones is looking up as if he is thanking God, for this tremendous outcome of the trial. Johnny is looking at me smiling and I'm smiling back at him and we both know that when we stand up, we will be walking out of here free agents. Free to do whatever we please and free to go wherever we want to go. The judge takes the gavel and announces that court is dismissed, as he gets up to go to his chambers.

"My baby. You're free," mama says, coming towards me and when she reaches me, she gives me one of the biggest hugs and kisses me on my cheek and everyone else is congratulating each other and we're all so happy, as we go from one to the other hugging and shaking hands. Sarah and Genny are smiling at me and wiping away tears with their hankies.

Jimmy comes over to Johnny and me as we are about to leave the Courtroom. The last place we want to be right now is in this place. We don't ever want to see another courtroom again.

"Thanks Jimmy. You came through for us. We owe you our lives," Johnny says, as he hugs his best friend the way men hug with first that handshake.

"You would have done the same for me, Johnny. We've always come through for each other, you me and Sly. I wish he could have been here to see this day."

"Yeah, me too."

"If you ever need anything, you know where I'll be. My home is always your home."

"We'll keep in touch," Johnny says, as he hugs Jimmy again.

Now the congregation from the church is coming over to us and hugging Johnny and me one by one and wiping tears from their eyes. They gave us hope by being here. Knowing that all these people cared about us, helped to keep our spirits up.

"How long will it be before you get back to Savannah?" Reverend Jones asks.

"As soon as we can drive there," Johnny says, with a big grin on his face.

After we all had congregated at one of L.A.'s finest restaurants, said our good byes, hugged and kissed everyone and thanked them for their support, me and Johnny are now leaving the restaurant arm in arm.

"Where do you want to go Mrs. Parker?" He asks me.

"Let's go home, Johnny. Let's go home."

Johnny and I drove the close to fifteen hundred miles in less time than it usually takes. We've been back in Savannah four months now and we are so glad to be back in Savannah Georigia, where we're continuing to live in the house connected to the church. We still maintain the grounds and keep them looking beautiful, as well as

Johnny helping Reverend Jones out from time to time, with the Sunday morning messages. Reverend Jones is planning to move to Florida for his health and he plans to leave the church in our hands, with Johnny taking over the pastorial duties, while he is away. Johnny is ever so thrilled about how his life has turned out and so am I. We plan to have a real wedding in two weeks and all our friends and relatives will be there. The drive up marriage at the chapel in Las Vegas isn't setting well with either one of us, so we plan to do it again with a big wedding to make it feel right. I'm going to have to have my wedding dress specially made, because I'm almost four months pregnant. We can't wait until our little bundle of joy arrives. We both couldn't be happier about us having a baby. Johnny already plans to name him Johnny Jr. He's very confidant that it will be a boy. If it's a girl, I plan to name her Sarah Jenean, after my two best friends, Sarah and Genny. I miss them so much, but they will be here for the wedding in two weeks and I can't wait to see them. Cynthia is coming in from New York as well. She never thought Johnny and me were right for each other, but she now admits she was wrong. Sarah and Genny have always been there for me, ever since we became friends in grade school.

Since we've been back in Savannah, everyone has been so kind to us, they don't seem to hold anything against us at all. They realize we were in a position that we didn't belong in and they have been ever so supportive. We love this town and all the people in it and they love us. Love is what really counts in this world. Without it, we'd all be a very lost society. That's why it's so important. Love is what keeps us all alive. I just wish more of it were spread around. Johnny and I, we have it all now. We have each other, we have the congregation and we have baby on the way. Life is grand, when it can be complimented with love. Johnny and I have so much love for each other and we've been taught by Reverend Jones, just how to make and keep that love strong.

"Callie, could you make some breakfast please?"

"Coming up."

I'm so nervous today. It's the day of our wedding. Our second time getting married of course. All our friends and family are here. Most of them came in last night. Cynthia came in this morning. She was such a dear, when I got to New York for the first time and she let me move in with her and we've been friends ever since. I was a scared lonely young woman in a big city too big for a country girl to be alone and God sent Cynthia and Johnny into my life at once. I'm trying to finish bathing, while everyone is waiting in the other room to help me get into my special made white wedding dress. One thing I did right, was that I was still a virgin, when I married Johnny in Las Vegas almost two years ago. Mama would have killed me if I hadn't been one. She always preached to me about that from a little girl on up. She never let me forget that it had to be that way.

"Callie are you done yet? Sarah calls from the other room. You have to get dressed. The wedding starts in less than forty minutes," she calls from the other room.

"Be right out." I can't help but think about how I got to this day. It's been a long journey, but one well worth the trouble. I'll be marrying my man the way I've always dreamed. I also have the man of my dreams and will never let him go until death do us part. I've been blessed all right. I can't think of anything I'd rather do than be Mrs. Johnny Parker.

"Callie are you all right in there?" I hear my mama call to me.

"I'm coming out now mama," I call to her.

The churchyard is so beautiful. Everything is fixed for a beautiful wedding to take place. As I walk out of the house in my wedding dress, I see all the people I love and that love me, sitting in chairs in the back yard of the church, just waiting for me to appear. I see Johnny standing with Reverend Jones, waiting for me to get to him, as the wedding march is playing loudly and everyone going ooh and ah, as they see me coming towards Johnny. Reverend Jones was one of the best things that has happened to us and the little church too. Johnny and I didn't realize that night in the tent meeting that we would wind up being dead serious about living a good clean and holy Christian life, but now we are truly alive. A joyous and happy life just begins, when you take Jesus as your personal savior. This is one of the happiest days of my life, as I see Johnny standing there with that big beautiful smile of his. The man of my dreams come to life. It won't be long, before we say our vows to each other again and I believe that we will feel the impact of those vows, that almost could not have taken place on today, if things had went different for us, but we're free to live our lives together now and nothing in this world can stop us. Maybe, just maybe he found me.

At the reception, Johnny and I are greeting the guests and they are giving us their best wishes and Johnny looks so handsome in his tux and I know I look good in my wedding dress made for two, me and the baby inside me of course, and now it's time to cut the cake. Guests are positioning themselves to take pictures, as Johnny and me are standing in front of the most wonderful five layered cake with the little man and woman in their wedding garb on the very top of the cake. Johnny's hand is on mine as we both begin to cut the first piece. everyone is saying smile to us, so they can get a good picture. Johnny is smiling at me, with the kind of smile that "says", I picked the right woman to spend the rest of my life with.

"Give her the cake Johnny," mama says, while positioning herself to take a picture. I'm smiling and I open my mouth, just in time for Johnny to stick a big piece of cake in my mouth and I hear a snap and see the flash on the camera. It must be a perfect picture.

Home is where the heart is and our hearts are here in Savannah Georgia at the little church, where we found our first hope, where we found peace and a life that made us feel free. A lifestyle, that is satisfying to the soul. I wish that everyone were as blessed and as happy as Johnny and I are right now. I got my cake and I can eat it too, because of the win-win covenant we have with Christ in our lives. We got a second chance, that only one that is able to surrender to the creator will ever find. Our hearts belong to each other, but our souls belong to God.

About The Author

VIRGINIA CONSTANCE MCKINLEY was raised in a town in the Midwest. A beautiful place in summer and especially winter, when there is snow. She earned a double degree in Sociology and religious studies from a Midwestern College. A mother of six, who are all adults, she lives with her youngest child. This is her first published novel, but have been offered awards for her published poem achievements.

www.ingramcontent.com/pod-product-compliance
Lightning Source LLC
Chambersburg PA
CBHW072012190726
48293CB00001B/249